TELL NO LIES

TELL NO LIES

JULIE COMPTON

St. Martin's Minotaur ❧ *New York*

www.minotaurbooks.com

Jack Hilliard's acceptance speech in chapter thirteen is based, in part, upon the U.S. Supreme Court case of *Berger v. United States*, 295 U.S. 78 (1935).

Library of Congress Cataloging-in-Publication Data

Compton, Julie.
    Tell no lies / Julie Compton.—1st U.S. ed.
        p.   cm.
    ISBN-13: 978-0-312-37875-2
    ISBN-10: 0-312-37875-0
    1. Public prosecutors—Fiction.   2. Adultery—Fiction.   3. Murder—Fiction.   4. Saint Louis (Mo.)—Fiction.   5. Psychological fiction.
    I. Title.

    PS3603.O487T45   2008
    813'.6—dc22

                                                            2008003667

First published in February 2008 in the United Kingdom by Pan Books, an imprint of Pan Macmillan Ltd.

First U.S. Edition: May 2008

10   9   8   7   6   5   4   3   2   1

In memory of Hyman and LaVerne Grossman

ACKNOWLEDGMENTS

I am truly indebted to Jo Bicknell, who selflessly took me under her wing and has been a constant friend and passionate advocate. She gave this novel a new life.

I am also deeply grateful to everyone at St. Martin's Press, including my editor (and fellow St. Louis native) Kelley Ragland, George Witte, Andrew Martin, and Matt Martz, and to all the folks at Macmillan, especially Maria Rejt, David North, Liz Cowen, Sophie Portas, and Anna Valdinger.

Many, many thanks go to the numerous individuals who provided invaluable advice, assistance, and support during the years I wrote and revised the novel:

Alison Hicks of the Greater Philadelphia Wordshop Studio, and all the members of her Monday night AWA workshop. Alison practically held my hand the entire way, acting as my friend, mentor, and inspiration when I was ready to give up.

Karen Voellmann, one of my closest and dearest friends, who acted as my first "nonwriter" reader.

Rob Livergood, who spent more time on the phone with me than I'm sure he had available, answering numerous questions about prosecutors and the criminal justice system. (Also, thanks in advance to the people of

St. Louis for granting me the literary license to use the technically inaccurate but more nationally known term—*district attorney*.)

Kathy McLaughlin, my Philly running buddy and a talented designer who was very gracious about the cover switch.

Ellen Cooney, who probably doesn't even remember me, but who was the first "real" writer I knew, who, with three small words on one of my short-story manuscripts—"Send it in!"—convinced me that maybe, just maybe, I could do this.

Andrea Chapin, who waded through my hefty first draft and immediately homed in on where the story truly begins.

The Dave Matthews Band, for a never-ending supply of music to write to.

I also owe enormous thanks to my daughters, Jessie and Sally, for not getting too upset when Mommy spent more time at the computer than with them. They are genuinely good kids and my greatest accomplishment in life.

Finally, and most important, I want to thank my husband, Rick, who is one of the most loving, generous, patient men ever to walk the earth, and for whom there is no rival. Without him, this writing life of mine would not be possible.

Good will, like a good name, is got by many actions, and lost by one.

—*LORD FRANCIS JEFFREY*

PART 1

SPRING

CHAPTER ONE

Jack drove his car a little too fast out of the parking garage, his tires screaming as he rounded the coiled curves of the down ramp. He fumbled with the radio, looking for a song to match his upbeat mood, all the while keeping his eyes ahead and his left hand on the steering wheel. A slight grin graced his face, though he wasn't aware of it.

That morning, the jury had returned a verdict in the most publicized murder case he had ever prosecuted. The case had been hard fought for two weeks, and he had worried about the outcome until the very end— even after his boss, Earl, came to hear closing arguments, complimenting him afterward, and even after a few of the jurors smiled at him on their way back to the jury box, just before the verdict of guilty was read. But Earl's belief that juries loved Jack Hilliard proved true again.

He'd called Claire as soon as he returned to his office. She'd listened and laughed with him as she always did, asking certain questions that only another lawyer would know to ask. Before they hung up, Jack announced that, for the first time in weeks, he'd be home in time for dinner.

Now he was already past the Innerbelt, far enough out of the city to smell the suburbs, fragrant with freshly cut grass and the overgrown lilac bushes that bloomed untamed near the off-ramp into Clayton. When his cell phone rang, he answered without bothering to look at the caller ID.

"Hiya, babe."

"Gosh, Jack, I never knew you felt that way about me."

Jack felt his face redden. "I thought you were Claire," he said. Even though he'd known Jenny Dodson for almost nine years, and he'd reached the conclusion early on that she talked this way to everyone, her flirtatiousness still unsettled him at times.

"Obviously," she purred. "Hey, *Mr. Hilliard*," she said then, speaking his surname in an intimate tone that transformed it into her own pet name for him, "I hear you won your case. Congratulations."

He smiled. "I did. How'd you hear?"

"Are you kidding? It was the top story on the five o'clock news. You're famous again."

"Yeah, so what am I doing hanging out with the likes of you?" he said, laughing.

"I won't dignify that with a response. Will I see you tonight? I'll buy you a drink to celebrate."

"Tonight?" But as soon as he said it, he remembered. The bar association was having its annual awards dinner, and Earl, the St. Louis District Attorney for more than thirty years, was to receive an award for his dedication to public service.

"Damn, I completely forgot about it." Earl hadn't mentioned it after the trial, Jack knew, because he hadn't wanted to take away from his moment of victory. One of the many reasons Earl was a great boss, and also one of the reasons Jack had to go to the dinner.

"Were you heading home?" Jenny asked.

"Yeah." He sighed. "But I'll be there. Why are you going?"

"You forget easily, Mr. Hilliard," she chided. "Not every lawyer in town has had the good fortune to jump ship from a big firm to the security of the DA's office. I still have to fish if I want to eat. It always helps to do a little mingling with the other sharks in town."

Both knew he hadn't exactly "jumped ship" from Newman, Norton & Levine. It was more like he'd been thrown overboard. But he *had* landed a plum job. Although he shared the title of Assistant District Attorney with twenty-four other lawyers, only Jack was seen as Earl Scanlon's protégé.

"Should be an interesting night," Jack said. "I'm sure his old-time bar association buddies plan to roast him." His mind drifted to the new logistics for the evening. "Listen, I'd better hang up and call Claire. She's gonna have to try to find a sitter. I'll see you tonight, okay?"

"Okay. Don't forget, first drink's on me. I'll see you tonight, *babe*."

She hung up before he could respond, and he shook his head and laughed, knowing she'd be pleased with herself for having found a way to tease him one more time about his earlier mistake.

The hotel was near the Mississippi riverfront in the heart of St. Louis. The evening was damp but warm for late April, so Jack left his car in the garage near the courthouse and walked the nine blocks to the hotel. The air was thick with humidity, and he smelled the pungent scent of the river. The rush-hour traffic had begun to dissipate, and the few cars still leaving the city drove too fast down Market Street. The road was still wet from an earlier shower; tires sprayed water as they rolled through puddles on the way to the highway entrance.

In the hotel, he immediately began looking for Earl. Most of the lawyers attending the event were still in the lobby, scattered like orbiting moons around the center bar, which served as their planet. It was a local businessmen's hotel; the reservations and check-in desk had been strategically placed at the top of the escalator on the second floor, leaving room on the main level for happy hour and even a small dance club with its own entrance from Fourth Street.

Jack spotted his boss near the escalator. He was leaning against a large, shoulder-height marble post that had an arrangement of exotic flowers on top of it. Earl stood only about five foot six, and the towering structure made him appear even smaller. He was with a group of defense lawyers from Clark & Cavanaugh. All of them were laughing.

"There's my man!" Earl said, setting down his drink. He grabbed Jack's right hand as he approached and patted him on the back. To the others, he said, "Jack Hilliard, gentlemen. Are you all familiar with each other?"

Was he familiar with them? Was Earl crazy? Two of the four lawyers standing with Earl were among the best-known criminal defense attorneys in the city, and Jack had tried cases against them on more than one occasion. The other two he recognized as senior associates from the same firm. They often sat at the defense table, second chairing cases. It was not unusual for the bigger defense firms to put two or sometimes three lawyers on a case. The attorneys in the DA's office joked that defense attorneys were only half as smart as the opposition, hence the reason there were always at least two of them.

"Yes, of course," Jack answered politely. "Good to see you again." He shook their hands as they congratulated him on the outcome of the trial.

The truth was, Jack couldn't wait to get away from this group with their custom-made suits and Rolex watches. One of the many reasons he loved being a prosecutor was that it demanded more substance and less style. He liked being an average Joe; it felt true, as if the outside finally fit the inside. When he had practiced at Newman, he'd always been on edge about how he looked. He didn't worry about that stuff anymore. As long as he wore a suit in the courtroom—sometimes even a sport coat was acceptable—it didn't matter whose name was on the inside label.

He stood there listening to the banter between them, feigning interest, but he began to suspect he'd interrupted something more than a cocktail conversation. What was Earl doing with these guys, anyway? They talked to Earl as if he was one of them, and he responded in kind. Jack's stomach flipped, the way it did when he feared he'd overlooked a key piece of evidence or forgotten to ask an important question. He felt as though everyone else knew something he didn't.

"Gentlemen, will you excuse us?" Earl said finally. "I'd like to talk to Jack in private."

This time it was Earl shaking hands. "We'll see you after the roast," one of them said, and they all laughed.

"Nervous?" Jack asked him once the others had walked off.

"Nah; this will be a piece of cake compared to what those guys have done to me in the courtroom over the years." He picked up his drink from where he'd set it on the post next to the flowers.

"So what's up with the goon squad, anyway?" Jack asked, but when Earl's smile faded and he looked down, Jack knew he'd said the wrong thing.

Earl took a deep breath. "I'm going to make an announcement to-night, but I wanted to tell you beforehand."

Jack narrowed his eyes. "Why do I feel the same way I did right before Newman laid me off?"

"You're not being fired, Jack."

"Oh, I know that. If I was, I'd hope you wouldn't make an announcement out of it."

Earl laughed; Jack didn't. They stood for a moment looking at each other and wondering who would speak next. Jack leaned against the post and crossed his arms in front of him.

"You're leaving, aren't you?" he said.

Earl nodded. "Yeah; I've accepted an offer to join Clark and Cavanaugh."

"I knew it." *Do the right thing, Jack.* "Well, congratulations," he said, cracking a smile and extending his hand.

Earl hesitated before shaking Jack's hand. "Thanks." He tilted his head slightly, studying Jack. "You know, I tried to talk to you this afternoon after Court. I wanted to tell you before now. But you were on the phone almost from the minute you came back to the office."

"Sorry about the 'goon squad' comment," Jack said.

Earl dismissed it with a shrug of his shoulders.

"So, are you going to clue me in on why you're leaving?"

Earl looked down again at the tumbler in his hand; except for small chips of ice, it was empty. "It's time, Jack. Time to let someone else lead the troops."

"Bullshit. What's that supposed to mean?"

Earl touched Jack's sleeve. "Come on," he said, turning toward the bar. "You look like a thirsty man, and I need a refill."

If only they knew what they were really congratulating you for," Jack said when they reached the bar, referring to the numerous interruptions along the way. He motioned to the bartender.

"Be with you in a minute, hon." She smiled, flashing a perfect set of white teeth at him.

Earl snickered. "I can't believe your wife lets you out of the house alone."

"I'm waiting."

"What can I say? I've been at the DA's office since right out of law school. It'll be nice to do something different." Jack was skeptical, and Earl knew it. "Look, they made me an offer that was too good to pass up. It'll be a nice, cushy job. I'll get to pick and choose the cases I want; I'll have a decent office for once in my life—big window, furniture that's not government issue, some real art on the walls . . ."

"Take it from me—the big window and nice furniture get old real quick." Earl laughed, but Jack continued, "And you get to pick and choose your cases now. When's the last time you tried one that wasn't high profile?"

The bartender approached and slapped two cocktail napkins on the bar. She leaned on her elbows, displaying her ample cleavage. "What'll it be, gentlemen?" she asked, eyeing Jack.

"Whiskey and Coke," he said, smiling just enough to be polite.

"Scotch and soda," Earl said to her, watching the exchange. "Try to put yourself in my shoes," he said to Jack.

"I just don't buy what you're telling me. I think I can honestly say this is the first time in your life you haven't been convincing."

Earl sighed and looked around the room. "I'm fifty-six years old. I've already put two girls through college, I've got one in there now, and the youngest one will start next year. Not to mention the weddings I'll probably be expected to pay for. I want to do it all for them, and so far I've been able to. But it ain't cheap. Helen and I also want to travel, see some sights before we're too old to enjoy them. Frankly, I don't want to worry about the money anymore."

Jack watched his boss. The crow's feet around Earl's eyes were pronounced even when he wasn't smiling, and his silver flattop was peppered with short strands of muted black. Jack felt he knew Helen pretty well—as well as one gets to know his boss's wife—and he'd seen their girls grow into women during his eight years in the DA's office. But he still had the distinct sense that there was a lot about this man he didn't know.

"Well, you're convincing me now," Jack said. "I'm beginning to wonder if I'm saving enough."

"Don't get me wrong, Jack. We're not in the poorhouse or anything. It's just that Helen's sacrificed a lot for my career, and I'd like to be able to spoil her a little in return." Earl grabbed the drinks and handed one to Jack, who had turned around to face the crowd. "I guess you could say I sold out, huh?"

"No, I wouldn't say that." Jack took a long swallow. The bartender had made it strong and the liquor burned his throat, but nevertheless he wished he'd ordered it straight. He was going to need it tonight.

"It won't be the same without you," he said.

"I was thinking the same thing."

"When will you leave?"

"I'll finish out my term, wait till after the election."

Jack leaned against the bar and looked out over the dwindling crowd. He tried to imagine who in the office could fill Earl's shoes. Although he had good relationships with most of the lawyers there, he couldn't picture any of them as his boss. For an instant he indulged in fantasy and imagined himself in the position, but just as quickly dismissed the idea as unrealistic. The effect of Earl's decision started to sink in. What if some lawyer from outside the office decided to run? That would be even more disruptive than having an insider take over. The office had a chemistry that Earl had nurtured during his years there, and the slightest change would upset it permanently.

Jack's thoughts were interrupted by the sight of Jenny coming through the revolving door. Even after all those years, the blackness, the absolute darkness of her hair, struck him. She had dark russet skin, and he remembered how, when he first met her, he'd thought maybe she was Hispanic. He'd been a little ashamed that he couldn't tell; he thought he should have been able to, but when she'd introduced herself—"Jennifer Dodson, Jenny's fine"—her all-American name had surprised him, and he'd never had the nerve to admit to her his ignorance.

Earl turned to see what Jack was looking at.

"A pretty girl enters the room and your eyes light up, don't they?" Earl said.

"No law against looking."

"True. But there's been plenty to look at all night, and you didn't blink till now."

Jack shrugged. "She's my friend, Earl." What more could he say? This evening *was* beginning to remind him a little too much of his days at Newman, when for a time his friendship with Jenny had been fodder for the office gossip mill.

"Speaking of pretty girls, where's Claire?"

"At home. We couldn't get a sitter; it's hard on a weeknight." He didn't add that they'd only started looking for one that night after Jack had called Claire from his car in a panic. "She sends her regrets." Jack's eyes followed Jenny as she joined a group of partners from Newman and ascended the escalator with them. He could feel Earl watching him.

"Can I give you a little bit of advice, Jack?"

He turned to Earl and laughed. "You've never given me bad advice, so sure, go ahead."

"You have to get that woman of yours out more. It's not good for her to be cooped up at home so much with the kids."

Jack rolled his eyes. It was true that they'd started a family just after they were married, while still in law school, and the weight of that burden fell on Claire. But they'd both been infatuated with the idea, rationalizing that it would be better to have a child while they were still in school so Claire wouldn't be pregnant while interviewing or just starting a job. Michael was born late the following summer, after their second year of law school. Of course, once they had him, they couldn't wait to have another, so Claire ended up being pregnant anyway during her first year at Marshall & Hawes. She'd quit practicing after having several miscarriages, though, and shortly thereafter had gotten the job at the law school teaching legal writing to first-year students. Jamie was born six years later. It had worked out well for her—she had a flexible schedule that allowed her to spend time with Michael, and later with Jamie—and it had worked out well for the school, as it was an untenured position.

"She's still teaching three days a week. With that and her volunteering at the kids' schools, she's probably busier than I am." Earl looked doubtful.

"Anyway," Jack continued, "no offense, but I think if she had a night out she'd rather be having a nice Italian dinner down on the Hill."

"I think I'd have to agree with her. I know the food would be better. Just take care of her, Jack. She's a good woman."

"I know that." Jack grinned. "That's why I convinced her to marry me."

Earl finished the rest of his drink in one swallow and set the glass on the bar. "Okay then, let's get upstairs."

Once in the ballroom, they split up. Earl moved to the front of the room and Jack joined a group of prosecutors at a large table. It was all he could do not to reveal to the rest of them what he knew; he suspected that Earl wouldn't have told any of them before letting him know. He was a little disconcerted, though, that Earl hadn't broken the news before to-night. But after years of watching him in a courtroom, Jack knew this method was consistent with Earl's way of doing things. Unlike Jack, who approached the judges, juries, and even witnesses in a quiet, if open, way, Earl preferred the power that came with catching people off guard.

The dinner was slow, with numerous presentations and awards. Once Earl stood to speak, though, he mesmerized everyone with his command-ing presence and dry sense of humor. Despite his small size, he filled the room.

After he accepted his award, told a few "war" stories and made a funny rebuttal to some of the jests made about him, Earl suddenly be-came humble. When his words started to suggest the conclusion of his speech, but before he actually said, "I'll be leaving the District Attorney's office at the end of my term to join Clark and Cavanaugh," a compre-hending hum settled over the room, and Earl had to fight against choking on his emotions. Jack had the urge to stand up and tell everyone that it was all a big hoax. Wasn't that Earl the consummate joker?

Instead, he sat with his arms crossed and watched Earl regain his composure as the hum gave way to applause and then organized chaos. If they'd planned on making any more announcements or speeches, the time had passed.

Jenny approached Jack's table as dessert was served and ignored. After hugging and congratulating him again on his trial, she sat in the chair next to him, abandoned only a minute before by another lawyer. She pushed an empty glass away and set her drink in front of her.

"Big news for you guys, huh?" she said to the group. To Jack: "You keep a good secret."

He opened his mouth to defend himself, but Maria Catalona, one of the newer prosecutors in his office, spoke first. "We didn't know. This is news to us, too."

Jack wasn't sure he would have been so forthright about their pre-announcement ignorance.

"We're placing bets on who will succeed him," said Frank Mann. "Care to make a wager?"

Jack suspected that Frank was hedging bets on himself. He'd been at the DA's office longer than Jack, and Jack had heard through several sources that Frank was envious of his close relationship with Earl. Frank probably viewed Earl's announcement as an opportunity to reassert his position in the office pecking order.

"Come on, Dodson, who's your money on?" Frank urged.

"Well . . . I don't know," Jenny said, pretending to think. "Let's see." She looked at Jack and nudged his arm with her elbow. "I think Jack would be a great District Attorney."

Jack nudged her back. "Get out of here, Jenny. Go back to your stiff suits."

"Yeah, like we didn't see that coming from a mile away," said Jerry Clark, another prosecutor.

Jenny took a sip of her martini. Jack could tell from the look on her face that she didn't like it that they weren't taking her seriously, even though she hadn't meant to be serious, and that she was preparing her response.

"I mean it. I'm not just saying that because we're friends, although that would be an added benefit, wouldn't it? If I ever got in trouble." She laughed, and the others laughed with her. "Really, though, Jack is perfect for the job." She paused, loading her ammunition. "There's no question he has the trial skills for the position, but what makes—"

"Now, Dodson, how would you even know that?" Frank asked.

"Well, *Mr. Mann,* I'm aware that he wins many more cases than he loses."

Jack's spirits dipped a bit; he'd thought that he was the only one she referred to as "Mister" in quite that way.

"I mean, just look at his most recent stellar performance." Jenny turned and winked at him.

"That he wins more than he loses doesn't mean anything," Frank snorted, "except maybe that he's smart enough to take a plea bargain on the difficult ones."

Jenny ignored him. "As I was saying, before I was so rudely interrupted . . ." She cleared her throat, took another drink, and glared at Frank. "What makes him perfect, in addition to his trial skills, is his administrative aptitude. After all, what's the most important job the DA has? Setting policy, knowing which cases to make a priority, and knowing when to play and when to fold." She lifted her glass and finished off her drink. "Don't you all agree?" she asked the others. They mumbled the obligatory assent. She was at the edge of drunkenness, and it was apparent to everyone there.

"Dodson, there's a gaping hole in your argument." Frank glanced at Jack and grinned at him, as if he thought they were teasing Jenny together. "Your friend's a dove. He even turned down the Barnard case."

Jack felt all eyes turn cautiously in his direction. Everyone at the table, even Jenny, knew exactly which case Frank referred to, because in the past few days it had become impossible for St. Louis residents to turn on their televisions or radios and not hear about it. Cassia Barnard was a twelve-year-old girl who'd been kidnapped and brutally murdered months before, and the cops had finally made an arrest earlier in the week. Every seasoned prosecutor in the office had lobbied Earl for the assignment—the case had the potential to make an attorney's career—everyone except Jack. He knew there was a good chance that Earl would seek the death penalty, and, for that reason alone, he didn't want it. It hadn't surprised him, though, when Earl offered it to him anyway. And it hadn't surprised Earl when Jack turned it down. Frank was the lucky runner-up.

Now everyone at the table looked at Jack with veiled pity, as if he hadn't played a part in his exclusion from the case.

"Well, I agree with Jenny," Maria said brightly, trying to quell the awkwardness that followed Frank's comment. "I think he'd be a great boss."

Brown nose, thought Jack.

As if bolstered by Maria, Andy Rinehart spoke up. "Jenny, Mann's just arguing with you because he wants the job for himself."

"Frank doesn't like to admit that we might prefer someone else," said Jeff McCarthy, one of Jack's closer friends in the office. They all laughed, except Frank and Jack.

The alcohol was starting to have its effect on everyone now. Jack remembered what one of the litigators at Newman, one of the few he respected, told him when he'd first started there: "Loose lips sink ships," he liked to say. Jack could feel this boat starting to take on a lot of water.

"I suspected as much," Jenny said, pleased they were beginning to come around.

"Well, *Jack's* not interested," Jack said, hoping to cut them off.

"Who's the hunk from your firm?" Maria asked Jenny, changing the subject because she was more interested in young men than office politics.

"Who?" Jenny seemed distracted.

"The guy you were sitting with." She lowered her voice. "The one with the bedroom eyes."

Jack turned to look. He recognized most of the other lawyers from her table, but he didn't recognize this guy. He was young, perhaps a new associate at Newman.

Jenny laughed. "Oh, you mean Lance," she said, putting emphasis on his name; and then she shrugged her shoulders as if to say, *What kind of name is that?* "He's new. He thinks he wants to work in the bankruptcy department, so I've been assigned to be his mentor, whatever that means."

Maria raised her eyebrows. "Lucky you."

"The way he's been hanging on you all night, Dodson, it looks like he has more than mentoring on his mind," Frank said.

Jack looked at Jenny to gauge her reaction to Frank's comment. She wouldn't date someone ten years her junior, would she?

"No, thank you," she said. "He's a little too . . . how should I put this? . . . compulsive for me. He's the type of guy who would insist on putting a towel down during sex to protect the sheets."

They all burst out laughing. Jack was a little embarrassed. He pitied the lawyer; he knew no one at the table would ever be able to talk to him without thinking of her comment.

"I'll be back," Jenny said, holding up her empty glass to indicate where she was heading. Jack grabbed her arm and pulled her down closer to his face.

"Cool it with Frank, will ya?" he whispered so the others wouldn't hear.

"All in good fun, Jack. Not to worry." And then she said again, "I'll be back."

After she left, Frank stood and came to Jack's side of the table to say good-bye. He placed his hand on Jack's shoulder and leaned close to his ear. "She's crazy about you, Hilliard. Someone better warn Claire."

Jack felt a blush rising. "It's a threesome, Frank, didn't you know?"

By the time Jenny returned from the bar, most of the lawyers at the table had scattered. Maria was still there, talking quietly to another woman from the Public Defender's office.

Jenny snapped her fingers as she sat down. "What are you thinking about?"

Jack shrugged.

"The next election?"

"No." He waved to Maria as she and her friend left the table.

"I don't believe you."

"Jenny, why are you pushing this?"

"Because you could do it, and you know it." Her voice was low but insistent. "Didn't you see the look on Mann's face when I said your name? He knows you could do it, too, and it kills him."

Jack pushed his chair away from the table. In all the years he had worked in the DA's office, he had given only a passing thought to becoming *the* District Attorney. He'd always dismissed it, though, because Earl was so clearly that man. Jack had figured it would be at least ten years before Earl retired, before anyone would have to think about his successor. Anyway, as Frank had so bluntly pointed out, Jack—unlike most prosecutors in the state—was deeply opposed to the death penalty. It was an obstacle that wasn't going away.

"I think I need another drink, too," he said.

Jenny followed him to the bar. "You'd be the perfect man, Jack," she said, her voice a little boisterous from the martinis she'd been drinking.

"You're crazy, Jen. And you're drunk."

As he stood at the bar trying to get the bartender's attention, she leaned in closer.

"You're only partly right. I'm drunk, but I'm not crazy." Jack smelled alcohol on her breath. It mixed with her perfume, a musky scent he'd noticed before. "Juries love you—your track record speaks to that. Earl would most definitely support you. What more could you ask for?"

Jenny shrugged her shoulders, lifted her glass, and raised it in a mock toast.

Jack laughed. "It's that easy, huh?" He put a tip down on the bar and turned away with his drink in hand. "Jen, you're forgetting something." He loved to prove her wrong; she was always so confident.

"Yes, Mr. Hilliard?" She raised her eyebrows, grinning back. She knew what he was doing.

"Would you vote for a prosecutor who didn't believe in the death penalty?"

Her grin disappeared, and despite her contrary position in the countless arguments they'd had over the issue, she answered without hesitation. "If that prosecutor was you, of course I would."

They stood for a moment, staring at each other. Jack instinctively reached up and moved a stray hair away from Jenny's face, but then remembered this wasn't Claire he was standing with.

What was he doing? "Sorry," he whispered.

Jenny pretended not to have noticed. "Jack, you're a good man," she said, still serious. "You do what's right, what's good. You wouldn't be swayed by politics or by friendships. You have a moral code that you live by, and God knows that's a scarce quality among the attorneys in this town. You'd make an excellent DA." She paused and furrowed her brow in thought. Then she laughed. "Drunk or sober."

Jack relaxed a bit, relieved that the smart-ass Jenny he knew had returned.

Maria approached them as they moved away from the bar. "There's a bunch of us going to the club downstairs in a little bit. I'm passing the word."

"Let's go; it sounds like fun," Jenny said.

"No, I've gotta get home soon."

She grunted in exasperation. "Come on, Jack. Your boss just made the biggest announcement of his career. He's going to want to celebrate. You have a lot to celebrate, too. Don't be such a party pooper."

Jack sighed. He always had trouble telling her no. "Only if he's going."

They found Earl not far from the dais, as though he'd made the effort but hadn't been able to break loose from the lingering throngs wanting to talk to him.

"So what's the report from the home front?" Earl asked. He smiled at Jenny.

"Don't tell me you haven't spoken to anyone yet?" Jack eyed his boss warily.

"Yes, I've spoken to some of them, but I want to know what they're saying when I'm not there."

"It's all good, Earl, don't worry," Jack said.

"Actually," Jenny piped up, "their biggest concern is who's going to succeed you."

"Really?"

Jack knew exactly where she was heading. He carefully moved closer to her, not wanting Earl to notice, and stepped on her toe. She let out a little "ouch" and glared at him. Earl looked at her curiously.

"Just the typical talk, Earl," said Jack, trying to pretend that he didn't know what her problem was. "They're just wondering about their future, that's all. We came over"—he looked at Jenny—"to see if you're joining the group downstairs."

"Yeah, I'll be down as soon as I can break away. You guys go on ahead."

The club was already jammed. The Thursday night happy-hour crowd had hung around even after the price of the drinks had gone up, and now lawyers from the banquet upstairs had joined them, too. The music, some sort of 1970s disco, was louder than it needed to be, and Jack wasn't sure he was in the mood to put up with it. He trailed reluctantly after Jenny, who'd worked her way through the mass of bodies to reach the bar. When the bartender turned his back to fix her drink, Jack laid into her.

"Jenny, what are you doing? You need to slow down."

"I'm thirsty." She tapped her fingers on the bar to the beat. She didn't look at him.

"So have a glass of water."

"Screw you, Jack. Can't I have a little fun? It's been a long time since I've had some fun. It's all work, work, work."

But Jack suspected that work wasn't what she was talking about. He assumed she was referring to her ex-boyfriend. Alex was an adjunct professor from the university where Claire worked; Jenny had met him years before at a summer party in Jack's backyard. After living with Alex for several years, she had recently left him.

"You're going to have to catch a cab home, then," Jack said. "You're not driving."

"Fine." She reached into the side pocket of her skirt and pulled out some money to pay for her drink. "Anything. Just leave me alone about the drinking."

Just then Earl came down, and Jack was relieved when Jenny found a lawyer from her firm to dance with, leaving him alone to shout over the music to some of the other prosecutors who had joined them. Earl didn't stay long, though; it was clear he was merely putting in an appearance.

"I'm too old for this," he joked when Jack tried to get him to stay because he felt he was supposed to.

The dance floor eventually thinned out, and Jack spied Jenny each time she made a trip to the other side of the bar. He smiled to himself; she probably thought she was being inconspicuous. But he knew she was keeping an eye on him, too, because when all the lawyers he'd been talking to finally left, she reappeared at his side.

"Dance with me." She grabbed his hand and tried to pull him onto the dance floor.

"You're spilling your drink." He reached for the glass in her other hand and took it away.

"Come on," she begged. "Let's have some fun. I just wanna dance."

"I'm not a good dancer, Jen," he protested. "I step on toes."

She lifted her arms above her head and swung her hips to the beat of the music. Her eyes were closed and he knew she wasn't listening to him; the music had completely absorbed her. He watched her dance, a little embarrassed by her drunken display but drawn to it nevertheless. The camisole under her jacket had come untucked when she'd raised her arms, and he could see her flat stomach. Her hair, that luminous black hair that held such a tactile attraction for him, oscillated in waves behind her. Her movements were fluid, uninhibited. *Like a stripper on the East Side,* he thought. He glanced around the club to see how many other guys were thinking the same thing. His eyes met Andy Rinehart's. They both laughed a little and Andy waved his hand like a fan in front of his face. Jack shrugged. He had to get her out of there before she became the talk of the town.

"Come on, Jenny," he said, catching her by the waist in midgyration. "You've got to work tomorrow. We need to get you home to bed."

She let her arms fall. Her face was inches from his and she stared at him, unwavering. "Well, that would be fun, too."

Her statement caught him off guard and his throat tightened; she had never said anything so directly sexual to him before. But then, she'd never been so drunk with him before.

"Where's your car?" he asked.

"In the garage," she said, still moving to the music as he led her out of the bar.

"*Which* garage, Jenny?"

"The same one I always park in."

He sighed. "Across from the stadium?"

She nodded. "But my keys are in my office," she said, giggling, as if somehow it was funny that she was in one place and her keys were in another.

Shit. It had been more than eight years since Jack had set foot in Newman's offices, and he didn't relish the thought of doing it now.

Somehow he managed to get her across the street and into the lobby of her building without running into anyone. The ride in the elevator up to the twenty-third floor felt familiar, as though several years hadn't passed since the last time he'd been there. Everything was the same, just as he'd remembered. The elevator looked the same—the mirrored walls, the chrome railing—even the midnight-blue carpet was identical.

His luck ran out when they stepped out of the elevator and into the firm's lobby.

"Jack! Is that you?" The voice boomed from down the hall to his left.

Oh, God, of all people. It was his old boss, Steve Mendelsohn. What the hell was he doing here at this hour? Mendelsohn, together with Rob Kollman, was a co-chair of Newman's litigation department. Jack quickly reminded himself that he had been away from the firm for more than eight years, during which time he had become a successful prosecutor; he had probably tried more cases in the past year than Mendelsohn had tried in the last ten. He had no reason to be intimidated by this man anymore.

Jack forced a smile as Mendelsohn approached.

"Hey, Steve, how are you?" Jack extended his hand.

"Jack, my boy, it's been too long."

Yeah, right, Jack thought.

"What brings you up here?"

"I'm walking Jenny to her car. We just came from the bar association dinner. She left the keys in her office."

Only then did Mendelsohn acknowledge Jenny's presence. His eyes traveled the length of her long body, both lecherous and disapproving at the same time. Jenny straightened her posture as she mumbled, "Hello," and Jack wasn't sure whether it was her way of defending herself or was an instinctive response to being looked at like that. Despite his earlier, internal pep talk, Jack felt himself getting worked up over the jerk.

"You two are still friends? That's great. I love it how you kids are able to have a social life outside of work. That's really great."

Jack wanted to tell Mendelsohn that he was thirty-five years old and had two kids of his own. But he knew Mendelsohn still thought of him as unformed larva, fresh out of law school. So he restrained himself—barely. "You should try it, Steve."

Mendelsohn looked at him curiously, then let out a deep, low laugh and patted him on the back. "How's life at the DA's office treating you? You keeping those drunk drivers off the streets?"

To hell with restraint. "Actually, I just tried the Adler murder case. I'm sure you read about it in the papers."

"Oh, that was you?" Mendelsohn asked.

"Yup, that was me. The jury returned a guilty verdict just today." Jack hoped Mendelsohn was beginning to realize that the man standing in front of him was not the same young lawyer he had fired years before on a night very similar to this one.

"Well, congratulations are in order." The fake smile had left Mendelsohn's face. "Shall I show you to Ms. Dodson's office, Jack?" He looked at Jenny once more. "I'm not sure she's in a condition to remember where it is."

Jenny glared and began to speak, but Jack interrupted her. "That's not necessary, Steve," he said. "*I* remember where it is."

Jenny cut loose as soon as they'd reached her office and she'd slammed the door behind her.

"The fuckin' asshole! I could poke his beady eyes out, looking at me like that! If he thinks he's going to oust me from this firm or screw up my partnership chances, he's got another think coming!"

"Jenny, calm down. What are you talking about?"

She continued to rant as she walked to the file drawer where she kept her purse. "He's trying to blame me for all the shit happening with Maxine Shepard, and I'm not going to let him. He's into something—I don't know what, yet—but I'm not going to let him make me take the fall for his crap!"

Jack searched through her purse as he tried to make sense of what she was saying. The only part that sounded familiar was the mention of Maxine Shepard. "Crazy Maxine," as Jenny always referred to her, was one of Jenny's least-favorite clients. She was a spunky widow whose husband had left her with more money than she knew what to do with. Sixty-two years old, Maxine wore Levi's and sweatshirts at the same time as she wore a three-carat emerald-cut diamond ring. She smoked Virginia Slims menthols incessantly and spoke with a permanent rasp in her voice. Maxine had come to Newman around the same time as Jenny, after her husband's children from his first marriage—a brother and sister—had contested their father's will and attempted to obtain control of the large estate that had been left to her. As told to Jenny later by Maxine, the children had disliked her from the day they were first introduced.

" 'I'm sure it had something to do with the coat I was wearing that day, some beastly old fur their father had given me—how was I supposed to know it had been their mother's?' " Jenny had mimicked Maxine's deep voice when she first told Jack about her.

Maxine prevailed, and with her caustic personality and seemingly never-ending supply of litigation work for the firm, she soon became a legend around the office. Jenny's first face-to-face meeting with her had occurred just last summer, after another of Maxine's investment deals had gone sour and Jenny was asked by Mendelsohn to "go after the crook that bilked her out of her money." When Jenny didn't immediately indulge Maxine's style, and Maxine didn't warm to working in the shadow of Jenny's youth and beauty, a cold war ensued.

"Are you having trouble with Maxine?" Jack asked. He handed her the purse, minus her keys.

"She fancies herself some worldly businesswoman just because she inherited all this money. But she doesn't have the business sense she needs to play the part. She refused to listen when some of the guys in Corporate suggested she hire someone to handle her investments. She keeps getting screwed, and if I'm not able to clean up the mess, she blames me." Jenny lowered her voice. "And Mendelsohn blames me, too."

"What did you mean, 'he's into something'?" Jack's voice was pressing, insistent; he didn't trust Mendelsohn either.

But Jenny only shook her head and didn't elaborate. She was winding down, and he let it go. He'd ask her about it later, when she was sober.

Her phone rang, and they both stared at it as if it'd just come to life.

"Who's calling you at this hour?" Jack asked.

She made a dismissive noise and waved it off. "Let it go."

This time Jack persisted. "You think it could be Mendelsohn?"

She ignored him and headed for the door, but he reached for the phone. She saw him do it, and before he had a chance to speak, she snatched it from his hand and hung it up. "It's not Mendelsohn, Jack. I'm certain it was Alex and I can't deal with him right now, okay?"

Before they finally left her office, Jack called for a taxi to meet him at Jenny's house in an hour. Plenty of time to get her car and drive her home. They walked along Broadway toward the garage. She was quieter now, but he knew from the skip in her step that the alcohol hadn't begun to wear off. Jenny seemed to have forgotten the run-in with Mendelsohn and the call from Alex. The streets had dried, but a damp smell still hung in the air.

They passed the open door of a sports pub, and Jenny tugged on Jack's sleeve to stop him.

"Uh-uh, no way," he said. "There's gonna be a cab wait—"

She shook her head and put one finger to her lips to quiet him, then pointed into the pub, over the bar. Jack looked up to see his own face on the television screen above the bartender's head. The bartender had his back to the bar and had paused in the middle of pouring a beer to watch. The faces of the three patrons sitting at the bar turned up toward the TV at the same angle.

"It's the eleven o'clock news. They're talking about your win today," Jenny whispered.

Jack fidgeted under the neon light above the doorway. His face and gestures on the screen were animated—"approachable," Earl called it— as he answered the reporters' questions about the Adler case. Jack always enjoyed the interviews while they were happening, but watching himself afterward made him uncomfortable. Tonight was no exception, particularly because the next questions were about the recent arrest of Clyde Hutchins, the accused in the Barnard case. He'd known Jenny Dodson long enough to know where that topic would take them.

"Come on, Jenny, I've already lived this episode," he joked, as Hutchins's photo appeared on screen. He took her hand and led her away from the doorway just as the reporter made the switch. But it was too late.

"They should fry his ass," she announced. When he didn't respond, she stopped on the sidewalk. "Oh, come on, don't tell me you wouldn't like to see that creep get what he deserves. The guy tortured that little girl! And then he left her out in the cold to die a slow death!"

Jack tugged on her sleeve to get her moving again. There was no use trying to have a serious discussion now, so he merely said, "Let's just get him convicted first, why don't we. Okay?"

"But if there was ever the perfect argument for the death penalty, don't you think this case is it?"

He sighed. "I don't think there will *ever* be the perfect argument for the death penalty."

A s they rode the parking-garage elevator to the fifth level, neither spoke. Jack watched Jenny; she kept her head down, looking at her hands. He wondered if the embarrassment of the bar dance was beginning to sink in or whether she was just thinking about Mendelsohn. Or Alex.

He saw her car, a bright red Jeep Wrangler, as soon as they stepped off the elevator. It was one of only a few still parked on that level. They crossed the cement, illuminated by the yellow overhead lights on the ceiling and the ambient glow of the lights of surrounding office buildings that filtered in through the open sides. Their footsteps echoed, and for a moment they walked in step with each other. When they reached the car, he retrieved her keys from his pocket and started to unlock the door. She reached down and softly touched his hand.

"Will you dance with me now?" she whispered.

Jack remained still, his eyes on their motionless hands, but he felt his heart beating wildly, uncontrollably in his chest. He knew, he just knew, what was going to happen, and he stood there frozen; he should just say no and open the car door as he had planned. But there was something in her voice, something that said, *Don't reject me again, like you did back in the bar.*

"There's no music."

She understood then that he had accepted. "That can be remedied," she said as she took the keys from him and, with much concentration, opened the door herself. She sat down in the driver's seat, her legs still outside, and put the key into the ignition. The music she had been listening to on the way to work began again. "Crash Into Me." She leaned over and turned up the volume slightly. The slow, gentle sounds of an acoustic guitar and brushed cymbals floated through the humid air of the garage and out into the night. Had he not known better, he would have thought she had planned all this.

She stood and took his hands, intertwining their fingers. They moved together away from the car, and she moved closer to him. For the first time in nine years he felt her body against his, and even with their clothes as a barrier, it was exactly as he'd imagined—and feared. He felt the fullness of her breasts as they pressed on his chest, and her hips as they brushed up against his. She began to sway to the music, taking him with her.

"Jenny . . ." He tried to speak, but it came out hoarse and he was forced to clear his throat.

"Shh. Just listen; move with the music," she murmured. She closed her eyes and rested her head on his shoulder.

He stared out at the lights of the city, trying to regulate his breathing. *This is the alcohol,* he told himself. He prayed she wouldn't let go of his hands, because he knew he would have no control over them.

She began to lead him around in slow, easy circles. His head reeled, but she seemed unaffected by it all, so relaxed, and he suddenly worried that this pas de deux had a whole different meaning for him than for her. Maybe she did just want to dance.

He tightened his hands on hers, discreetly taking the lead. He felt her tense up and knew she had sensed the switch. He stopped the turning, led them back to the car as slowly as she had led them away, and backed her up against it. She lifted her head and looked at him, startled by his sudden authority.

"You don't step on toes," she said.

"No, I don't," he said, admitting his lie.

Her dark brown eyes were black tonight, and he stared into them, trying to see behind them. She met his stare, as if they were locked in a contest, but finally gave in and looked away.

"Look at me." He turned her cheek so that she faced him again. "What are you doing?"

"What are *you* doing?" she replied without hesitation.

He asked himself the same question as he bent his head down to meet hers. As he felt her lips and then her tongue, he finally submitted completely, his fingers caressing the heavy strands of her silky hair.

His tongue explored her mouth, slowly and gently, without urgency. He felt her hands move to his shoulders, and she exerted light pressure in no particular direction, as if she was unsure whether to push him away. He disregarded it, determining her intentions instead from the hungry response of her mouth.

Later, he wondered how they hadn't heard the elevator cables moving, how they hadn't heard the doors opening and then closing, hard and resolute. They hadn't heard the footsteps or even, unbelievably, the opening of the car door on the other side of the garage. It was the start of the car's engine that startled him and caused him to back away from her, and only because, for less than an instant, he imagined the sound had somehow come from Jenny's car.

"Come on." He grabbed her arm and led her quickly around to the passenger side. The spiral ramp that led to the exit was on their side of the garage and he wanted them inside her car before the other one reached them. She seemed not to have the same sense of urgency. The soporific effects of the alcohol had kicked in, and she stumbled as she tried to get inside.

"Jenny, please," he begged. Without looking, he could see the headlights approaching. He turned his back to the car as it passed slowly behind hers. *Keep going, keep going,* he thought, knowing that had he been the driver, at this hour, he would stop, wondering if the woman was there willingly.

It passed without stopping, and he thanked it and cursed it at the same time, hoping it was indicative of his good fortune and not some girl's bad luck in the future. He waited until it drove onto the ramp before walking to the other side of Jenny's car. When he got in, he looked over at her; she had her head back against the headrest with her eyes closed. He leaned across her to grasp her seat belt, taking care not to let their bodies touch again. As he struggled with the buckle, he watched her face, wondering if she had fallen asleep. And then he saw it. A tear. Just one, in the outer corner of her eye, pooled in the space between her upper and lower eyelids, caught heavy in flight by her black lashes.

Jenny lived in one of the rehabbed Victorian duplexes on Lafayette Square that lined the streets around the park. The taxi was already parked outside, waiting for him, when they arrived. He touched Jenny's hand to wake her.

"I'll be right back," he said to the driver before helping her up the front stoop. The taxi driver nodded in understanding, as if he had watched the same scene unfold numerous times before. Jack fumbled with Jenny's keys, trying a few to determine which opened the door. One finally fit, and he shoved the door open with one hand while balancing her with the other. They were greeted by a Siamese cat; it mewed insistently as it wound its body first between her legs and then his. He pushed it gently out of the way with his foot and kicked the door closed.

It was dark inside, and he felt for a light switch on the wall. He debated whether to try to get Jenny upstairs and into her bed, but thought better of it and steered her to the couch. She immediately rolled onto her side, drew her legs up, and grasped the throw pillow under her head with both hands. He went upstairs, forgoing the interior lights this time in favor of the soft, dim glow of the street lights below. He stopped in the doorway to her bedroom, startled by the imposing mahogany four-poster bed in front of him.

He remembered there had been no bed when he and his son, Michael, had helped her move; she'd lived with Alex, of course, before moving here. Now, she'd dressed the bed to rival any linen catalog. And pillows. There had to be at least seven or eight pillows at the head, and a white scarf was draped from post to post. His eyes were drawn to the room's tall windows, which were framed by long white sheers that matched the bed scarf. He smiled a little, amused by the evidence of the difference in their disposable income; he and Claire still slept on the old bedroom set handed down from her parents. And after five years in their house, the bedroom windows were still covered by roller shades.

He walked around the end of the bed and looked at the items on her dresser. He picked up a picture, one he'd seen in a box when they'd helped her move. It was an old photo—of Jenny, he presumed—taken when she was a little girl. Despite the difference in age and the lighter hair color, the lips on the little girl in the picture were unmistakably hers. She must have been playing dress-up. She wore a billowy, oversized dress shirt—her father's, perhaps—gathered at the waist by a skinny belt. She had adorned herself with a pillbox hat with a large, glorious bow in the front, and jewelry everywhere. She wore black high-heeled pumps with sharp, pointed toes that, because of the camera angle, actually seemed to fit her tiny feet. What struck Jack most, however, as he studied the picture, was the makeup. This little girl, who looked to be no more than five or six, had on the makeup of a grown woman.

He continued to study the photo. The little girl stared back at him, cocky and self-assured even then. Everything was the same but the hair; he couldn't figure out the hair. He knew hair became darker as one grew older, but from amber to black? He was sure she didn't dye it. He set the picture back down, puzzled.

At the end of the dresser, on the floor, a discarded bra and pair of panties lay carelessly at the edge of the area rug. Their intimacy embarrassed him, and he suddenly remembered why he had come up there.

He turned and tugged the comforter from her bed, disturbing another cat, this one a skinny orange tabby curled up in the middle of the pillows. As he gathered the comforter in his arms, something black between the mattress and box spring caught his attention. He stepped closer to the bed and lifted the mattress a bit. A semiautomatic pistol—he recognized it as a Walther PPK .380—rested on the white cotton top of the bed skirt. He immediately thought of Alex, but then dismissed the thought and figured it was just her way of feeling safe in the city. It bothered him, though, that she had never mentioned it to him. But then, why would she?

He returned downstairs and covered her, then squatted next to the couch and moved the hair off her face as an excuse to touch it one more time. "I'll see you later, Jen," he said softly, unsure whether she heard him.

He opened the front door to leave, but her voice whispering his name stopped him.

"Don't deny yourself what you really want." She mumbled as she spoke, from alcohol, from sleep. "It's so close."

"Jenny . . ."

"Jack, do it. Run for DA. Just do it."

Without looking back, he stepped into the quiet still of the night and closed the door behind him. He locked it and dropped her keys through the mail slot.

He settled into the back of the cab and tried not to inhale the sickeningly sweet scent of the peach-shaped air freshener hanging from the rearview mirror. And he wondered how one night in his life could have so drastically altered his view of the world.

CHAPTER TWO

By the time Jack got home it was after midnight; most of the porch lights his neighbors turned on at dusk had been turned off for the night. He decided to leave the car in the driveway to avoid setting off the automatic garage door. The rumble might wake Claire and the kids.

He opened all the car windows and turned off the engine. He reclined his seat and looked at the black sky through the open sunroof. The night had cleared and he stared at the stars but didn't see them. He could see only Jenny's face, the intensity of her dark eyes, and her lips, slightly parted. He closed his eyes, trying to block out her image, to no avail. The noise of the cicadas in the trees behind his house magnified; their relentless high-pitched droning became louder and louder. "Cheat-er! Cheat-er! Cheat-er!" they sang out at him.

"It was just a kiss," he muttered to himself.

He lay there for a while; he didn't know how much time had passed. He started to think about when he and Claire had first started dating, the heady feeling of those first few months. He'd met her almost immediately upon starting law school; it had been Claire's first year, too. He'd seen her from afar during the second, maybe third week. He'd just come out of his Torts class and was still worked up over a debate with his professor. Claire was sitting in the Pit, the sunken, common area in the center of the school where the students gathered between classes to socialize or study.

Once he saw her, he forgot all about Torts class. He suddenly let go of every bit of skepticism he'd ever had about love at first sight; those stories he'd heard about knowing, upon first meeting a woman, that she'd be the one you'd marry. It was the late 1980s, and Claire sat there on the worn, modular furniture in the Pit amid students dressed in khakis and polo shirts or oxfords, the guys with hair shorn close and the women with neat, chin-length bobs, guaranteed to look appropriate with their interview suits. But not Claire. She looked like a leftover hippie who hadn't yet realized Reagan was in office, much less nearing the end of his second term. Her curly blond hair had been even longer then, almost to her waist, and it cascaded carelessly over her shoulders and down her back and arms. Every once in a while, in an apparent effort to keep it behind her, she'd gather it with her hand into a makeshift ponytail and then flip it down against her back. She wore a print sundress made of a gauzy material; its mottled blues and greens reminded him of the ocean on a still day, the subtle colors illuminated in the reflecting flashes of the sun. Some sort of woven rope bracelet graced her wrist. A trace of red lit her cheeks and shoulders, as if she'd been in the sun earlier that day.

When he thought back on it, he was surprised that he'd scored well on his exams that first semester, given how distracted he had become by his pursuit of her. She hadn't been easy to snag, either, not like the other girls he'd dated. At the beginning she'd been uninterested in him; she told him later that he seemed like too much of a "pretty boy." He'd had to work on her, and he hadn't even realized at the time that his boyish good looks were a handicap. It was almost Halloween before he finally persuaded her to have lunch with him. To this day he remained convinced that she agreed only because he promised to make the lunch himself for a picnic in Forest Park, where she could bring her dog, and she didn't really think he'd follow through.

"Jack?" Claire's voice was soft, faraway. "What are you doing out here, babe?"

Jack shot up suddenly, surprised to see Claire standing right outside his car door. He realized he'd fallen asleep.

"Hi." He blinked to bring her into focus. She stood on the pavement in an oversized white nightshirt, her face scrubbed bare of all makeup. She'd pulled her hair back into a braid at the nape of her neck, as she did every night to keep it from getting tangled while she slept. But now, stray curls stood out against the halo of backlight from the lamps over the garage.

"Are you all right? What's the matter?" Claire opened the car door.

"I fell asleep." It sounded as good as anything else he could have said at that point.

"I can see that," she said, laughing a little bit. "Why didn't you come into the house?"

"How'd you know I was out here?"

"I was half asleep when I thought I heard you pull into the driveway. Later I got up to go to the bathroom and saw it was three, but you still weren't in bed yet. So I came looking for you."

Jack opened the door and swung his legs out, but decided against standing up just yet. He stared straight ahead into Claire's shirt, the white cotton glowing against the black of the sky. He reached out and grabbed her hips, pulling her to him. He turned his face and pressed his cheek into her stomach. Although still flat, it was soft from her pregnancies and gave a bit when he leaned into it. He liked that. He inhaled the clean scent of the shirt.

"I missed you," he said without looking up at her.

"I was only a few steps away. Funny you should decide to sleep in your car."

"It's been a weird night." He lifted the shirt and ducked his head under it. Now, skin to skin, his cheek against her stomach, he could smell her scent, the indescribable essence her skin gave off when she was sleeping. He just needed to be honest with her. After all, it was simply a kiss. "Jenny got really drunk tonight. She's upset about something happening at Newman, and probably about Alex, too. I had to drive her home." Did he imagine her muscles tense? When she didn't say anything, he added, "And Earl's quitting."

"What?" Now Claire backed up, forcing Jack's head out.

"He announced it tonight. Says he's going to Clark and Cavanaugh. He claims they made him an offer that's too good to pass up."

"Wow," she said quietly, looking over his head and down the dark street. Jack knew Claire was as surprised as he had been. She knew how long Earl had been in the DA's office. Every lawyer in town had assumed he would retire there.

"What do you think this means for you?" she asked finally. He understood her question. They'd both seen the turnover at other state offices after someone new took over.

Jack turned around and reached for his briefcase on the passenger seat. "I don't know," he said, getting out of the car and quietly closing the door. "It's late, Claire. Let's go to bed. I'm too tired to even think about this now."

He sensed her watching his face, but he didn't look at her. He hadn't meant to sound so abrupt; she probably had a lot of questions, but he couldn't think about Earl's announcement without thinking about what had happened that night with Jenny. He needed time to figure out how to tell Claire.

They didn't talk when they went into the house. She went back into their bedroom while he brushed his teeth and checked on the kids. Michael slept as usual, his body curled up in the fetal position, with the covers pulled up close near his chin. It was his three-year-old son, Jamie, who caused him to pause. Jack stood next to his bed, staring at his small body lying uncovered on a tangle of sheets and blankets. His mouth was open, his still-girlish lips forming an imperfect circle. The guilt from Jack's long-abandoned religious upbringing surfaced, and he hated that he still allowed it to haunt him. Finally, he sighed, bent down, and kissed Jamie's sweaty, sweet-smelling forehead.

When he returned to his bedroom, Claire was still awake, sitting up in bed in the dark, waiting for him. He climbed in next to her, but in the room's blackness the images of Jenny returned. He rolled over on his side, away from her. The cicadas had stopped for the night and the room was still.

"Jack?" Despite the softness with which she spoke, her voice shattered the fragile silence.

"Yeah?"

"What is it? There's something else on your mind."

"Yeah."

She didn't say "tell me" or "what is it?" or anything at all. She just waited. Jack wondered whether relief would come once he'd told her the truth. But what happens if you tell your wife that you kissed another woman? She'd be hurt, he'd say he was sorry—it didn't mean anything, and then it would all just blow over, wouldn't it? After all, he reminded himself again, it was just a kiss.

"I've been thinking . . . what would you think about me running for District Attorney?"

The next day, Jack slept in. The first time he woke, around seven, the bed was empty and he could vaguely hear Claire getting Michael and Jamie ready for school. He smelled coffee and he knew this was Claire's way of tempting him to get up; she didn't drink it. He knew he should drag himself out of bed and go down and have breakfast with them, especially since he hadn't seen his children last night. But he didn't feel he could face his wife. He wondered if he would ever be comfortable around her again, and felt a sick kind of admiration for men who had real affairs and seemed unaffected by them. It was just a kiss, he reminded himself once again. Resolving to just forget about it, he pulled the covers over his head and tried to go back to sleep.

By the time he woke for good, at close to ten, the house was quiet. As he stood in the shower, running the water as hot as he could bear, he thought about what he would say to Jenny the next time they talked, and he wondered when that would be. Should he just pretend it had never happened? Maybe she had been drunk enough that she wouldn't even remember.

He closed his eyes and let the water pour down over his head. The insides of his eyelids burned from the lack of deep sleep. He suddenly wished that Claire were there in the shower with him. He would make slow love to her standing up against the cold, wet tiles, and then maybe any suspicions she had would dissipate in the steam. Would that be enough? Was the nervous weight in the bottom of his stomach merely the manifestation of his fear that Claire would find out, or was it something else?

He thought back to the night he and Jenny had first met. He remembered how it had taken him a while to realize she could flirt with him and not mean anything by it. He'd been at Newman only about a year at the time. He remembered it vividly because he'd spent the day away from the city, touring the remains of a blown-up farmhouse for a product liability case he'd been working on. By the time he'd arrived back at his office, around quarter to six, he was exhausted and behind on everything else. After calling Claire to tell her he'd be late, he'd propped his feet up on his desk, shut his eyes, and folded his arms across his chest. He told himself that after a quick nap he'd be able to get some work done. He had almost dozed off when he heard a steady rain begin. The water drops sounded like the fast, nervous tapping of a hundred fingertips on his window.

"Hypnotic, isn't it?"

The woman's voice startled him. He turned his chair around to see Jenny standing in his doorway. He knew a new associate had been hired in Corporate, and he'd heard talk that she was a looker, but the term didn't do her justice. She was tall, lean, built. She wore a stylish black suit like something from the pages of a magazine, not like the shapeless suits worn by many of the other women lawyers he knew. Her skirt was just slightly shorter than he was used to seeing; her legs were taut and dark even beneath her panty hose. The neckline of her off-white blouse followed the same V shape as her jacket, and he didn't stop his eyes from briefly following it down to the point. Her black hair was smooth, and it shimmered in the fluorescent light.

"Hi, uh . . ." Jack hesitated, trying to remember her name.

"Jennifer Dodson. Jenny's fine." She leaned back into the hallway and pointed to the nameplate on the wall outside his office. "And you're Jack Hilliard." He nodded and stood to greet her. "Nice to meet you, *Mister* Hilliard," she said, walking across his office and extending her hand. He shook it, then they stared at each other across Jack's desk. He searched his brain for something intelligent to say. "I'm sorry, did I interrupt you?" she said finally, breaking the silence.

"No, no, of course not," he managed. He heard the rain coming down even harder and he glanced at the clock. It was almost seven thirty. Despite his good intentions, he hadn't touched a file on his desk and knew at this point he probably wouldn't. "I was just about to go to the lunchroom to pour myself a cup of coffee. Would you like to join me?"

She tilted her head and smiled. They both knew the only thing he'd been about to do was fall asleep. "Sure, I'd like that."

They'd spent the next hour and a half leaning against the counter in front of the coffeepot, talking. Not since Claire had Jack met anyone who put him so at ease. When he asked how she'd ended up at Newman, Jenny explained that she'd gone to law school at Yale and had spent a year practicing in New York before returning to St. Louis.

Jack raised his eyebrows. "New York to St. Louis?"

She shrugged. "I grew up here. I always intended to come back." Jack looked at her without responding, and she smiled. "Is that hard for you to believe?"

"You're just, well, different," he said, grinning. "Where'd you go to high school?"

They both laughed, and Jack knew by her understanding of his parochial joke that she was telling him the truth. It was the question every native St. Louisian asked each other upon first meeting. Suddenly Jack really liked her.

"Do you want to know?"

"No, it doesn't really matter, does it? There's not a high school in this city for which you fit the stereotype." He laughed. "Maybe when I get to know you better, I'll be able to figure it out."

"I doubt it," she said.

"Well, I hope you'll give me the chance," Jack blurted. He suddenly felt foolish, and worried that he sounded as though he was trying to hit on her. He felt himself blushing.

"Well, the firm willing, I hope to be here for a while." She shifted her stance against the counter, and her shoulder lightly grazed his. When she moved, her hair moved, too, and then, so close, he had the urge to reach up and touch it. He looked down at his coffee cup instead, so she wouldn't think he was staring at her.

"Are your parents still here, then?" he asked.

"No, they're dead." He was startled by her lack of euphemism. She didn't offer more, and before Jack could ask, she changed the subject. "Can I ask you a personal question?" she said.

"Sure."

"Does it bother your wife that you work this late?"

"My wife?"

Jenny chuckled. "You know, you're pretty funny." He didn't know if she meant "odd" funny or "humorous" funny. "Yeah, your wife." She pointed at his hand. "Your wedding ring. Usually it's a dead giveaway."

"Oh," he said, looking down at his hand. "Well, she doesn't like it, but she understands, if that's what you mean." Then he added, "She's a lawyer, too."

Jack worried again that she might think he'd been hitting on her, and the question had been her way of letting him know it. Then it suddenly occurred to him that maybe *she'd* been hitting on *him*. He stood up straight and looked at his watch.

"I didn't realize how late it was," he said.

Jenny straightened, too, as if on cue. "Yes, it is late." She walked to the sink and washed out her cup. "Well, it's been nice chatting with you. Maybe I'll see you tomorrow, Mr. Hilliard." And Jack knew he had been dismissed.

Almost nine years had passed since that first meeting, but now, standing in the shower, letting the water get so hot that it almost burned his skin, Jack again felt the imbalance, the inability to grasp the meaning of what had happened between them. Their friendship had survived its uncertain start years before; in fact, it had flourished. He'd eventually understood that her subtle playfulness was merely her way of putting the male lawyers on notice that, although she enjoyed being one of the boys in a firm dominated by men, she was still a woman underneath.

He reminded himself that even Claire liked Jenny. She'd immediately accepted her as his friend; she'd never been the possessive or jealous type. Although they'd never developed a friendship with each other separate from Jack, Claire regularly invited Jenny to their house for dinner, and

Jenny had even babysat the kids a few times when he and Claire went away for the weekend.

They *were* just friends; they would always be just friends. He'd just gone a little bit further than he'd intended. He'd been buzzed and he'd let his inhibitions down. Their flirting hadn't meant anything way back then, and he had to believe it didn't mean anything now. He stepped out of the shower stall and grabbed a clean towel hanging from the rack on the shower door. Claire had put it there for him, he knew. He buried his face in it and smelled the same just-washed scent he'd detected last night on her T-shirt. He hurried then. He had to get out of the house and to the safety of his office. Maybe then everything would get back to normal.

When he arrived at the office, Beverly, a secretary who had worked in the DA's office even longer than Earl, pounced on him.

"Jack!" she said, coming around her desk to greet him. In her hand was a large stack of pink phone messages. "You're a popular man today." After she handed the messages to him, she reached up and touched his chin. "Ooh . . . trying to grow a beard?"

He pushed her hand away. She relentlessly teased him about his youthful face after he'd once been carded at a bar where the office had gone to celebrate a victory.

"Anybody important?" he asked, fingering through the papers.

"Depends who you think's important," she said, shrugging. "Jennifer Dodson's been trying to reach you all morning. Says she really needs to talk to you. After she kept pestering me, I finally told her to just leave a message on your voice mail."

The weight that had lifted briefly when he'd first entered the familiar surroundings of the courthouse was back. "Who else?" Jack said, trying to skim over the mention of Jenny's call so that Beverly wouldn't think it was important, at least not to him.

"A couple of reporters called, wanting to get your reaction to Earl's announcement. I got the feeling they'd already talked with Earl." She paused, as if in thought. "And one wanted to talk to you about Barnard."

"But I'm not handling Barnard."

"I tried to tell him that." She shrugged. "Oh, yeah, and Earl's been looking for you."

In his office, he looked carefully at the messages Jenny had left. The first one was pretty basic—Beverly had simply checked the little box next to RETURN CALL AT YOUR CONVENIENCE. The next, left only twenty minutes after the first, had the same box checked, but Beverly had also handwritten "important" on the memo line. A half hour later, Jenny had called again. Beverly hadn't bothered to check off any boxes on that one; she'd merely scrawled in capital letters across the paper "NEEDS TO TALK TO YOU ASAP!!"

Jack glanced at his phone and saw the message light blinking. He wondered how many of those calls were also from Jenny. He dialed and took a deep breath as he heard her voice.

"Jack, I'm just wondering why you haven't called me back." Her voice oozed artificial calm. "I've been trying to reach you all morning. Could you give me the courtesy of a return call?"

He skipped a few more messages from others and then listened to her next, and last, one.

"Jack, where the hell are you? Why haven't you called me back? Don't tell me you're one of those jerks who refuses to call a woman back because he wants to pretend something never happened. I'm not Glenn Close, you know. I'm not going to stalk you or anything." Her anger trailed off at the end. "I just want to say I'm sorry."

Jack laughed at her comparison. Despite Jenny's ranting, the maniacal character from *Fatal Attraction* would never have entered his mind. He knew Jenny just hated being vulnerable. He pressed the switch and waited for a dial tone. He hit the speed dial for her direct line, even though he knew the number by heart. The phone rang only once before she picked up.

"Jennifer Dodson." Her voice was all business.

"Jenny, it's me."

She let out a huge sigh. "Goddammit, Jack, where the hell have you been?"

"If you wanna be my campaign manager, you'll have to clean up that potty mouth of yours."

She laughed with relief. "You've reconsidered?"

"No, I was just razzin' you."

"Where have you been?" she asked again.

She must still have thought he'd been avoiding her calls.

"I slept in. I just got here about ten minutes ago."

"It wasn't that late when we left last night."

"Yeah, well, long story."

"Is everything okay?"

"Yeah."

The phone line fell quiet. Jack knew she was expecting him to say more. He considered telling her how he had fallen asleep in the car—leaving out the role she had played, of course—but he didn't think he could even say Claire's name out loud to her right then.

He heard Earl's voice down the hall, talking excitedly to someone about his plans. Despite his own misgivings about the future, Jack had to admit that the prospect of a new career seemed to have pumped extra life into his old boss.

Jack took a deep breath. *Here goes,* he thought. "Jenny, about last night—"

She cut him off. "Jack, you don't have to say anything. It's okay, really."

"I know we were a little drunk, and—"

She did it again. "No, Jack, *you* were a little drunk; *I* was a lot drunk. I was out of line and I'm sorry we even have to deal with this. It never has to be mentioned or thought about again."

It happened so smoothly, so quickly, that he didn't even realize at first she had just turned the tables on him. Although she spoke apologetically, as if taking full responsibility for what had happened between them, he knew she was saying, in effect, *I was drunk and indiscriminate; you weren't and you chose me.*

While he sat there trying to think of something to say, he heard a brief knock on his office door. It swung open, on its own, it seemed, as if a ghost had entered the room. Earl was obviously right outside Jack's office. "Don't worry, I'll go easy on you guys for a while," Earl said to someone else. The statement was followed by his low, deep-throated laugh. After a moment, he stuck his head in. Jack was forced to be decisive.

"You're right, Jenny," he said, waving Earl in. "I'm sorry, too. We'll just forget about it."

"Is someone there?" Jenny had heard the change in his tone of voice.

"Yeah, Earl's here. He's been looking for me, too, apparently."

"Okay, go on, then. We'll talk later, about that candidacy of yours." She laughed and her voice was lighter. Jack laughed, too, but it felt forced. When he hung up, Earl closed the door behind him and sat down in one of the chairs opposite Jack's desk.

"Jennifer Dodson?" Earl said, motioning to the phone.

"Yeah."

"Good-looking girl."

He shrugged. "Yeah, I guess."

Earl smiled slightly. "Good lawyer, too, from what I hear."

"Having worked with her for a few years, I'd agree with that. She's very smart."

"You two spent a lot of time together last night. You're good friends, huh?"

Jack grew impatient. "Yes, Earl." He sighed. "You know we're friends. I'm not on the witness stand. Where are you going with this?"

Earl remained silent for a minute, folding his fingers forward over his wide palms to study his nails. "Nowhere in particular, I guess," he said. "I'd just hate to see you end up somewhere that you didn't even know you were going." He looked straight at Jack, and Jack understood why his boss had been a successful DA for so many years. Despite his own talents in the courtroom, he wouldn't want to face Earl from the witness stand.

"You have nothing to worry about," Jack said. "I know exactly where I'm going."

"Okay." Earl stood up and started to wander around the small office, looking at the diplomas and bar licenses on the wall. "You like it here?" he asked suddenly.

"Yes . . ." Jack said cautiously. *Here it comes,* he thought. The invitation to follow Earl to Clark & Cavanaugh. As much as he liked working for him, Jack had no desire ever to practice in a private firm again, but he didn't relish the thought of trying to explain that now. Working at one of the big firms had never been in his plans; frankly, when he'd first started law school, he hadn't even given it any thought. But, like many of his classmates, Jack had succumbed to the enticements of a big, high-paying firm. He and Claire had later joked that being wooed by the big firms was a bit like entering the Hotel California: Until, that is, they didn't want you anymore. "I love my job, Earl. You know that."

He swiveled around in his chair, his eyes following Earl as he made his way around the office. Earl nodded and picked up a picture of Claire from a file cabinet. It was Jack's favorite picture of her. He had taken it in Amagansett, on Long Island, shortly before they were married. It was June; they had gone up for the wedding of a friend and it had been the first time on the East Coast for both of them. It had rained all weekend; neither had realized how cold it could be there at that time of year. On the last day, the rain tapered off to a mist and they decided it would be their only chance to get to the beach. They walked along the shoreline holding hands, adjusting the direction of their stride to avoid the waves that broke on the sand at their feet. The picture was black-and-white, a close-up of Claire's face. Her head was tilted down slightly; her eyes looked up to the camera. She had only the slightest hint of a smile on her face. The wind had been strong that day, and Claire's long, curly hair blew to the side, most of it around the back of her head, toward the ocean. What Jack liked so much about the picture was the way a few stray strands had blown in front of her face and caught on her lips; he had snapped the picture just as she was about to reach up to pull them away.

"She's a beautiful woman, Jack," he said, setting the picture down.

"I know."

Earl crossed his arms and leaned against the cabinet. "How's she feel about your career?"

"What do you mean?"

"Well, some women expect their husbands to bring in a bit more money than you'd ever make at the DA's office."

Jack smiled. That was it, he thought. Earl was going to try to talk him into going with him. "You know she's not like that. She knows how miserable I was at Newman."

"So you plan on staying here awhile?"

"If the next guy wants me, yeah."

"Have you ever thought about being that next guy?" Earl grinned.

Jack laughed. If only Earl knew who else had suggested the same thing to him. He debated whether to risk bringing up Jenny's name again.

"What's so funny?" Earl asked. "You can't tell me you've never thought about it yourself."

Jack couldn't resist. "Actually, I hadn't, at least not seriously, until last night, when the same idea was pitched to me by none other than Jenny Dodson."

"So that's what you two were huddled together talking about."

"Yup, that's it." He was feeling bold now. "Contrary to your suspicions, we weren't planning which motel to meet in."

"I didn't say that."

"You implied it. Give me some credit, will you?"

"I just don't want you to mess things up for yourself."

"I'm married to a 'beautiful woman,' as you say, who I love more than life itself, and I've got two unbelievable kids. I'm not going to do anything stupid." As he said it, Jack had almost convinced himself that he'd done nothing wrong. And then, giving himself that one last push, he added, "Jenny and I are just friends, and we've got the stamp of approval from Claire."

Earl raised his hands in defense. "Okay, okay. Point taken. I won't bring it up again."

Jack took a deep breath and sighed. Earl had always treated him as the prodigal son; now he felt like a spoiled teenager who had rebuffed a parent's generous attempts at guidance.

Beverly knocked on the door and stepped into the office.

"Earl, there's another reporter on the phone for you. You want it in here?"

Earl furrowed his forehead and scratched the short fuzz on the back of his head. A veteran, he always looked like he still got his hair cut by the army.

"No, not now," he said. "Jack and I still have some things to talk about." When Beverly left, Earl said, "Will you give it some thought?"

Jack wanted to say yes. He wanted to think about it, to dream about it.

He knew he was a good lawyer and that, except for one minor—no, major—detail, the job was well suited for him. But, as he'd told Jenny, he knew no city in this state would elect a DA who didn't believe in the death penalty. It was an unspoken prerequisite for the job.

"They've asked me who I want to follow in my footsteps." "They" meaning the reporters, Jack knew. "I gave them your name, Jack."

"You shouldn't have done that without talking to me first."

"I didn't say you were going to run, or even thinking about it. I just said you'd be my pick."

"Well, I'm flattered." Jack meant it. "But the answer's no."

"Jesus . . . Why, Jack?" Earl walked back to his chair.

"Well, let's see, there's that one little problem I have with the death penalty."

"So what?" Earl said, waving his hand in dismissal. "It's not even a factor."

"Of course it is. It will be the first question they ask me. Especially with the Barnard case. Everyone's out for blood, and if you don't give it to them on Barnard, they're gonna make damn sure they get it from the guy who takes your place."

"You've been thinking about this," Earl said quietly.

"I'm just being realistic. It's coming." Jack paused for a minute. "You know, Earl, it's one thing being an Assistant DA. We always knew you'd just keep me off the death penalty cases if that's what I wanted. But it's another thing to suggest someone like me could head up this office. It just won't happen."

"Maybe you're right. But I'd like to believe otherwise."

"That's what I always liked about you, Earl," Jack said, laughing a bit. "You always believed we'd win those cases that seemed impossible to win."

"Don't forget . . . sometimes we did."

"Yeah," Jack conceded. "Sometimes we did."

CHAPTER THREE

The scent of simmering wine and beef broth greeted Jack when he entered the house. He forged into the family room, where he found Claire sitting cross-legged on the floor in front of the built-ins that held their television and stereo. Videotapes, compact discs, and old, dusty cassette tapes surrounded her. The bottom doors of the cabinet were open, and he could see where she had begun to replace the videotapes in an organized array. David Bowie sang "Let's Dance" on the cassette player; the sound was poor and scratchy. One of their old tapes.

He threw his briefcase on the couch and squatted next to her. She turned to him, and he pecked her on the cheek.

"What's up?" she said. "That was the lamest kiss ever."

"Sorry." He forced a smile and gave her another, better one.

"You guys went out after work?" she asked, turning her attention back to the tapes.

"Yeah, just the office. Our own little celebration with Earl." He sat on the floor with her. "Smells good. What's for dinner?"

"Beef Stroganoff. Hungry?"

He hesitated. "Yeah, I guess." He pointed at the mess in front of her. "What are you doing?"

"I don't know. I started to put away some of the tapes the kids left out, and then I just decided to organize the whole thing while I waited for you to get home." She turned the videotape in her hand over to read the title and then searched for its case.

Jack ran a hand through his hair and sighed. He smelled the smoke from the bar on his clothes and thought about taking a shower before dinner. "What happened to you this morning?" he asked. "You didn't wake me to say good-bye."

"I just didn't have the heart. You looked dead to the world. But you know, you had this really pained look on your face, so I almost thought I should."

He picked up a magazine on the floor next to the couch and began to leaf through it mindlessly. "It didn't feel like I got any sleep at all."

"This thing with Earl's really getting to you, isn't it?"

"I don't know. I guess." He tossed the magazine aside. "Today he asked me if I wanted to run. He said he'd already told some reporters that he wanted me to."

She turned around, her eyes wide and smiling. "Really? Wow, that's good, isn't it?" She stopped sorting the tapes and scooted closer to him.

"Yeah, in a perfect world."

"Why do you say that? I thought you said you were thinking about it."

"Well, I was. I am, I guess, or I'd like to." Was he? Or was he just covering, still, from last night? "I'd love the job, but I'd never get elected. Not in the current climate. With Barnard all over the news, they'll want someone who's willing to go for death."

He stood and went into the kitchen. Claire called after him, "If you want the job, just give it your best shot. Just be you and let the voters decide."

He laughed as he poured himself a glass of water at the sink. She wasn't that naïve. "Yeah, let's see," he said, walking back. "When they count the votes, there'd be mine, yours, maybe Earl's." *And Jenny's.*

She laughed, too. "Oh, Jack, you're exaggerating just a bit, don't you think? There are as many people who agree with you as disagree with you."

"Maybe," he said. "But it's the ones who disagree with me who will get out the vote this year."

She kept silent to acknowledge that maybe he had a point.

"Where is everyone?" he asked. "It's so quiet."

"Jamie's upstairs in his room playing. Michael's off Rollerblading somewhere. He knows to be back by seven for dinner."

Jack lay down on the couch, using his feet to kick his briefcase onto the floor. "What's with the retro music?" he asked, singing along under his breath to the Police's "Every Little Thing She Does Is Magic." It was unlike her to be nostalgic.

She stopped what she was doing again. "Don't you know what these are?" Claire grabbed a handful of the cassettes off the carpet and held them up. "They're the tapes you made for me. Don't you remember doing that? When we first started dating."

"Yeah," he conceded quietly. He did remember making those tapes. He remembered sitting in his apartment, in front of the dual cassette players—one to play and one to record—and trying to choose just the right mix of songs for her. He remembered recording this very song, this tape, for their first picnic in Forest Park. He'd wanted to subtly convey his attraction to her. *So much for subtlety,* he thought, embarrassed now by his youthful intentions.

"Of all the things you've ever given me, I've cherished these tapes the most," she said.

He rolled onto his side and propped his head on his hand. "Really? Why?"

Claire moved closer to the couch and sat on the floor in front of his face. "Jack, you've always been such an eloquent speaker, for the right audience. I remember you in mock trial, how you sounded like you'd been speaking to a jury all your life. Even in class, I remember Professor Buckley calling on you, and you were so cocky when you debated with him, the only one in class that he didn't scare the shit out of that first year. But when it came to me, you just lost it. Try as you might, you couldn't say what you wanted to. So these tapes are like old love letters to me."

Okay, so she had realized. He caressed the back of her head and kissed her.

"Hmm," she mumbled from her throat. She pulled away and scrambled up to the couch, stretching out on top of him. She loosened his tie and started to unbutton his shirt.

"Let's go upstairs," Jack suggested between kisses.

She giggled. "We've gotta feed the kids and get them to bed first." She climbed off him and headed for the kitchen. He closed his eyes and listened to her putting the glass he'd left on the counter into the dishwasher. Then he heard Jamie's voice from upstairs and suddenly had the urge to be with him.

He found him seated on the floor of his bedroom, his miniature dinosaurs and zoo animals lined up in front of him. He held two, a T-rex in one hand and a stegosaurus in the other, and he had them engaged in some sort of combat. Jack stood in the doorway and watched him a bit before announcing his presence.

"Hey, buddy."

"Daddy!" Jamie shot up and hugged Jack's legs. "Come on, play animals with me."

"Are you kidding? That's why I came up here. On my way home from work today, all I could think about was getting here so we could play animals together."

Jack lay down on his side next to the line of animals and asked Jamie to choose which animals he wanted him to be; Jamie handed him a brontosaurus and a bear. As they played on the floor together, Jack felt his eyelids getting heavy and he kept dozing off. Jamie jumped on Jack to rouse him, which worked a few times, but he gave up eventually and resumed playing alone. Jack heard Claire calling up to them once or twice, but he couldn't summon the energy to answer her. He eventually rolled over onto his stomach and gave in completely to the exhaustion. At some point he felt Claire touching his shoulder; he stood, half asleep, looked around the now dark room, and saw Jamie asleep in his bed.

"What time is it?" he asked Claire as she led him out of the room.

"After ten."

Damn, he'd missed seeing Michael for two nights in a row.

"What about dinner?" he muttered, falling backward onto their bed. She'd already pulled the covers down for him.

"We saved you some. You can have it for breakfast."

She laughed at him, but he didn't mind. He closed his eyes. She pulled off his shoes and removed his tie. She unbuttoned his shirt the rest of the way but didn't bother trying to get it off. Then he felt the palm of her hand on his cheek. He opened his eyes and looked at her in the dark as she caressed his face.

"You've got to start sleeping in your own bed, Jack."

Sweet Claire. He felt then that everything would be okay.

On Monday morning, the racket from angrily chirping birds outside the open window woke him at quarter to six. The approaching dawn crept through the thin line of space between the shade and the window frame, and in the faint light he watched Claire's face as she slept. He wondered if she'd want to make love. She usually liked to in the morning. She'd once told him that the sensation of a full bladder heightened her body's sensitivity during sex. He'd laughed, but something about the fact that she'd even admitted it excited him.

Now he reached up, pulled the rubber band out of the end of her braid, and spread apart the plaited strands. He gently rubbed her temple with his thumb.

She opened her eyes and rolled over to face him better. "Morning."

"Hi."

"It's early."

He looked at the window. "I was going to run."

"Too bad." Yeah, she wanted to.

He traced his finger down her arm. When he reached her hand, he picked it up, turned it over, and, like a palm reader, lightly caressed it.

"I'm in no hurry." He lifted the blanket and sheet, pulling it down a bit to expose the top half of her naked body. He placed his hand on her warm belly.

"Claire?"

"Yeah?"

"You know I love you."

A small smile. "I know."

Pushing the covers down farther as he went, he slid his hand over her hip and then to her inner thigh. He stayed there a minute, teasing her. He climbed over her and lay on the other side of the bed, using his foot to push the covers off completely. He kissed her, and as he began to run his hands over her body, all he could think about was that he needed to do this; he'd needed to do this so badly since Thursday night. He needed to get back to wherever they'd been before that night, and this was the only way he knew how.

He felt that she sensed his desperation, and even though she couldn't know its origin, she responded eagerly. He kept his eyes open, watched her underneath him, kept his mind on one road, the road back. He kept telling himself that this was his wife, this was the woman he loved, had always loved, would always love. He was almost there . . . almost there. But then she cried out, and he felt every muscle in her body tense; it was as if someone had knocked him out of his lane and into the oncoming traffic. He closed his eyes, tried to get back the control, but couldn't. His mind raced down that other road—the road right into the garage. And standing there, at the end, was Jenny. When he saw her, he shuddered and cried out, too, and then whatever strength he'd had, whatever self-restraint he'd managed to hold on to, was gone.

In the middle of the parking lot outside the Child Advocacy Center, Jack unlocked his car and sat in the driver's seat. The captured heat suffocated him and he closed his eyes briefly, oddly enjoying the sensation. He'd just come from an interview with a young girl who'd been sexually abused by her mother's boyfriend. The police report indicated she was eight years old, but she'd been quiet and withdrawn and had spoken with the vocabulary of a child of four or five.

From the beginning, sex crimes had been the hardest for Jack, because more often than not they involved children. He had trouble falling asleep at night because he couldn't shake the faces of the kids as they reticently told him their tales. They were completely unaware that what had happened to them hadn't happened to every other kid on their block, and yet they knew, subconsciously, that it wasn't right.

He struggled with his inability to reconcile his opposition to the death penalty with the emotions he felt when he thought about Michael or Jamie falling victim to some predator. If the unthinkable happened, he insisted to Claire, he would hunt down the perpetrator and kill him with his bare hands. Claire thought he was merely grandstanding; she claimed that reason would prevail and they would handle it together in a level-headed manner. He knew she was right, that's what they *would* do, but it wasn't what he would *want* to do. And yet he knew these same types of emotions motivated those in favor of the death penalty. How could he hold everyone else to a higher standard than he held himself?

What bothered him now, ironically, was that over the years he had become somewhat desensitized to the cases. Everyone told him that it was completely normal, that it was a defense mechanism and was to be expected after years of prosecuting child sex abuse, but his numbness disturbed him nevertheless.

Now he was just relieved to have the interview over with; it was not the way he wanted to start the week. Maybe the day would begin to improve. He left the door open to cool the car off while he called Beverly on his cell phone.

"Don't come back to the office, Jack," she said. "Earl wants you to meet him at the Noonday Club for lunch. He says it's important."

The restaurant was on the top floor of the Metropolitan Square building. Earl was waiting for him as he stepped off the elevator.

"I assume you're buying," Jack said, surveying the extravagant lobby.

"Come on," Earl said, leading Jack into an empty room across the lobby from the main dining room. "I want to talk to you alone before we go in." He closed the double doors.

"Alone?" Jack walked to the window and looked out. It faced west; Jack could see the government complex where he'd been that morning and, just past that, Forest Park. "Aren't we having lunch alone?" he asked.

"No. We're having lunch with some guys from the party. I wanted them to meet you."

"The party?"

"Don't be so naïve, Jack. The Democrats. The ones who will make sure you win the election, if you decide to run."

"Dammit, Earl," Jack said, his jaw clenched tight. In all the years he had worked for Earl, he couldn't remember ever really getting angry at him. But now he was fuming. "Didn't we go over this on Friday? What are you doing to me?"

"Sit down." Earl pulled out a chair, but Jack glared at him and ignored the command. "Relax, will you? It's not what I'm doing to you. It's what I'm doing *for* you."

"You spring this on me when I get off the elevator? That's not doing something for me. That's sandbagging me. You could have at least told me ahead of time."

"And you would have come, right?"

Jack crossed his arms and turned back to the window.

"That's what I thought." He paused for a minute. "Look, Jack"— Earl's voice was tamer—"all I'm asking is for you to have lunch. Just meet them. Let them ask you a few questions, see what you're all about."

Jack focused on the monstrous compressor on the roof of the building below them, mesmerized by its whirling fan. "Why bother?" he said.

"Because I think you want the job; I think you can taste it. You're just afraid it's impossible. I want you to see it's not."

"It is."

"It's not. Trust me. There are ways to deal with the death penalty issue."

Jack wanted to call Claire, ask her what he should do. Calm, wise Claire.

"What have you told them?" he asked.

"A lot," Earl confessed. "I've been talking to them about you for a while. Did you think I just came up with this idea last week? Not quite."

Jack couldn't help but feel flattered. He turned, started to straighten his jacket. He wasn't wearing a suit that day. "Look at me. I'm not dressed to be meeting these guys."

"Christ, Jack, you're a prosecutor. They don't expect you to look good."

They both laughed, and Jack felt his muscles beginning to ease. But Earl wasn't finished.

"Now listen to me. This isn't the time to bring up your opposition to the death penalty, you got it? First win them over, and we'll address that issue later. And you don't need to tell them how you left Newman. If they ask you about your past experience, just tell them you were there two years before coming to my office." He headed for the doors.

Jack shook his head in disbelief. "You amaze me."

"What?"

"You believe in me enough to do all this, but then you stand there and lecture me about what and what not to say."

"Just my nature, Jack. You know that. You just be sure to turn on that Hilliard charm, and I don't think it matters what comes out of your mouth."

When they entered the main dining room, the quiet noise of subdued conversation and silverware against fine china embraced them. The table was in a corner, next to a window overlooking the Mississippi and the Arch. Jack glanced down at Jenny's building and wondered if she was there. The three men at the table stood when Jack and Earl approached. One of them, the tallest of the three, looked vaguely familiar. Jack thought he recognized him from the news, always at the Governor's side or something.

"Earl, how are you, ol' boy?" said the tall one, shaking Earl's hand. "It's been too long." He turned to Jack. "You must be Mr. Hilliard."

Jack smiled and extended his hand. "Please, call me Jack."

"Gregory Dunne," he said. "This is Stuart Katz and Pat Sullivan." He motioned to the other two.

Jack did a quick appraisal as he shook their hands. Gregory was the only one of the three whom Jack would have mistaken for a Republican. Most Democrats would have just called themselves "Greg." And with his close-cropped hair and expensive suit, he just looked too, well, conservative.

The other two fit the stereotype that Jack had in his mind of liberal politicians. Stuart Katz, too, wore a suit, but it was probably bought off the rack at Macy's. His brown hair was also short, but not as styled as Gregory's. Pat Sullivan had on a navy sport coat and tan slacks; small round spectacles rested on the bridge of his nose. His sandy hair was a tad on the long side. Had his clothes been more well worn or a little bit rumpled, he would have looked like a professor.

They made small talk while they waited for the waiter to take their orders, and despite his earlier objections, Jack found himself enjoying the harmless banter and looking forward to the food, which the others kept raving about. Maybe this was going to be as easy as Earl had made out.

When the waiter set his plate in front of him, Jack had to restrain himself from digging in greedily, as he might have if he'd been with one of the guys from his office. The slow, polite bites he took only made him hungrier.

"So, Jack," said Gregory, "Earl's told us a lot about you."

"Earl's been very supportive of me. I couldn't ask for a better boss. Or friend."

"You've been at the DA's office, what now, ten years?" asked Pat.

"Eight. Two years at Newman, Norton and Levine before that." Maybe he should have just said "eight," and left out the Newman part. Of course, they'd probably done their research and just wanted to make sure his answers were consistent.

They nodded, as if they understood.

"Saw you got the conviction in the Adler case," said Stuart. "When's the sentencing?"

Well, that was easy. They didn't even ask why he'd left Newman.

"It's scheduled for next month sometime."

"What are you going for?" asked Pat.

Jack looked at Earl before answering. They usually made it a habit not to talk about cases unless they had some planned response for the media. He wasn't sure if Earl would expect him to make an exception for these guys, or whether this was some sort of test to see if he kept his mouth shut despite the importance of his audience. But he couldn't read him.

"I'm not sure we've decided that, yet. We're still mulling it over."

"Are you handling the Barnard case?" asked Stuart.

This was beginning to feel like Twenty Questions. "No; Frank Mann handled the arraignment. Either he or Jeff McCarthy, or both, will handle the rest of it, right, Earl?" He looked straight at his boss now, hoping he would help steer the conversation in another direction. "Or maybe our DA will decide to try it himself, go out in a blaze of glory."

They laughed, and Jack relaxed.

"Whaddaya think, Earl? If you don't do it yourself, you're not going to put your best man here on it?" said Gregory.

Okay, Earl, now you're on the hot seat, Jack thought. *Let's see how you like it.*

"I'd love to, if I could," Earl said, leaning back to one side of his chair and placing his arm across the seat back. "Jack's already got a lot on his plate, so I'd have to take him off a few things to put him on Barnard, and then I'd have to figure out who could pick up where he left off. The judges don't like it when I start moving everyone around in the middle of a case. Sure, I'd prefer Jack, but either Mann or McCarthy's capable." He picked up the napkin from his lap and wiped his mouth. "Anyway, Jack might be too busy this summer, huh, boys?" He turned to Jack and winked at him.

But they weren't letting up. "Well, I'm sure you two are aware that there's some pressure to seek the death penalty in the Barnard case," Gregory continued. "Has the time arrived, Earl?"

They all stopped eating, anticipating the answer.

Earl shrugged. "We'll see." He wasn't giving anything away.

"What do you think, Jack?" Gregory pressed on.

"I don't think it's my place to decide. That's still Earl's job, for now." *To hell with this.* He didn't want the job, anyway. Why was he having this conversation?

"Look," Pat spoke up, "we're only asking because it's going to be an issue in the election. It's important to know where you stand."

"I haven't even decided to—"

Earl interrupted. "He works in the DA's office, for Christ's sake—where do you think he stands?"

What on earth was Earl doing? Jack stared at him, trying to make eye contact. Earl's nostrils flared and Jack knew he was trying not to lose his temper. He obviously hadn't expected this discussion at the first meeting.

But they weren't taking Earl's word for it. Gregory pressed on. "Jack, we understand you might not want to comment on a particular case. But, in general . . ."

He started to think that maybe Earl was wrong; maybe he should just be straightforward, tell them now where he stood, and let them decide if they wanted to get behind him despite his views. Put the issue to rest.

"Look, I think there are a lot of problems with the death penalty that need to be addressed. Do you realize that since it was reinstated in this country, almost two-thirds of the trials that ended in death sentences were later, on appeal, ordered to be retried because so many mistakes had been made?" He glanced at Earl to gauge his reaction. He watched Jack, but his face didn't betray his thoughts. Jack wasn't looking forward to their private conversation after lunch.

"You can interpret those statistics several ways, Jack," Gregory stated. "Some would say that they prove the system is working. The mistakes are being caught before it's too late."

"Not all of them," he replied. "DNA tests show that innocent men have been put to death."

"That was before DNA," Stuart interjected. "Now those mistakes are easily prevented."

Tell that to the ones already executed.

As if he'd read Jack's thoughts, Earl spoke up. "Well, that doesn't help the others, does it, Stuart?" Jack looked at him in amazement, acknowledging his support with a thankful glance.

"No, but we're talking about the future. We can't change the past."

Jack felt his own agitation increasing as they spoke.

"But DNA's not enough," he said. "You can send a person to death in this country without any physical evidence. You can send someone to death on circumstantial evidence alone. That's outrageous."

Pat, who had been quietly eating throughout the discussion, finally spoke. "Come on, guys. I think we all know Jack's preaching to the choir." Jack wondered if this was their "good cop, bad cop" routine. Pat turned to him. "I think we understand where you're coming from, and I, for one, agree with you. Indeed, some think the tide's turning across the country, thanks to our neighbor Governor Ryan in Illinois. But the fact of the matter is that the people of our own fair city are going to insist that Earl's successor be willing to seek the death penalty, if the case calls for it. This string of cases that we've had recently has upset the public and they want to hear some tough talk. The Republicans know this and will use it to their advantage. We've got to take that into account."

Well, I'm not your man, then, Jack thought.

"Listen, Jack, once you're in, it'll be up to you to decide whether it's appropriate to seek death," Gregory said.

Once you're in.

Pat spoke again. "We just need to know, theoretically, if the right case came along, you know, given the statute . . ."

Jack nodded; he knew where they were going. They had him pegged; they were now posing this as an ethical question. Would principled Mr. High and Mighty Jack Hilliard follow the law?

"Theoretically," he began hesitantly, "I'd be loath to seek it. But"—*did he just say "but"?*—"as with a judge or a jury, a DA is charged with the duty to uphold the law, and if the facts warrant, as required by the appropriate statute, he would have to weigh those facts and make a proper determination in accordance with that law." *What* did he just say? And did he really just say almost all of it in the third person? He was sure he hadn't said he was in favor of the death penalty in some cases, but it was apparent that everyone else at the table thought he had. Earl beamed.

Gregory nodded and grabbed his drink and then leaned back in his seat before taking a sip. "That's exactly right, and that's what the voters are going to want to hear," he said. Was this guy a fool? Jack himself didn't understand what he'd just said; he seriously doubted the voters would buy such a convoluted response.

He had to get away from them for a few minutes to gather his senses.

The men's room was empty and unnecessarily large and ornate. Jack leaned against the brown speckled marble in front of one of the four sinks and stared at himself in the mirror. He ran his hand through his hair. He wasn't sure what had just happened in the dining room. Clearly they thought he'd said he would be willing to seek the death penalty in the right case. Or did they? Maybe they just thought he was willing to *say* he'd do it. Maybe they didn't even care what he did once he was in the position to decide.

The door to the bathroom opened and a man walked in. Jack nodded to him, washed his hands as if he'd just used the john, and then walked back into the hallway. He'd go back to the dining room and get the damn lunch over with as soon as he could. And then, when they got back to the office, he'd tell Earl to lay off, to leave him alone. He had no intention of running for District Attorney. Period.

They loved you; are you out of your mind?" Earl's voice rose as he slammed the door to his office.

"That's because they think I'm in favor of sending everyone to the electric chair." The volume of Jack's voice almost matched Earl's. "Thanks to you," he added sarcastically.

"Goddammit! You're really starting to piss me off, you know that?" Earl moved a file off his chair and slammed it onto the desk. "They weren't even paying attention to me. You told them exactly what they wanted to hear, once you got off your soapbox." He pointed at Jack, his eyes narrowed. "If you don't like that, you have only yourself to blame." His face was tight and red.

Jack remained stubborn. He sat with his legs crossed, his hands in his lap, his fingers intertwined, his thumbs tapping against each other, one foot swinging nervously. He *hadn't* said what they all thought he had.

"Maybe Mann's the one I should be talking to," Earl said then, taunting Jack.

"If that's who you think you should talk to, then I guess that's who you should talk to." He refused to play the game.

Earl sighed angrily, but the red began to fade. "Look, Jack, I'm not going to beg you. If you really have no interest, fine." He pulled his chair closer to the desk and leaned forward on his elbows. "But here's the thing—I think you do. You wouldn't have said what you did at lunch if you didn't. That was your own little way of keeping your options open. I have no problem with that. The only problem I have is that you won't even admit it to yourself."

"Okay."

"Okay what?"

"Okay, you're entitled to your opinion."

Earl shook his head, pursed his lips. The red crept up again. "Get out of here, then. We'll talk later, once you've had a chance to think about this."

Jack felt as he had when he was fifteen, after his father had quietly chastised him for letting a friend copy his test answers. But there'd never been a discussion with his dad. Jack just did what he was told. "You told me you'd respect my decision," he reminded Earl.

"I will, when it's an honest one. Now out." Earl picked up some mail from his desk and began to read it.

Jack sat there for a moment, staring at the top of his forehead behind the letter, wondering why Earl even cared.

Earl finally looked up, pointed at the door. "Out."

CHAPTER FOUR

That evening, Jack and Claire stayed up late talking. He told her about the lunch, including his statement about how he'd handle a potential capital case and their interpretation of it. Unlike Earl, Claire didn't view Jack's statement as a concealed effort to keep his options open. She thought he'd merely stated the obvious. "A DA *does* have to make those decisions in accordance with the law," she said. "What's wrong with saying that?" For her, the question he had to ask himself was whether he could, in fact, ask for death in a case that met the statute's requirements, regardless of his personal beliefs. If he couldn't, she thought, he had to be forthright about his position and let the voters decide if they still wanted him, or he should forget about running altogether.

As the week wore on, his feeling of abandonment grew, and he found himself wondering why he hadn't heard from Jenny since their brief call on Friday. By the time he arrived at his office on Thursday morning, he'd decided to ask her to lunch. Maybe he'd even score some points for being the one to call first.

He hesitated for only fifteen minutes—the time it took to open his mail—before he picked up the phone. But she wasn't there, and he didn't leave a message. After all, what would he do if he asked her to call back and she didn't?

It was almost ten before she finally picked up, on his seventh try.

"Hey, it's me." He tried to sound nonchalant, undemanding.

"Hi." Sometimes she said, "Hi, me," but not today. Her voice sounded distracted, as though she was in the middle of drafting a brief and it was still on her computer screen and she was only half listening to him.

"What are you doing?"

She laughed a little bit, derisively, he thought. "I'm training for a ten-K race."

Goddammit, she knew what he meant. "Where were you earlier? I tried to call you when I first got in." *And several times thereafter.*

"I went straight to Bankruptcy Court this morning. I had a hearing with Judge Fields. The creditors are trying to get him to dismiss my client's case because they haven't been able to put together a plan of reorganization. I had to go beg on their behalf to get one more chance."

He thought of her sitting in her chair, phone wedged between her ear and shoulder while her hands worked the keyboard. He knew she hated the speakerphone and used it only when others in the room wanted to be in on a call. He wondered what she was wearing. When she'd mentioned court, he'd immediately thought of what she called her "lucky suit." It was an odd green color, sort of minty like the original Crest toothpaste but maybe a shade lighter. On anyone else it would have looked ridiculous, but with her dark skin and black hair she could pull it off. In fact, on her it was stunning.

"A debtor?" he asked, teasing her. Newman didn't usually handle debtor work.

"Well, this isn't just any debtor." She was serious still, ignoring his teasing. "It's Mertz."

"Oh." He understood. The Mertz Corporation was a longtime client of Newman's and it was owned by a prominent St. Louis family. Newman would never have turned down the work. "Well, did you succeed?" he asked.

"Of course" was her immediate reply. He knew she wasn't bragging about her skills, or even referring to her good relationship with Judge Fields, but merely to the fact that a bankruptcy judge didn't like to dismiss a debtor's case unless he had absolutely no other alternative.

"Listen, Jack, I'm sort of in the middle of something right now. I don't have a lot of time to chat. Is there something specific you wanted?"

He swallowed. She'd never been so abrupt with him before. "Yeah, I . . ." He hesitated, and wondered if he should just try another time. Maybe it was too soon. "I thought you said you just got back from court?" he asked instead.

"I did. But Stan laid a new case on me last night before I left, and he wants us to try to get appointed as creditors' counsel. I need to put together some sort of proposal by tomorrow." Stan Goldberg was her boss, the head of the corporate and bankruptcy department at Newman.

But she had to eat, didn't she? "Well, do you have time for lunch?"

"I brought my lunch today."

In all the years he'd known her, he couldn't remember her ever bringing her lunch. If she didn't go out for lunch, she just skipped it.

"Can't you save it for another day?" he suggested. And then he thought of a way: "I wanted to talk to you about, you know, Earl's job."

He could hear her sigh and knew it had worked. "All right. How about outside in the plaza, then? At noon. But half an hour is all I can spare."

"Okay, noon in the plaza." A half hour would do. A half hour was all he needed to get everything back to normal.

At eleven forty, his phone rang and he just knew it was her calling to cancel.

"Jack Hilliard." His voice rose at the end, as if it was a question, and the question was, *Okay, what's the excuse?*

"Jack? Gregory Dunne here."

"Hi, Gregory." He instinctively stood up from his chair and tried to recover quickly. Had he given Dunne his direct dial? Maybe Beverly had just put it through. "How are you?"

"Good. Good. I enjoyed our lunch on Monday. All of us did."

"Yes, I did also. Thank you, again." He looked at his watch. Unless he got off quickly, he'd never make it by noon.

"I spoke to Earl this morning. He says you're still undecided."

Jack bit his lip to suppress his amusement. And surprise. He wouldn't have expected that from Earl, given his cold treatment all week. "He said that, huh?"

"He did. He thought we should get together again, talk a little about the process, you know, about what's involved between now and November. He's a little concerned that your uncertainty might stem from a lack of knowledge."

"Really?" Jack paused as he tried to decide how to respond. A lack of knowledge of what? How easily the voters would buy a lie? "Well, I suppose being more informed might alleviate some of my concerns." *Some, not all, Dunne.*

"I know that November seems a long way off, but you'd be surprised how quickly it sneaks up. We have to name our candidate fairly soon. We'd need to start getting the money lined up by the end of May at the latest. Don't want to be slow out of the starting gate."

Jack dropped to his chair. Until that moment he'd felt like a kid play-acting, pretending that he could be District Attorney. It had all seemed so hypothetical, until now. Until Dunne mentioned money. Money made it real. Money meant someone deciding that he was worth the risk.

"No, I guess not," he said quietly.

"Are you available early next week? Earl said to fit it around your schedule."

Jack stared at the open calendar on his desk, but nothing registered. He'd spent the last eight years at Earl's beck and call, and Earl had said to fit it around Jack's schedule? Was it really only one week ago that Earl announced his resignation? He glanced at his diplomas on the wall, and then rotated his chair to look at a picture resting on the credenza behind him, next to the one of Claire that Earl had picked up last week. It had been taken on the day of their law school graduation. They had their black robes on, and their caps, both adorned with the extra gold tassel that recognized their positions in the top tier of the class. They had their arms around each other's shoulders, and they smiled broadly. God, they had been so young. He remembered thinking, How could they let twenty-five-year-olds be lawyers? He still felt too young, like an impostor. Would they really let a thirty-five-year-old run this office?

"Jack?"

"Yes?"

"Is something wrong?"

He swiveled his chair to face his desk, and sat up erect. "No, no. Actually, everything's great. I'm looking forward to meeting with you again. How's Tuesday?"

By the time they finished their polite chitchat—Dunne was especially talkative—it was almost five minutes after noon. He managed to get down the elevator, out of the courthouse and east seven blocks to the plaza by quarter after. It took another few minutes to find Jenny. She wore navy, not mint green, making it more difficult for him to locate her in the lunch crowd. She sat on the top step at the far end of the plaza, closer to her office than to his. She held a half-eaten sandwich in her right hand and a bottle of water in her left. A paper lunch bag rested on the step next to her. She really had brought her own lunch.

She didn't look up when he approached. "You've got ten minutes, Jack."

Before he could apologize, she added, "You could at least have called."

"Relax, will you? I couldn't call you; I was on the phone. I got a call as I was leaving from a guy I couldn't just blow off, all right?"

She bit into her sandwich, took her time chewing and swallowing. "Couldn't you call him back? In fact, why'd you even pick up the phone if you were on your way out?"

He sat down next to her and lowered his voice. "Frankly, I thought it was you, calling to cancel."

She crumpled up the plastic sandwich bag and shoved it into the paper bag. She pulled out a banana. He took her silence to mean that maybe she had actually considered canceling.

"Well, who was so important?" she asked finally.

He looked at her, her gaze on the banana as she peeled it. They still hadn't made eye contact since he'd arrived. It occurred to him that her anger was merely a cover for her nervousness. He softened.

"Gregory Dunne." She shrugged and waited for more. "From the Democratic Party."

She whipped her head up, finally looking at him to see if he was joking. "You're serious?" He nodded. "What'd he want?"

"I had lunch with him Monday, him and some other guys."

"You're shittin' me."

"No."

"God, Jack, you've been holding out on me."

He watched an ant crawl on the ground between his feet. "Well, I haven't heard from you."

She grunted. "So pick up the damn phone! What, am I supposed to call you and ask if you've had lunch with the Democrats yet?"

She was right. He had been silly, he realized now. If he'd had something to tell her, he should have just picked up the phone and called her.

"So what happened? How come you had lunch with them? What did they say? Did you tell them about the death penalty thing? Are you going to run? What—"

He held up his hand. "Whoa! Slow down. I can only answer so much in my allotted . . ." He paused, looked at his watch dramatically. "What do I have left? Seven minutes?"

She nudged his leg playfully. "Screw you, Hilliard."

He cast a sideways grin at her. The Jenny he knew was back.

He spent the next twenty minutes telling her everything that had happened in the last week, including the phone call from Dunne moments before.

"Jesus" was all she said when he finished. They both gazed out into the center of the plaza, where a street musician with a guitar butchered Beatles tunes in the hope of a few coins in his guitar case. "Jesus," she said again. "It's yours, Jack." Her voice was low, reverential. "I mean, all you have to do is say the word, and it's yours."

She looked right at him. He studied her face and thought about how, if things were different, it'd be so easy to lean over and kiss her. He mentally chided himself for the thought. She was still talking; she couldn't know what he was thinking.

"I had no idea, when I said that Thursday night, that it was this real. I had no idea. I knew you could do it, I meant that, but I had no idea that

Earl was thinking the same thing, and that he was already working to make it happen for you. And then when I saw your name being mentioned in the paper . . ." She paused for a moment. "It's yours."

"Jenny, I can't just lie outright. What am I going to say?"

"You'll say whatever you said to those party guys to convince them. Sounds like it did the trick."

"It's not that easy."

"Bullshit it's not. It's only hard if you make it hard." She shook her head in disbelief. "What more do they have to do for you? Dispense with the election altogether?"

When he didn't answer, she said, "You're a fool, Jack Hilliard. I think that's what Earl's been trying to tell you."

"Well, I've been called worse." As he said it, he spotted Frank Mann and Andy Rinehart walking toward them.

She tracked Jack's eyes; Frank and Andy came closer.

He leaned over close to her ear, lowering his voice as they approached. "What I told you is just between you and me." Her familiar scent filled his nostrils.

"Well, if it's not the dancing queen and her escort," quipped Frank when he stood in front of them. Jack wondered what Andy must had told him about Jenny's suggestive performance in the bar. He glanced over at her. She glared at Frank.

"Good to see you again, too, Frank." In a more pleasant tone, she said, "Hi, Andy."

"Did you guys close down the bars across the river last week?" Andy asked, trying to make up for Frank's rudeness. He sat down on the step in front of Jenny.

But Jenny wasn't buying it. "No, having a real job, I had to work the next day."

"Dodson, from what I hear, you weren't in any condition to be doing any work, at least not the legal kind." Frank laughed at his own comment. Jenny looked as though she were about to explode.

"We came over to see if you two wanted to get a pizza with us," Andy said. Maybe he believed that, but Jack was certain Frank had torment on his mind.

Jenny held up her empty lunch bag. "How unfortunate. I've already eaten."

"So what *did* you two do when you left that night?" Frank asked, raising his eyebrows.

"What do you think?" Jack said. "We went home."

"*You* drove?" Frank said to Jenny, ignoring Jack.

"Oh, you gonna report me to the police, Mr. Mann?"

"*I* drove," Jack said, figuring it'd be better to admit it than have Frank catch them in a lie.

"Really? Mmm, interesting." Frank turned away and faced the middle of the plaza.

Jack thought of the car in the garage, wondering if it could have been Frank's. But that night he'd left much earlier than the rest of them, so Jack decided that Frank just wanted to give them trouble.

"Look, if you guys don't mind, Jenny doesn't have much time today and we were in the middle of a discussion"—he looked at the back of Frank's closely shorn head, hoping he knew that the statement was directed at him—"a *private* discussion."

"Is she helping you plan your campaign strategy?"

Andy stood. "Come on, Mann. You're being a jerk. Can't you tell when you're not wanted?"

"Frank?" Frank turned around at Jack's voice. He was oblivious to the imminent ambush. "I didn't know he had me in mind for the position. I'm not trying to take anything from you."

Frank's eyes dropped for a moment and then he looked up again. "Yeah, I know. I was just needling you. I didn't mean anything by it." He stood. "I'm sorry if it came across wrong." He really did sound repentant, as if he realized for the first time that Jack could be his boss in a few months.

As they walked away, Jack glanced over at Jenny; she pretended to be occupied with the cap of her water bottle. It occurred to him that they'd just talked more to Frank and Andy about the night of the dinner than they had with each other. They sat for a while, listening to the music.

"I don't like that guy," she said finally. But Jack didn't want to discuss Frank.

"Jenny?" She looked at him. "Why were you so hostile to me on the phone, and when I first got here?"

She sighed, and he realized his mistake in asking her an open-ended question. "I'm having a really hard time at work right now, Jack. I'm sorry. You know that I'm up for partner this fall. I feel like Stan's testing my commitment or something. He's loading me down with work. I'm billing more hours than I did when I first started. You'd think I was still in New York. Sometimes I think he asks me to do something at the drop of a hat just to see if I will."

"Have you talked to him about it?" he asked.

"No. He works long hours himself. I don't think I have a right to complain."

He sensed she wasn't telling him everything. He thought of her outburst after they'd seen Mendelsohn at Newman's offices that night. "Is Mendelsohn giving you trouble?"

She shrugged and was quiet for a moment before she answered, "Just the usual for him. You, of all people, know how he is."

"What happened with me was different." He paused. "Jen, that night"—he looked down—"you said something about Mendelsohn trying to screw up your partnership chances . . . something about Maxine Shepard."

She fiddled some more with the bottle cap and then took a drink. "It's nothing. I guess he just doesn't think I'm doing a good enough job for her. That's all."

He waited. She finally met his stare.

"Jack, really. You know Maxine and I are like water and oil. She gets her jollies from trying to make my life miserable."

"In what way?"

"Mendelsohn says she's been complaining about me." She shrugged, as if to suggest she didn't care. "Really, that's all. Okay?"

"You said something about him being 'into' something."

She pretended not to have heard him. "What really pisses me off is that some of the guys are starting that crap again about how Newman has a reputation for only hiring good-looking women. As if that's the only reason I was hired. As if it doesn't matter that I do a damn good job."

"Oh, come on, Jenny. You've never been one to let stupid talk like that bother you." He accepted that he wasn't going to persuade her to talk about Mendelsohn just then. "Anyway, it's not like you don't use your—how shall I say?—physical attributes to your advantage, when you need to." And then he thought that maybe he shouldn't have said that, given their current precarious situation.

But the Jenny he admired, the tough one who consistently proved his first statement right, responded. "Yeah, look who's talking, Mr. Flashes His Dimples on Demand."

"What dimples?" he said and gave her a big grin.

She shook her head and laughed. And then, as if she suddenly remembered something, she eyed her watch. "Now don't get upset; I'm not being hostile. But I do have to scoot." She placed her hand on his knee, using it as leverage to get up. Maybe everything really was back to normal. "Will you call and let me know how your Tuesday meeting goes?"

"I'll even call you before that."

The corner of her lip curled in the start of a smile. She looked pleased, as if she thought everything was okay, too.

Jack's mood dropped like a stone when he returned to his office and found Earl sitting in his chair. Earl held a paperweight in his hand, a large egg-shaped rock that Jamie had painted at preschool and given to Jack as a Father's Day gift. Earl turned it over in his hand, inspecting the boy's work. He wasn't smiling.

"What are you doing?" Jack asked, his tone more accusatory than he intended.

Earl pushed the chair away from the desk, leaned back, and crossed his arms. He furrowed his brow and looked at Jack. "What am I doing? Well, let me see." He spoke slowly. "I'm trying to figure out what it's like to be Jack Hilliard. I'm sitting here, and I'm thinking, Now, what could be going through his mind? What could he be thinking? How does he view the world? He's got this boss who practically wants to hand him his job on a silver platter—a job that, by the way, any of the other attorneys in his office, and some others around town, would kill to have—but Jack doesn't seem to want it." He paused. "At the same time, though, he hasn't taken any calls, or returned any calls, from the reporters who keep trying to reach him, so that he can tell them he doesn't want the job. For some reason, he hasn't told them that he's not going to run. And he also schedules meetings with the very people who can help him get the job—you know, the job that he doesn't want." He tilted his head back and looked at the ceiling. "So what is Jack Hilliard thinking?"

Jack remained standing. From his spot against the door he could hear voices in the hall, some secretaries back from lunch.

"Tell me, Jack, why'd you go to law school?"

Jack shrugged and let out a short laugh. "I don't know, why does anyone go to law school?"

"Come on, seriously. I know you. I don't think it was for the money."

"I don't know, Earl." His voice was louder now. He knew Earl was leading him down the primrose path, but he also knew he needed to go there. "Like I said, probably for the same reason everyone does. We all have this romanticized idea of what a lawyer does, don't we? You know, like we're all going to become Atticus Finch, fighting the good fight."

"Do you feel like you're fighting the good fight?"

He nodded. "Yeah, most days."

"Give me the name of a politician you admire, one you respect. Past or present."

"Can't think of one."

"You haven't even tried."

"Well, if you're talking about recent memory, I liked Jimmy Carter."

Earl grinned, as Jack knew he would. He knew he hadn't chosen the most *effective* one he could think of. But that hadn't been the criteria.

"Because of his honesty?"

"Yes."

"He was a good man?"

"Is. Yes."

"Anyone else? From the past, maybe?"

Jack finally sat down in one of the two chairs in front of his desk.

"Truman, I guess. It's hard to grow up here and not respect Harry Truman."

Earl looked pleased with Jack's choice. "Despite him having dropped the bomb?"

"You're the military man. I shouldn't have to defend that decision."

"But you still admire him?"

"Yes." They looked at each other across Jack's desk. "Look, I know where you're going with this."

Earl removed his feet from the desk and leaned forward. "Where am I going, Jack?"

"You want me to say something like 'the ends justify the means,' right?"

"Do they?"

God, he'd walked right into that one. "You know what? I'm behind on everything. I have a lot of work to catch up on." He stood up. "Can I have my desk back?"

"Sit down. It'll wait."

"Easy for you to say." He sat back down. "You'll be out of here soon."

Earl picked up the rock again and turned it in his hand. "Well?"

"Well, what?" But he knew.

"Do they?"

"I don't think you can compare dropping the A-bomb to deciding whether to run for District Attorney." He couldn't help but laugh, it was so ridiculous.

"No, you can't; it was a much more monumental decision, wasn't it?"

"Yeah, just a bit."

"That's my point, Jack."

He thought he'd followed Earl all along, had cut him off at the pass, but now he felt really stupid, as if he should have already known the point, but didn't. "What?"

"He made a decision of that magnitude, knowing the terrible consequences, and yet he's still an admired, respected man, even by someone like you. You still think he's a good man."

"Don't you?"

"What I think isn't relevant just now."

"He did what he thought was *right*, that's why I respect him."

"No. He did what he had to do to achieve certain goals, but that doesn't mean he gave up his principles."

Jack looked away in frustration. Earl always had a way of making anything he said seem logical. He could coax a mouse into the mouth of a lion if he wanted to.

Earl set the rock down a second time and crossed his arms. "On second thought, maybe you're right." He paused, knowing that statement would get Jack's attention. "Maybe he did do what he thought was right, but 'right' is relative."

"I'm listening."

"What's right or ethical depends on the particular situation at hand. Don't you think?"

"Sounds like a cop-out to me."

"So you think Truman's decision was a cop-out?"

When Jack didn't respond, Earl continued. "Look, Jack, sometimes you just have to work with the system you've got, and accept that. You just do the best you can. There will always be those who think we should ask for death in certain cases; you'll never change that. You know I'm thinking seriously about it in Barnard. I hesitate because I think the man who makes the decision to ask for it should be the one to try it, and I might not be here to do that."

"Well, doesn't that just prove the arbitrariness of it all?" Jack asked sarcastically. "I mean, the Pope comes to town and whispers in the Governor's ear, and the next thing you know, the next guy in line is spared. How friggin' crazy is that?"

Earl ignored Jack's example. "But there are still things you can do in my position that you can't do in yours. Good things. You can set policy in this office, choose the type of cases you want to make a priority. Those child-abuse cases that drive you crazy? The ones where you think I shouldn't send defendants to jail without any provisions for counseling? Well, go for it. If you want the judge to impose counseling, then you can make it your policy to ask for it, or to cut deals, if you want, to require it.

You don't have that leeway now, but in my job, you would. But first you have to get here."

He paused to study Jack's reaction.

"And even the death penalty. You've got a problem with how the statute's written? Then do something about it. You can have an effect on state legislation, if you want. It'll be a lot easier from my chair. You may not change anything, but at least your voice has a better chance of being heard."

"But it's like you said, first I have to get there."

"That's right. But it doesn't have to be so hard, Jack. Stop making it so hard."

Jack looked past Earl to his and Claire's graduation picture. What would Claire say to Earl's little speech? Would he have convinced her? He thought of his dad; he remembered his dad telling him on graduation day that he had the smarts, the skills, and even the drive to succeed, but how far he went would depend on whether he finally gave up his need to please everyone. Jack had been insulted at the time—since it was his dad whom he was always trying to please—but now he realized that it sounded just like something Earl would say. Or Jenny.

"Sounds like you and Jenny have been talking," he said to Earl.

"No, but if she's telling you the same thing, she's a wise girl."

"Look, let me digest what you've said. Fair enough?" Earl nodded. "And I'm doing what you want. Obviously, you know I'm set to meet with Dunne on Tuesday."

Earl came from behind the desk and stood against the front of it. "That's where you keep getting hung up, Jack. You keep telling yourself you're doing what *I* want you to do. Once you accept that you're doing what *you* want to do, everything else will get a lot easier."

CHAPTER FIVE

By the time he and Earl started out on foot for Dunne's office the following Tuesday, Jack had decided there was no point in keeping his options open if he didn't take the time to explore them. He would clarify his position, as he and Claire had agreed he should, but then he would listen to their advice and at least consider whatever he'd need to do, within reason, to win. After all, maybe he was unrealistic to think he could run for office without any compromises.

The clock in the foyer struck eleven when they arrived, but a receptionist led them into a conference room where lunch was already laid out. Dunne, Stuart Katz, and Pat Sullivan were admiring the food when Jack and Earl entered. Dunne approached Jack to shake his hand as Katz and Sullivan casually greeted Earl.

"Jack, how are you?" Dunne asked enthusiastically, his free hand on Jack's back. He pulled out a chair for him as he momentarily directed his attention to the receptionist. "Kelly, get this man a drink, will you?" To Jack again: "What'll you have?"

Jack tried to digest the unexpected attention being lavished on him. Had he not known better, he might have thought they believed he'd already decided to run.

. . .

They spent most of the meeting going over the mechanics of the election. Everything seemed much more grassroots than Jack had imagined, and he was relieved. A few fund-raisers, flyers, yard signs, possibly some short interviews or profile pieces. When he expressed his surprise, they reminded him that the election of a DA was small potatoes in the grand scheme of things. He wondered if Earl had told them to stress that fact. The less consequential the election, the less consequential the sellout.

"You'll want to choose some people you trust to help you out. You need someone to handle your PR, and someone to keep track of the money." Jack noticed that Dunne spoke as if he had already decided to run. "And, of course, you'll need a campaign manager. Someone to oversee everything so you can spend your time at fund-raisers and just getting your name out there. Plus, you'll want to have the time to keep doing what you do best—trying cases. Every case you win will help your PR."

"How much time are we talking about? At fund-raisers, I mean." Jack had never been one to enjoy the forced camaraderie of large legal functions, and he imagined fund-raisers to be ten times worse.

"Believe me, Jack, you'll grow to love them." It was Katz talking now. "People want to be associated with a winner, and if they think you're that winner, they fawn over you. You'll be amazed at how good a fund-raiser can make you feel."

Jack doubted the accuracy of Katz's claim, and he didn't like to think he might be susceptible to such false flattery even if it was true.

Earl must have sensed this; he jumped in. "Don't worry. It's just a few months between now and November. We're talking District Attorney, not President." He smirked, and Jack knew he was thinking back to their conversation on Thursday. "There won't be too many events. You'll still have time to go out with your wife on the weekends."

Nice thought, except Jack couldn't even remember the last time he and Claire had hired a sitter so that they could go out alone together. He'd been gently nodding his head in agreement with whatever they'd been saying to him, even though, deep in his thoughts, he wasn't paying attention. But when he heard Stuart jokingly mention the Barnard case, it had the effect of someone splashing cold water on his face. He sat up straighter and tried to piece together the conversation. He relaxed only slightly when he figured out that Stuart had addressed Earl.

"That's not how I make my decisions, Stuart," Earl said.

"I'm just thinking it might take the heat off Jack a bit." Stuart shrugged.

"Jack can take the heat. I'm not going to let Barnard be influenced by November's election." Earl's tone was steady, but firm.

Jack guessed from Earl's cold response that Stuart must have suggested that Earl ask for death in the Barnard case to quench the public's thirst before the election. The idea disgusted Jack, and he decided this was a good time to bring up his own concerns, when there might be a chance that Earl would sympathize with him.

He braced himself for their reaction. "Since you've brought it up, let's talk about me taking the heat. What about the death penalty?"

"What about it, Jack?" Dunne leaned forward, his hands clasped together on the table.

"You know my views about it." He hesitated. His next sentence should have been, *I won't misrepresent myself to get elected,* but instead he said, "How am I supposed to reconcile those views with the public's desire to elect someone who's in favor of it?"

Dunne started to speak again but Pat Sullivan motioned with his hand to interrupt him. "Jack, the way I understand it, you don't like the law, but you know you're ethically bound to follow it, and will do so if the situation calls for it. Is that right?"

"Yes, but—"

"Then you've already reconciled it. It's that simple." Pat grabbed a handful of peanuts and sat back. "If the issue comes up—"

"*When* the issue comes up," Jack interrupted.

"Okay, I'll give you that. It probably will come up this year, with the Barnard case all over the news. When it comes up, you just reiterate what you've explained to us. No one is asking you to say you support the death penalty. You need to understand that."

Jack saw Dunne purse his lips and stare at Earl with impatience. The meeting had taken a turn that Dunne obviously hadn't anticipated.

"I do understand that," Jack said suddenly.

Dunne turned to him. "Good. It's very important you understand that." He leaned his elbow on the table and pointed at him. "But it's more important for you to understand that you can't come right out and say that you oppose it, either. Like it or not, Mr. Hilliard, running for office is like walking a tightrope."

Jack swallowed. When had they reverted to a more formal, last-name basis?

Dunne stood and walked over to the food. "If you aren't ready to master that skill now, you should give up. Don't waste our time." As he talked, he placed a sandwich on his plate without inviting the others to join him. Jack scanned their reactions. Dunne clearly had the floor and they were deferring to him.

"This country is pretty much split down the middle on the issue, as I'm sure *you* know," Dunne continued, as he piled on more food. "The majority leans one way or the other depending on whether there's been a gruesome crime in the news lately. Unfortunately for you, the tables are currently tipped in favor of the death penalty. I'm sorry about that. There's nothing I can do. So you just have to make up your mind whether you want to deal with it, or wait another four years and hope the climate changes." He turned to face them, balancing his full plate in one hand as he motioned with the other. "Of course, by then you'll also have to deal with running against an incumbent without the support of this party."

Jack forced himself to remain calm. "Once I make the decision to run, I'll be more than ready to master the skill, Mr. Dunne," he said. "But I'm not going to make that decision without knowing exactly what's expected of me, what 'mastering the skill' means. If you believe that's tantamount to wasting your time, so be it. I'll have my lunch and be on my way."

As he pulled out a chair next to Earl's, Stuart said, "Jack, what you're saying is—"

"Excuse me," Dunne said tersely in Stuart's direction. He was finished massaging the potential candidate. He turned to Jack. "It means being able to address the issue without polarizing the public. That's the only way to get elected. Do you think you can do that?"

Jack relaxed slightly. Dunne hadn't called his bluff. He struggled not to let Dunne see his relief.

"I *know* I can do that, Mr. Dunne. I just haven't made up my mind if I *want* to."

Dunne glanced at his watch. "Well, let's see. We're already into the middle of May. Do you think you could make up your mind by the Friday before Memorial Day?"

"If that's when you need to know, then that's when you'll have your answer."

The meeting had lasted longer than expected. By the time they returned to the courthouse, Jack had just enough time to grab a file from his office before heading to the eighth floor for a hearing in Judge Lehman's courtroom. He was a half hour into the hearing when the defendant's attorney requested a break to deal with an emergency on another case. Jack approached the bench to chat with the judge and his clerk while they waited for the other attorney to finish his calls in the hallway.

"Did you decide whether to run, Jack?" Judge Lehman asked. He took his glasses off and rubbed the lenses with a small, white cloth.

"Not yet. What do you think, Judge? Are the rewards of winning an election worth the gruel of a campaign?"

The judge smiled and placed his glasses back on the bridge of his nose. "Can't help you there. Judges know that the only ones who even bother to vote for us are the lawyers, so a campaign like you'd face is practically nonexistent." He looked at something behind Jack's shoulder and raised his voice for his next statement. "Mr. Hilliard, I think you have your own little cheering section." He nodded to the benches behind Jack.

Jack turned around and grinned; Claire was sitting in the back row of the empty courtroom. "Excuse me, Judge," he said and went to greet her.

"We'll resume in ten minutes," the judge announced and exited a side door to his chambers.

"Hey there." Jack slipped into the row with Claire, and she stood to greet him. He touched her cheek and kissed her briefly. "This is a pleasant surprise. What are you doing here?"

She smiled, too, clearly pleased that he was happy to see her. "I don't know. I decided it'd been a while since I'd seen you in action."

He kissed her again. "No class?"

"I canceled it. Justice O'Connor was speaking on campus today, so I knew no one would show up anyway."

His eyes widened in disbelief. "And you didn't want to go?"

"Well, it *was* a tough choice. Handsome husband or stodgy old jurist."

"You flatter me." He nudged her foot teasingly with his own. "We'll be done soon. You can wait in my office if—"

"No, no. I want to watch."

He held her hands down low in the space between them. She still wore her work clothes, or what for Claire constituted work clothes. Her dress was a terracotta color, a shirtwaist style that loosely followed her figure. She seemed out of place in the courtroom, although at one time she'd spent long hours there, too. But it wasn't just her clothes; her body language lacked the defensiveness that many attorneys unconsciously carried with them at all times. "You look pretty."

"How did it go this morning?"

Jack realized, somewhat guiltily, that he hadn't even thought to call her to report on the meeting. Not that he'd had the time.

"It went well, I think." He squeezed her hands. "I got a good lunch out of it."

"Did you make up your mind?"

"Without talking to you? Of course not."

"What'd they say when you clarified your position on the death penalty?"

Jack glanced back at the clerk. She was on the phone and paying them no attention.

"Jack?"

"Listen, when I'm done here we'll go get a bite to eat and I'll tell you everything we talked about, okay?"

Her shoulders fell and she took her hands back. "You didn't talk about it, did you?"

"Yes, we talked about it."

"What'd you say?"

"I'm in the middle of a hearing."

"No, you're in the middle of a ten-minute break from a hearing. Plenty of time to explain the gist of what was said."

He leaned against the seat back and crossed his arms. He turned his head again briefly to look at the clerk. "We talked about it. We talked about how to deal with the media on the issue—you know, how to answer any questions."

"You need them to tell you how to do that? How hard can it be? You answer honestly."

Jack shook his head in frustration. "You're not that naïve, Claire. Give me a break."

"It's naïve to want you to be honest?"

"No one said I'm going to be dishonest."

"Maybe you should start over, then." Her tone was sarcastic. "I've misunderstood."

He grunted. "Maybe you should—" He stopped himself. *Leave,* he was going to say. *Get off your high horse. Join the real world.*

"What?" She put her hands on her hips. "Maybe I should what, Jack?"

He breathed deeply and reached for her hands again. "Maybe *we* should do what I first suggested. Let's talk afterward, okay?"

She looked past him at the bench. For an instant, he wondered if she missed being in the courtroom herself, and that's why she'd stopped by. The defendant's attorney came through the double doors then and nodded to them as he passed. Claire forced a smile.

Jack lowered his voice. "Didn't you ever work on a case where you made arguments that you didn't completely buy yourself? But you made them because you still believed, on the whole, your client deserved to win?"

She shook her head. "You're rationalizing."

"Isn't that what matters, ultimately? That the right party wins?"

"No matter how he does it? Is that what you're saying?"

"You didn't answer me. Didn't you ever have a case like that?"

She sighed. "I don't know, Jack. I'm sure I did." She shrugged. "Maybe that's why I work at the law school now."

The door from Judge Lehman's chambers opened and he emerged, his black robe flowing behind him. "Are you gentlemen ready to continue?" he asked as he took the bench.

Jack waved to indicate his readiness. Turning back to Claire, he said, "I've gotta go. We'll talk more when I'm done, okay?"

"Ms. Hilliard?" The judge's good-natured voice carried easily to the back of the courtroom. "Are you here to decide whether you'd bother voting for this guy?" He motioned to Jack, who was on his way back to his seat at the prosecutor's table.

She laughed. "Oh, he knows he has my vote no matter what."

"Then he should work extra hard to make you proud."

Jack desperately wanted to slide down in his chair and hide under the table. He turned to look at Claire, but she ignored him and focused on Judge Lehman.

"You know what, Judge?" Only then did she look right at Jack. "I couldn't agree with you more."

CHAPTER SIX

Jack sat on the steps of the front porch, a paper grocery bag between his legs and a stack of corn on the cob beside him. Jamie sat next to him on his other side. Jack picked up an ear and handed it to Jamie, then reached for another for himself. They both began to rip the husks, methodically peeling them off.

"Look, Jamester, you have to grab it like this at the top, sort of divide it with your fingers, grab a clump, and then tug the whole thing down. That's how you get the silks off at the same time." Jamie stared at him, perplexed. "The little yellow hairs," Jack clarified.

"Like this?" He shoved his ear in Jack's face, proud of his slow progress.

"Yeah, like that," Jack said, dropping his own peelings into the bag. "You've got it now."

After several moments of silence, broken only by the sound of shucking and the occasional rustle of the bag, Jamie announced, "I love Mommy's corn."

Jack laughed. As if she had grown it. "Jamester, it's our corn this time. We're the ones doing all the work."

"Does that mean you'll be cooking it, too?"

Jack turned around at the sound of Claire's voice. She stood in the doorway, behind the screen. "How long have you been standing there?" he asked.

"Long enough," she said, smiling. She opened the screen door and stepped out onto the porch. She squatted behind Jack and wrapped her arms around him.

"Who taught you how to shuck the corn?" she said, her lips brushing against his ear.

"My mom."

"Liar."

"You."

"Exactly." She leaned toward Jamie now. "Which means, Jamie, honey, that it's still Mommy's corn, by proxy."

Jamie giggled, not because he understood, but because Claire tickled Jack's waist and caused him to squirm. She pushed aside the unshucked corn to make a spot for herself next to him and then bent forward to pick weeds from the mulched bed next to the steps. Jack lightly rubbed the back of her neck under her hair and leaned down to kiss the top of her head. She turned and smiled at the unexpected gesture.

"What time is Mark coming?" he asked.

"Around four."

"I hope Uncle Mark brings me a toy," said Jamie.

"Don't be begging him for toys, Jamie," Jack scolded. His brother was a sales rep for a toy company, and Jack hated the way he spoiled the kids with new things every time he came over.

Jack finished the last ear. He watched Claire for a while; she'd turned the weed picking into a full-time job and had moved into the middle of the bed. When the phone rang inside the house, she stood and brushed the dirt from her hands.

"Just let it go," said Jack, who didn't want the moment to end.

"I can't," she said. "We've got company coming."

"So?" But she'd already run into the house, letting the screen door close behind her. He gathered up the corn and followed her into the kitchen.

"No, I'm fine, I don't need anything." Claire snapped her fingers to get Jack's attention. She pointed to the front of the house. Jack shrugged, confused.

"No, really, I'm set. Just come on over around four."

Jack determined it was his brother, although her tone was less familiar than usual. Claire covered the mouthpiece with her hand and whispered to him, "Jamie."

Jack darted outside. Jamie hadn't left the yard. He sat on the ground cross-legged with his purple bucket next to him, using his red shovel to dump dirt into it. He looked up when Jack came out. "I'm making soup," he declared.

Jack opened the screen for Claire when he heard her coming through the front hall. "Well, was it company?" he teased.

"Yes," she said, in a tone that said, *I told you so*.

"What'd he want?"

"*He* didn't want anything. *She* wanted to know if I needed anything."

"He's bringing someone?"

"No, I invited Jenny."

Jack's muscles tensed. "You invited my brother."

"I also invited Jenny."

Jack sat back down on the steps. "Why didn't you tell me?"

Claire shrugged. "Because I knew how you'd react. I know what you think about my matchmaking." She sat, too, this time in one of the wooden rockers.

"Is that what you call it? Well, let's see, Claire, maybe you should remember what happened the last time you set her up." He heard the sarcasm in his voice.

She picked at some loose paint on the armrest of the chair and brushed the flakes away. "Jenny and Alex had a fairly long relationship, if you remember correctly. Just because it didn't end in marriage doesn't mean it wasn't worth having."

"It caused her a lot of pain."

"'Between grief and nothing, I will take grief,'" Claire quoted smugly.

"You're sick, you know that? It's her life, not some book." He hated how Claire, with her English- and American-literature degrees, always had some relevant quote for everything. "And it's not your choice."

"I'm not trying to choose anything. I'm just providing opportunity."

Jack shook his head in disgust. His brother, of all people. What was she thinking?

"She just moved out of Alex's a month or so ago, you know."

"I'm aware of that. But she's not a widow. If I'm not mistaken, there's no mandated mourning period after breaking up with someone."

"If she wanted to date, she's got plenty of opportunities at Newman and all over town. She's surrounded by men all day. It's not like she can't find a man."

"I'm well aware of *that,* too."

For a moment, from the way she said it, Jack thought she was somehow accusing him, or hinting that she knew about the incident in the parking garage.

"You know," she continued, "it's easy for you to say this with your cozy little house in the suburbs and your wife and two kids. Did it ever occur to you that she'd like a family, too?"

"I think she's capable of creating it without your help."

Claire turned away. They sat there wordlessly, looking at anything except each other.

"Tell me something. Were you going to wait until she pulled in the driveway to tell me she was coming?" he asked after a few moments.

"No." Her voice sounded unsure. She got up and went to sit next to him. He scooted over a bit, as if to make room, but both knew it was his way of saying he didn't want to be so close to her at that moment. "Jack, what are you so angry about? He's so much like you, I just thought it would be a good match."

"What's that supposed to mean?"

She hesitated. "I don't know. . . . You and Jenny are such good friends, and you and your brother are so similar . . . I don't mean your looks, although that, too, I guess, but your personalities. . . . It just seemed natural that she'd take a liking to him."

"He's not like me," he said, ignoring the obvious implications.

She fingered the honey-colored hairs on his leg; he pretended not to notice. "He is. You don't see it because you're too close. But anyone who knows you both thinks so."

Jamie, sensing the tension, came over and Claire reached out to him. He climbed up into her lap and rested his head on her collarbone.

"I just don't see what you're getting so upset about," she said to Jack. "It's just a barbecue."

He watched her hand stroke Jamie's blond head. What *was* he so upset about? Initially, it was the thought of spending a few uncomfortable hours with Claire and Jenny together. He was beginning to think this was some sort of punishment for his transgression. But what was really bugging him, he knew, was the fact that he wanted Jenny nowhere near his brother.

Mark arrived first, as Jack knew he would; he'd never known Jenny to be on time for anything, not even court. Jack and Michael were shooting hoops when Mark pulled up. He drove a black BMW Z3, just washed. The hubcaps flashed in the sun when he turned into the driveway.

"Hey, bro." Mark greeted Jack with a twelve-pack of Budweiser. He waved to Michael, who tossed the ball to him, trying to catch him off guard.

"Still driving this piece of shit?" Jack asked, smiling. Mark loved his cars. He had trouble keeping one for more than a year or so, always tempted by newer models or faster engines.

"Yeah, well, it's been good to me. No tickets, yet."

"I wondered why I hadn't heard from you in a while."

Mark laughed. "I think all the cops know me by now, so they don't even bother." He looked over Jack's shoulder and then handed him the beer and started walking to the open garage. Jack turned to see Claire approaching.

"Hey," Mark exclaimed as he hugged her. She kissed his cheek.

"Maybe they just mistake you for Jack," she said, picking up on their conversation. She glanced at Jack, raising her eyebrows as if she'd just scored extra points in their spat.

Mark, unaware of Claire's double entendre, stood back and pretended to appraise her. "Looking good, as usual, Claire. I'm taking her home with me," he said to Jack.

His younger brother was right—she did look good. She had changed into a lightweight jumper, its gossamer fabric hanging easily on her slim body. Her skin glowed from an afternoon in the sun the day before. She had pulled back the front of her hair in a low barrette; the rest hung loose, its gilded curls just grazing the middle of her back. Jack set the beer down and wrapped his arms around Claire's waist from behind. She smelled good, too: lemony. "I might have to share my friends with you, but I'm not sharing my wife." He felt her relax; she'd accepted his overture.

Mark jumped in front of Michael and stole the ball from him. "So *where* is the black-haired beauty with the big dark eyes?" he sang, taking another shot.

"Late, as usual," Jack said. He watched Mark dodge back and forth behind Michael, trying to get the ball as Michael dribbled it in front of him.

Claire picked up the beer and went into the house. Once she was out of earshot, Michael said, "You'll like her, Uncle Mark. She's hot."

Jack's jaw dropped. Michael had not yet shown much interest in girls; the comment surprised him and smacked of disrespect. He nudged his son's arm to indicate his disapproval, and Mark snickered.

Jack glared at him. "He's not even twelve. He shouldn't talk about women like that."

"Yeah, whatever," Mark said. He grabbed his brother's arm and led him back to his car, away from Michael. "Why don't *you* tell me a little bit about her, in that case?"

Well, let's see, Mark, we had a little make-out session in a downtown parking garage a few weeks ago, and frankly, I don't like the thought of you doing the same.

"There's nothing to tell you." Jack paused. "Just do me a favor, will you? Just stay away from her. I don't know where Claire got this ridiculous idea to set you up."

"She hasn't arranged a marriage. It's just a barbecue."

"Yeah, well, after the barbecue, just forget you ever met her, okay?"

"I'll decide that after the barbecue." Mark leaned against the car and crossed his arms, defiant.

"I'm asking you to decide it now."

"What's it matter to you, anyway?" Mark narrowed his eyes at Jack.

"Look, we're good friends; we have been for years. Your track record with women is not great, and when you eventually dump her, it's bound to affect our friendship."

Mark laughed. "God, you are so transparent. No wonder Claire's trying to set us up."

Jack leaned against the car, too, his palms on the hood, his fingers drumming on the flawless finish. He wanted to respond, but he feared his voice would betray him.

Mark taunted him. "You can't have her, so you don't want anyone else to, either."

Jack remained silent. He began to wonder just what, exactly, Claire had told Mark about Jenny.

"Ah, the ever-articulate orator is speechless." Mark slapped his hand against the side of his own head. "But, of course, I almost forgot, the jury is always told the defendant's silence is not indicative of guilt, isn't that right?"

"Fuck you," Jack managed to say.

"Nice try, Jack, but the answer to your request is no. If I want to see her again, I will." He leaned over, his mouth next to Jack's ear. "And don't worry, your secret's safe with me."

Jack wondered what level homicide he'd be charged with if he reached over, slammed his brother onto the hood of the car, and choked him right there. Surely nothing higher than voluntary manslaughter. He imagined, at least, a fight like the ones they used to have as kids, rolling around on the hard ground in their backyard, grunting and panting as each struggled to gain control, Jack always ending up on top and threatening to smear dog shit in Mark's face. He wished now he had done it at least once. He tried to remember what those fights had been about; nothing specific came to mind but he was sure it had always been some sort of provocation by Mark. He stared at Michael and told himself that but for his son's presence, he would have hauled Mark onto the grass and taken him on a little trip down memory lane. Instead he stood, fuming, his fists clenched in balls.

"Here she comes," Michael announced. They turned to see Jenny's Jeep coming down the street, the soft top off. When she saw them notice her approach, she honked the horn and then maneuvered the car against the curb.

As she climbed out, Mark whistled under his breath. She'd left her hair down and it was tousled and tangled from the wind; she appeared not to care. She wore a short black skirt that showed off her legs and a soft pink sleeveless turtleneck. Jack noticed how the armholes curved in a bit, accentuating her shoulders.

"From a distance it was hard to tell you two apart," she said as she sauntered toward them.

Jack sighed. He knew it was her way of trying to make light of the situation Claire had put them in, and that she had no way of knowing the conversations he'd had that day—first with Claire and then with his brother—but he wished she had chosen something else, anything else, to say.

"Yes, but now that you're close, you can see I'm the more handsome one, don't you think?" Mark said, reaching out to shake her hand. "Hi, Jenny. Mark Hilliard."

She laughed and shook his hand, and then she touched Jack lightly on the arm. "Hi there," she said to him. He was glad of the intimacy of her gesture, and he almost wished he were ten again so he could stick out his tongue at his annoying brother.

"Where's Claire?" she asked. Claire. He'd almost forgotten there were other issues to contend with. Well, he might as well get the worst over with.

His anxiety over the approaching moment proved to be worse than the moment itself. Jenny seemed entirely comfortable, and given her friendliness to Mark in the driveway, Jack found it a lot easier to be affectionate with Claire. After a bit, his tension eased.

"Hey, Mark. Did Jack tell you his boss is quitting?" Claire spoke from the far end of the deck, in front of the barbecue grill. Jack went to her and traded her spatula for a cold beer.

"What's that mean?" Mark asked.

Jack and Claire looked at each other knowingly. They both knew that Mark never read a newspaper and probably didn't even vote.

"It means there's an opening for the top job," Jenny said.

"Jack wants to run." Claire sat next to her.

Jack couldn't see Jenny unless he turned around, but he felt her dark eyes boring into him. The last she knew, he was still resisting the idea. And really, he still was. "I think it's more accurate to say Earl's trying to convince me to run," Jack called over his shoulder.

"Earl's the boss?" Mark asked.

"Yeah," Jenny and Claire said at the same time.

"But?"

Jack closed the lid of the grill and joined them. He grabbed some chips and leaned against the railing. "But, I'm the only one who seems to care that my moral beliefs are antithetical to the position."

"Yeah, he thinks monsters who rape, choke, and tie little girls to trees, leaving them to die from the elements, should be allowed to live." Jenny winked at Mark after she rattled off her version of the Barnard case.

Jack was amazed at how quickly she had figured out his brother. She seemed to know instinctively she had an ally.

"I think his feelings are a little bit more complex than that," Claire said quietly.

"That's exactly what his problem is, Claire," Mark said, coming to Jenny's defense. "He thinks about everything too much. If he wants the job, he should just go for it."

"And what would you have him tell the voters when they ask his position on the death penalty?" Claire said.

"I think he should do what every other politician does to get elected. Tell them what they want to hear and then do what he wants once he gets in." Mark smiled at Jenny.

"Jack, what he's suggesting isn't as bad as it sounds," said Jenny. "I think what he's trying to say is that to get into a position to make any difference, you sometimes have to compromise."

"He makes a difference now." Claire stood and walked back to the grill. Jack's eyes followed her.

"Of course he does," Jenny said. "But just think of what he could do as head of that office."

"What's your boss say, Jack?" Mark asked.

Jack pretended to be surprised that Mark spoke to him. "Oh, I'm sorry. I didn't realize what I think about this subject might be relevant."

Mark, unable to resist an opening, retorted, "It's not. Just what your boss thinks."

"The food will be ready in a minute," Claire announced as she went into the house. Then, through the screen: "Can you help me a second, Jack?"

He stood to follow her. "He thinks I'm a fool if I don't do it." He glanced at Jenny, wondering if she'd remember calling him that.

"Don't let him get to you," Claire said inside the house. "He's just in performance mode for her." She moved closer and leaned against him.

He played with her curls. "Do I look like I'm letting him get to me?"

"You're unusually quiet."

He shrugged. He didn't want to tell her he was starting to believe that maybe they were right. Despite their tiff at the courthouse, he knew Claire really had no problem with his running; she just didn't want him to misrepresent himself to get elected. But maybe Earl was right; maybe Jenny and Mark were right. Once elected, it would be up to him to decide how to handle cases. If he never saw a set of facts that convinced him the death penalty was appropriate, well, he'd just never ask for it. He knew that wasn't fair, though, because implicit in this was some sort of bargain, some promise that if someday he came across a heinous enough crime, he'd ask for the death penalty. But he knew himself enough to know, no matter the facts, no matter the crime, he never would. And Claire knew that, too.

He bent his head and kissed her lips lightly. "I'm fine."

The screen opened and Jenny stepped in, but stopped suddenly when she saw them. Jack stood straighter and took a step back.

"Oh, I'm sorry." She pointed toward the bathroom. "I was just going to wash up and see if you wanted some help, Claire."

"That's okay." She looked from Jenny to Jack. He looked down at the ground. "Come back when you're done, and I'm sure I can find something for you to do."

"Why don't I put on some music?" Jack said after he heard the bathroom door close. Claire grabbed his arm as he turned to the family room and yanked him back.

"Hey, what was that all about?" she hissed in a whisper.

"What do you mean?"

"Is there some law against kissing your wife? You two acted like a couple of teenagers who just accidentally walked in on their parents having sex."

"I guess it just made her uncomfortable, that's all."

"What's your excuse?"

Jack felt like he was being backed into a corner from which there was no escape. In trial, sometimes the only thing to do in that situation was to go on the offensive.

"You're being paranoid, Claire. Lighten up." He shook his arm and she released her grip. After turning on the radio he went back outside with Mark. *Let Jenny deal with it,* he thought, and opened the cooler to grab a beer.

After dinner, the four adults sat at the patio table and talked. Michael and Jamie hovered nearby in the yard, waiting for Claire to bring out dessert. Jack was ready for Mark and Jenny to leave; he thought the worst was over and he just wanted the evening to end. But then Jamie asked for a cup of water, and Jack went inside to get it. Through the window above the kitchen sink he could see Jenny and Mark flirting. Claire was sitting on the other side of the table, out of his line of sight. The radio was turned up loud so that they could hear it outside. The bass vibrated in his chest, and he heard only their voices over the music, not decipherable words.

The song ended, and over the beginning strums of an acoustic guitar, the DJ announced the next one. Jack didn't need to be told the name, though; he could have named that tune in two notes. He remained motionless, staring out the window at Jenny, hoping that she'd been drunk enough not to remember the song they'd danced to.

But she remembered. She fidgeted in her chair, crossed her legs, uncrossed them. Took a long drink of her beer. And then what he feared most: she looked up and saw him in the window. For a moment their eyes locked, each too nervous to know what to do. Jenny looked down at the bottle in her hands, into its long neck, and began to pick at the wet label. Mark said something to her; she smiled slightly, politely patronizing him. Mark must have sensed something, because he looked up, too, and Jack's and Mark's eyes met briefly just before Jack spun around, his back to the sink. He wished that somehow he could see Claire without her seeing him. What was she doing? Did she see what was happening? Did she understand? And then he heard Jenny laugh, a spontaneous, easy laugh, followed by another from Claire, and he turned again to see his brother jumping around on the deck, like some character in a cartoon trying to walk across a bed of hot coals. What was he doing?

"Yow!" Mark hollered. "Is it gone? Do you see it? It was a big sucker." He swatted at the air.

"I never did see it." Jenny giggled. Jack could tell that she knew it was an act, but she played along.

"Jack, your son's dying of thirst out here," Claire called, still laughing at Mark. He looked down; to his surprise, he still held the cup. He stepped back outside and sat in his spot next to Claire. Jamie ran to him and guzzled the water. The music still played but now it seemed that he was the only one to hear it. Jenny had taken advantage of his brother's little show to compose herself, and she appeared relaxed. Claire, thank God, was clueless. But Mark wasn't letting him off that easily.

"Tell them, Jack, about the time I had that allergic reaction to a bee sting."

"How come I've never heard this story before?" Claire asked.

Fine, Jack could play this game, and he could play it better than Mark. "Yeah, I remember. What I remember is when they gave you that god-awful shot with that enormous needle to administer the antidote. You screamed in pain and then cried like a baby. Even though you were like, what, thirteen or so?" He paused and glanced at Jenny. She had her beer bottle at her lips to cover her smile. She understood exactly what Jack was doing. "Yep, now that I think about it, I remember it vividly, Mark." He shook his head slowly, as if he were sympathizing with his little brother all over again. "You were thirteen, but you cried like a baby. Just like a little baby." And then he leaned back, put his arm on the back of Claire's chair, and tried in vain to enjoy the laughs he got out of Claire and Jenny at his brother's expense.

Jenny left first, and later Jack walked out to the driveway with Mark.
    "Mark . . ." Jack began when they reached his brother's car. Just as he had decided to fabricate some story to explain the odd behavior, Mark saved him the trouble. He raised his hand.

    "I don't want to know." He poked his index finger hard against Jack's chest. "You'd just better get your shit together." He used his finger to push him back, away from the car door. "Don't think for a minute I did that bee routine for you. I did it for Claire." He opened the door and got in. Closed it hard. He backed the car out of the driveway and stopped just as he'd turned the car in front of the driveway entrance. "And I'll make it easier for you, Jack," he called from the open window. "I think I'll ask her out."

CHAPTER SEVEN

On the third Wednesday in May, Jack woke to the loud, low slap of their bedroom door slamming shut. Sleet pelted the bedroom window, and tiny, needle-sharp pellets of ice and water blew sideways through the five-inch gap below the window, which they'd opened the night before to catch a cool breeze. Now, the temperature in the room reminded him of the walk-in freezer at Dierbergs, the grocery store where he'd worked years before as a bagger.

"You've got to see this," he said to Claire from the window.

The slamming door must have startled her, too. She appeared at Jack's side, fully awake. Together they gazed at the three large maple trees surrounding the deck, their new leaves, spring green and still tender, hanging heavily, encased in ice. "It's freaky," she said. "It's going to kill everything."

Jack knew she was thinking of the many hours she'd spent in the yard last weekend. On Sunday she'd planted rose bushes. After begrudgingly allowing Jack to dig the postholes for her—she'd wanted it to be her project, and hers alone—she'd installed two perpendicular sections of post-rail fence in a sunny corner of the backyard and planted the climbing roses all along the front of it. That they would become casualties of this freakish storm, as she called it, he knew caused her the most distress.

"Just think of how neat it will look, though," he suggested as he pulled her close. "The ice on the new buds. We can go out with the camera before it melts." He thought this would help; it bothered her that he didn't use his camera much anymore.

She leaned against him, her arms crossed tightly in a vain attempt to ward off the chill. "I'd better go shut the kids' windows." As she opened the door to leave the room, she added offhandedly, "I think Mother Nature is a little bit confused."

Join the crowd, he thought.

He had two days left to make his decision.

When the schools announced a two-hour delayed opening because of the ice storm, he offered to go in late so that Claire could still make her ten o'clock class; classes at the university would be held regardless of the weather. But he had an ulterior motive. He planned to dig his camera out of a box in the back of their closet and take some pictures of the ice storm after she left. If he was fortunate enough to get a good shot before the temperature started its inevitable rise, he would enlarge a print and save it for her birthday in September.

After Michael scrambled out the door to catch his bus, Jack got Jamie dressed quickly. He searched the hall closet for his coat, sensing that any delay would cause him to miss out.

The grass crackled under their feet as they started over to the far side of the yard, where Claire had spent most of Sunday. Jamie tagged behind, stopping several times on the way to investigate a branch that had fallen from the weight of the ice or some crispy brown leaves left over from fall. Jack finally realized these little pit stops provided some good photo ops, so he stopped, too, and began shooting. When Jamie saw what Jack was doing, he began mugging for the camera. He smiled wide, his top lip stretching to show not only his baby teeth but his gums, too. The mist settled on his face, and Jack tried to get in close enough to capture the beaded droplets that blended with the faint freckles on his nose and cheeks.

Jamie decided he'd rather be photographer than model. He stretched out his arm for the camera, but Jack whisked it out of his reach before Jamie's wet hands touched the lens. The interruption reminded Jack of the reason why he'd come outside.

"Come on, Jamester, let's go see what Mommy's flowers look like," he said.

Jamie followed Jack to the fence, where they both pondered the scene before them. The rose bushes were pruned low, but a spattering of tiny green buds sprouted from the almost leafless canes. Ice still coated the bushes and the fence, but it was wet and glassy, as if someone had applied a clear varnish. It would be gone in less than an hour, Jack knew. As he squatted and began snapping, Jamie approached the fence, stuck out one finger, and touched it lightly.

"It's like God wanted to freeze the day," he said quietly.

Jack lowered the camera and regarded Jamie, a little awed by his statement. It was just the type of insight Claire would have had, had she been there with them. An insight to reinforce his belief that she viewed the world differently from everyone else. That she saw it with more clarity.

"Yeah. It is, isn't it?" he said.

He grabbed Jamie by the sleeve of his coat and pulled him closer, between his legs. He held the camera in front of Jamie's face, focused for him, and showed him which button to press. Jamie tried to grasp the camera between his hands, but he was caught off guard by its weight and almost dropped it. Jack caught it and put it back into his hands, this time looping the camera strap around his son's shoulders. He placed Jamie's small fingers in the right spots, then stood close as the boy pointed it first at the bushes, as Jack had, and then at the woods farther back, and then at the ground and the sky, taking a picture of each view. He laughed when Jamie finally turned around and snapped a picture of Jack, at the most ten inches away.

"My turn now, buddy," Jack said. "We've gotta finish and get you to school."

He took a few more pictures, approaching the roses and the fence from different angles, and then he took some of the maples, too, because he doubted he'd ever see them like this again in his lifetime.

"I guess Mother Nature has just about made up her mind, hasn't she, Jamie?" he whispered in his son's ear. And Jamie smiled that illuminating, gummy smile again, as if he knew exactly what Jack was talking about.

On the drive to work after dropping Jamie at school, Jack thought of Claire, and the kids, and how he'd been in his own world the past several weeks, a world in which they weren't even invited to visit. Once he and Jamie had stepped into the yard, though, he'd remembered why he once enjoyed photography. The ability to zero in on one thing, to concentrate on the moment to the exclusion of everything else. When he saw Jamie through the viewfinder, Earl disappeared, Jenny disappeared, Gregory Dunne disappeared, the entire courthouse, and all the judges and the DA's office disappeared. The noise that seemed constantly to dwell in his head evaporated, and the only sounds that had mattered to him were the words spoken by his son as he crouched in the yard talking to himself. He'd forgotten the camera had this effect on him. But Claire had remembered. She always knew. She knew back when she was the only subject at the other end of the lens, and later, when she shared the space with Michael. By the time Jamie came along, though, Jack had all but abandoned his old Nikon, and Claire took the family's pictures with a fully automatic camera.

When he finally pulled into the parking garage around eleven thirty, he'd made up his mind to abandon any fantasies of running for DA. He was eager to tell Earl of his decision. Once in front of his own office, though, he hesitated. He knew Earl would not accept the news happily, despite his promise to Jack.

Finally he went into his office and closed the door. He decided he just wasn't ready to endure Earl's wrath.

He'd tell him later, right before he went home to share the good news with Claire.

The letter lay on his desk, hidden among other mail that had arrived that morning. It caught Jack's attention because his name and address were handwritten. The top left-hand corner, where he would usually see the name and return address of some law firm, was empty. He looked the envelope over. The writer had used black ink and written in small, scratchy letters, all caps. Except the *J* and the *H*. These letters were larger than the rest, almost twice the size. He looked at the postmark. Nothing unusual: St. Louis.

He opened the letter. The handwriting inside matched that on the outside: same color ink, same small, sharp, capital letters. Monday's date was written in the upper right-hand corner. The writer began, *Dear Mister Hilliard*.

> You wont remember me. You did my daughters case more than three years ago, but I seen your name in the paper and I want to tell you that you would be a good man to run for Mister Scanlons job. I will vote for you. My girl Sheryl was shot by her no good husband and his no good lawyer tried to say it was self defense but you proved it was not.

He did remember, though, as soon as she mentioned the name Sheryl. He remembered because the case was the first time he'd ever seen the name spelled with an *S* instead of a *C*. And he remembered the daughter. He remembered the pictures the mother had brought him, because she hadn't liked that he knew her daughter only from the bloody crime-scene photos.

> If not for you he would have got away with it and my granddaughter would have to see him or even live with him. But you showed he was lying. You showed that it didn't happen like he said, that it couldn't happen like he said. And you put him in jail for life. How can I ever thank you?

Jack remembered the details of the case more clearly as he read. Sheryl's daughter, the letter writer's granddaughter, had been in the room when her father shot her mother. He remembered the grandmother's agonizing throughout the trial, because she feared that if her son-in-law prevailed, he would gain custody of the girl. Jack had feared the same thing, and that fear had motivated everything he did on the case.

I read that you have not decided if you want to run for Mister Scanlons job. I hope you do. That is why I am writing to you. I want to tell you that I will vote for you, that I hope you do not let me and my granddaughter down.

During the investigation the grandmother had repeatedly asked him to seek the death penalty, and he had kept putting her off, trying to tell her it was up to Earl and that Earl was not inclined to seek it on that type of case. He finally convinced her that the execution of her son-in-law would only add to her granddaughter's trauma, and that the girl might someday want to confront her father about his crime.

You are a good man and we need a good man to take over for Mister Scanlon. Please do it, Mister Hilliard. Don't let us down.

The letter was signed *Sinserely, Mrs. Betty Waters,* and it was the only part of the letter that was written in cursive script. He reread the letter several times and then set it on the desk in front of him. He picked up the envelope to check again for the return address. There wasn't one. He'd have to get the file from downstairs to find it.

Leaning back in his chair, he closed his eyes and tried to picture Jamie's face through the viewfinder. Tried to picture Claire's face if he pointed the camera at her. What would she think if she read this letter? Would she be proud of him? Would she agree he'd made a difference? *He makes a difference now.* The noise was back. *But just think of what he could do as head of that office.* He could already hear Jenny: *See, even this lady thinks you're a fool if you don't do it.* He opened his eyes, but the noise was still there. The noise wouldn't go away.

He wanted it. Why was he so afraid to go for it? *To get into a position to make any difference, you sometimes have to compromise.* He tried again to imagine the camera in his hands, his finger lightly on the button, ready to shoot, but he couldn't focus it. Claire stood right in front of him, but he couldn't focus. *You still think he's a good man.* Why couldn't he focus it, dammit? *Doesn't that just prove the arbitrariness of it all?* Then he imagined photographing Jenny; he'd never had occasion to take a picture of her. *I think he'd be a great boss.* When he adjusted the lens, just slightly, the blur faded, vaporized like the morning's mist, leaving in its wake a view of Jenny, her dark skin and dark hair in sharp contrast to the white sky behind her. *Stop making it so hard.* He could see her perfectly. She had on her green suit, the minty one. *What more do they have to do for you?* Her eyes stared down the camera. *But you first have to get here.* She never opened those eyes to him, not really. *I first have to get there.* But he held the camera now; he held an X-ray machine. *Don't deny yourself what you really want.* He could see clearly now. He could see behind the eyes. *It's so close.* He could see right into them; everything else disappeared. *All you have to do is say the word, and it's yours.* Where had all his so-called principles gotten him, anyway? Look what had happened at Newman. He'd already lost a job over his goddamn principles. *All you have to do is say the word, and it's yours.* No one else seemed to care.

He reached for the phone and dialed Earl's extension. "You got a minute?"

After a moment of quiet, Earl said, "Yeah, I've got a minute. My door's open."

But Jack didn't want to wait the thirty seconds it would take to get to Earl's office.

"I'm coming down. We'll call Dunne together."

"And what are we telling him?" But Earl knew. Jack knew that he knew.

"We're telling him I want your job." And then he laughed, it sounded so funny. He laughed because he felt the relief he'd expected to feel earlier. He laughed because he felt light, and a little weak. He laughed because he liked the way it sounded; he liked the way *he* sounded when he admitted it to Earl. *I want your job.* He sounded like an honest man.

They called Gregory Dunne together. After the initial congratulations and banter, they scheduled a meeting, and then Dunne asked Jack's permission to contact the media. Jack, who should have known better, who'd had plenty of experience with the speed with which news could travel, made the mistake of giving Dunne the go-ahead.

When they finished with Dunne, and after another round of congratulations with the rest of the office, Jack was finally left alone to get back to work. His efforts were fruitless, though, because within the hour his phone began ringing. The news had traveled faster than he'd expected. It started with a reporter or two calling to confirm the rumor, but then he began receiving calls from other attorneys, defense attorneys he'd tried cases against, attorneys he knew from law school, and attorneys he'd worked with at Newman. He received calls from a few judges and from some judges' law clerks. He even received a call from Steve Mendelsohn, who politely congratulated Jack and informed him that Newman would support him in his run, which Jack took to mean they'd contribute financially to his campaign. Except for Mendelsohn, he wasn't surprised by any of the callers, but the continuous outpouring throughout the day stunned him nevertheless. As soon as he realized how the word had traveled so fast—not through reporters but from one attorney in his office to another outside it—he began to answer the calls in anticipation of hearing Jenny's voice. Especially after he'd heard from Newman attorneys. She had to know.

The call he didn't anticipate came midafternoon, several hours after he'd first picked up the phone and called three offices down to Earl. He was being congratulated by an investigator when he saw the red light of the other line begin to flash next to the steady green. He quickly concluded the conversation, not wanting to miss the incoming call in case it was Jenny.

He instantly recognized the female voice.

"Well, I guess I'm supposed to say congratulations, but it would have been nice to have heard it from you first."

Jack took a deep breath and let it out. "Claire." God, he was an idiot.

"Thanks, Jack. Thanks a lot."

"I'm sorry. I'm really sorry. I've been on the phone nonstop since telling Earl. I—"

"You knew when I left this morning and you didn't mention it to me?"

"No, I hadn't made—"

"Thanks, Jack. How do you think it felt when one of my students, *one of my own students,* says to me, 'Oh, I heard your husband's decided to run for DA.' How do you think that felt?"

"I'm sorry."

"And I think it's just more of the same talk, you know, until he says he saw it on the Internet. He saw it on the fucking Internet!"

"What?" He didn't know what surprised him more, her cursing or her mention of seeing the news online. Claire just didn't curse.

"So I run down to my office and pull it up, and there it is, on the *Post-Dispatch* site, that my husband has announced he's going to run for District Attorney. God, isn't that nice?"

"I'm sorry, I didn't know."

"Fuck you."

"Claire, it wasn't like that. It all happened so quickly. I didn't have time to call you."

"Shut up. Just shut up."

So he did. But she didn't say anything either, and as the silence lengthened, he started to worry that maybe he was supposed to say something even though she'd told him not to.

"Claire, just listen to me a minute, okay?"

"What'd you tell the *Post-Dispatch* about the death penalty, Jack?"

"That didn't come up."

"Yet."

He sighed. "I'll deal with it, okay?"

"Yeah, I bet you will."

"Listen to me. I didn't decide until I got in this morning, after dropping Jamie off. I told Earl, and then, before I knew it, it got crazy in here. I didn't have time to call you. People kept coming in, and the phone kept ringing. It was crazy. I was going to call you."

"When?"

"When I had a minute."

"You were going to fit me in, huh?"

"Claire, it wasn't—"

"God damn you, Jack. I should have been the first person you told, even before Earl."

"I know; I'm sorry. I'm really sorry. What do you want me to say?"

"You go to work, and poof! you just decided you were going to run?"

"No, not *poof!*" He mocked her use of the word. "I think you know it's been on my mind." His own anger was starting to build now.

"Oh, I know. Trust me, I know. How could I not know? Our life for the past month has revolved around you and your fucking decision."

"Well, excuse me. Remind me next time and I won't involve you."

"Fuck you!" She yelled it this time and started to cry. He felt bad all over again.

"I think you're making too much out of this," he said softly, trying to let her know he wasn't mad, despite his earlier tone. "It was an innocent mistake. I just let the time get away from me. I had it in my mind to call you the whole time." He could hear her trying to stifle her sobs. The other line started flashing again. "Claire? Don't be mad, okay? I really am sorry."

"I feel like you keep everything from me lately."

"Claire, listen—"

"I have to get home before the bus comes."

"Don't hang up yet."

"I'm not in the mood to play beat-the-bus."

"He's old enough to let himself into the house. If you're a few minutes late, it won't kill him."

"It might. He might burn the house down making a snack."

"You're trying to change the subject."

"I'm leaving now, Jack. I'll see you when you get home, whenever that may be."

"Claire, come on."

"Bye. I love you." She always said "I love you," even when she was angry at him. It was one of her unwritten rules for making a marriage work. Make your spouse feel extra guilty by telling him you love him even when you're mad because he's been a jerk.

"Don't—"

But it was too late. He heard the click of the receiver, followed by silence and then a dial tone. As he hung up the phone, he caught sight of the letter from Betty Waters. He picked it up and read it again. Then he crumpled it into a ball and tossed it, in a grand, sweeping arc, into the toy basketball hoop that hung from the back of his door.

At five fifteen Jack was sitting in his office, wondering if Claire would still be angry at him when he got home. The high he'd felt before she called had all but disappeared, and he hadn't felt like talking to anyone

since. He left the door closed, using the excuse that he had to catch up—
he could hardly remember the last time he'd done any real work—and
told Beverly he wasn't taking calls.

There was a knock at the door, and then: "Jack?" Beverly poked her
head in. When the door opened, he watched it push the crumpled letter
across the floor. "Jennifer Dodson's on the phone. Said to tell you it's her."

"Thanks, Beverly, go ahead and send it in." He reached for the phone
in the middle of the first ring. "Hey!"

"Hey, you! What's this I hear, you're going to be the next District Attorney?" He laughed, and she let out a scream, high-pitched and contained. "Jack, I'm so excited for you! I knew you'd do it, I just knew it.
When did you make up your mind?"

"Just today."

"I can't believe it. I just got back from bankruptcy court. I was there all
day for a confirmation hearing, and I get back, and everyone's saying to
me, 'Oh, did you hear about Hilliard?' and I'm like, 'What about Hilliard?'
I couldn't believe it. This is so exciting, isn't it? You're a shoo-in. You're
going to be the DA, you know that?"

The smile was back, and the laugh. "Well, I wouldn't—"

"You are. You know it. I can't believe it."

"Thanks, Jen."

"Tell me about it. Tell me what made you decide. How did you decide?"

"Truthfully?"

"Of course."

"You'll think I'm crazy."

"No, I won't. Tell me."

"You promise?"

"I promise. Tell me."

"I got a letter this morning in the mail."

"And what did this letter have to do with you deciding to run?"

"Well, that's the part I really can't explain. It was from this lady, the
mother of a woman who'd been murdered by her husband a couple of
years ago. I told you about it then, I think. The granddaughter of the lady
who wrote the letter saw her dad shoot her mother."

"Oh God."

"Yeah, it was a bad case. Anyway, the little girl's grandmother wrote me this really nice letter."

When Jenny was quiet on the other end, he said, "I told you that you'd think I was crazy."

"You're not crazy. Just sweet. Incredibly sweet and vulnerable."

He didn't respond; the comment felt too intimate and made him a little nervous. As if she realized it, she added, "Little old ladies have an effect on you."

"Yeah," he mumbled, trying to find something to say.

"Let's celebrate," Jenny said suddenly. "I'm taking you to lunch tomorrow. My treat. Some good food, too. Where should we go?"

"I'll go wherever you take me."

In the split second of dead air, he recognized that the words he spoke might be true, in a much deeper sense than she understood. Just as quickly he dismissed it; it was a fantasy that lately he'd been indulging in a little too often, a little too much for his own good. But he wanted to see her. She'd brought him back up and he didn't want to wait until tomorrow.

"Jenny, come on over and let's go get a drink. Celebrate now."

"When?"

"Now. Or in an hour. Whenever you can get away."

"I don't know, Jack. I haven't even opened my mail from this morning. I just got back."

"Come on. I want to celebrate now."

"Shouldn't you be heading home? Claire's probably fixed your favorite meal."

She was serious. She wasn't making fun of Claire. She was trying to keep him in line.

"I doubt it." He paused, and Jenny remained quiet. "She's a little pissed at me right now."

"She thinks you're going to compromise yourself, doesn't she? The death penalty thing."

"Yeah, probably. But on the surface, no. She found out from a student about me running."

"Ouch."

"Once I told Earl, I just got caught up, you know? I never thought she'd hear about it before I had a chance to call her."

"You should go home. Talk to her. She'll be happy for you, once she realizes you weren't trying to exclude her."

"I know."

"We'll celebrate tomorrow."

"Just one, Jen. Come on."

"What about your office? Go with someone from your office and then head home. It'll be too late by the time I can get over there."

"Everyone's on their way home. Come now, just for one, and then go back. I'll meet you halfway."

She didn't respond then, and he suspected he'd almost worn her down.

Finally, she exhaled a long sigh and said, "Jack."

"Come on. Just one." He thought he could almost hear her shaking her head, one of those "what am I going to do with you" type of head shakes. "Jen."

"Just one."

"Just one."

"I'll meet you at Shanahan's in twenty minutes."

"Okay. Shanahan's. Twenty minutes."

"Jack?"

"Yeah?"

"Congratulations."

CHAPTER EIGHT

Once he arrived at the restaurant, Jack realized he would rather have met Jenny somewhere else, perhaps outside the downtown area, where there was less of a chance of seeing someone they knew. There were things he wanted to talk to her about, things not having to do with his running for DA. Like whether his brother had asked her out.

They sat in a booth across from each other. Despite his protests that he just wanted a beer, she insisted that they order champagne to toast his decision. He surprised himself by finishing his quickly, and then the things he wanted to say came more easily.

"Did Mark ever call you?" he asked after the waiter walked away.

She studied the bubbly liquid in her fluted glass. "Yes, as a matter of fact, he did."

"How come you didn't mention it to me?"

She slowly raised her eyelids and stared at him. "Why would I?"

"Why wouldn't you?"

"You think I report to you about every date I go on?"

"Well, this was probably the first time the date was a close relative of mine."

She took a sip of champagne and then set the glass down, picked up a piece of bread from a basket on the table, and broke off a smaller piece.

"Earl thinks there's something going on between us." The sentence was in his head but he hadn't thought he would actually have the nerve to say it.

"Really?" She tried to look unfazed by this, but after nine years he knew her poker face by the involuntarily widened nostrils and the way one eyebrow rose just slightly.

"He suggested as much to me the morning after he announced his resignation."

"And what'd you tell him?"

"The truth, what else? That we're just friends, that we've always been just friends."

"Right."

The waiter approached with Jenny's food and a beer for Jack. She smiled and thanked him, lightly touching her hair to move it away from her face as she talked. When he left, she picked up her knife and fork, but stopped just as she was about to cut.

"Jack," she said, "I thought we agreed to forget about what happened that night."

That night. That's what it had become to them in thought and conversation. *That night.*

"We did," he said, trying to sound nonchalant. "And I have."

"Okay." She nodded slowly. "Good. So have I."

She ate in the awkward silence that followed. She asked him if he wanted to try her food—she'd ordered the special, grilled tuna—but he declined because he was almost afraid she'd tease him by feeding him from her fork.

"So where'd he take you?"

"Huh?" And then she laughed, realizing that he was referring to Mark. "Are we still on this?"

"I'm just curious. Just want to make sure he's not embarrassing me."

"He's not embarrassing you. He was a perfect gentleman. We rode our bikes up to Augusta and spent the day at the winery."

Of course. That was just like Mark. His idea of a date always involved something physical—tennis, biking, rock climbing, swimming the English Channel. He'd once explained to Jack that he learned so much more about a woman when they were engaged in an athletic activity. Fitness, competitiveness, sense of fairness, vanity. Jack had decided that Mark just liked his women sweaty.

"And?"

"And then we rode back, although it was a bit more slow going. You know, the wine, and all." She giggled, as if she was remembering something funny from their trip.

He shook his head. "I meant, what did you think of him?"

"I liked him. Like I said, he was the perfect gentleman."

He resisted the urge to make a face. "Well, watch him. He's got a habit of getting a girl attached to him, then dumping her. He loses interest once he no longer has to work at it."

She tilted her head and eyed him suspiciously. "I'm a big girl."

"I'm just telling you."

"Okay, Jack." He knew she was patronizing him.

"Are you going to see him again?"

"I already did. He came downtown and took me to lunch."

He wanted to ask more, but she resumed eating, and Jack sensed she wasn't going to tolerate any more questions about his brother. So he merely nodded and took a bite of a roll.

When Jenny finished her meal she ordered coffee, and Jack ordered another beer. He liked that about her, how she lingered over coffee after a meal, sipping it slowly and not hesitating to have another cup when she finished the first.

"We're here to celebrate you running," she began, stirring the coffee slowly as she talked, "but you haven't told me a bit about what this summer has in store for you. What's going to happen? What's your next step?"

"I need a campaign manager, a treasurer, and a PR person. Which would you like to be?"

Her look of surprise told him she hadn't considered that he might ask her to be involved.

"Jen, I'm serious."

"I don't know anything about organizing a campaign. Are you crazy?" She shook her head, but he could see that she liked the idea, even as she denied it.

"Neither do I. They'll tell us what to do. I just need someone to make sure it gets done."

"I don't know."

"Actually, I had you in mind for treasurer. You're the bankruptcy lawyer." He winked at her. "If you can't keep me in the black, then who can?"

She stared into her cup. "I'm not sure you want me. I might tarnish your image."

"Why?" She wouldn't look up at him. "Jenny," he persisted, "why do you say that?"

She began to rub the tablecloth with her index finger, back and forth. As if to control her fidgeting, she picked up her cup and took another sip of coffee.

"Jenny?"

She waved her hand. "Oh, it's just firm stuff."

"Firm stuff."

"You're supposed to be celebrating, not listening to me grouse about my job. I'll tell you about it some other day."

"I'll only agree to that if you'll agree right now to be my treasurer."

He waited for her to look at him. When she did, she pursed her lips.

"Okay. Do you remember that night"—there was that phrase again, *that night*—"in my office, when I told you I thought Mendelsohn was up to something?"

"I remember." He raised one eyebrow. "I'm surprised *you* do."

"I remember everything, Jack." They locked eyes in silence, each challenging the other to take the discussion in a different, more dangerous direction. She dodged it by continuing with the topic of Mendelsohn. "Anyway, I think I'm figuring it out. Or at least I'm getting warm." She leaned forward and lowered her voice. "You know that Maxine is Mendelsohn's client, right? He's in charge of all her work, from a litigation standpoint, at least. And he keeps his hand in her other work, too."

"Yeah. So?"

"Well, since I've been working on trying to recoup some of her money from the lousy investment deals she gets involved in, I've noticed, from looking at old files, that all the attorneys who worked on her stuff at one time or another have been fired."

"Why are you looking at old files?" Jack asked.

"Initially, to defend myself. It seems Maxine doesn't like how I'm handling her cases. Remember that day we met for lunch in the plaza, when you accused me of being hostile to you?"

Jack suddenly felt bad all over again for the way he'd treated her, always assuming that her moods had something to do with him. He nodded.

"Well, I didn't tell you everything that happened that morning." The waiter approached again, and she paused until he'd topped off her coffee and walked away. "When I returned from court, Mendelsohn pulled me into his office and laid into me about how I was handling her work. He told me she was very upset with me because I kept encouraging her to settle for less than one hundred cents on the dollar. According to Mendelsohn, she claimed I wasn't aggressive enough." Jenny rolled her eyes. Her dislike for Maxine hadn't mellowed in the months she'd been working for her. "Can you believe that? Me? Not aggressive enough?"

Jack laughed. "Well, not really."

"He tried to intimidate me, you know, telling me the only reason I still had a job was because of Stan, and that he'd be watching every move I made, blah, blah. I was so mad, I was shaking." Jack saw her hand tremble as she retold the story. "I went straight to Stan's office afterward and told him what Mendelsohn said. I found out then that Stan already knew about Maxine's complaints, because Mendelsohn had gone to him trying to have me fired! Stan told him where to stick it, of course, and he thought that was the end of it, until Mendelsohn couldn't help himself and decided to threaten me. I don't think he believed I'd ever go to Stan."

Jenny's eyes were narrowed in anger, her brow furrowed. Jack admired her for having the strength to stand up to Mendelsohn in her own way, by going to Stan after being attacked by him. It was a strength Jack hadn't possessed years before, when Mendelsohn had played the same type of intimidation game with him and he had let Mendelsohn win.

"Anyway, Stan's the one who suggested I look at the old files, to see if the other attorneys who'd worked on her cases had handled them differently.

You know, to see if they had been settling them, too, and if so, for how much. I did, and that's when I realized that the attorneys who'd handled Maxine's collection cases were no longer with the firm."

"Did you point this out to Stan?"

"No, not yet. I'm still investigating, if you know what I mean."

"You think Mendelsohn pushed them out." It was a conclusion, not a question. "Why?"

She laughed sarcastically. "That's the ten-thousand-dollar question, isn't it? I intend to find out the answer."

"What about Maxine?"

"Well, I'm hoping I can keep her at bay until I figure out what's really going on. It shouldn't be a problem, because getting to the bottom of this will mean not settling any of her cases, which is what she claims to want. It'll give me more time to dig. I just have to convince her that, despite our differences, I'm really working for her when it's all said and done. I need to show her that she needs me, at least for now."

They sat in silence for a few moments, neither taking their eyes off the other.

"Why didn't you tell me all this that day?" Jack asked. "I asked you."

She shrugged. "I don't know, Jack. You seemed so excited about everything that was happening at the DA's office, with Earl pushing you to run, and your meetings with those politico guys. I didn't want to spoil it for you. I'm only telling you now because I think you should know what you might be getting yourself into if you have me join your team. I suspect that if Mendelsohn thinks I'm onto him, he'll make my life miserable, and possibly yours, too."

"You've only given me another reason to involve you. Nothing would give me greater pleasure than to win the election with your help and shove it down Mendelsohn's throat."

She shook her head. "I don't know, Jack. I'd hate to see you get dragged down with me."

"He's not going to drag you down."

"I'm not so sure."

"I am. He called me today, to congratulate me."

"So?"

"He offered money." When Jenny eyes widened, he added, "He offered to support me in my run, is how he put it. Which I'm sure means money. Which, I'm also sure, after what you've said, means he's getting a little nervous about his past catching up with him." He laughed.

"What?"

"I'm just thinking about how we ran into him that night. He probably didn't realize we were still friends. Now he's probably wondering what stories we've shared about him."

He leaned forward over the table, nodded his head so that she'd come closer. "Say you'll do it."

"I don't know. I just don't know if it's a good idea, for many reasons."

"Just think, it'll look good on your résumé." Her fingers were curled around the handle of her cup. He reached up, briefly touched her hand, and grinned. "Plus, if you're my treasurer, no one can get the wrong idea when we have lunch together, right?"

She lifted the cup to her lips and smiled over the rim of it. She liked that, Jack realized. They'd progressed from not talking about what had happened *that night* to talking around it, to finally, in a way, making jokes about it.

"Right."

As if it didn't mean a thing. As if it hadn't really happened.

Their tête-à-tête was interrupted by a familiar voice, and Jack immediately leaned away from Jenny upon hearing it.

"I was told I could probably find you here." Earl smiled at Jenny, but from the look he shot Jack, Jack was fairly certain he'd witnessed the last few minutes of his and Jenny's huddled conversation. He started to get up, but Jenny stopped him.

She scooted out and greeted Earl with a handshake. "I see a guy at the bar I need to say hello to. He works for one of my bank clients. You guys have a beer together and I'll be back later."

They watched her leave, but before Earl had a chance to chastise Jack, the waiter arrived to take Earl's order and other attorneys joined them. After hearing Jack's news, one round turned into two and then three. When it got close to seven and the last of them had said good-bye, Jack decided it was a good time for him to slip out, too.

"I'm gonna tell Jenny I'm leaving," he said to Earl. "You coming?"

"Yeah, I gotta hit the head. I'll meet you over there in a minute."

Jack approached Jenny, and she dutifully made introductions. Then she grabbed Jack's arm and pulled him close. "Are you okay to drive?" she asked in a low voice. "Can't have you arrested for drunk driving before you've even kicked off your campaign."

He glanced at the guy and wondered what she'd told him. Had he recognized Jack's name when she introduced them? "I'm fine, Jen. You're the lightweight. I thought you had mail to open."

She released him and shrugged her shoulders. "Oh, well, I've been detained," she said, smiling at the banker.

Earl appeared, and as they started to leave, Jenny surprised Jack by reaching out to stop him. "Jack." Her hand was suddenly on the back of his head, pulling him nearer. "Congratulations," she whispered, her breath tickling his ear. "Don't forget me these next few months." And then she kissed him, her lips just brushing his cheek.

It was still light out when Jack and Earl stepped out of the restaurant's relative darkness and onto the sidewalk. They walked in silence to the courthouse. The streets seemed unusually quiet, as if everyone had left town a few days early for the long weekend. Jack knew that Earl had something to say. He could tell it from his gait, from the absence of any expression on his face.

"Jack."

"Earl, you don't have to—"

"Stop. Don't get defensive on me. I'm not going to attack you." Jack motioned with his hands as if to say *Okay, okay, go ahead.* "It's more important now than ever that you watch yourself."

"She was just a little buzzed. That's all."

"Maybe. But she's smitten with you. It's written all over her face."

Jack grinned slightly; only someone of Earl's generation would say *smitten.*

"She's just a flirt. She's always been like that."

"Look, I'm not questioning your intentions. I'm just saying that you need to think about every move you make. What might be innocent to you can come across differently to outsiders."

"Like you?"

"No; you told me nothing's going on, and I trust you." He paused. "But think about it. You met her alone in a bar, and when I come across the two of you, you've got your heads together like you're planning some secret conspiracy. A reporter sees you sitting together like that and it's on the front page of tomorrow's paper. You're fair game now."

"I'm not allowed to have a drink with a friend?"

"Not if the friend's female, no."

They reached the courthouse steps. Jack knew Earl was right. It seemed Earl was always right. He thought maybe Jenny knew this, too, and that's why she'd said what she had.

When Jack arrived home, he found Michael and a friend playing basketball on the driveway. Instead of going inside, Jack joined them for a few shots and then leaned against the trunk of his car to watch. The door from the garage to the house opened and Jack turned to see Claire in the doorway. He could tell she was tired by the way she leaned one shoulder against the wall.

"Kevin, it's time for you to go home," she called before noticing Jack. "Oh. Hi." He gave her a little wave. "When did you get back?"

"A few minutes ago."

Michael and Kevin started down the street. "Don't be long, Michael," Claire called to him. "You've still got some homework."

"Come over here with me." Jack motioned to her. He knew from her tentative step that she didn't want to fight but she still wanted him to work for her forgiveness.

"Where have you been?" she asked. She stood against the trunk next to him, a few inches away, facing the driveway in his same crossed-arm stance.

"We had a beer before I left downtown."

"Who's 'we'?"

It didn't seem worth it to mention Jenny and take the risk of killing any chances of reconciliation.

"Earl and I."

She nodded. The neighborhood was quiet; everywhere seemed quiet tonight.

"Listen, Claire—"

"You know, you used to call and tell me when you were going to be late."

"I figured you weren't in any hurry to see me."

She pursed her lips and raised one eyebrow, as if to tell him he'd figured right.

He faced her, moved in close, and stood between her legs so they both leaned as one against the car. She wore sweats and he could feel the shape of her body through the loose fabric. He started to feel a little horny, with their bodies touching and their hips resting against each other's.

He reached down and took one of her arms by the wrist, placed it around his waist, and then did the same with the other arm. She left them there, limply, but he detected the start of a smile, if only in her eyes. "Come on, I know you want to hug me."

She pushed at him, trying to maintain a serious face. "Sometimes you make me so mad."

"That's good, don't you think?" She still stared at something behind him. "It'd be really boring otherwise, huh?" He moved his head to block her view, to make her look at him.

She shook her head. She wasn't ready to forgive him so easily.

"Hey, look at me." She did. He was close enough to see the blue speck in the green of her right eye. "I'm sorry, okay? I am. I didn't mean for it to happen like it did. I just wasn't thinking."

"No, you sure weren't," she agreed and looked away again.

"Claire, come on, look at me." He leaned his head in closer, stopped briefly to see if she was going to let him do it, and then he kissed her.

"You guys are gross." They both looked up to see Michael coming back up the driveway.

"Go finish your homework like your mom asked," Jack said.

"And do it quietly," Claire added. "Don't wake Jamie."

They watched him as he took his time going into the house. Jack turned back to Claire and tried to remember where they'd left off. She smiled a bit, but it was a smile about Michael. He touched her lips. "You know I wouldn't purposely do anything to hurt you."

"I know."

"How can I make it up to you?"

"Change your mind."

God, she didn't even hesitate. "I thought you supported me. I thought you were the one who told me to give it my best shot, if I really wanted it."

"Yeah, I did. But not the way you're planning to do it. What are you going to say when they start asking you the inevitable questions?"

"I'll worry about it when the time comes. I'll roll with the flow."

She sighed and stood up straight, pushing him away in the process. "Are you hungry? I didn't think you'd be this late, so I put the food in the oven to keep it warm for a little while. It's probably all dried out now." She walked away from him, toward the house.

"I won't do it if you really don't want me to."

She stopped abruptly and turned. "Oh no, I'm not going to let you lay that on me. I don't want you to make a decision based on what I want. You're the one who has to look in the mirror every morning. You're the one who will take the questions and come up with the answers. If you have no problem with it, then I have no problem with it. Pretend I never asked."

She left him standing there, gazing at the empty space between his body and the car and wishing he could explain that Harry Truman stuff to her as well as Earl had explained it to him.

Later that night in bed, after they'd turned out the lights, she asked him to rub her back. He gathered her hair in his hand—she hadn't braided it—and tossed it to the side so he could rub her neck, too. She'd never told him so, but he always took her failure to braid her hair as a sign to him that she wasn't ready to go to sleep just yet. When he drew a big, invisible heart on her back, she laughed softly. He then pretended to play dot to dot with her freckles and moles, and she laughed at that, too, because she knew he claimed that when he connected the dots it formed a gigantic *J*, and that she was marked for him. Maybe everything between them *was* okay.

He finally decided he'd rubbed her back long enough and had made his way over the curves of her behind, to the backs of her thighs, to the backs of her knees, to the insides of her thighs, and was on his way back up again, when she spoke.

"So what was the impetus?"

"Hmm?" His eyes were closed and he wasn't really listening as his hand kept moving, only inches from its intended destination.

"What made you finally decide?" She rolled over to face him, and he felt his hand slide over her leg and land on the mattress between them. He opened his eyes and they stared at each other.

"What do you mean?"

"Oh, come on. You know how you are, a little impulsive. You might have been thinking about it for a long time, but something happened to make you decide. Did Earl say something to you?"

He rolled onto his back and stared into the dark. "Is there a reason we're talking about this right now?"

"I just thought of it. I'm curious."

He wondered whether to tell her about the letter. At any other time he wouldn't have hesitated; she would have understood completely. But something about her demeanor, how she'd been so hot and cold ever since their phone conversation earlier in the afternoon—caused him to be almost embarrassed that he'd let the letter affect him as it had. But this was Claire, and he had to believe that she'd get it, that she'd comprehend its significance to him.

"I got a letter today from the mother of a murder victim in a case I tried a few years ago." She rested her arm on his chest in anticipation—she wanted his reasoning to be heartfelt, if not sound—and it spurred him on. "She encouraged me to run. She wanted me to run. I thought . . ." He remembered that he'd shoved it into his pants pocket before leaving to meet Jenny. He threw the blankets off, grabbed his pants from the floor, and dug out the letter. "Turn on your light," he said.

She reached for the paper, squinting a little, and said, "Why's it so wrinkled?"

Instead of replying, he watched her read it and tried to gauge her re-action. Twice she raised her eyes, without comment, to look at him over the top of the letter. It took her a long time to read it and he thought that maybe she was reading it more than once, as he had. This was Claire. She had to get it.

When she finished, she set the letter on her nightstand and turned off the light. She scooted over to him, snuggled in tight, and sighed. "I'm sorry, Jack. I jumped to conclusions."

She started to say something else, but he put his finger to her lips and pulled her closer. He was tired and he'd lost interest in anything else but sleep. He drifted off, a slight smile on his face, feeling again like an honest man.

PART 2

SUMMER

CHAPTER NINE

The blacktop driveway was already hot under Jack's bare feet when he dashed out early to grab the morning paper. As he sat down at the table with his coffee, the headline screamed up at him. OUTGOING DA MUM ON WHETHER HE'LL SEEK DEATH IN LAST CASE OF HIS TERM.

"How can you drink that when it's so hot outside?" Claire asked. She stretched to get a glimpse of the headline.

He barely heard her. "It's like he's purposely dragging this out to make my life difficult. They're going to descend on me when I get to work today."

Jack knew the honeymoon was over. After announcing his candidacy, he'd braced himself for a barrage of high-pressure questions from reporters, but they'd never come. He'd received plenty of calls, of course, and had been interviewed several times for profile pieces, but, amazingly, no one had pushed him on the death penalty.

He now suspected the media had merely been waiting for the most opportune moment to spring the issue. They would take advantage of the public's combustible emotions resulting from the Barnard case and then throw Jack's position into the mix and wait for something to ignite. He pushed the paper away without finishing the story.

"Oh, come on." Claire was skeptical. "Isn't that inevitable regardless of when he decides?"

"I guess." Although usually he admired her for her reasonableness, he resented it just then. "I just feel like he's milking the issue. He enjoys playing the media."

She ruffled his hair. "I think maybe you're the one he's playing, Jack." He tilted his face to her, but she slipped away to the sink and began putting dishes in the dishwasher.

"What's that supposed to mean?"

"Maybe he's trying to force the issue. Maybe he wants to make sure you can handle it before it gets too close to the election." She spoke without looking at him.

"He knows I can handle it."

"Then why are you so worried?"

He drew the paper closer to him and turned to the sports page. He tried to read an article but the words stuck to the paper like glue, refusing to find meaning inside his head.

"You know what?" he said. "We can't talk about this. It always ends up this way."

She shut off the water and grabbed a dishtowel. She turned to him as she dried her hands. "What way?"

"With you challenging everything I say."

He rose from the table and searched for his keys in the cabinet. He called up the stairs to Jamie, who emerged at the top still in his pajamas. "Come down and say good-bye to me," Jack said, his tone softer. When Jamie reached the bottom, Jack grabbed him and lifted him into the air. "Are you gonna go to the pool with Mommy?" he asked, tickling him under his shirt. Jamie shrieked with pleasure.

"I don't mean to," she said, as if they were still the only two in the room.

"Yes, you do." He set Jamie down. "Go put your suit on." He kissed his head. "I think you're waiting to see me squirm."

"Jack . . ."

"It's true. I'm not doing this exactly how you wanted me to, so you want me to pay."

"That's not true." She crossed the kitchen and gently touched his shoulder.

He picked up his briefcase and headed for the garage. She followed, but stopped in the doorway as he climbed into his car.

"Bye, Claire. Thanks for your support."

He took the stairs instead of the elevator from the third floor of the parking garage, but regretted it as soon as he stepped into the rank stairwell. The odor of urine and discarded beer cans hung in the stagnant heat, remnants of the city's July Fourth celebration a few days earlier. He emerged on the sidewalk expecting relief, but stopped abruptly at the corner when he noticed a small crowd at the bottom of the courthouse steps. He knew without being told they were there because of Barnard; the only question was whose side were they on.

The light changed to green but he didn't cross. Feeling someone at his elbow, he mumbled, "Excuse me," and mindlessly took a step to the side to let the person pass.

"Come on, we'll walk right by them together."

He turned at Earl's voice. "Oh, it's you."

They crossed together and Jack waited for an explanation, but none was forthcoming.

"I can't do this," he said, more to himself than to Earl.

But Earl kept walking. "You don't have a choice. Anyway, you don't deserve to be DA if you can't do this."

As they neared the group, the homemade signs made it clear they were there to protest the possibility of Earl's asking for the death penalty. The largest of the signs encouraged Earl to "take the more humane approach to justice." That was okay with Jack, of course, except that now he couldn't very well express his sympathies with them, could he?

The group had enough of a presence to attract a news truck. A single reporter stood with the crowd, her cameraman tailing her every movement. Jack glanced sideways at Earl to gauge his reaction, but Earl merely nodded to the crowd in greeting and kept going. The cameraman motioned to the reporter. Seeing Earl and Jack, she yanked the microphone away from the face of the young man talking into it and started in their direction.

"Keep walking as if there's nothing unusual going on," Earl said quietly to Jack without changing his expression or his pace. They began to climb the steps.

"Mr. Scanlon! Mr. Hilliard! Can I have a moment, please?" Jack heard the tap of the reporter's heels as she followed just behind them. Despite Earl's instructions, he couldn't just pretend he hadn't heard her. He stopped and turned, forcing Earl to do the same.

"Of course," Jack answered, smiling slightly. A drop of perspiration trailed down the back of his neck; the collar of his shirt felt tight. *This is it.*

"Mr. Scanlon"—the light on the camera came on and she shoved the microphone in Earl's face—"have you made up your mind whether to seek death in the Barnard case?"

"No, ma'am, I haven't. I hope to complete my review of the evidence and the statute by the end of the week. I will announce my intentions then."

Earl was well aware of the evidence in the case and could recite the relevant section of the statute by memory, if he wanted to.

"So it is a possibility?"

"It's always a possibility in a first-degree-murder case."

"There have been very few cases in your tenure for which you've sought death. Why's that?"

Sweat ran down Jack's back as if someone had turned on a faucet. The questions may have been pitched to Earl, but Jack was on deck.

"Despite the sometimes apparent heinous nature of the crimes that have crossed my desk, there have been very few for which I thought the circumstances justified the death penalty under our statutes. My job for this city has been to prosecute criminals to the fullest extent of the law, as that law was written by our state legislature. I can't substitute my own wishes or the wishes of a few vocal citizens for the intent expressed by our elected representatives."

It sounded good to Jack, but this lady wasn't having any of it.

"Well, Mr. Scanlon, if the Barnard case doesn't satisfy the requirements of the statute, what type of case would?"

"As I explained, I'm still deciding whether Barnard does, in fact, satisfy the requirements of the statute." Then, with finality, Earl declared, "I'll have that decision for you within days."

Jack considered whether to turn and continue up the steps, as if he, too, believed the interrogation was over. Earl would like that. Some sort of decisiveness on Jack's part, an effort to take control. But maybe not. He thought of what Claire had suggested: *Maybe he wants to make sure you can handle it before it gets too close to the election.* He could handle it, Earl knew that. It was Claire who doubted him.

Jack looked the reporter in the eye to acknowledge that he knew the next question would be directed to him, and that he welcomed it. The microphone moved swiftly from Earl to Jack.

"Mr. Hilliard? I'm sure the electorate would like to know how *you* would handle this case."

He considered lobbing a pat response about how it wasn't his decision to make, but he knew she'd persist, and by not answering the question right away, he would be seen as evasive and weak. Anyway, hadn't he been expecting this question for months? He was ready for it.

"Ma'am, I'm not going to stand here and tell you I like the idea of the death penalty. I don't." He intentionally looked past her at the small group of protesters so that he could also steal a glance at Earl. He was listening to Jack but without any evidence of concern for what he might say. He'd completely, with full trust, relinquished the floor to him. Emboldened, Jack continued.

"Although I know some people believe otherwise, I really don't think any prosecutor relishes the thought of asking for the death penalty. But despite a DA's personal views about the appropriateness of such a punishment, he or she is ethically bound to follow the laws of the state in which he prosecutes crimes." He attempted a deep breath but, because of the stifling heat, managed only a shallow intake of air. "So to answer your question, how would I handle this case? I would handle this case in the same way any conscientious and ethical DA would handle it. Like Mr. Scanlon, I would review the totality of the evidence in light of the statute and make the difficult but informed decision as to whether the facts of the crime indicate it should be a capital case."

The muscles in Jack's shoulders began to relax and he almost imagined a cool breeze tickling the nape of his neck. But then the young man who'd been talking to the reporter when they'd first approached spoke. "That's bullshit," he sneered, his voice easily carrying over to them in the morning's relative silence.

The reporter ignored him but used his comment as an excuse to press on. "And, in your opinion, Mr. Hilliard, do the facts of the Barnard case indicate it should be a capital case?"

"I don't—"

"Surely you are privy to all the relevant facts. You're asking this city to let you wear Mr. Scanlon's shoes. Aren't the voters entitled to know where you stand?"

"Yes, of course they are." He felt the tension rising at her insinuations. He struggled to follow the first advice Earl had ever given him, years before: don't let a reporter goad you into anger. "I think—"

"Clyde Hutchins kidnapped twelve-year-old Cassia Barnard at her bus stop, then raped, tortured, stabbed, and strangled her. Then he left her out in the brutal elements of a January winter to die, just in case that hadn't already been accomplished. I'm merely asking, Mr. Hilliard, is this a case for which *you*, as a candidate for District Attorney of this city, would ask for death?"

What *would* he do? Jack remembered the conversation he'd had with Jenny that night, so long ago, it seemed: *If there was ever the perfect argument for the death penalty, isn't this case it?* And what had his answer been? *I don't think there will ever be the perfect argument for the death penalty.* And then he thought of Dunne's comment: *Your goal is to get elected, not to make everyone think like you do.*

He looked at the group again. They stood quietly, ready to pounce. How to make them understand he was on their side? Maybe he was asking too much. *Your legacy will be made in office, not on the campaign trail.* There was only one response to the question. He stared hard at the reporter before answering.

"Absent mitigating circumstances of which I may not be aware, since I'm not working on the case"—he paused, not for effect, but to gather the nerve required to say what he planned to say—"I think it may be an appropriate case." He ignored the rising murmur and looked at his watch. "If you'll excuse us, I have a meeting in ten minutes," he lied.

The reporter made an effort to ask more questions, but Jack and Earl turned together and trotted up the steps to the entrance of the courthouse as if they had previously choreographed it.

It was the comment of one of the protesters—a female this time—that caused Jack to stop abruptly just as he gripped the handle of the massive door.

"Then you're no better than Cassia Barnard's murderer!" she called, her voice laced with contempt.

Before Jack could react, Earl spoke quickly and quietly to him. "Don't respond. Don't even turn around or you'll erase every gain you just made down there." When Jack still didn't move, he commanded, "Open the door."

They'd passed through the metal detector and stepped into the empty elevator before Earl spoke again. "You know," he said with a chuckle, "getting you through to November is a little like trying to thread a rope through the eye of a needle."

Jack glanced at him, expressionless, and then, as if the force of his touch would make them get there faster, pressed the elevator button hard. He crossed his arms, leaned against the wall, and stared at the chipped linoleum tiles on the floor of the elevator.

"Don't look so miserable. You handled that well."

"Yeah, well, put in a good word for me if you get to the gates of St. Peter first."

"Spare me, Jack. You knew you'd have to put up with comments like that."

He couldn't deny it—he had known he'd get comments like that. But that didn't mean he had to enjoy them. He thought again of what Claire had said that morning and suddenly wondered whether he'd just been set up.

When they stepped off the elevator, Jack said, "I didn't say I'd ask for death."

"No, you didn't," Earl agreed.

He expected Earl to say more. Instead, they walked down the quiet corridor toward their offices. Jack stopped short at the door to the men's room. Perspiration drenched his shirt and he wished he kept an extra one in his office for times like these. Right, times like these. Despite the city's sweltering summers, he couldn't remember ever sweating like this before.

In the bathroom, he wet a few paper towels with cold water and wiped his face. His cheeks were flushed, the way they looked after a long run. He folded the towels and placed them on the back of his neck. He remembered that Newman had showers in the men's room. If he won the election, maybe he'd have showers put in these offices, for everyone. He laughed, because he knew it wasn't even an option. He'd have the first say over whether defendants should live or die, but he wouldn't have the power to get a shower installed for his staff.

"What's so funny?"

Earl stood in the doorway. Jack hadn't heard him come in; he wondered how long he'd been there. He'd assumed Earl had continued on to his office.

Jack shrugged. "I don't know. Everything. Life. Death. This summer. The campaign. The reporter. That girl's inability to read between the lines."

"Nope. She doesn't even realize that you're her man, does she?" He paused, and then grinned when he saw the hint of a smile on Jack's face. He stepped all the way into the bathroom and let the door close behind him. "People hear what they want to hear, what they expect to hear."

Jack nodded as he pulled down more towels from the dispenser and began to wipe his face and neck all over again. "Maybe I have no right to ask, but what's her mom want?"

Earl remained quiet for a moment. He knew Jack meant Cassia's mother. "I don't know."

"Maybe you should ask her."

Earl smiled a bit and nodded. "Okay." Then: "Jack, I meant it when I said you handled it well."

"I know." He unbuttoned his shirt halfway and rubbed the towel down his neck. "Hey, do you think I'd be able to get showers put in if I win the election?"

Earl laughed. "You could always try, I suppose."

"What would you have done differently?"

"Huh?" The question seemed to have caught Earl off guard, and Jack realized he thought he was referring to Earl's time as DA. Jack leaned against the sink, facing Earl.

"My response to the reporter's questions. Would you have handled it any differently?"

"You were perfect, Jack. Keep it up and before you know it you'll be moving your junk into my office."

November seemed a long way away.

CHAPTER TEN

On the Thursday afternoon before the weekend of the state bar's annual Bench & Bar Conference, Earl called Jack into his office. Jack was certain he wanted to discuss Barnard; for anything else he would have just stopped him in the hall. He wondered if Frank Mann had been invited to the meeting, too.

He found Earl sitting behind his desk, his feet propped on the corner. A stapled packet of papers rested on his lap but he wasn't reading. His eyes were closed, and Jack thought maybe he'd dozed off, although that would have been very uncharacteristic. He rapped softly on the door.

"Close the door behind you," Earl said, skipping any greeting.

Jack motioned to the papers in Earl's lap. "Pleasure reading?"

"Psychological report."

"Barnard?"

Earl nodded.

"Why isn't Mann in here for this meeting?" Jack asked.

Frank had been ecstatic when Jeff McCarthy first accepted Jack's invitation to be his campaign manager, because Earl had pulled Jeff off the Barnard case as second chair and Frank figured he wouldn't have to share the glory. Jack knew Frank wouldn't appreciate a meeting about the case in his absence.

"Because right now this has to do with your campaign. I'll invite him to join us in a few minutes."

Jack sat across from him and waited.

Earl brought his feet to the floor and leaned forward over his desk, hands clasped. "I want you to try it."

Jack shifted in his seat. All the reasons he *shouldn't* try it began to explode like fireworks in his mind, but he was determined to stay calm.

"More importantly," Earl continued, "Dunne wants you to try it. He thinks it's a ready-made publicity opportunity we can't squander."

Jack nodded slowly. They both knew he wasn't agreeing to anything; he was merely indicating he understood Dunne's position. He motioned again at the report. "Did you make any decisions yet?"

"Yes. But I want to know if you'll try it regardless of my decision."

At that moment Jack knew that Earl intended to ask for death.

"And if I say no?"

Earl shrugged. "Then I guess perhaps you will have given Steve Schafer quite a gift."

Jack looked away at the mention of his Republican opponent. Steve Schafer was an older trial lawyer, the founder of a small defense firm with an excellent reputation. Schafer himself had forged a Perry Mason–like persona over the years; even as he represented defendants, he always appeared to be on the good side of the law: "Of course I'm in favor of putting the bad guys behind bars, but my client's not the bad guy" seemed to be his motto. In line with this philosophy was his expressed support for the death penalty when appropriate. Jack thought it all seemed a bit too convenient.

"Look," Earl said. "I'm not asking you to decide whether this should be a capital case. I'm merely asking you to take my decision and run with it. Win the case. Someone in this office is going to; it might as well be you, since you're the one trying to get elected."

"What happened to 'the man who makes the decision should be the one to try it'?"

"I'm making an exception." Earl stared hard at Jack, reminding him that the exception was being made for his benefit.

Jack tried to imagine Claire's reaction if he agreed to do it. Would it matter to her that the decision had been Earl's? Was it enough of a distinction for Jack, even? Could he live with himself, knowing he'd played a part in the outcome, even if the choice of outcomes hadn't been his?

"The slippery slope just keeps getting steeper, doesn't it?" Jack tried to keep the sarcasm out of his voice, but he didn't succeed. He took a deep breath. "The answer's no. I won't try it regardless. I'll try it only if you're asking for life." With a raise of his eyebrows, he added, "Can I see the report?"

Earl sighed, though he didn't seem too surprised by Jack's response, and tossed the papers across the desk.

Jack picked up the packet and flipped to the back page for the summary of findings. He scanned the last paragraph of the report. Someone, Earl perhaps, had highlighted the defendant's IQ score with yellow marker. It bordered on mental retardation.

"When did you get this?" he asked Earl.

"Late last week."

Jack stared at Earl angrily, the sense of having almost been tricked growing larger with each minute. "Isn't this what the defense has been saying all along? The guy's not all there. No one seems to care. Obviously you don't."

"It's the first bit of real evidence to back them up. So what do you think?"

"Does it matter what I think?"

"I won't be the last to want to know."

Jack threw the report on Earl's desk. "Earl, it's no mystery what I'd do if I were in your shoes. Yes, I'd use this as my hook. So what?"

"Is that what you want me to do?"

"It doesn't seem to matter what I want. You said yourself you've already made your decision."

"True, although you've been making a lot of assumptions about what that decision is." Earl stood and came around to the front of the desk, near Jack. "Everyone's expecting me to ask for death in this case. If I don't, you'll be the one to take most of the heat. You realize that."

"Of course I do." Jack grunted. "What? You think I'd rather you go for it just so that I can breeze through to November? That's insulting." Jack had to look up to meet Earl's gaze. "Well, are you going to let me in on your big secret?"

"I am."

"And?"

"And I'm going to ask for life. With no parole."

The case was Jack's.

Jack had to admire Earl. He'd timed his decision on Barnard just right. He called the defense attorney, Millie Rubin, on Friday morning to advise her of his decision, and within the hour he began taking calls from reporters. Most of the attorneys in the DA's office, including Earl, were scheduled to leave for the Lake of the Ozarks that morning to attend the Bench & Bar Conference. Although neither Jack nor Earl would be able to avoid the press completely even at the lake, the pressure on them would be substantially less. And by the time Jack returned to St. Louis for a fundraiser on Sunday afternoon, the story would be approaching old age.

With Earl's blessing, Jack left town early and was halfway to the lake before the onslaught began. He'd invited Jenny to ride along with him, but a nine o'clock hearing in court prevented her from leaving any earlier than noon. She'd originally planned to skip the conference; attendees were overwhelmingly state-court practitioners and judges, and her practice was almost exclusively in federal court. But Earl—against his better judgment, Jack suspected—insisted that Jack's entire campaign team be there to meet and greet some of the state bigwigs. Jack readily agreed. Jenny had always been better than Jack at schmoozing, anyway; he knew the older men would love making fools of themselves over a cocktail with her.

Later that night, after the welcome dinner and a short swim with other attorneys, Jack returned to his room and left the rest to continue partying. It was only eleven, but he could tell they were poised to stay up into the wee hours of the night, drinking on the deck and taking turns in the cool water of the kidney-shaped pool and the steaming froth of the hot spa.

The room was too cold. After turning off the air-conditioning, he opened the slider to the small cement balcony overlooking the pool. His room was only four floors up. When he stepped outside he must have been visible, because someone in the pool, Jeff maybe, called his name, and then the rest of them began to hoot and holler for him to come back down. Their voices and laughter echoed off the green, illuminated water.

He ignored their playful heckling and went back inside. He turned out the light and watched their antics in the pool as he called Claire. Her voice was slow when she answered and he feared he had woken her. She denied it and claimed she was reading in bed while she waited up for his call.

"I was afraid it was going to be another reporter," she said.

"They've been calling our house?" he asked. "I wonder how they got our number." It had been unlisted since he'd started at the DA's office.

"I don't know, but they're anxious to talk to you."

"What'd you tell them?"

"The truth. That you were at Bench and Bar and wouldn't be home till Sunday. I didn't want them bugging me all weekend."

He watched Jeff, Andy Rinehart, and Jerry Clark lift Maria Catalona from the spa and carry her, kicking and screaming, to the pool. Jenny was still in the spa with another lawyer from Newman. She leaned her back against the edge, her arms outstretched on the deck behind her and her long legs floating in the water. One hand held a beer bottle. Maria's screaming rose a few decibels as they swung her by her arms and legs, threatening to toss her in. Jenny laughed, seemingly unaware that she would probably be next.

"Where *are* you?" Claire asked. "What's all that noise?"

"I'm in my room, but the door to the balcony's open and there's a bunch of them getting a little rowdy down at the pool."

"Yeah, that sounds like the Bench and Bar I remember." She laughed. "So what are you doing in the room?"

"My youth is probably already a concern for some in November. I don't need to add immaturity to the mix."

"Ah, yes, but sometimes the immature get to have more fun."

"That is true."

"Where's Earl?"

"We had dinner with some politicians and a few judges. They were talking about a poker game in one of the judge's suites, I think."

"You should go join them."

"Nah. It's all the old guys."

"No, I mean in the pool. Don't worry about November. Go have some fun."

"Maybe. I'll see."

Jack turned away from the open balcony door and lay down on the hard bed. The beer that made them rowdy had made him sleepy. "I'm tired," he whispered into the phone to Claire. "Tomorrow's gonna be a long day, and this bed sucks."

"Okay. Go to bed, sleepyhead." It was the phrase she always used with the kids.

He wanted to say something to let her know he appreciated her not bringing up *why* the reporters called. Since their spat earlier in the week, he could tell she'd tried to ease up on him. She'd even commented that night at dinner that she'd seen the courthouse interview on the news and she thought he'd handled the questions well. She didn't mention the taunt from the protester, and he realized later when he saw the tape that the news station cut it, or else the cameras hadn't been rolling when the woman made her accusation.

"I wish you were here with me."

"Me too." Her voice was barely audible.

Jack undressed and lay back down on the bed. He must have dozed off, because he jerked awake when he thought he heard a soft tap on the door. He'd been having a dream, one of those panicky dreams similar to the ones he'd had when he was still in law school. In it, he sat in one of the big lecture rooms with a blue book on the table in front of him, trying futilely to answer questions on a test for which he hadn't studied, for a class he hadn't attended in weeks.

Another knock and the panic he'd felt from the dream came back. It was ridiculous, but he imagined a reporter on the other side of the door.

He searched on the floor for something to put on, but came up with only his damp swim trunks. He stood and grabbed the trousers he'd worn to dinner from the chair.

Another knock. "Jeez, give me a minute," he mumbled.

He tried to look out the peephole, but either it was broken or whoever stood outside his door had covered it. He left the chain on as he cracked open the door, but released it once he recognized the person on the other side.

"Hi, Mr. Hilliard." She gave him a slow, lazy, lopsided smile. "Hope I didn't wake you."

"Jenny." She stood in the threshold, her arms folded, shivering from the chill of the air-conditioning. Her hair was wet, she still had her bathing suit on, although she'd pulled on a pair of cutoffs over it, and a white hotel towel hung around her neck. Goose bumps dotted the length of her arms. The way she leaned against the doorjamb so nonchalantly reminded him of the first night they'd met, when she'd stood in his office doorway the same way. Except now, he was sure she was slightly under the influence. "What are you doing?"

She reached up and tousled his hair. "You look pretty cute with bed head, Jack."

"Jenny . . ."

"Relax. I'm here with a completely innocent proposal."

"What happened to the others?"

She gave a little wave of her hand, dismissing them. "They're no fun." Again she touched his hair. "This little piece, though, just doesn't want to stay put." He smelled the chlorine from the pool on her arm.

"What is it? If someone sees you standing in my door at this time of night, I'm toast."

She moved forward, causing him to back up, and then shut the door behind her. "There. Problem solved."

His survival instincts had kicked in the minute he saw her standing at his door, and now they switched into high gear. He could barely see her in the dark, but he knew that her charcoal eyes stared at him, unwavering, while she waited for his reaction. He felt on the wall next to the door and turned on the light.

"Is that what you sleep in?" she asked, pointing at his pants.

"No, this is what I answer the door in at three in the morning."

"For your information, Jack, it's only one or so."

He wondered if she was right.

"Jenny, morning is going to come sooner than you think. Go get some sleep." He began to open the door. She stopped him, her hand covering his on the doorknob.

"Come to the lake with me."

"What?" He pulled his hand away.

"You heard me. Come to the lake with me. I rented a boat when I got in this afternoon. I want to go out on the lake."

He couldn't help but laugh. Only Jenny would have thought to rent a boat.

"You're something."

"I know." She took a step closer; he took a step back. "Come on. It'll be fun."

"What kind of boat?" Why was he asking her this? He had no intention of going out on a boat alone with Jenny Dodson at one in the morning.

"A pontoon boat. I thought it'd make a good party boat, but no one wants to party."

"Somehow I would have taken you for a speedboat type of gal."

"Yeah, well, some other weekend, maybe." She shrugged. "Come on, Jack. I never came here as a kid, like I'm sure you did. My parents were dead, remember? I want to get out on the water. Please."

He was taken aback by the blasé comment about her parents. He *didn't* remember, because she'd never told him when they'd died, or how. Just that she was an orphan. He wondered what else she hadn't told him.

"Jenny, I can't."

"Why not?"

"Do you need me to spell it out?"

She lowered her eyes, and he worried he'd been too blunt. Then she looked straight at him, her expression solemn. "I'll be good, I swear." She gave him the slightest grin. "Scout's honor." She raised one hand in the air as she tried to figure out how many fingers to put up. He reached over and arranged her fingers in the right configuration. Her hand was cold.

"Three fingers," he said.

"I knew you must have been a Boy Scout."

"I wasn't."

"If you won't come with me, I'll go alone."

"No, you won't."

"I will, and I've been drinking."

"Really? Who would've guessed?"

"Okay, Jack," she said with exaggerated resignation. She turned and gripped the doorknob. "I'll wave to you from the middle of the lake, under the glittering stars."

Something in her tone convinced him she *was* going, with or without him. What would be worse? His treasurer found drowned in the lake, or the two of them being seen together in a boat in the middle of the night? She'd backed him into a corner, and she knew it.

He sighed and touched her shoulder to stop her. "Give me a minute to get dressed."

He searched in his suitcase for dry shorts. "Here, put this on," he said, tossing her a sweatshirt. "Your skin's like ice."

He went into the bathroom to change. He kept telling himself, *This is crazy, this is crazy,* even as he pulled on his shorts and T-shirt. He could just walk her to her room and stay there until he was sure she'd fallen asleep, but that option posed problems of its own. The two of them in a wide-open boat was preferable to the two of them in the privacy of her room. Both of them alone in their own rooms would have been best, but that scenario didn't seem likely. *God, when had it become such a dilemma just to be alone with her?*

When he came out of the bathroom, he found her lying on his bed, on her stomach, surfing through the TV channels with the remote in her hand. She'd put on his sweatshirt.

"Ready?" she chirped.

At the door, he stopped. "Wait," he said, slipping into the bathroom one more time.

He remembered that he still hadn't brushed his teeth.

They crept down the back stairs because he was afraid they'd run into someone in the lobby. Outside, in the muggy air, they scurried to the docks like teenagers sneaking out after curfew, Jenny trying not to giggle after he admonished her for making so much noise.

Jack found the right boat and stepped onto its rear platform; he held out his hand to help balance Jenny as she did the same. She grabbed his wrist, and he noticed that the few minutes in the warm air had returned her skin to a normal temperature.

He put the gear in reverse and carefully backed out of the slip. As he edged out of the small harbor, he glanced back at her. She was on her back, with her knees bent, gazing at the sky. He set the throttle at a low speed and made minor adjustments to their direction with one finger. Despite the slow pace, it didn't take long before the lights of the resort became nothing more than a lambent glow in the distance and then, once he turned the bend and brought them into the open expanse of the lake, disappeared altogether.

After a while, she came up front and sat in the seat adjacent to his. She didn't speak, and they both watched the gentle waves of the black swollen water. He finally started to relax. He steered the boat into a large cove where the water was calmer. It wasn't until he shut down the engine that she came out of her trance and looked at him questioningly.

"I thought maybe you'd like it without the noise," he said.

She smiled. "Yes, I would."

"You really never came here as a kid?"

She turned to him and waited a moment before answering. "No."

He sensed there was more, an explanation, because hadn't every kid who'd grown up in Missouri been to this man-made lake at least once?

"My parents died when I was nine, Jack. There were a lot of things I didn't do." She stood up, pulled the sweatshirt over her head, and dropped her shorts. "Let's swim."

Before he could respond, she'd climbed over the railing and was poised to dive in. He stood just in time to see her sinewy body cut a hole in the water with barely a splash.

She hooted as her head popped out of the water. "It feels great! Come on in!"

Her voice echoed in the still air, and he looked around as if someone else might have heard her. But the only sound was the ripple of her gentle treading in the warm water. He wanted to tell her he was sorry, wanted to ask more about her parents, but she'd made it clear she didn't want that. So he dropped anchor, pulled off his shirt, and dived in with her.

When he came up out of the water, he laughed from the sheer joy of what they were doing. How long had it been since he'd swum in a lake in the middle of the night? And apparently this was a first for her.

"How far is Bagnell Dam?" she asked. They treaded water close to the boat, and the invisible hollow that formed between the water and the boat's aluminum side caused her words to reverberate.

"Far."

"Can we go see it?" she persisted.

"Jenny, it'd take all night. It's at least an hour up and then another hour back." She looked skeptical. "Anyway," he added, "there's not much to see. Trust me. It's not Hoover Dam."

She scrunched her face in disappointment.

"Did *your* family come here a lot?" she asked.

"A lot? No. But every so often. And I spent a few weeks at camp somewhere down here. I'm not even sure where, exactly."

"Mark, too?" She stretched out and swam farther from the boat. He followed.

"Yeah."

"Are you two close?" She ducked under the water, came up with her face to the sky to smooth her hair back.

"You saw us together. What do you think?"

"Well, if you were really, really close, I would have met him before now, I think. But yeah, I think you're close, in a drive-each-other-crazy sort of way."

"Sort of like us?"

She smirked, and swam away again. He watched her measured strokes; they were strong and smooth, practiced. It hadn't been on the lake, but she'd learned to swim well somewhere. She spoke again when she was a good twenty-five feet from him. "Yeah, sort of like us." And then, "You wanna race?"

No, he didn't want to. But he knew if he declined, she'd take it as a sign of weakness.

They decided to start the race by diving off the back of the boat, one on each side of the propeller. They'd swim to a buoy near shore and then double back.

It was at least two hundred feet to the buoy, and for the first one hundred or so, they swam head to head. Every few strokes he'd check her progress against his own, and if he felt she was gaining on him in the slightest bit, he pushed himself harder. But he reached a point where he couldn't do more; he was operating at full capacity, and still she was pulling ahead. The lake water was earthy-tasting and he struggled not to swallow it. She reached the buoy a few feet before him and executed a turn like the kind he'd seen on television.

On the way back she seemed to lose her energy, though, while he kept pushing himself, kept circling his arms like a turbine engine in the belief that she might have the skill but he had the endurance. The gap between them began to shrink, and for a moment he thought he was going to do it. The boat loomed near, but he was only a foot or two behind her.

Then she grinned at him. Or did she? He was sure he'd seen it through their chaotic splashing. A devious, *tricked-you* grin. His gains evaporated as she sprinted for the finish and touched the boat a full body length before him. When he emerged, jerking his head to shake off the excess water, she was smiling broadly, panting from her exhaustion and exhilaration.

"I'm sorry!" she said between breaths. "I couldn't resist."

"You're good," he said, exhaling loudly. The combined rhythm of their labored breathing unnerved him, and he turned from her when he realized why. It was the sound that immediately followed vigorous love-making.

He dunked his head into the water. The humiliation of being beaten, and now these thoughts invading his head. "You ready to go back?" he asked when he came up. "We shouldn't be here."

Her face fell. "No, why?" She swam around the motor to his side. "Jack, why? You're not mad at me for beating you, are you?"

Water beaded on her dark eyelashes, forming shiny black triangles. He wondered how long they would dance around it.

"No, of course not," he said finally. "It's just that we have a long day tomorrow. We should get some sleep."

"But I like being out here alone." He sensed that she didn't mean alone with him, but instead was alluding to her isolation from the world at large. He wondered if things had gotten worse for her at Newman. "I think I could stay here forever, actually," she added, laughing slightly at the absurdity of the idea.

"Jenny? Is everything okay at Newman? With Max—"

She cut him off. "Don't worry about it. I've got everything under control. I'm not going to mess anything up for you."

"That's not what I meant," he said slowly, a bit taken aback by her aggressive tone.

She dipped under the water and swam to the ladder. "Come on, then, let's go," she said. Her muscles were toned and slick with lake water as she pulled herself up. She pretended her sudden acquiescence wasn't sudden at all, and her refusal to meet his eyes told him to back off.

In the boat, they realized they hadn't brought dry towels, so they shared the damp one Jenny'd had around her neck when she'd first shown up at Jack's door. She put on his sweatshirt and took her seat again in the front, next to him, but the silence they shared was awkward now.

"You just don't see stars like this in the city, do you?" she asked.

"You don't see stars like this as an adult," he said. She turned to him, and he knew she understood what he meant.

After another fifteen minutes of silence, she asked, "How much farther?"

Jack shrugged. "Forty, forty-five minutes."

"To the hotel? Did we come that far?"

He looked over at her. He wanted to give her whatever she wanted, whatever he could.

"To the dam."

The humidity still hadn't lifted when Jack woke the next morning and headed to the main lodge for breakfast. The sky was cloudless but blurred hot with haze. He was tired and running late, but he was in a good mood. He felt that the night before with Jenny had been a test of his fidelity, and not only had he passed, he'd done so with flying colors. After all, if he'd really wanted to pursue something more with her, last night would have been the night to do it. The temptation had been high, and the risk low, but he hadn't succumbed. His behavior on the boat had been beyond reproach.

His mood, though, proved to be short-lived. Jim Wolfe was standing outside the lodge, leaning against the valet stand, when Jack approached. Wolfe was the legal reporter for St. Louis's largest daily newspaper. They made eye contact from a distance, but as Jack got closer, Wolfe bent down and pretended to retie his shoelaces.

Jack planned to walk by with just a nod, hoping that Wolfe wasn't there to talk to him, but he made the mistake of trying to stifle a yawn as he passed.

"Good morning, Mr. Hilliard," Wolfe said, standing up straight again, his tone a little too friendly. With one finger he pushed his wire-rim glasses farther up his nose. "Late night?"

"Excuse me?" Jack said. He tried to muster a smile so that Wolfe wouldn't sense his discomfort at the question. The automatic doors that had opened when Jack first stepped on the hotel's large welcome mat now stood gaping at attention, waiting for him to pass through into the cooled air. In his mind he kept replaying the picture of walking with Jenny back to their rooms from the dock. Except for the small ground lights that lit the path, it had been very dark. The deck and pool lights had been turned off hours before, and most of the rooms were black, too. He was sure no one had seen them.

Wolfe shrugged like a little kid. He reminded Jack of Radar O'Reilly from *M*A*S*H*.

"You yawned. I was merely joking in reference to your yawn, Mr. Hilliard. I apologize if I offended you."

"No, no," Jack stuttered. "You didn't." He struggled to recover. "I just didn't hear you properly, I guess."

"I was just wondering if you had a few minutes to discuss the Barnard case." Wolfe's tone was still friendly, but he reached for a Dictaphone in his shirt pocket, so Jack knew he planned to ask the questions regardless of whether Jack intended to answer them.

"Certainly." At that moment Jack was happy to discuss anything if it would draw Wolfe's attention away from his own lack of sleep. He just couldn't get rid of the image of him and Jenny strolling back to the hotel together. He tried to remember if they'd touched or given any other indication of being anything more than friends. He knew it didn't matter; just being alone with Jenny at that time of night would be incriminating evidence to someone like Wolfe.

"Well, I'm sure you're aware of Mr. Scanlon's decision not to seek death for Cassia Barnard's murderer—"

Jack interrupted. "Her alleged murderer, yes." God, now he sounded like a defense attorney.

"Her *alleged* murderer," Wolfe agreed easily, shrugging his carefree Radar-like shrug again. "I'm wondering if he consulted you prior to making his decision, and whether you believe it was the right decision to make."

Out of the corner of his eye Jack glimpsed other attorneys coming up the walk—St. Louis attorneys, and he recognized many of them. He felt the rapidly rising sun on his face and wished that Wolfe had conducted his stakeout inside the hotel.

"We talked about it, of course. I'm not at liberty to share our conversations with you. I *will* tell you that I think he made the right decision. I believe it was the only decision he could make after being presented with all the available evidence of Mr. Hutchins's diminished mental capacity."

The group of attorneys slowed as they neared, some nodding to Jack or smiling in silent greeting. He returned the gesture once, intending it for the whole group. Wolfe ignored all of them; he was the outsider and he knew it. He focused his attention on Jack.

"Absent the evidence of his low IQ"—he noticed that Wolfe had reworded Jack's description of the defendant—"do you think Mr. Scanlon would have asked for the death penalty?"

"I'm not privy to the inner workings of my boss's mind, Mr. Wolfe." He smiled in a friendly manner as he said it. He knew he was being smart with the guy, but he also knew the small crowd that had gathered to watch the exchange enjoyed it.

"Well then, I'm sure you're privy to the inner workings of your own mind, aren't you, Mr. Hilliard? I'm also sure that you're aware this is a very hot issue in the upcoming election. So what would you have done? Would you have asked for death?"

"A hot issue for a hot day, huh, Mr. Wolfe?" He smiled again, directing it at one of the female lawyers in the crowd who'd just lifted a curl of thick chestnut hair off her neck in an effort to stay cool. She smiled back. All of them were on his side. Despite their differences in the courtroom, they would stick together against a common adversary.

But then she yawned. It was a silent, wide yawn, politely covered, but Jack saw it and it proved as contagious as the flu. He felt the involuntary movement of his jaw as his mind ricocheted once more to the two of them standing in his doorway, trying to deny their attraction to each other.

Wolfe laughed. "Mr. Hilliard, are you *sure* you weren't out late last night?" He narrowed his eyes as if he, too, was in on the secret.

Jack tried to remember the question before his yawn. He had to divert Wolfe back to Barnard before he began to inquire more about Jack's evening. He didn't want to be forced to lie outright.

"Mr. Wolfe, to answer your question, the one that I think you really want an answer to—" He would tell Wolfe exactly what he wanted to hear. "I do think that if Clyde Hutchins had an IQ like me, or you, or any of these ladies and gentlemen standing here with us, Mr. Scanlon would have been justified in asking for the death penalty."

Even as he spoke these words, words so contradictory to what he really believed, he knew that he couldn't stop now. "And if I were in his shoes," he continued, purposely using the phrase the woman from the television news had used, "I, too, would be justified in asking for the death penalty."

"Justified," not "right." Justified was different from right, wasn't it? But his throat tightened. He sensed that he'd just given away something that he could never get back.

CHAPTER ELEVEN

As summer neared its end, the campaign picked up speed. In addition to the activities scheduled during the day, Jack's nights were increasingly being eaten up by functions that, according to Dunne, required his appearance. Even the weekends became hectic after Dunne saw a picture of Jack's family in the paper, taken at a festival, and decided he wanted Claire to attend as many events as possible. "She's got a certain quality about her, a genuineness," he'd stated matter-of-factly. "There are certain people who will vote for you simply because of her." Claire acquiesced. Whatever misgivings she had about the campaign—and she had many, as Jack's expressed position became more opposed to what he really felt—she saved for home, and he discovered that he enjoyed having her along; he enjoyed showing her off.

But he was eager to leave the campaigning behind and return to the courtroom. The Barnard trial was scheduled for early October, and the date was fast approaching. In the weeks leading up to it, the late nights began to exact their toll at home. The routine wasn't unusual; he'd always prepared for his big trials at night, when the office was quiet and it was easier to concentrate. Claire had always understood, but this time her patience gave out quickly. They both were exhausted from the campaign, so he tried to ignore her sighs when he called to say he'd be late. But it soon became an escalating cycle that they couldn't break. He'd have to work late, she'd complain, and then, to avoid further conflict, he'd make less of an effort to get home to her.

One morning in mid-September he left early for work, pulling out of the driveway before the sky began to lighten. Claire was still sleeping, and he didn't wake her to say good-bye. They'd fought the night before over something silly and had gone to bed with little conversation, back to back, not touching. By the time his anger had dissipated and he'd whispered into the dark for her to come closer, she'd fallen asleep, or at least had pretended to.

But the thought that she might still be angry gnawed at him, so at lunchtime he called her.

"Hi," she said, immediately dropping the professional tone she used at work. She sounded tired. "What do you need?"

He swallowed. As if he called only when he needed something. "Nothing. I just missed you"—he decided to take a chance—"and hoped that maybe you missed me, too."

Her response, delivered without humor, wasn't what he'd been fishing for. "I've been missing you for a while, Jack."

"I know." He looked at the picture of her on the beach in Amagansett and wished she were in the room with him. "I'm sorry about last night. The trial and the election's making us crazy, but they'll be over soon, okay? A few more weeks. And I'm leaving at five tonight, come hell or high water. I promise."

The line was silent for a moment, and then she said, "You left so early this morning."

"Yeah, I wanted to get here before the office opened so I could work without any distractions. I just wanted to be alone for a while, that's all."

He could tell by her silence that she'd taken it the wrong way, as an indictment of her. Maybe, in a roundabout sort of way, it was. "Claire, I don't mean to—"

"I've gotta go. My class starts at five after."

He sighed again. No matter how hard they tried, it seemed that lately every discussion ended this way, with him trying to explain himself and her misunderstanding, and then cutting him off before they could reach some sort of resolution. "Okay" was all he said.

For the umpteenth time, the line fell silent between them.

Finally, she spoke. "Okay, I guess I'll see you when you get home."

"Yeah, okay." He picked up the picture frame with his free hand and studied it. He was certain that if they were in the same room they'd be able to get past this. "I love you."

"Is that all?"

Is that all? She'd been expecting something else but he didn't have a clue what it might be.

"Claire, I told you I was sorry."

"Yeah, you did, didn't you? Never mind. I'll see you tonight." The words were cold, without feeling or intonation. And for the first time that he could remember, she hung up without telling him that she loved him, too.

At quarter to five Jeff barged into Jack's office after only a halfhearted attempt at a knock.

"What now?" Jack asked, tossing him a nasty look.

"You've been a little crabby lately." Jeff grinned like the Cheshire cat, as if even Jack's foul mood wasn't going to spoil his own good one. "Not getting enough sleep?"

"No, now that you mention it, I'm not. Which is why—"

"Well, don't expect to go to bed early tonight."

"That's exactly what I plan to do."

"Uh-uh. Not tonight. Dunne just called, and he's got plans for you. Wait till you—"

"No. Stop. I don't care what plans he has for me. I'm going home"—Jack looked at his watch—"in about fifteen minutes. I promised Claire."

The phone rang and they ignored it.

"Don't worry about Claire. She'll understand. The Dems are in town, the big ones." They talked over the second ring as they waited for it to flip to Beverly. "Dunne's arranged a little meeting for you, it seems."

"No. I told you, I'm going home."

"You're not listening, Jack. These are the big guns, out of Washington. He's arranged for them to meet you, and if all goes well, you might land a coveted endorsement from the House Minority Leader himself. I'm talking a TV spot with him telling everyone to vote for you."

"Yeah, how much is my campaign paying for this 'coveted endorsement,' if I might ask?"

Jeff laughed. "Aw, Jack, you've become such a cynic in your few months on the campaign trail."

"I prefer 'realist.'" Jack stood and started putting the files on his desk into some semblance of order. "It doesn't matter. I'm going home. I don't need any endorsements."

A buzz from his phone interrupted them, and then Beverly's voice filled the office.

"Jack, I know you didn't want to be disturbed, but it's Mr. Dunne, and he's insisting on talking to you or Jeff. I can't find Jeff, so what should—"

"He's in here with me. Just put him through."

Jack motioned with his hand for Jeff to take the call. "Tell him I left for the day," he mumbled as he sat back down in his chair, resigned to another twenty minutes in the office. Jeff pressed the button for the speakerphone.

"Hey, Greg. I've got Jack here with me," he said, his voice more animated than usual. Jack wondered if Jeff had started calling Dunne "Greg" on his own or whether he'd been instructed to. "He's ecstatic about the plans for tonight."

Jack glared at Jeff; there hadn't been even a touch of sarcasm in his voice.

"Hey, Jack!" Dunne's low voice reverberated from the small speaker on the phone.

"Hi, Gregory. You've outdone yourself."

"Yeah, how 'bout that? Do I take care of you or don't I?"

"You do. You do." Jack laughed a bit. "There's only one problem."

"Hold on, Greg." Jeff quickly pressed the mute button, and the smile left his face. "Don't you dare, Jack. Do you have any idea what strings he's pulled for you? You get on that phone and you ask him when and where and you tell him how grateful you are. Don't be an idiot."

Instinctively, Jack looked at the photograph again, and Jeff saw him do it.

"I don't have a choice," Jack said. "I need to go home."

Jeff's tone softened. "I'll call her and explain, if you want me to. But you've gotta do this. You are right about one thing. You *don't* have a choice."

Moments later, Jack agreed to meet Dunne at the Ritz-Carlton in Clayton at six thirty so Dunne could prep him for a meeting at seven. Dunne and Jeff continued to talk, but Jack had trouble following their conversation because of an overwhelming preoccupation with figuring out what he was going to tell Claire. His ruminations were cut short when Beverly came in and slipped a note in front of him. "Michael's on line 2," it read.

That was strange. Michael never called him at work. In fact, it seemed that in the past six months Michael wanted as little to do with him as possible.

He interrupted Jeff and Dunne and, after ushering them quickly through their farewells, he picked up the handset to talk without Jeff hearing both sides of the conversation.

"Michael, what is it?" His voice sounded more alarmed than he'd intended.

"Dad, how come you haven't left yet? Mom said you were leaving by five today."

"Yeah, I was, but—"

"Don't forget you're supposed to pick up the cake."

The panic in his gut hit him immediately and hit him hard. He looked at Jeff. "Oh fuck," he thought, and then realized he had spoken it aloud, and both Jeff and Michael had heard it. *Is that all?* Her question reverberated in his head. "Claire's birthday. Today is Claire's birthday." Jeff rolled his eyes, but Jack couldn't tell whether this was meant to express his displeasure at having another problem to deal with or whether he was just commenting on Jack's apparent incompetence as a husband. "Oh fuck," he repeated.

"You mean you forgot?" Michael's voice rose an octave.

"Michael, listen to me. Where's Mom? Is she home?"

"Yeah. I can't believe you forgot her birthday."

"What's she doing?"

"Right now she's sitting out on the deck with Marcia." He paused.

"They're drinking wine." He said it as if he had top-secret information and Jack was lucky to be privy to it.

"Does she look mad?"

"I don't know, Dad! She's just talking."

Jack scribbled a note and shoved it across the desk to Jeff. *Call Dunne and tell him I won't be there.*

Jeff began to shake his head.

"Go get her," Jack said into the phone. "I need to talk to her."

He heard Michael set down the phone; as he waited, he tried to take a deep breath. "Fuck," he said one more time.

Jeff pushed Jack's note back across the desk. "I'm not calling him, Jack. You're going. Claire knows how important this campaign is. She'll get over it."

"No. She won't." He stood, suppressing the urge to make some smart-ass remark about the reasons why Jeff was still single. "Get out of here. I want some privacy."

But Jeff didn't move, except to shake his head in disbelief. Before Jack could repeat his demand, Claire was on the phone. "Hi." She didn't sound mad, just apathetic. Maybe damage control was still possible.

He motioned for Jeff to leave and then turned around and sat on the desk with his back to the door. "Hey, happy birthday. Starting the celebration without me?" The line was silent but he pretended he didn't notice. "Did you have a good day?"

"Thank you. Yes, I did."

He glanced over his shoulder and watched Jeff close the door behind him.

"I've got a surprise for you." He knew what he was about to do was extremely risky, but, as Jeff had said, he didn't have a choice.

"You do?" She sounded skeptical, but interested.

"I booked us a room at the Ritz. We've got eight o'clock dinner reservations, and then we're going to stay the night at the hotel. How's that sound?"

"Jack"—the skepticism was waning—"my parents are coming at seven, remember? They're having dinner with us. You said you were leaving by five. Shouldn't you be on the road now?"

"My lovely wife, you're so gullible." He winced at the irony of his statement even as he teased her. It would be a miracle if he pulled this off. "That was just a ploy. They're coming over to watch the kids for us."

"Really?"

He could hear her warming up to the idea. "Yes, really."

She sighed. "I sort of thought we'd all get a chance to be together tonight."

He jumped on that comment. "I was thinking we needed a chance to be alone. Don't you think we need that?"

"Well, yeah, I know we do." She paused, he knew, to weigh her decision. "And here I thought you'd forgotten, the way you bolted out of here this morning."

"I like to keep you guessing." She giggled then, and he gave silent thanks to God that she'd decided to share a bottle of wine with their neighbor. "I wanted to come home early to pick you up, but I realized I'll get in late tomorrow, so I need to hang around and wrap some things up, okay? How much wine have you had? Can you meet me at the hotel around quarter to eight?"

"Just a glass. I'm fine." If he were there with her, she'd be looking at him with her eyes narrowed and a little smirk on her face as she tried to decide whether or not to believe him. He glanced at his watch to determine how much time he had to negotiate all the arrangements he'd promised. "Okay, I'll be there," she said finally.

When they finished with the details, he asked to speak to Michael. After explaining the plan to ensure that Michael didn't blow Jack's cover, he hung up and dialed Jeff's extension. "Call Dunne and tell him I have a half hour to spend with those guys, and that's it. Come seven thirty I'm out of there."

He hung up before Jeff had time to protest. Next he called Claire's mom and begged, and then he called the restaurant and begged some more. And finally, when all the other arrangements had been made, he called the hotel and booked a room. He didn't have to beg, though—he merely had to pay the price.

CHAPTER TWELVE

The Barnard event—and the media had truly turned the trial into an event—began every morning exactly as Jack expected, with a mob on the courthouse steps to greet him. He'd known when he first agreed to take the case, back in early August, that it would be like this. And yet every morning he still had to brace himself as he turned the last corner on his short walk from the parking garage.

He was accustomed to such scenes. He'd tried many cases in which he'd been forced to push through a crowd of spectators just to get to the front doors of the courthouse. But he'd never had to make the journey as a candidate for office who was prosecuting the most emotionally charged case to hit the city in years. And on this final day of the trial, before the jury retired to deliberate, walking the gauntlet had been particularly unsettling.

Once inside the courthouse, though, once he took his seat at the prosecution table, he forgot about the crowd outside. He even forgot about the crowd inside. He knew everyone was there, of course—not only the spectators but the reporters and family members of the victim and the defendant, too—but for Jack, entering the courtroom always felt like coming home. Whereas some attorneys saw the courtroom as a dangerous, foreign country to be conquered, Jack felt like a native son who spoke the language fluently and was able to translate it effortlessly for the people who mattered most—the jurors.

Earl had always claimed that "jurors simply love Jack Hilliard," and if the current trial was any indication, his claim held true. Jack had developed a rapport with the jury during the long voir dire—two and a half days long because of the pretrial publicity that had saturated the city— and none of the defense efforts so far had been able to break that. Once he'd begun to put his witnesses on the stand, the trial progressed quickly. He'd built his case methodically, as a carpenter builds a house, laying a strong foundation and then carefully framing each component until the structure couldn't be knocked down. He'd begun by letting the cops tell the story of their discovery of Cassia in the woods, and then he'd questioned each investigator, each lab technician, each eyewitness, each piece of the puzzle that had led them first to Cassia and then to Hutchins. And then, when the skeleton had been laid, he'd brought it to life with the testimony of those closest to Cassia: her mother and father, her brother, even a teacher, and her best friend. After a week, he'd rested his case and passed it to Hutchins's attorney, Millie Rubin. It was now Thursday morning, and Millie was ready to call her last witness. With any luck, they would present their closing arguments after lunch, and then the waiting would begin.

But first he had to get through the last witness.

"Your Honor, I'd like to call the defendant, Clyde Hutchins, to the stand." Millie's voice was strong over the loud whispering that swelled from the gallery.

Jack hadn't expected Hutchins to take the stand; murder defendants rarely did unless they had an alibi or pleaded self-defense. But the day before, after Judge Baxter had adjourned for the day, Millie had pulled Jack aside and given him the news: against her advice, Hutchins insisted on testifying. Jack had seen from the honest worry in Millie's eyes that she hadn't been sandbagging him. He almost felt bad for her, because the defendant's testifying in such a case—in which the crime was brutal and the evidence overwhelming—was akin to sealing the prosecution's case with a kiss and putting a pretty bow on top for good measure. So, although the news had come as a surprise, it hadn't really concerned him. He'd merely nodded sympathetically and returned to his office to plan the next day's cross-examination.

But as night fell, and the background noises of computer keyboards and ringing phones became less frequent but more noticeable, and the soft bell of the elevator down the hall signaled another person leaving for the day, Jack grew inexplicably nervous about Hutchins taking the stand. He found himself unable to sit still in his chair, even though his notes for the cross-examination hadn't made it past the first page of a clean legal pad. He made a trip to the bathroom; he made a trip to the vending machines. He called Claire and asked to speak to the kids to say good night. He even stood in the doorway to Earl's dark office, gazing at his unusually organized desk, and began to miss him already.

The reason for his discomfort became apparent, finally, after he accidentally startled Gwen, the night cleaning lady, who'd been humming to herself as she made her way from office to office.

"Oh! Excuse me, Mr. Jack!" she said, addressing him in the semiformal way she'd adopted after he'd asked her, years ago, to call him Jack. The words came out slowly and muffled, as if she had a mouthful of marshmallows. This was not unusual or surprising—all her words came out this way: she suffered from mild mental retardation.

Jack stared at her in a daze. Only when her face scrunched up in confusion at his failure to respond did he issue an emphatic apology and insist he'd been entirely at fault.

On the way back to his office, he suddenly realized the source of his agitation: Gwen's voice. Despite the fact that he'd heard it many times over the years, and despite the fact that its owner was a well-adjusted middle-aged woman who held a full-time government job, Gwen's voice always evoked just the slightest hint of pity.

And it was that same, reflexive pity Jack feared the jury would feel when Clyde Hutchins took the stand.

Jack trusted the jury to understand that Hutchins's slightly diminished mental capacity didn't have any bearing on guilt or innocence; an insanity defense wasn't at issue. But he knew that logic and emotion seldom agreed, and he feared the effect on his case, however subtle, if the human evidence of that diminished mental capacity was paraded right in front of them.

So he studied the jurors' faces as Hutchins trudged to the witness box. His intent was twofold: he wanted to gauge their reactions to the defendant, and he also wanted to maintain the connection he'd developed with them throughout the trial. When the clerk administered the oath, Jack felt only minor relief by his inability to identify any speech impairment from the defendant's one-word response. He knew it might still manifest itself under the pressure of questioning.

His confidence began to build again, though, as Millie walked her client carefully through the events leading up to the abduction and murder. The defendant's speech *was* slow, but he enunciated clearly, so the slowness could as easily have been part of his style as it could have been related to his mental disability. Overall, it didn't seem to have any effect on the jury, other than causing a few of them to glance at the clock.

What assured Jack the most wasn't the lack of a noticeable speech impairment. Rather, he had no idea what Hutchins intended to achieve with his testimony, and he could tell from Millie's demeanor that she didn't know either. As far as Jack was concerned, the defendant was giving the State a gift that surpassed even the written confession he'd signed just after his arrest. He kept expecting Hutchins to start making excuses for what he'd done, or even somehow to attempt to pin the blame on Cassia Barnard—an unbelievable tactic, to be sure, in this particular case—but none of Jack's conjectures came to pass.

Perhaps Jack's ignorance should have caused him some uneasiness. At the very least, it should have caused him to decline to question Hutchins when Millie finished her direct and passed the witness without any hint of damage to the State's case. But Jack didn't like the idea of ending the testimony with a murderer having the last word. He wanted to drive home the point that the guy understood exactly what he'd done, both before and during the execution of the crime. With the written confession as backup, he couldn't imagine any scenario in which he'd be caught unaware.

He rose from his chair when the judge looked at him, and he ignored the whispered "What are you doing, Jack?" from Frank, who sat at the prosecution table with him as second chair. He walked to a spot just near the back corner of the jury box, where he felt particularly at ease. After a brief nod to its occupants, he turned and faced the defendant.

"Mr. Hutchins." He stared at the small, skinny man, waited until he looked him in the eye. He wanted so badly just to ask the guy, *Why are you testifying against yourself? What could you possibly hope to achieve?* But Jack was more than familiar with the age-old rule that every trial lawyer knew and ignored at his peril: don't ask the witness a question unless you already know the answer.

So instead, he began simply. "You've just described to us what happened on the day of Cassia's abduction and murder, is that right?"

A simple yes and a cold glare was all Jack received. He'd expected no more and no less; it was the beauty of cross-examination. He thought back to the written confession, to things Hutchins had told the police but Millie had conveniently skipped. Jack had covered them with other witnesses during the State's case, of course, and the document had already been admitted into evidence, but to elicit the same information from the defendant on the stand would be the coup de grâce.

"Mr. Hutchins, isn't it true that you picked Cassia out as your intended victim?"

The defendant tilted his head. "What do you mean?"

Jack reminded himself of the reason why Earl had declined to make this a capital case, and he started over.

"You worked as a custodian at Cedar Hill Middle School, didn't you?"

"Yes."

"And you first saw Cassia Barnard at that school?"

"Yes."

"She was a student there?"

"Yes."

Hutchins was bald but he had a dark moustache, and Jack noticed he kept rubbing at it, smoothing it down with his thumb and forefinger.

"And you *chose* her, didn't you, from all the other students?"

"Yes."

"And you followed her for several weeks before you actually abducted her, isn't that correct?"

"Sure." *Sure?* His voice held no remorse.

"You knew where she lived?"

Hutchins nodded, and Jack said, "I'm sorry, Mr. Hutchins, but you have to speak your answer for the court reporter."

The defendant's eyes narrowed and he reached for his mustache again. "*Yes.*"

"You knew where her bus picked her up and dropped her off?"

"Yes."

"You even knew the exact times of day the bus came, didn't you?"

"Sure."

Every time he said "sure," it sounded to Jack like the guy was proud of himself for knowing the information.

"And you knew, in the afternoons, Cassia was the only child to get off the bus?"

"Yes."

"She had a good half mile to walk home, didn't she?" Before Hutchins answered, Jack added, "Alone."

"Yes." His one-word answers had shifted from a blithe monotone to apparent impatience.

"And on the seventeenth of January this year, you waited for her to get off her bus, didn't you?"

"Yes."

"You didn't even hide, did you? Isn't it true that you sat on a bench at the entrance to her neighborhood, and even waved to the bus driver as you greeted Cassia, as if you were a relative or family friend who'd come to meet her and take her home?"

Jack knew this fact was one of the most painful for Cassia's parents. It was that one moment in the whole horrific scenario—and every case had such a moment—that forced all the parties involved, whether it was family, police, investigators, or prosecutors, to think, *If only*. "If only" the bus driver had confirmed Hutchins's identity as a waiting parent. "If only" Cassia had hesitated, thus perhaps tipping off the bus driver that not only did she not expect this person, she didn't even know him. "If only" it hadn't been thirteen degrees with a light snow, and Hutchins's face had not been obscured by the large parka hood of his jacket, thus enabling him to be identified before the trail to Cassia, slowly freezing in the deep woods, had gone cold.

Hutchins didn't answer immediately, and Jack worried again that his compound question should have been worded more simply. He was about to rephrase it when the man leaned forward in his seat and said, "She *wanted* to go with me." He spoke the sentence with the slightest glimmer of a sardonic grin, almost as if he was bragging about the fact.

Another low buzz grew in the gallery. Jack felt his face grow hotter at Hutchins's smug answers. He looked over at Frank and met his eye, and the anticipation on Frank's face made it clear that he now fully supported Jack's strategy, however ill conceived he'd believed it to be minutes before.

Jack glanced at the faces in the jury box, and then, barely hiding the contempt in his voice, said to Hutchins, "Why don't you tell the ladies and gentlemen of the jury *why* twelve-year-old Cassia Barnard wanted to go with you."

Jack knew the answer to the question, of course, and he wanted the jury to hear it. He wanted them to realize, in the same way he had so despairingly realized upon first reading the confession, that all a parent's rules, and warnings, and threats, and scare tactics, all of them are so easily forgotten by a child in that "if only" moment.

But, fueled by the intensity of his desire, he'd disregarded the corollary to the first rule: never ask an open-ended question on cross, or you risk losing control of the witness altogether.

Jack's question had been wide open.

Hutchins sat up straighter, obviously enjoying the chance to share his clever plan with the rapt audience. "I told her I found a puppy freezing in the snow, and I asked her to help me find its owner." Jack knew that Hutchins didn't even understand the irony in his scheme; he hoped the jury did. Hutchins tittered a bit, setting off a new reaction from the crowd. Jack heard appalled commentary and uncomfortable repositioning. Judge Baxter gave one knock of his gavel to settle them.

"And I *did* have a puppy. I brought it with me. It was waiting in my truck." He smiled, raised one eyebrow, and added, "I didn't lie to her."

Jack became incensed. *He's having fun up there. He wanted to testify because he wanted to gloat over his crime.*

"No, you didn't *lie* to her. Instead you *tortured and murdered* her, didn't you?" His spontaneous remark, which was really more of a snide comment than a genuine question and which he immediately regretted, sparked a loud objection from Millie and a burst of angry chatter from the gallery. A lone voice shouted above the din, "He's a murderer!"

"Quiet!" the judge ordered, banging his gavel again. He gave it a few more sharp blows until the noise settled to a simmer, and then he turned to the attorneys.

"I'm going to overrule the objection." He fixed his gaze on Jack, who understood the look. The last question *wasn't* objectionable, technically, but Jack knew they both were thinking the same thing: This wasn't how Jack Hilliard treated witnesses; this wasn't how he conducted himself in a trial. While other lawyers enjoyed courtroom theatrics with their clever turns of phrases and over-the-top sarcasm, he had built his reputation on maintaining decorum, on being respectful. He nodded contritely and was about to resume with a more properly phrased question when Hutchins decided to answer the last one.

"Of *course* I murdered her. What choice did I have? She kept crying and screaming. She wouldn't shut up."

Millie shot out of her chair. "You can stop, Mr. Hutchins; you've answered the question."

Hutchins looked at her but gave no sign of having heard her. "The bitch scratched me and bit me. I still have scars to prove it." He jerked his arm up and shoved it forward. He made as if to show Jack, and then Millie, and then finally the jury, as if he believed they'd share his disgust. "That's why I used the rope. She wouldn't sit still." He made a scoffing noise from his throat. "The bitch."

Jack heard wailing from the row behind his and Frank's table and knew it was Cassia's mother. He heard Millie begging the judge to put a stop to her client's narrative, but her voice was lost in the cacophony of even louder voices that had exploded in the courtroom. He heard the shuffling of feet as the crowd rose from their seats and many began to shout invectives at Hutchins: *Murderer! Scum! Devil! Fuckin' retard! White trash!* He heard the pounding of the gavel grow harder with each blow, and Judge Baxter shouting, "Order in the court! Order! Quiet down

immediately or I will have the bailiff remove each and every one of you!"
He heard Hutchins's continued rant about Cassia, though no one was listening to him anymore.

And like a wind that changes direction, the crowd's anger shifted ever so slightly, and Jack realized some of them were angry not only at Hutchins, they were angry at him. The ones who had shouted at him on his way into the courthouse that morning were now shouting at him as he made his way back to his table. He heard, "He should have been gassed!" come from the row behind Cassia's parents, and when he looked in the direction of the voice, his eyes were drawn to the hunched-over figure sobbing in the front row: Cassia's mother.

Within moments, sheriffs came in to assist the bailiff, and the courtroom was cleared. Jack watched the jury being led out, too, and he knew from the looks on their faces that closing arguments weren't even necessary. The State had just won the case.

Later, after the lawyers had been called back to chambers and Millie had made a motion for mistrial, which the judge had denied, they waited quietly at their tables for the trial to resume. The courtroom was empty except for the court personnel, the attorneys, the defendant and his family, Cassia's family and a smattering of reporters.

"Mr. Hilliard?"

Jack turned at the sound of the soft voice behind him and rose quickly to meet Mrs. Barnard at the bar. Though she wasn't much older than Jack, the past year had obviously taken its toll. She spoke with her eyes down, and he had to strain to hear her.

"I wanted you to know . . ." She hesitated, and Jack waited. "I was pleased when Mr. Scanlon told me you were going to handle the trial, even though, you know, it would mean . . . I had accepted that maybe he would suffer more if he sat in prison for the rest of his life, thinking about what he did. But after hearing that"—she made a small motion in Hutchins's direction—"I do think he should die for what he did to Cassia." She began to sob gently. "But—"

"Mrs. Barnard, I'm so sorry, I—"

She touched his hand where it rested on the bar. "No, no, I know it's too late for that now. What I'm trying to say is . . . you've done a good job. You showed him for what he truly is—a monster."

She turned to join her husband, as Jack whispered an inadequate "Thank you."

He felt Frank studying him when he took his seat. After several minutes of uncomfortable silence, Frank mumbled, "They're right, you know." His arms were crossed in front of him and his eyes monitored the door where the jury would be brought back in. "We should have asked for his ass to be fried."

Jack looked at him but didn't respond. He wasn't sure if Frank was goading him or just making small talk.

"Earl crapped out on this one," Frank continued. "He wanted you to try the case so badly that he forgot who his client was."

"What the hell is that supposed to mean?"

"Oh, come on, don't give me that bull. You know as well as I do that if the election wasn't weeks away, Earl would have tried this case and he would have sent this asshole to death row." Frank finished his sentence with a disgusted grunt.

"The guy's got an IQ of sixty-eight, in case you hadn't noticed. *That's* why Earl's not sending him to death row."

"Yeah, you keep telling yourself that. Maybe it'll make it true." He laughed derisively. "Whose side are you on?"

Jack was still staring at Frank in disbelief when Judge Baxter returned to his bench and asked the bailiff to bring in the jury. The room was silent except for the sound of their shoes marching solemnly across the wooden floor of the jury box. One by one, they took their seats, each stealing a glance at Jack as they made themselves comfortable in the small black chairs.

"Mr. Hilliard?"

Jack looked up at the judge. The judge nodded in the direction of the witness stand. "He's still your witness. Any more questions?"

Jack glanced at Frank once more as he considered whether to continue with Hutchins. He wanted to ask the defendant about his mental disability. Somehow, he wanted everyone in the courtroom to understand *why* the State had not made this a capital case. Millie had covered her client's mild retardation on direct, and earlier in her case she'd had a mental-health expert testify about it, too. But there'd been no useful testimony about how it affected his personality and whether it might have been responsible for the complete lack of remorse they'd witnessed moments before. Jack wanted to believe it was; he wanted the jury and Mrs. Barnard to believe it was. Because otherwise, maybe the crowd was right, maybe Frank was right, and if so, Jack had had no business trying the case.

"The people are waiting," Frank said under his breath, and Jack understood. Earl might have forgotten who the client was, but Jack wouldn't make the same mistake.

He stood and addressed the court. "No, Your Honor. No more questions."

PART 3

LATE FALL

CHAPTER THIRTEEN

Jack woke on Election Day expecting to feel different, but everything seemed the same. It was still dark outside when he went downstairs to search for his running shoes. After stretching in the kitchen, he turned to grab his sweatshirt from the stair railing and started when he saw Claire sitting on the fifth step up, her chin propped on her hands, her elbows on her knees. She wore a slight smile—the smile she sometimes had when she caught the kids sneaking raw dough from the cookie sheet before she put it in the oven.

"Were you having trouble sleeping?" she whispered.

"I slept well, actually. I just wanted to run."

"At four in the morning?"

He turned to look at the clock above the stove. Sure enough, the green digital numbers shone brightly against the black glass front of the microwave: 4:06. Maybe things were starting to feel a little bit different.

He sat next to her on the step and rested his hand on her knee. "I'm wide awake," he said. "I thought it was six."

"Are you nervous?"

"I didn't think so."

"You know Schafer isn't even a factor."

"I know. It's not the election. It's that . . . I don't know."

She touched his face. The furnace in the basement went off and the house seemed to sigh in the silence that followed.

He pulled her closer. "Have I disappointed you?"

She leaned away to see him better, her brow furrowed. "Of course not."

"I shouldn't have tried that case."

"Why not? Because some people thought Earl made the wrong decision? You didn't have anything to do with that. Your job was to get the conviction and you did. You put a bad man away for a long time. For good."

He could have argued the point—of course he'd had something to do with the decision, just not in the way she'd meant—but instead he just nodded. "I know you would have liked me to handle the whole campaign differently."

"Jack, no." She sighed. "I know I'm too idealistic. I'm sorry if I made you feel that way. I understand you needed to play by their rules if you wanted to be in the game."

He moved some hair away from her face and kissed her lightly on the lips. She might not have realized it, but she'd finally given him the blessing he'd wanted so badly.

The small ballroom was packed and hot by the time Jack and Claire arrived at close to seven that evening. They already knew, thanks to a brief call from Dunne, that early reports showed Jack was ahead at the polls, but nevertheless the roar of cheers and applause that greeted them was overwhelming. He couldn't deny that he enjoyed the reaction, but it made him feel self-conscious in a way he'd never felt as the main event in the courtroom.

The crowd split to form a path as he and Claire walked forward. It was slow going; arms stretched out from all sides waiting to shake hands. He recognized many faces but others he didn't. Dunne hadn't advised him on protocol so he just did what felt right, shaking every hand and stopping to talk.

When the time came, Earl insisted on the honor of announcing the result. Jack was so focused on mentally rehearsing his acceptance speech that he barely heard a word Earl said. He knew Earl was finished and it was his turn to take the mike only because of the applause and cheers from the decreasingly sober crowd.

He'd spent numerous hours over the past few days writing and revising his speech. As recently as that afternoon, on the way to the polls with Claire, he'd tweaked phrases here and there in his head. So when he stepped up to the mike, the words that started to come out of his mouth were the ones that he'd actually planned to say.

But then something happened. He became aware that his mind was taking him to a different place.

"You know," he said, "I've just decided to say something other than what I originally intended."

Silent confusion worked its way through the warm room. He was aware of it, but it didn't deter him. Mark, who stood between Claire and Jenny, leaned toward Claire's ear and she shrugged her shoulders. Jenny seemed oblivious to Mark and Claire's exchange; she stared at Jack, her eyes lit with anticipation.

"I know my prepared speech might have been more what you expected to hear, but I think I'd rather use this unique opportunity to say something unique, too." He shifted his weight from one foot to the other and smiled. "After all, it's not every day you get to stand in front of such a large, captive audience and say whatever strikes your fancy."

The crowd laughed, and it spurred him on.

"When I started law school a little over fourteen years ago, I couldn't possibly foresee that one day I would be standing up here giving an acceptance speech after winning the election for District Attorney. I'd be lying if I told you I'd ever thought about running back then, or about working in the DA's office. The truth is, when I started law school I had no idea what I intended to do with the degree I'd earn three years later; no idea even of the type of law I wanted to practice. Even once I graduated, I didn't have any specific goals with respect to my legal career." He grinned. "Unless, of course, you count getting my student loans paid off." He paused to allow more laughter.

"I suppose the point I'm trying to make is that sometimes the best things in life, the things that are the most satisfying both professionally and personally, are the things you least expect to happen. Life sometimes takes you places you didn't expect to go, yet when you get there you realize just how right it is for you. That's how I feel about this position you've entrusted to me. It feels right. It feels like a job I was meant to do, even if I didn't know it fourteen years ago.

"Last spring, when I was first approached about becoming a candidate for District Attorney, I dismissed the idea. But a good friend said something that made me reconsider."

He stopped again, because the words in his brain were the words Jenny had spoken at the banquet. He glanced at her; she still had the look of expectation, and he felt certain that she knew he was talking about her. But she'd been very drunk; would she remember what she'd said?

He began once more, avoiding pronouns that would identify the gender of the friend. He didn't have time to think about why he made this effort; it just felt necessary.

"What was said to me was this: 'Jack, you'd be perfect for the job. You have a moral code that you live by; you would do what's right, and what's good. You wouldn't be swayed by politics, or friendship.' I was flattered, of course, to be thought of so highly, and I must admit that pride was my first emotional response." He purposely kept his eyes trained above the heads of those nearest to him: Earl and Helen, Claire and her parents, Mark, Jeff, and Jenny. He didn't want to be distracted by the expressions on their faces. But his curiosity got the better of him, and he let himself look at Jenny. For a moment, just one brief instant, he felt they were the only ones in the room, and he knew she remembered.

"The comment stuck with me for days, but not as the compliment it was meant to be. Instead, I began to think about what it meant to be those things, to continue to aspire to be those things, for someone holding public office. I decided that voters would rather vote for someone they believe will be guided by principles of honesty and righteousness, than for someone who just happens to hold the same views on various issues as they do. I think that's what my friend was trying to tell me, because God knows we disagree on many issues." He paused to allow the laughs—this time unexpected—to dissipate. As he did, the speech began to grow even larger in his head. He remembered a Supreme Court case Earl had insisted he read when he'd first started the job—about a prosecutor's duty not only to the state but to the system as a whole—and decided that its message fit right in with what he was trying to say.

"Most people, when they think of those who hold positions of power in the legal system, think of judges. But I've learned something in the years I've worked in the DA's office. I've learned that in many ways, a prosecutor has more power than a judge. A prosecutor has what we call 'prosecutorial discretion.' He's a gatekeeper, in a sense; he decides which cases to pursue, and which cases to let go. The judge hears only those cases that the prosecutor has decided to bring before him. The District Attorney is not only a representative of the state, he is a representative of an entire system. He represents a sovereignty whose obligation is to govern impartially, and in a criminal case the sovereignty's interest is not that it will win a case, but that justice will be served. And he is a servant of the law. His goal is twofold: that guilt will not escape, but also that innocence will not suffer. The integrity of the system he represents depends on the integrity of the exercise of his discretion, on the integrity of the process he uses in determining how to exercise that discretion.

"The opportunity to run for this position began to represent much more to me than an incredible career opportunity—it was also, I realized, an incredible public-service opportunity and an incredible personal opportunity. I stand before you tonight and make a promise: I promise to exercise my discretion with the utmost integrity. I will take those words spoken by my friend and use them as my guide. No matter what decisions I make with respect to individual cases or larger issues, I will strive to follow a simple precept—to do what's right, and good, and not to be swayed by politics or friendship. And then, hopefully, I will have done a job that's worthy of the trust you have placed in me."

Someone began to clap, and then slowly, but with growing momentum, others followed suit. Jack waited patiently for the applause to die down, but the noise only increased, and he realized that they thought he was finished. The room lit up with camera flashes and the music began again. Suddenly Earl was on the platform with him, hugging him and patting his back. The rest of his campaign team followed, each with his own words of congratulations. He managed a final thank-you into the microphone before he was carried on the wave of the crowd down to the floor, where he was greeted with even more congratulations. An anonymous arm stretched through the wall of people surrounding him and handed him a glass of champagne; he swallowed it in two gulps.

Everyone hugged him and told him what a great speech it was. He grabbed Claire and kissed her, whispering a private thank-you in her ear. "I'm so proud of you, Jack," she whispered back, reaching for his hand and giving it an unseen squeeze. Their eyes met and for a moment he felt the same connection he'd felt that morning. But the demands of the crowd intervened, and when the next break in conversation came and he looked around, he noticed she was gone. She'd managed to slip discreetly into the crowd, he knew, to allow the moment to be his alone.

Everyone except Jack, it seemed, was drunk by the time they made it up to the suite. The room was large and spacious, unlike any hotel room he'd ever been in, even on Claire's last birthday. A wall of windows faced east toward the river and the Arch. In the foreground, the lights of office buildings and streetlamps appeared to dance in the black sky, and down below, the automobiles on the highway were glimmering ribbons of red and white. The entire city was visible, but no one except Jack was looking.

Two large sofas were arranged at a ninety-degree angle in front of the windows to provide a prime spot to view the city. Nearby, a long marble-topped dining table groaned with sandwiches, cheeses, fruits, cakes, caviar, and more champagne. French doors opened to the bedroom, where the windows continued, and even the massive Louis XIV four-poster bed seemed small.

"This is obscene," Jack said to Earl. "You've outdone yourself."

Uncharacteristically, Earl was a little buzzed, too. "It'll be back to the pauper's life soon enough. Enjoy it while you can." He grinned as he twisted the wire off the cork of a bottle of champagne. They both laughed when the loud pop caused a swell of cheers from the group. Someone turned on music.

A round of toasts followed and then the dancing. Jenny didn't even bother trying to get Jack to dance, as in the spring. She approached Mark, who had been hanging with her all night, and they joined some of the younger lawyers and staff from the DA's office. With Helen's blessing, Beverly pulled a reluctant Earl up from his spot on the sofa. He protested that he was too old for "this nonsense," but she persisted and prevailed. Jack decided to use the john before he got pulled into the fray.

He met pressure when he tried to shut the bathroom door.

"Hey." Claire laughed as she pushed on the door and poked her head in. He stepped back, and in an instant she was in and had closed the door behind her. "I don't believe I've had the chance to congratulate you properly." Her lids draped lazily over her blue eyes, and she leaned heavily on the door. It had been a long time since he'd seen her like this.

"So you resort to cornering me in the bathroom?" he teased.

"I think it's the only way I'm going to be alone with you tonight."

She reached out and pulled him close. He touched his lips lightly to hers, but she grasped his head and reciprocated with a strong, deep kiss. He fumbled to lock the door behind her, but then he remembered why he'd gone in there. He pulled away before the task became impossible.

He called to her as he stood in front of the toilet, "So what do you think? First headline after the election: new DA caught fornicating with wife in hotel bathroom while victory party continues in next room."

Her response came quickly: "Better your wife than some other partygoer."

He whipped his head around to look at her. She stood in front of the long sink, fishing through a little basket of miniature soaps and other toiletries. He relaxed when he saw the smile on her face. She'd been joking, not accusing.

"What do you think of this?" he asked. He hoisted himself onto the counter in front of her after washing his hands.

"Hmm?"

"The room."

"It's nice. You're lucky to have someone like Earl." She lifted the flap of a small packet to inspect the contents. After discovering a tightly folded shower cap, she replaced it in the basket.

"I am," he said, and covered her hand with his to stop her fidgeting. "I'm even luckier to have someone like you."

She stared at their hands a moment and then peered up at him. "Are you happy now, Jack?"

Her tone lacked sarcasm—she was sincere—but the question took him by surprise.

"Of course I am." He pulled her closer, between his legs. "Why do you ask that?"

"I don't know. You've just been so restless these past months. I worried that you didn't really want this, but had gotten yourself in too deep to turn back."

"Hey." He lifted her chin so she looked directly at him. "I really wanted this. The hard part's over. Now the fun begins." He tilted his head. "I'm very happy. I'm overwhelmingly ecstatic. Okay?"

She pecked his lips. "Okay."

"Good." He jumped down from the sink. "Come on, let's go celebrate."

By three thirty in the morning, the party had quieted only slightly. The size of the crowd had diminished, but those remaining gave no indication of slowing down. Claire and Jenny reclined together on one of the sofas, their heads at opposite ends. Each had a glass of champagne in her hand and from a half-seated position on the edge of the other sofa, Jack eyed them talking and giggling like schoolgirls while he attempted to carry on a conversation with the others.

He paid closer attention when his brother joined them. Mark squatted behind the sofa near Jenny's head, his arm crossed over the sofa back and his chin resting on his hands. Jenny swam in Mark's attention, throwing her head back when she laughed or coyly challenging something he said. Claire looked pleased that she'd apparently made a successful match.

Jack used the next interruption to join them.

"Well, I think I deserve the most credit for his victory," Jenny was bragging just as Jack sat on the edge of the sofa next to Claire.

"Excuse me?" Jack said.

"It's true," Jenny said. Claire's eyes widened. "If it hadn't been for me, he probably would have wimped out and not even run." She spoke of him in the third person, as if he weren't sitting there with them.

Claire and Mark laughed, but Jack asked tentatively, "Is that so?" Jenny drunk could mean trouble.

"Yes, that's so, Mr. Hilliard." She turned her head to Mark and smiled at him. "Not you. The other one," she said, then laughed at herself. She put her index finger to her lips and furrowed her forehead in thought. "Where was I? Oh, yeah. I decided you needed a little prodding, you know, something to make you shit or get off the pot."

Jack and Claire glanced at each other and waited. Jenny's dark eyes glinted and she leaned forward as if she was letting them all in on a big secret.

"It was me. I was the letter writer." She announced it as if she were a contestant on a game show, loudly, and proud of herself for having the right answer.

"What do you mean?" Claire asked. "What letter?"

But Jack knew immediately, as soon as the words left her lips. His throat tightened. She'd duped him and now expected him to be grateful. Or else she was too smashed to care one way or the other and just wanted to be sure she got credit for the end result. A look of recognition washed over Claire's face as her memory came back to her. Her mouth turned up on one side in the start of a smile.

"*That* letter?" Claire said, her eyes big with disbelief.

Jenny nodded. "Yep, that one." She looked at Jack to gauge his reaction.

Claire covered her mouth with her hand and started giggling, and Jack felt that he'd been betrayed twice—first by Jenny and then by his wife. How could she think this was funny? To his mind, Jenny had slapped not only him but Claire, too, because they'd done this together as a family, hadn't they? But Claire seemed not to mind. She started asking Jenny questions: *How did you know about that case? How did you get the details so perfect?* And complimenting her on the content of the letter: *It was so convincing! Your handwriting and grammar were just right*. And then they were joking about Jack, about how easy he was, and how, yes, he'd needed something like that letter to force him to make up his mind. He sat there, numb, listening straight-faced to their banter without revealing the anger boiling inside him. His mind reeled back to the day he received the letter and made the decision to run. He remembered how mad Claire had been, but she'd instantly forgiven him when she read it. She'd believed it, too; she'd been tricked, too. Didn't that bother her in the least?

He felt Claire's hand on his arm. He looked down at it, but it was as if his arm belonged to someone else.

"Where's your drink?" she asked, her tone light and breezy. She was oblivious, or maybe just indifferent, to his fallen mood. "This calls for a toast to Jenny."

He turned to the table beside him. He didn't know what had happened to his glass and he didn't care. He feigned a brief search. "I'll be back," he mumbled and left them to their revelry.

But he didn't go back. He joined another, more sober group seated around the dining table, picking at food and talking quietly. He looked back at the sofa once. He saw the back of Claire's head where it rose behind the arm of the couch, but Jenny's face as she continued her show was in full view. He watched her from across the room until she noticed him, and they locked eyes. The smile on her face faded slightly. Maybe he only imagined it, but he thought he saw a trace of remorse in her eyes.

Jack woke to the six a.m. toll of distant church bells. It took him a minute to get his bearings, but then he remembered that he'd collapsed on the bed fully dressed around five. He heard voices at the door, talking about where to meet for breakfast. He recognized his brother's voice, and Jenny's, and he thought maybe Maria's and Andy's. He heard Earl saying that he and Helen wouldn't be joining them. Someone closed the door, and their voices became more distant as they made their way down the hall toward the elevator. He shut his eyes when Claire entered the bedroom.

She approached his side of the bed and bent down close to his ear. "You awake?"

"Yeah," he muttered without opening his eyes. "Sort of."

He listened as she fumbled around with something on the nightstand, and then he heard the groan of the motor as she used a remote to close first the sheers and then the room-darkening drapes that lined the large windows.

"There," she said. "We can pretend it's nighttime as long as we want." She disappeared into the bathroom, closing the door behind her.

Jack rose and went to the window. He searched for the seam between the drape panels and peeked out. The cloudless sky graduated from dark pink on the eastern horizon to deep blue above; the sun had not yet made an appearance and stars were still visible. Steam rose from tall stacks on the far side of the river. It billowed incessantly, like a genie being let out of his bottle.

He thought about Claire's question last night in the bathroom. He *was* happy, now that the election was over. He had the job he wanted, even though it wouldn't seem real until he actually stepped foot in the office. Earl had already told him he wouldn't stick around and would immediately name Jack as Acting DA until the new term started in January. It had been the compromises of the campaign, not the new job, which had caused the distress sensed by Claire.

Why was he bothered so much by what Jenny had done? She'd embarrassed him, that was true, but he thought it must be something more. It seemed to him that the whole thing—the campaign, the election, even the party afterward—was somehow based on a false premise. Would he have made the same decision but for the letter? Would he have been able to answer the countless questions about the death penalty so skillfully, so believably, *so easily,* if that letter hadn't always been at the back of his mind?

He stepped out of his pants and headed back to bed. He heard the faucet running and Claire brushing her teeth. He decided not to bring it up; he wondered if she would.

As he was about to lie down, he heard a thump in the hall and giggling. He opened the door and heard a short gasp. Down the hall, next to the door that opened into the living area of the suite, stood Mark and Jenny. Jenny's back was to the wall, and Mark faced her, one arm stretched above her shoulder with his palm propped against the wall. His other hand held one of hers. Jack sighed and crossed his arms as if he'd just caught one of his kids misbehaving. He raised his eyebrows and waited for an explanation.

"Nice boxers, Jack," said Mark, and Jenny suppressed another giggle. Jack didn't move.

"We're sorry if we woke you." Jenny tried to modulate her voice.

"Why don't you just get a room?" Jack said, his own voice edged in sarcasm.

A shadow crossed her face and she glared at him. She opened her mouth but Mark squeezed her hand to stop her. "We're going out to breakfast," he said. "We're just talking a bit before we meet up with the others."

"Good. Talk away. Have fun." He slammed the door. He grabbed the remote on the way to the bed and, once he'd climbed under the covers, opened the drapes. When Claire came out of the bathroom, she looked at the window in surprise.

"I wanted to watch the sun come up," he explained.

She burrowed in close to him. She smelled good, though different, more spicy. She must have tried one of the soaps in the bathroom.

"Relax, will you?" She slipped her hand under his shirt. "Your body is so tense."

She tilted her head up to him, and they looked at each other from a much further distance than the little physical space between them. Had what Jenny done really had no effect on Claire whatsoever?

"What is it?" she asked.

He didn't speak; he just shook his head.

"We're not going to let this bed go to waste, are we?" She began to unbutton his shirt. "You can't sleep in this."

"I already did."

She finished the task and then helped him wriggle out of his undershirt, too.

"Claire . . ."

"Relax, I said. Just lie there and enjoy yourself." If she knew what bothered him, she didn't plan to talk about it.

He closed his eyes as her hands traveled his body. But he couldn't forget Mark and Jenny in the hall, Mark pressing up against Jenny like he owned her, and Jenny letting him.

He opened his eyes and looked at Claire's face above him. She straddled his waist, her eyes closed and her hands caressing him. He pulled her down close and rolled over quickly so that he was on top. She opened her eyes, surprised by the apparent sudden change in his mood. He kissed her before she had a chance to speak.

His mind was back in the parking garage with Jenny, but this time he didn't fight it. He'd been fighting it for seven months now. He had been winning, sort of, but it had been exhausting and now he felt entitled to just give in. If he let himself think the forbidden, then maybe it would go away. His thoughts hurtled between the real kiss in the garage and an imagined one in the hotel corridor. His cheek brushed Claire's and he heard her utter his name from deep in her throat, but he suppressed his voice for fear of what he might say. He closed his eyes tightly, and the taut muscles responding to his touch became Jenny's. He thought of them together on her large bed, her hands pressed firmly into his backside. He heard a faint voice in his head—his own—telling him to come back, but another louder, more insistent voice—also his—prevailed.

As their bodies rocked together in a fast, rhythmic motion, he grabbed Claire's arms and held them above her head, gripping them by the wrists with one hand while the other pressed into the hot skin of the small of her back. She wriggled a bit underneath him and he tightened his grasp. He knew she didn't like to be held like this, but he felt strangely indifferent to what she wanted just then. She didn't protest aloud but she squirmed some more and tried to free her hands, her body and her mind disagreeing even as she continued to move with him. She grunted loudly and said, "Let me go!" He loosened his grip just as she jerked her arms down. For one brief instant she pushed against his shoulders, then relented and gave in to the needs of her body.

He continued as if nothing had happened. He was all but gone.

Later, there was a rap on the door to the suite. Jack lay prone, one side of his face smashed into the pillow. He opened one eye to look at the clock on the nightstand. Eleven a.m. Through the open French doors he saw Claire sitting on the sofa, looking out the window, her bare legs bent and pulled up close to her body. She had on a long green silk camisole, and her hair cascaded over her arms. She didn't move to answer the door, so he decided the noise had been a dream.

The knock was repeated and then a voice called, "Room service!"

She turned her head toward the door and sighed so loudly he could hear her from the bed. To his surprise, she answered the door without first putting on the hotel-supplied robe.

"I'm sorry, but we didn't order room service," she said quietly.

"Mr. Scanlon ordered it last night for you, ma'am."

"Oh," she said, sounding surprised but pleased. Jack heard the valet roll the cart in.

He climbed out of bed and pulled on his shorts. By the time Claire shut the door, he was standing in the doorway from the bedroom, watching her.

"Morning," he said.

She lifted the covers to peek at the food without answering.

"Anything good?"

"Earl knows you well, doesn't he? Eggs and bacon. And they're over easy."

It seemed like a normal conversation, but he knew from her flat tone that it wasn't.

"When did you get up?" he asked, moving toward her.

She shrugged. He waited but she didn't elaborate. He wrapped his arms around her from behind. "Don't I get a hug?"

She nudged his arms off and walked away. "I think you got whatever it was you wanted a few hours ago."

Stung, he watched numbly as she pulled up a chair to the edge of the small cart.

"You'd better eat before it gets cold," she said without emotion.

He didn't move. He stared as she spread a napkin on her lap, removed the silver lid from the plate in front of her, poured maple syrup on the strawberry pancakes Earl had ordered for her, and picked up her fork and began to eat. He tried to gather his thoughts, determine his next move, but he couldn't get past deciding whether to sit down with her or retreat into the shower. She made the decision for him.

"Jack?"

He grabbed a chair from the dining table and sat across from her. He didn't think he'd be able to eat, but once he'd taken a bite of the eggs, he realized he had that ravenous, grease-craving hunger that always follows a night of drinking. They ate in silence without looking at each other. Despite her head start, he finished first. He fiddled with things on the table while he sipped his coffee and waited for her to finish. He noticed a folded note card: "Take your time, the room is yours as long as you want it." It wasn't Earl's handwriting, but Jack knew the message was his. He lifted the card and held it in front of Claire's face so she could read it. She eyed it as she chewed, but didn't react. He contained a sigh and suspected he was going to need at least until midafternoon to warm her back up.

He picked up a miniature ketchup bottle and read the label. "Do you know anybody who actually puts ketchup on his eggs?" he asked.

She gave him a disgusted look.

"What?" He felt himself sinking further and couldn't seem to grab hold of anything to pull himself back up.

She shook her head. "Is that all you can think to say to me?"

Her eyes were becoming glassy and her bottom lip quivered. He didn't want to end their stay in the room like this. He wanted to say something, but he didn't know what. How had they gotten to this point? This was supposed to be a good day.

When he didn't answer her question, she calmly placed her napkin on the table and stood up. "I'll be ready to go home in a half hour," she said.

He stared at the yellow yolk drying on his plate, barely registering the loud slam of the bathroom door. What was he supposed to say? *I'm sorry, I was thinking about another woman when I was making love with you?* Right. Anyway, she'd probably done the same thing at some point in their marriage, hadn't she? No one was perfect. He knew, though, that there'd never been a time when he felt she wasn't right there with him. With his elbows on the table, he cradled his head in his palms and closed his eyes. He wished that the day were already over.

He finally went into the bedroom. He held his ear to the bathroom door but didn't hear anything. He knocked on it softly. "Claire, can I come in?"

There was silence for a moment, and then: "Sure, you're king of the world. I guess you can do anything you want."

He glanced at the ceiling. This wasn't going to be easy. He turned the knob and opened the door; at least she hadn't locked it. She was sitting in the empty tub, looking out the window. She'd taken a blanket from the bed and had it wrapped around her.

"I think you forgot the water." He tried to say it softly, teasingly.

"Fuck you, Jack," she said.

In the thirteen years they'd been married, she'd said that to him on only two occasions, both having to do with his run for DA: the first when he announced his candidacy, and now, after he'd won. He'd deserved it each time.

He approached the tub cautiously and squatted next to it. He almost reached over and touched her, but decided to wait. "I'm sorry."

She didn't respond, didn't even acknowledge that she'd heard him. He knew why: she wanted to hear *what* he was apologizing for. Just to make sure, say, he wasn't apologizing for his dumb comment about the ketchup.

"I'm sorry about last night." Finally, a look in his direction. But she still wanted more. "I guess I just got carried away."

Her eyes narrowed. "Carried away?"

He looked at her manicured feet sticking out from under the blanket. He couldn't look her in the eye. "Well, I—"

"I felt like I was being raped, Jack." He looked right at her then. He opened his mouth to protest but she stopped him. "I'm not saying that's what it was. I'm just saying that's what it felt like." Her eyes filled and he couldn't look away. "I don't know who was in bed with me, but it wasn't Jack Hilliard." Tears began to run slowly, silently, down her cheeks. They glistened in the warm sunlight beating through the bay window.

"Claire, you've gotta believe—"

"You're different. Ever since your decision to run for DA, you've been different. I don't know you anymore."

"I'm not. It's just—"

"You are. And . . . and I'm afraid now that you've won, it'll just get worse."

"It won't. I promise."

"But will it get better?"

"Yes."

"I tried to tell myself you were under a lot of pressure. I tried to make it easier for you." It seemed that she was talking to herself now. "And last night, I realized you were upset about what Jenny had done." His pulse quickened at the mention of Jenny's name. "It took me a bit, but I did realize it, once I sobered up some. And I was trying to make you feel better. I felt bad for you. I know you felt like you'd been tricked." He reached up and with his thumb wiped tears from the side of her face. She gripped his hand. "But it felt like you were taking all your anger out on me. That's what it felt like. You were so angry. *It* was so angry."

"I'm sorry," he whispered.

"The Jack I know isn't an angry person. You've never been an angry person."

"I'm sorry," he repeated. He meant it, but he couldn't give her a better explanation. He had been angry, but of course it had been about more than the letter. He couldn't tell her anything to make her understand how angry he was at himself for not having control of his emotions.

"What is it about her, Jack?"

Her question took him by surprise. She'd suddenly turned a corner, taken a new, more direct route to a destination he'd been trying to avoid. He couldn't find words fast enough.

"There's something different about both of you. Something different *between* you." She held his eyes; there would be no circling around the issue. "And I'm not the only one who thinks so, either."

He swallowed, and it felt like a walnut going down his throat. "What do you mean?"

"Just what I said. People have said things to me."

He shook his head, denying any understanding, denying the accusation. "What are you talking about? Who? Who has said things?"

"Well, the most recent was Maria."

Jack let out a soft grunt, and Claire continued as if he were no longer part of the conversation.

"I think her exact words were: 'You are such an awesome wife not to be bothered by how close Jenny and Jack are.' Yes, I'm sure she used the word *awesome*."

Jack relaxed a bit; if that was her evidence, she didn't even have a case. "Well, she's right," he said gently. "You are awesome. A lot of women would be bothered by our friendship, I guess." She didn't appear flattered; more like skeptical. "That's it?" Jack asked.

She shook her head. "Frank."

"Frank?"

"Yeah."

"What did Frank say?"

"He claims that you told him we had a threesome going on."

His jaw dropped and he pulled his hand from her grip, averted his eyes. "Unbelievable. Frickin' unbelievable."

"Well?"

"Well *what*?" The question came out loudly and much angrier than he'd intended.

"Did you tell him that?"

He grunted again, shaking his head in denial, but unable to say no truthfully. "How in the hell did it come about that Frank said something like that to you?"

"He was drunk," she said flatly. "It was at one of those fund-raisers this summer. He had a few too many drinks in him, and you know how obnoxious he is anyway. You were talking to her, and I guess he thought I was feeling neglected or something. I don't know. He—"

"Were you?" He forced himself to look at her again.

"No." She stared back for an instant before she continued. "He started rambling about how he thought Jenny had the hots for you and that when he suggested that to you, you told him we . . . well, you know."

"He's such a fuckin' asshole," he said, looking away once more.

"Did you tell him that?" she persisted.

"Yes, but it wasn't like that."

"Like what?"

"It wasn't some sort of veiled acknowledgment about me and Jenny, for Christ's sake. He was being obnoxious, so I was just being obnoxious back at him."

She nodded; she was willing to accept that.

They both fell silent, as if neither knew where the discussion had led them or where they should go next. Jack heard maids in the hall, cars honking on the street outside the window.

"Claire?" She turned to him. She'd stopped crying for now, but wiped at the expectant tears still poised for release. "Does it bother you? My friendship with her?"

She shrugged sadly. "It didn't used to. I trusted you. I even trusted her." She paused. "But then people started saying things like that to me, and I began to wonder if maybe I'm just naïve. Or too trusting." She shrugged again. "And it's just that, what she did with the letter . . . that she could make you react so . . ." Her voice trailed off and she looked right at him. The late-morning sunlight made her blue eyes appear transparent, and he imagined she could see straight into his soul with those eyes. "I don't know. *Should* it bother me?"

In that instant he recognized that Jenny had become an obsession. He knew it now, as he knew the color of his eyes or the date he was born. He hadn't wanted to admit it because that was exactly what had happened with Claire, that day he saw her for the first time in the Pit. He hadn't wanted to believe he could feel that way again, that there was anyone other than his wife who could inspire such emotions in him.

Will it get better? He needed to believe it would; he needed Claire to believe it would, that *he* would. If Jenny was an obsession, he could control it. It was a choice to make, and he determined right then to make the right one. He reached for Claire's hand.

"No. It shouldn't bother you." He touched her hair. "Okay? Nothing about me and Jenny should bother you."

CHAPTER FOURTEEN

He went back to the scene of the crime. That's what inexperienced criminals did, wasn't it? It took him just over a week to get up the nerve, but he went back. He was relieved to see her car in its usual spot, despite the late hour.

He sat on the hood and waited for her. What a difference a few months made. The air, which had been heavy and wet the last time, now filtered coolly and easily through his nostrils. The garage seemed darker. When he lay back against the windshield, he noticed that the light fixture on the ceiling was broken. Something had shattered the dingy plastic globe that covered the bulb—a gunshot, or perhaps a rock. All that remained were the sharp, jagged edges of half the globe and the dangling filaments of the bulb. He pulled his coat tighter.

He tried to think of what he would say when she arrived. How to tell her that he had to stay away from her? How to explain that, despite their promise to each other, he couldn't forget what had happened in this garage and that her presence in his life was messing with his mind? Should he just come right out and admit that he couldn't stop thinking about her, and the only way he knew to solve the problem was to banish her completely? Or would that make it worse? Maybe the thing to do was lead her in the other direction, blame the situation on everyone else. He wondered whether to tell her about his conversation with Claire, to explain that others were starting to talk and that he'd decided the only way to protect Claire, to preserve his marriage—which, he needed to make her understand, meant more than anything to him—was to end his friendship with her. But how could he say this without hurting Jenny or, worse, making a fool of himself if he'd called it all wrong? After all, perhaps what he thought of as an unspoken but undoubted attraction between them was really one-sided on his part. Maybe he'd turned a simple kiss into something much more. What if she didn't even know what the hell he was talking about?

He turned when he heard the elevator. Jenny stepped off, walking tall and moderately fast. She wore a long black coat over her black pantsuit. Over her shoulder she carried a black bag large enough to hold files. Her black hair was gathered behind her head. Except for her face and hands, all he could see was black.

When she saw him, still some distance away, she hesitated. She turned to see the two others from the elevator get into a car together. She approached cautiously, shoulders erect. As she came closer, her body relaxed. "Jack?" she called softly.

He didn't respond. The other car passed him on the way to the ramp; oddly, the possibility that he might have been recognized didn't worry him as it had the last time.

When she reached the car, she stayed a few feet away, next to the driver's side door.

"What are you doing here? What happened? Is something wrong?"

He shook his head. *Nothing's wrong, everything's wrong.* What should he say?

"What is it?" she asked, her voice more urgent. "You're scaring me."

"Where have you been?" The words came out more accusatory than he'd intended.

She looked behind her again, as if watching for something. "I . . ." She hesitated. "I had a late meeting."

He jumped down from the hood and extended his hands to her. "We need to talk."

She set her bag down on the ground and stepped closer. When their hands touched, he realized he'd misstepped. If he was going to rid himself of an obsession, he shouldn't have touched it. He shouldn't have even gotten near it. The words—the absolutely wrong words—tumbled out.

"I need to dance with you again."

It wasn't at all what he'd intended to say, but once he'd said the words, he knew they were true. He felt goose bumps travel like an unstoppable tidal wave up his legs and down his arms and he could think of nothing except being with her. Not just being in her presence, but being with her as one, feeling her body lean against him as it had when they'd danced in this same spot last April. He wanted to make everything else disappear and sway to the music again with her, go round and round until they fell down laughing from dance-induced vertigo. He wanted to lie down on that gigantic bed of hers, sink with her into the layers of blankets and pillows and comforters she had piled on top, and hold her head as they made love so she couldn't look away. He wanted to drown in the vortex of her eyes.

They stared at each other and he could see her breath in the air. She didn't answer him, and he started to panic. He realized, with horror, that he'd just propositioned her.

"Jenny, please." He just wanted her to say something, anything.

She looked down with eyelids slow and heavy. "Get in. We'll talk when we get there."

They drove in silence for the ten minutes it took to get to Lafayette Square. He glimpsed her profile out of the corner of his eye, but she just stared at the road and gripped the steering wheel. He asked himself what he was doing, but he couldn't come up with a sensible answer.

"Be careful, the cats might try to get out," she said at the front door, as if he were merely a girlfriend she'd invited for dinner. But the cats were nowhere to be seen, and after they went in and she'd locked the door behind them, she turned on a light and walked around closing the blinds. She hung their coats in a small closet near the front door.

"Did you have dinner?" she asked. On the way to the kitchen, she kicked off her shoes and threw her suit jacket over the stair railing.

"No; I'm not hungry."

"You will be." She opened a drawer and fished around for a take-out menu. "Thai okay?"

He nodded. He watched as she placed the call without asking him what he wanted. When she hung up, she took a bottle of wine from a small rack on the counter and searched a different drawer for a corkscrew. She poured two glasses and handed one to Jack.

"Have you thought this through?" she asked.

"Some things you shouldn't think through." Even as he said it, he knew he was wrong.

"This isn't one of them, Jack." When he didn't respond, she said, "Where are you supposed to be right now?"

"On my way to Jeff City for a seminar tomorrow."

She took a long sip of her wine. He heard the clock ticking on her kitchen wall.

"You're very selfish." Her voice was matter-of-fact. What did she mean? Was she talking about Claire? He didn't want to think about that right now. "You only think about what you want, and you plow on ahead, oblivious to how your actions might affect others. You think if you just turn on that charm, then it's all okay."

"Jenny, I'm willing to accept the consequences, if I have to. But it doesn't have to affect anyone else. No one ever has to know." With these words he realized that somehow he'd already moved beyond worrying about the ramifications.

Her eyes narrowed. She set her wine down hard; a few drops splashed onto the counter. "Goddammit, I'm not talking about Claire. What about me? How do you know I'm willing to accept the consequences? Did you ever think about me?"

"Jenny, you're all I've been thinking—"

"Stop it. Just stop it. Don't you understand what I'm trying to say? Tomorrow you'll go back to your perfect little life, but what about me? I'm not interested in being someone's mistress." She paused, blinking to hold back tears. "Especially not yours."

When he made no response, she said, "What do you think? Because I'm single, it's not a big deal for me? Just another fuck?"

"No. I know it's not like that."

She put her hands on her hips. "What's it like, then? Tell me."

But he couldn't tell her. Because she was right—he hadn't given it much thought from her point of view. *All you have to do is say the word, and it's yours.* Maybe he'd misunderstood. Maybe he'd read much more into that statement than she'd ever intended.

What should he do now? He would get on his knees and beg to stay, if he had to. He couldn't imagine leaving. Nothing would ever be the same, but in a different way than if he left the following morning. If he didn't find the words to explain himself right then, he'd never have the chance, much less the nerve, to explain tonight's actions later.

"It's like . . ." he began, not knowing what to say, just fumbling his way through.

She put her hand up. "No. Please, don't say anything." She gently rubbed the outer corners of her eyes. She picked up her wine again and took a long drink. What was he supposed to do? He wondered if he should call a cab. He waited for her to tell him to leave.

"I don't know," she said finally. "It just seems so calculated."

He wanted to laugh, but didn't. Nothing had seemed calculated to him, at least until he'd gotten into her car at the garage. How could he explain to her why he'd ended up there, waiting for her on the hood? How could he explain that he hadn't intended this to happen? But he sensed an opening, so he stepped closer to her.

"Jenny, I didn't plan this. I swear. I've thought about it for a long time, but I didn't plan it. I went to the garage tonight to tell you that we need to stay away from each other. I didn't go to end up here. You have to believe that. Something just happened, I don't know what. I know it sounds ridiculous, but it just seemed so right. It felt so right that night last spring in the garage, too. I've been going crazy for months, thinking about it. I know it's ridiculous, I know it's wrong. I just can't explain it, really, not in a way you'll understand."

"That's the problem, Jack," she whispered. "I do understand." She wouldn't look at him. He moved even closer, and she let him. He rested his lips on her forehead and closed his eyes. She looked up at him, and he kissed her, just once. Her mouth was sweet from the wine.

"Do you want to go upstairs?" she asked.

Her resignation stung. How could he make her understand it wasn't just sex? He wanted to spend the night with her, talking like they always did. He wanted to feel her warm body against his as they drifted to sleep and then wake together at sunrise and talk some more over morning coffee.

"No. Let's drink our wine and eat."

She glanced at the clock on the wall. She finally nodded and poured him some more, and then she topped off her own. She played with a button on his shirt, studied a scratch on the counter—anything not to look at him. He rubbed a tear from the corner of her eye and licked his finger to taste it.

"It's almost gone," he said, nodding to the bottle on the counter.

"Yeah."

"We could open another."

She pursed her lips. "I think we'd better wait until the food comes."

He felt as though they were two virgins who were just figuring it out as they went along.

"There it is now," she said when the doorbell interrupted their awkwardness. He followed her to the door, where she peeked through the peephole. "Uh-oh. You'd better go back in the kitchen."

"Why?"

"It's Alex."

"What's he doing here?"

"I don't know. I didn't invite him."

"Does he stop by often?" Jack asked, feeling the old jealousy return. The bell rang again.

"Jack, will you get in the kitchen? Or better yet, upstairs. We can talk about this later. I need to answer the door."

"Why? Just pretend you're not home."

"My car's outside. He's not stupid."

"Someone could have picked you up."

"All the lights are on." She shook her head. "Why am I arguing with you? Get upstairs."

He climbed to the first landing, where the stairwell turned, and continued up. He sat on the top step of the second landing, out of view but within earshot. He heard her slip the chain off its lock and turn the dead-bolt.

"Hi, Alex." Impatience oozed from her voice.

Jack recognized her former boyfriend's voice, but all he could make out was something about coming in.

"What do you want? I'm a little busy."

"Someone here?" His voice was louder now; Jack could tell that he'd stepped into the living room.

"No, but I don't think that's any concern of yours."

"Then why are you so busy?"

Jack heard Alex's footsteps on the hardwood floor, his voice moving through the house.

"I'm trying to edit an appellate brief that's due next week. You mind?"

"Maybe I could help you."

Jack strained to hear her response. After a long silence, she said, "Alex, what do you want?"

"Just wanted to see you again. I was surprised to see your lights on. I thought you'd be back at work."

"It's nine thirty. I'm not usually at work this late."

Why doesn't she just tell him to get the hell out of here?

"Did you talk to Maxine?"

"Maxine is Maxine. I deal with her, okay?"

"Just wondering. We've gotta get it resolved."

Jack felt his muscles tense. *We've?* He heard them as they passed the bottom of the stairs.

"Did you eat yet? We could have dinner together."

"No, we couldn't. I want you to leave now."

There you go, Jen. Their voices were fainter; it sounded like they'd moved into the kitchen.

"I thought you said no one was here." Alex's tone was verging on angry.

"They're from earlier."

There was silence for a moment, and then Jack heard the clink of glass against the counter.

"The glasses are still wet."

"Alex, you're getting on my nerves. Who are you, Sherlock Holmes? I want you to leave now. Don't tempt me to call the police."

For some reason, he laughed at her threat.

Jack wondered if Jenny had given him one of her "if looks could kill" looks, because then Alex said, "Okay, okay," and Jack relaxed a bit. But he added, "Can I use your bathroom first?"

Shit. The lone bathroom was upstairs. Jack stood quietly and looked around for a place to hide. He hoped the wooden floor underneath him didn't creak when he walked.

"You're five minutes from your house. You can't hold it?"

Jack could go into her bedroom, but if Alex thought she had someone there, he'd no doubt take a look.

"Come on, Jenny. I'll leave. Just let me use your john."

Jack slipped into a small closet that held her water heater.

"Fine." God, she must have trusted Jack to find a quick hiding place. Or maybe she thought he deserved to sweat. "Two minutes, Alex, and then I'm calling the police. I'm not kidding."

Jack listened as Alex climbed the stairs and went into the bathroom. After a minute he heard the toilet flush and then the faucet run. But he hadn't heard that distinctive, telltale sound of urine hitting the water in the bowl. The bathroom door opened, but he didn't hear Alex go down the stairs. Where was he? Jack held his breath and listened more closely, but he couldn't hear anything. He started to get nervous. What if Alex opened the closet door?

Jenny called up, "Alex, you have five seconds."

"Relax. I'm coming right now."

Where had Alex gone? Her bedroom? Once he was sure that Alex was downstairs, Jack tiptoed back to his spot on the steps. The doorbell rang again. *There* was the food.

"Busy night, huh, Jenny?"

"It's my dinner. So why don't you just show yourself out while I get it?" Her voice was sarcastic, angry.

She opened the front door; Jack heard her pay the deliveryman.

"What are you doing?" she said suddenly. Even from upstairs, Jack heard the quiver in her voice. He stood, ready to go down.

"I didn't know you'd started to wear men's trench coats. Looks like something your favorite prosecutor might wear."

"Get the hell out of here." The closet door shut hard. "And stay the hell away from me. The next time you knock on my door, I'm going to get a restraining order against you. I'm sure my favorite prosecutor can arrange that."

"Jenny." His voice was apologetic, as if he'd realized too late that he'd taken the wrong tack.

"Get out. Now." Alex was still protesting as he stepped outside. She slammed the door and after a moment called up, "The coast is clear."

Her face had paled. For the first time that night, she fell eagerly into his arms. He held her firmly, and it reminded him of how he sometimes held Jamie to calm him down. His stomach tightened; he felt his guilt trying to break through.

"I'm glad you were here," she whispered. "He was starting to give me the creeps."

"What's with him? Has he been bothering you a lot?"

"He's an asshole" was all she said.

"Does he stop by often?" He'd asked the same question earlier, but his motivation for wanting to know had changed. "What did he mean, he wanted to see you *again*? Have you seen him recently?"

"He's just an asshole," she said again. Whatever was going on, she didn't want to tell him.

He decided to try a different approach: "How would he recognize my coat?"

"He doesn't really know it's yours. For all he knows, it belongs to any guy. He's always been insanely jealous of you, of our friendship. He was just trying to get to me."

Now he was getting somewhere. As he stood there thinking of the next best question, inhaling the jasmine scent of her hair, she said, "It always drove him crazy how much time I spent with you."

She lifted her head to look at him. After a moment, she rested it back against his shoulder.

"But since we broke up, I don't know, he's been out of control."

"In what way?"

"I don't know. Do we have to talk about him? It's ruining my appetite."

"Yes."

"It's not what you're thinking. It's nothing physical or anything. He's just a pest, constantly calling me and stopping by unannounced. I made the mistake of—" She stopped abruptly.

"What?"

She sighed and shrugged apologetically. "I met with him, earlier. The meeting I mentioned."

Jack stared at her. He had no right to have an opinion, but they both knew he had one.

"It was a mistake. He just doesn't seem able to let go."

"Why haven't you ever mentioned this to me before?"

"You're not my dad, Jack."

No, he wasn't. For a moment, he wondered if she was wishing she had a dad to call. But what was he, exactly, to her? He wasn't her husband, he wasn't her brother, he wasn't even her lover. He was just a guy she was going to sleep with, and he wasn't even sure she wanted to.

"No, but I'm your favorite prosecutor."

She looked up again and grinned. The color had come back to her face. He bent his head and kissed her. Not like in the kitchen, but in the garage. This time she was decisive. She gripped his shoulders and pulled him closer.

Her urgency fed his. He tugged her blouse from the waist of her slacks and reached under to touch her skin. Just feeling the ridge of her lower spine roused him to kiss her harder, and she let out a murmur from deep in her throat. With his other hand he unclipped the large barrette holding her hair. But when she reached for his belt, he pulled back.

"Not yet. Let's eat, have some more wine."

She groaned. "You're killing me, Jack." She grabbed the bag of food from the table by the door. "Okay, why don't you get our glasses and another bottle of wine and meet me upstairs. I'll get this stuff ready."

"Okay." But again, they just stood there. She started laughing.

"Come on, Mr. Hilliard," she said, and he followed her like a puppy.

Upstairs, he left the light off. He set the wineglasses on the nightstand next to her bed and opened the new bottle. He reached behind the sheers and opened each window just a crack. The air was crisp; he breathed in deeply.

"It's dark in here." Her voice filled the room.

She turned on the stereo, and light from the receiver softly illuminated the room. As she chose a CD, he came up behind her and wrapped his arms around her waist. It felt so natural, so easy, touching her this way, as though he'd done it a thousand times.

When she turned to face him, he didn't hesitate. He felt like a child opening the first present on Christmas morning.

"The food's getting cold," she said, grinning, and watched him trying to unbutton the small pearl buttons of her blouse.

"Yeah." He knelt down to unfasten her slacks. On the way back up he brushed his lips against her exposed stomach. "I told you I wasn't hungry."

He led her to the bed, and when they lay down together, he just looked at her. Her black hair was spread out like a geisha's fan. The skin of her breasts was almost as brown as the rest of her, but he saw faded tan lines from a bathing suit. Her nipples were small, dark. His gaze traveling down to her stomach, he thought back to the bar and how he'd glimpsed that stomach when she danced.

"Jack, don't hurt me," she said. The words startled him. "After tonight, I mean. If you for one minute avoid me, or treat me differently, I won't be able to take it."

"I wouldn't do that."

"I know. I'm just telling you, I don't think I could take it."

He looked into her dark eyes and saw immense sadness. "I think if we were playing strip poker, I'd be losing," she said, and he knew that was her signal to move on.

He refilled the wineglasses and handed one to her before shedding his clothes. He took a brief sip, but she emptied hers quickly.

"You're not getting drunk, are you?" he asked.

"Maybe just a little."

"Don't. I don't want you to use the wine as an excuse to apologize tomorrow for what happens tonight."

She nodded in silent agreement.

He dipped a finger into his wine and brought it to her lips. Starting at her mouth, he traced a line down the middle of her body. He traced over her chin and then her throat as she tilted her head back. He traced down the small hollow where her collarbone met the base of her neck. He traced down the center of her chest, but before reaching the valley between her breasts he took a small detour to inspect a mole at the spot where her right breast began its rise. He resumed his journey then and continued down between her breasts, watching her nipples grow hard. His finger moved between her ribs and down onto her flat stomach. He let it fall briefly into her navel and continued until he reached the top of her underwear. He lingered there for a moment, drawing invisible circles on her skin. She raised her hips slightly and he knew where she expected him to go next, but to tease her he dipped his finger again and started the process all over.

"You know, I was thinking of something today," he whispered. Her eyes turned to him but her body remained still. "You never did tell me where you went to high school."

A small smile formed on her lips. "It might be a disappointment to you."

"I don't think you could do anything right now that would disappoint me."

They stared at each other, paying respect to the gravity of what they were doing.

"Tell me," he said.

"I was home schooled." The smile widened; she was pleased with herself for having fooled him for so long.

He stopped at the mole again, leaning closer to inspect it.

"What are you doing?" she asked.

"Just looking. Memorizing." When she laughed, he asked, "What's so funny, Jen?"

"You. You're funny." He knew this time she didn't mean ha-ha funny.

He brought his hand to her face and turned it slightly toward him. "You always say that to me. You said that to me the night we met, do you remember?"

"Yeah, the infamous night. The second worst night of my life."

The comment stung. He frowned and pulled his hand away. "Why do you say that?"

She shook her head. "Never mind. I didn't mean it like it sounded." Her tone of voice told him she wasn't going to say more.

"I want to know."

"No. Never mind."

He waited. "What was the first, then?" he asked instead.

She sat up, her back to him, and poured herself another glass of wine. Her smooth skin glowed brown in the light of the stereo.

He touched her back lightly. "Jenny."

"Jack, did you come here to talk or to fuck?"

He gasped. She suddenly reminded him of the teenage girls he sometimes interviewed, the ones who tried to act as if nothing mattered. "If I have to choose, I'll choose talk."

Jenny whipped around and narrowed her eyes at him. "Okay, fine. When I was nine, my parents and my sister were murdered while my brother and I hid in a closet and watched the whole thing." She said it evenly, without emotion, without pause, without taking a breath. When she'd finished the sentence, she turned away from him.

He stared at her back in shock. His mind first raced to the picture on her dresser. Her sister. He didn't know what to say or what to do. Or what she'd want him to say or do. The facts themselves were not that shocking to him; he'd worked on enough cases that not much really shocked him anymore. But this was different. This was Jenny. Why hadn't she told him before?

"Jenny, I—"

"You wanted to know. I told you. You don't have to do the whole 'I'm sorry' routine."

He grabbed his shirt from the end of the bed and draped it around her shoulders. He took the glass from her and set it on the nightstand and then held her hands. "But I am sorry. I'm sorry for you, but at the risk of sounding selfish"—he paused, knowing that she would remember calling him that—"I'm also sorry that you never felt close enough to me to tell me."

She shook her head contemptuously. "Sometimes you are so dense. I've always felt—" She stopped. "It would have been selfish of *me* to get that close to you. I'm being selfish right now for allowing you to be here. This is so wrong. If I weren't so buzzed, I'd probably ask you to leave. But I guess it's a little late for that now." She fell back onto the bed, and a haunting, bitter laugh erupted from her throat. "I mean, look at me, I've already got my clothes off." She lifted her shoulders in an exaggerated shrug. "We might as well take advantage of it."

He lay down by her side and opened his arms to her. She moved closer and curled up next to him. She started to shake and then sob quietly. He reached for the edge of the comforter and covered her with it. They lay there like that for a while; he stared at the sheers blowing in the wind while she cried softly. Neither spoke. When she quieted down, and he was certain she had fallen asleep, he allowed himself to join her.

He woke to find her straddling him. She had his hands pinned on each side of his face, and she was nibbling one of his earlobes. She smelled of fall, of burning leaves, and the hair brushing his cheek was cold, almost damp. He inhaled it all and became intoxicated.

She'd changed the music. Pink Floyd's *Dark Side of the Moon* played. He looked over at the clock on her nightstand; it was ten to two. She must have opened the windows all the way because the sheers billowed with abandon and the room was colder. He shivered.

"Jack." Her voice was eerily intense, different than he'd ever heard it before. He didn't move, didn't say anything. "I want you to fuck me until I scream, understand?"

His throat constricted and he felt a hard-on growing from her words alone. But at the same time he knew he'd made a grave mistake in coming there. He knew then that he couldn't keep his promise to her, the one about not hurting her, about not being different around her the next time they met. He knew he should leave. But he also knew that what she'd said earlier was right; it was a little late for that now.

"Understand?" she asked again, more insistently. Her breath was hot in his ear.

Later he would remember—at the last possible moment, when there was still time to turn back, when he still could have done the right thing—he would remember looking into her eyes and thinking: *What have you done to me?*

I'm starving," she said afterward. They lay side by side on the bed, staring at the ceiling.

"Me too," he said. He was also freezing.

She sprang from the bed, grabbed his hand, and pulled him up. He searched for his shorts. She used a fork to poke the cold food, turning up her nose at it.

"I don't think we should eat this." She headed for the doorway. "Come on."

He followed her, watching as she strode naked down the steps, head held high, shoulders back. It was warmer in the kitchen. She opened the refrigerator and peered inside.

"There's not a lot in here, I'm sorry to say." She handed him a piece of Swiss cheese, folded another piece for herself, and took a huge bite out of it. "You like fried bologna?" she asked.

"I can't say I've ever had it." He was taken aback by her rapidly changing moods. Was this the same woman who just hours ago had confessed that her family had been murdered in front of her?

"Ah, then you don't know what you're missing." She threw a pack of bologna on the counter, retrieved a jar of mayonnaise from the door of the refrigerator, and then bent down for a small frying pan under the stove. "Can you hand me the bread?" she asked, pointing to a bread box behind him.

"Gosh, it's like being in the kitchen of a five-star chef." He couldn't help but tease her.

"It's usually best to wait until after your belly's full before making fun of the food," she retorted. "Otherwise, you might go hungry."

He stood behind her at the stove as she assembled the sandwiches right in the pan, resting his chin on her shoulder as he watched.

"I bet you were one of those girls who slept naked at slumber parties, shocking all the other girls with your brazen lack of modesty."

"I've never been to a slumber party."

"Hmm." He let his hand wander down between her legs. As he touched her, she stopped what she was doing and braced her hands on the edge of the counter. Her wetness surprised him, and then he realized what it was. He removed his hand quickly.

"Jenny?" How could he have been so stupid? It'd been so long since he'd had to worry about such things. "Are you taking . . . ? I mean, we didn't use anything. . . ."

"Don't you think you should have asked me this a while ago?" She turned around to face him. "I trust you, Jack. Can't you trust me?"

"What are you talking about?"

She directed her attention back to the stove. "There's a lot more to worry about nowadays than just making a baby." She flipped the sandwiches. "You're here, and you're not supposed to be. I really don't know where else you've been, now do I?" she added.

He backed away from her and leaned against the opposite counter. He wasn't going to legitimize her comment with a response. But she looked over her shoulder with a sad smile on her face, and he realized that she'd just been playing with him. She moved the pan off the heat and went to stand with him.

"Well, do I?" She pecked him on the lips.

"Tell me you didn't mean that. Tell me you already know the answer to that question."

"No, I didn't mean that. Yes, I already know the answer to that question."

He wrapped his arms around her and pulled her closer. "Tell me you already know you drive me absolutely wild. That you know as you walk around here without a stitch of clothing on you're making me crazy, and that I've lost my appetite, because when I'm with you I don't care about food, and I want to make love to you again, right here, right now. Tell me you already know I want to stop the clock, because I don't want tomorrow to come, because I don't know what I'm going to do—what we're going to do. Tell me you already know all this, Jen."

"I already know all this."

"So what are we gonna do?"

"I don't know." She paused, as if she really was considering what they could do, that they had options. "How's the song go? 'Humor me and tell me lies.' "

She was trying to make light of their situation but it wasn't working. He wanted a better answer.

"I don't know," she said again, more seriously this time. "But I do know that right now you're going to sit down and try my sandwiches, because if you don't, I'm going to be upset that I made them for you and you didn't eat them."

So they sat across from each other at her table and ate the sandwiches. She'd made three for him, anticipating his ravenous hunger. Neither spoke, but he felt her eyes on him at all times.

"Do you want to know what happened?" she asked, finally breaking the silence. He'd wondered since waking when, if ever, she'd come back to it. He nodded.

Perhaps she thought he'd say no, that she didn't have to tell him if she didn't want to. Perhaps that was the kind, gentlemanly response she'd come to expect from him, but things had changed so much between them in the last six hours. She breathed in heavily and then let out a long sigh, as if she needed the extra oxygen to sustain her through the story she was about to tell.

"It was early summer. School had just let out a few weeks before. It was hot. Very hot already for that time of year. Our house wasn't air-conditioned. It was a Friday evening. To stay cool, Andrea and I were playing on the front porch while we waited for my dad to come home. He'd promised to take us for ice cream at a little stand down the street from our house."

She stared out the window that faced the rear courtyard, although all she could possibly have seen was the black, wet night. He had the distinct sense that she was no longer in the room with him.

"It wasn't like now. Back then, going to get an ice cream was a treat. A special night." She paused, as if more memories were developing, as if the picture was becoming clearer the more she thought about it. "It was almost eight thirty when he got home; he'd been working long hours that week. But it was still light out. There was still about a half hour of daylight left."

Jenny turned to him as if she just remembered that he was there. "You know that strange quality of light you get some nights, close to sunset? When the sky glows pink and gold on the horizon? When it looks so achingly beautiful that it's hard to believe it's real? It's from the pollution. Did you know that? The most beautiful sunsets are caused by pollution."

He mumbled "Yes," but stopped short of saying the rest of what was on his mind: He wasn't sure if he wanted to hear what she was about to tell him. The sorrow growing inside him was different from hers, he knew, yet he felt that somehow they were related.

"I remember when he finally got home, he seemed distracted. But who knows? Maybe I just think I remember he was distracted. Maybe I've made it up to somehow convince myself that there were signs of what was to come, that maybe if someone had seen the signs, they'd all still be alive." She paused again, perhaps realizing she'd gotten slightly off track. "We walked the six blocks to the ice-cream stand; it was just us three. I don't know where my brother Brian was—probably in the park playing ball or something. My mom stayed home. She never came. She didn't like the attention she and my dad attracted when they went out together."

She said it as if he would know what she was talking about. He didn't, but he didn't feel it was the time to remind her of that.

"The entire time we were at the ice-cream stand, he seemed nervous, you know? It's like he knew what was coming but didn't know how to prevent it. I remember Andrea and I kept vying for his attention. We both kept trying to be the silliest, the cutest, the loudest. But he really didn't notice either of us that night, not really." She was silent for a moment, her face betraying doubt about what she'd just said. "Or maybe it was just me."

He understood what she was trying to say—as the youngest child, Andrea didn't need to. Yet, it was hard for him to imagine Jenny ever having to compete for attention. In the years he'd known her, she'd always been the most magnetic force in any group.

"I wonder if my memories are skewed by what I learned later," she continued, "by what they claimed happened." He started to ask, "Who's they?" but she kept talking. "But I don't believe it. He was so . . ." She stopped, searching for the right word, and then looked straight at Jack as if he was the clue. "He was so . . . honorable." Her expression scared him. "Do you know what I mean? He was such an honorable man. I just can't believe what they said was true.

"By the time we got home, it was dark. My mom was waiting for us on the front porch. I remember that in the stillness of the night I could hear the creak of her rocker from a block away. I couldn't see her, though, until we were almost at the base of the porch steps, because she had all the lights out. She used to do that in the summer. She'd turn the inside lights off to keep the house cool and she'd turn off the porch lights to keep the bugs away.

"When we approached and my dad saw her there, he flew off the handle. He was very upset. He yelled at her and told her to get inside. He said he didn't like her sitting there alone in the dark when he wasn't home. I remember she was so wounded by his tone. And surprised. All of us were. He never spoke to her like that. He never spoke to any of us like that, even Brian. He was always so gentle, so soft-spoken, even when he was disciplining us. It just wasn't his nature to speak harshly to anyone."

She stood and moved to the window. She crossed her arms to cover her breasts; for the first time that night, she seemed self-conscious about her nudity. "I'm cold," she said.

He jumped up from his chair. "I'll get you something."

He grabbed his suit coat from the living room, but as he started back for the kitchen he noticed a throw folded over the back of the sofa. She smiled as he draped it over her shoulders. He tried to pull her to him, to tell her she didn't need to say more if she didn't want to, but she rebuffed his attempts to comfort her.

"Do you think he knew?" she said. She paced in front of the window. "I don't think I—"

"I can't believe he did. He would have done something, I think; don't you?"

Her tone was insistent. He wondered if she believed, in some distorted way, that she'd already told him everything he needed to know to answer her questions.

"What happened, Jen, after you got home?" He made his question as insistent as hers.

"We started to get ready for bed. We took showers to cool off. Me and Andrea with my mom and Brian with my dad." She laughed gently, but somewhat bitterly, Jack thought. "My mom was very weird about that, you know—the boys and the girls taking their showers separately. I mean, my God, we were just kids."

All Jack could think was that Jenny hadn't inherited her mother's modesty.

"It took me a long time to fall asleep. Andrea and I slept together and she always jabbered and sang to herself every night for at least an hour before she'd fall asleep. Usually, it didn't bother me. In a way it was like my own personal lullaby. But not that night. I sensed something was different, I think.

"Of course, that's another one of those memories that perhaps I've made up. I think to myself—how could I have remembered that? Maybe I've concocted it in my head with the passage of time." She stopped pacing and sat down. "I guess in a way it doesn't really matter, does it? Anyway, at some point I heard Andrea get up. I guess to get a drink of water."

Her back was to him now and he placed his hand on her shoulder. To his surprise, she reached up and grabbed his hand with both of hers and pulled him around to the chair next to her. She continued to hold his hand, tracing and studying the veins on top and then turning it over and doing the same to the creases on his palm. The action saddened and aroused him at the same time.

She breathed in deeply again, and he watched her shoulders rise and fall rhythmically. He knew she was very close, and he questioned where he was taking her, and why.

"Jenny, you don't have to tell me. It's okay." But maybe it was his fear, not hers, that made him want her to stop. Now that he'd gained her trust, what if he couldn't give her what she needed? What if he couldn't keep his end of the unspoken bargain?

"I think that's what did her in, you know? Her thirst." It was as if she hadn't even heard him. "How does that happen, huh? A little kid is thirsty, so she gets out of bed to get a drink, and she ends up dead. How does that happen?" She began to cry then. Once her tears started, they came fast. She was still holding his hand and the tears dropped onto it, hot and wet. "Seems she interrupted some negotiations. They said that she became a bargaining tool. Brian and I saw it because I heard yelling and got scared. Andrea wasn't in our bed so I went to Brian's room, and we snuck down together. The house was dark, but the moonlight lit the room enough to see."

Jack was beginning to understand that Jenny's father must have known his assailant, but other than that fact, the connection between them hadn't been explained.

"We hid in a closet, and we could see them lying on the floor, the three of them."

Her voice was hard to understand through her crying. He leaned in, his face inches from hers, both hands on her face, and tried to calm her.

"Shh," he whispered. "Jenny, shh. You don't have to do this. It's okay."

"He had the gun to Andrea's head," she said, her voice breaking. "She was first."

Jack shut his eyes to block the mental image that accompanied her words, but it didn't work.

"My dad's eyes . . . God . . . I've never seen anything like it." She paused. "The whole time, in my mind, I'm getting ready to run if I have to. I wasn't thinking about what I could do to help. I was thinking only of saving myself. Brian told me later, much later when we were grown, that I was shaking and whimpering like a dog left out in the cold, and he had to clamp his hand over my mouth to stifle the noise. I have no memory of that. He told me that the guy searched the upstairs, presumably suspecting or perhaps knowing that Andrea wasn't the only child. I find it ironic that it was Andrea, in a way, and not my parents, who saved us. Don't you?"

Jack was unable to answer her question. Instead, he found himself wondering what he would do in the same situation, what Claire would do. Would fear paralyze him, as it apparently had Jenny's father, or would he find the courage somewhere within himself to put up resistance? And what about Claire? She was always so strong, in her own quiet way. Would she submit to execution without a fight? He didn't think so, but he envisioned her version of a fight as an attempt at reason, a negotiated settlement.

He'd been staring at his hand, at Jenny's fingers nervously weaving their way through his without any awareness of the movement. Whom was he betraying just then, by thinking about his family, about Claire? Surely Claire, merely for his being there. And Jenny? Did her sharing this with him elevate their obligations to each other to an even higher level than their actions just an hour before? He knew that it must, yet he didn't know what she expected from him, and he was afraid to ask.

"Really, I have no memory of anything past the actual gunfire," she continued. "Everything else I learned from Brian, or later from the news stories and police reports."

"Was he prosecuted?" It seemed like a logical question when it was in his head but out loud the words sounded ridiculous. As if that could matter to her, really.

"Well, they caught him."

The ticking of the clock on the wall behind her punctuated her sentence. He jumped when one of her cats rubbed up against his leg, and as a result, he missed the nuance of her answer; it wasn't until much later that he would realize his mistake.

To his surprise, she smiled slightly. "You're behaving like I'm telling you a ghost story, Jack. You're all jumpy." Her smile lingered and he returned it, but he didn't know what to say. He'd asked to carry her burden and she'd let him; now he didn't know what to do with it.

"The picture. It's your sister?" he asked.

She knew without explanation which picture he was referring to. "Yes."

"So who schooled you at home?"

"An aunt. My dad's sister. For some strange reason, she thought it would be too hard for us to go back to school. But that was exactly what we needed."

"Yale, Jenny. She must have done something right."

She shrugged. "Yeah, well, I'm not talking about the academics. You want some more OJ?"

He nodded and handed her his glass. Just like that, she'd moved on. Did she sense that he couldn't hear more? Or had she finished? But she hadn't explained her father's connection to the murderer. She hadn't explained the "interrupted negotiations."

She stood, letting the shawl fall onto the chair behind her. She went to the refrigerator and refilled his glass. He'd never seen a woman so comfortable in her own skin. He wondered what the aunt had been like. Who had instilled all this confidence?

"Do you have pictures?" he asked. "Of your family?"

"Upstairs. Come on, I'll show you."

Her bedroom seemed warmer now. The wind still blew, but the air it pushed in felt almost tropical compared to earlier. He smelled rain as he cranked the casement windows, leaving them open just a crack. She waited for him on the bed with an old photo album.

"That's my mom and dad," she began when he joined her, pointing to a picture. "I have to admit that it's hard to know which of my memories are real and which I've created from looking at pictures. But I remember my sister so well. Isn't that funny?"

Jack looked at the man and woman in the photo. His eyes immediately focused on the woman. There it was. There was what he'd seen in Jenny the first night they'd met, what in his white-bread ignorance he couldn't identify. There was the darkness, the black hair.

"She was born in India, in Kanpur," Jenny explained.

"And your dad?"

"Oh, he was a full-fledged American. As Waspy as they come. Like you, Jack." He couldn't tell if he'd just been insulted. "According to my aunt, neither set of parents was too excited when they married. His didn't speak to him for a few years, but finally softened when us kids came along. Hers disowned her, but she was already in the States by then, so there wasn't much they could do to stop it."

Jack looked at the man in the picture. He appeared to tower above his wife. Jenny might have received her coloring and her lips from her mother, but Jack could see that her other features most definitely belonged to her father. The sharp little nose, the prominent cheekbones, her height.

"How'd they meet?"

"She was in the States on a student visa."

"Show me your sister," he said.

She flipped a few pages, searching, and then stopped when she found the page she wanted. Jack saw the same little girl from the photo on her dresser, but in these pictures she looked more childlike, more innocent. In one picture she played on the floor with two kittens, her mouth wide open in endless giggles. In another, Jenny sat in front of a birthday cake with a big pout on her face, her sister on one side of her, Brian on the other. Frosting and more giggles lit her sister's face; the cake in front of Jenny had been poked and the culprit wasn't trying to hide anything.

"She was younger than you."

"Yes, by almost three years."

"More of a troublemaker than you, huh?"

She smiled, just barely. "It seems so, doesn't it? I think I just took over where she left off."

A gust of wind slammed one of the windows shut. Jack turned at the sound, but Jenny's voice brought him back. "He had a mistress."

"What?" The statement took Jack by surprise. She was still gazing at the picture from her birthday, and the only "he" in the picture was her brother.

"My dad. They said he had a mistress. But she denied it."

Jack swallowed. "Jenny, I don't think—"

"You know what the only real memory I have of him is? You know, a memory that's not overshadowed by that night? He built this raft with us. Told us we were going to be just like Tom Sawyer and Huck Finn and take that raft out on the river. My mom thought he was crazy—swore he'd have us all drowned before it was over. But we could all swim well, we weren't worried." She shrugged. "My mom didn't really understand the allure of the Mississippi. It wasn't the Ganga so it held no meaning for her."

"The *Ganga*?"

"Hindus believe that bathing in the waters of the Ganges River will wash away their sins," she explained.

"We'll have to book a trip soon, then."

She gave him a bittersweet smile but didn't say anything.

"Do you miss them?" he asked.

"I don't know. I barely knew them."

"I guess." He watched her turn the pages of the album slowly without really looking at the pictures. "You seem sort of mad at them."

She turned to him, glaring. "Why would I be mad at them, Jack?" Her tone was smart, challenging him. But the answer seemed obvious to him.

"I don't know." He tried to speak gently. "You just seem angry. At your dad, especially, like it was his fault."

Her eyes pierced into him. He heard himself swallow. He wanted to take back what he'd just said.

"You are fucking amazing, Jack Hilliard. Who the hell are you to analyze me and my dead parents? It's taken you nine years to even acknowledge that my skin is darker than yours, but you think you can come in here and in five minutes psychoanalyze our relationship?"

"What are you talking about? Nine years to acknowledge your skin is darker than mine?"

She grunted. "Give me a break, will you? You think I don't know why you're so attracted to me? Like I'm some dark, exotic thing compared to your lily-white wife."

"You're wrong," he said quietly, shocked.

"Yeah, why don't we analyze that, since you seem to want to play amateur psychologist tonight? Why don't we analyze why you're here instead of in Jeff City, where you're supposed to be? Huh? Or, better yet, why aren't you at home, in bed next to Claire?"

The use of Claire's name made him wince in a way that her use of the generic term *wife* hadn't. He reached for her left hand, but she raised it and shook it to brush his away.

"Fuck you, Jack. You've got a lot of nerve."

He rolled onto his side, propped his head up on his left arm, and watched her staring blankly at the photo album. They lay there like that for what seemed to him forever, while he waited for the tension in her jaw to relax and her eyes to clear. When he thought she wouldn't rebuff him, he reached up and touched her hair, tucking it behind her ear. She let him, closing her eyes as he did. "This is so wrong," she mumbled.

He leaned close to her face. "Jenny, I'm sorry," he whispered. "I just thought you wanted to talk about it."

She nodded and spoke without opening her eyes. "You want too much from me, Jack. You're moving way too fast."

"I'm sorry," he said again. When he laughed a little, she turned to him. "First you complain that it takes me nine years to notice the color of your skin—"

"Acknowledge," she interrupted, correcting him.

"And then you tell me I'm moving too fast." After a moment, he said, "Tell me something."

"What?"

"Did it float?"

"What?"

"The raft."

"You're changing the subject."

"Did it?"

"I don't know. We never got the chance to take it out before that night."

"What happened to it? Afterward, I mean."

"I don't know that either. Maybe my aunt put it out for the trash one day. Brian and I never asked. Didn't want to know, I guess."

Rain began to fall outside, gently at first, and then picked up force. No more wind, though; the sheers hung still. Despite the horror of the story she'd told him, this, finally, was how he'd imagined it: her opening up to him, letting him in.

"Jenny."

"Hm?"

"I think we've got a problem."

"Yeah, and what's that?"

"I think I've fallen in love with you."

She tensed visibly and turned her head back to the album. "Jack—"

"Don't say anything. There's something else." He grinned. "I want to do it my way now."

She turned on her side and looked relieved that he hadn't mentioned love again.

"Really? And what's your way?"

He closed the album, carefully set it on the floor, and then gave her a lazy kiss. "Slow. Slow and easy. Like the Mississippi."

She seemed to like that answer. She closed her eyes and let him roll her over onto her back. When he climbed on top of her, she opened her eyes to him and he felt that he had fallen in, that he was sinking into the swirling eddy of their blackness. It startled him at first, the speed and the depths to which he fell. But he went willingly; he didn't even make an effort to save himself.

When he woke the second time, daylight had arrived. But it was still raining, thundering. He heard the water hitting the pavement on the street outside; every once in a while a car slowly drove past. They were under the covers, snuggled as if in a cocoon.

"Jenny?" he whispered. She lay with her back to him. He wondered if she was awake yet.

"What?" She spoke softly, but he sensed impatience in her voice.

"Do you believe in soul mates? You know, that everyone has a soul mate somewhere?"

She was quiet and he waited for her to answer. When several moments had passed and she still hadn't responded, he brushed the hair from her back and traced his finger between her shoulder blades. He saw red marks on her back and for a moment felt ashamed, remembering how furious, almost violent, their lovemaking had been the first time.

"Jenny?" Had she drifted off? He caressed her arm and felt the muscles tense.

"Don't make this into more than it was." Her voice was cold, unrecognizable. He removed his hand from her arm and leaned over, trying to see her face. "Yeah, I believe in soul mates—and yours is home right now wondering where you are while you're here fucking me."

Her expression matched her voice. Her eyes pierced the wall across from her, refusing to meet his. Was she playing some sort of sick joke on him?

"I'm not your soul mate, Jack," she continued. "We're just two people who have been dying to get into each other's pants since the day we met and we finally broke down and did it. It's as simple as that. Like two animals in heat." She finally turned to him, and he looked into her eyes, but nothing was there. He tried to gulp air, but it was as if every life-supporting mechanism in his body had shut down. "A couple fucks do not a soul mate make," she said.

The oxygen in the room seemed to compress, and he felt as if he was about to pass out. He wanted her to stop talking, to let him catch his breath, but her cruelty seemed relentless. She sat up, and the sheet that had draped her body fell to her waist, exposing her breasts. He wanted to lean over and cover her nakedness, it seemed vulgar now, but she had rendered him incapable of movement, incapable of speech. He wished that she had rendered him deaf, too.

She reached up and took his chin in her hand, roughly, as if to guarantee that he wouldn't look away. "You're a hopeless romantic, Jack. You're the type of guy who thinks there has to be some cosmic purpose for everything." She released him and lay back down, rolling onto her stomach with her sinewy arms stretched above her head, as if she were going to take a long nap. "The woman who loves you isn't here right now—so if that's who you're looking for, I'd suggest you get dressed and go home."

He stared at her bare back, and for a moment he thought of the raw intoxication he'd felt when he was inside her. And then he was outside himself, above them both, watching as they writhed on the mattress, twisting and pushing the sheet at their feet until it had fallen off the bed. *Like animals in heat.* He shivered and his stomach began to spasm violently. He sprang up and into the bathroom across the hall, where he fell in front of the toilet and began to vomit. At first it was only the sandwiches she'd made for them, and the wine, but as he knelt there, groaning with each spasm—not from the contractions of his stomach muscles but from the pain of her words—he began to lose it all. All the lunches, all the late-night dinners at Newman, every cup of coffee. And like a volcano finally erupting after resting dormant for many years, it wouldn't stop. With each convulsion, he felt as if something were reaching into the depths of his stomach. He continued to lose everything else, too. Every meal that Claire had lovingly prepared for him: the fried eggs and bacon that she made him every Sunday morning, the carrot cake—his favorite— that she baked from scratch every November for his birthday. The pretzels and popcorn he and Michael devoured together in the bleachers at Busch Stadium; the burnt Toll House cookies the kids baked for him; the chocolate-covered ants Michael made at camp one year and dared him to eat; the watery Kool-Aid on the deck; the cotton candy that Jamie insisted on sharing with him at the carnival each summer. It all came up against his will, burning his esophagus with contempt as it made its journey. He was helpless to stop it. When it finally ebbed, when he thought at last it was over, he vomited one last time and imagined that he had expelled his heart, that it floated there in the bowl below him, red and withered, amid the debris of his life.

He didn't know how long he crouched there, how much time had passed before he heard the creak of the bedsprings and assumed that Jenny had stood up. He lifted his head to listen, but he didn't hear footsteps. Summoning the energy to pull his heavy body off the tiled floor, he stood and flushed the toilet. His vision blacked out briefly, and he steadied himself against the sink until he could see again. He turned on the cold water and hovered over the sink, taking care not to look at his reflection in the mirror. He rinsed his mouth, splashed some water on his face; and after only a second of contemplation he grabbed her toothbrush, squeezed some paste onto it, and brushed his teeth. When he was finished he almost tossed it into the waste basket, but a touch of orneriness caused him to replace it in its holder.

Gathering strength, he returned to the bedroom. She was in the same position as he'd left her, but she lay uncovered this time, the sheet and comforter underneath her. One of her cats, the Siamese one, was curled up in the crook of her arm, as if it had been lying in wait, ready to take Jack's place. He leaned against the doorway.

"Did you write that speech ahead of time?" he asked. His throat was raw, his voice barely audible.

When she didn't respond, didn't even move, he went to her side of the bed and sat on the edge. His hip brushed against hers. He grabbed her shoulder and rolled her over; the cat, disturbed, pounced onto the floor. She didn't resist but she didn't help him, either. Her body was limp and spiritless, but the intensity of her eyes almost punctured his resolve.

"I said, did you write that speech ahead of time?" His voice was stronger.

She shook her head slightly.

He knew then that he could place his palm on her skin and run it gently along the contours of her body while he began to kiss her, and she would let him. He knew that he could climb on top of her and split her open. And he knew that this would probably be the last chance he would have to lie down with her again and feel her nakedness against him. But something in him had changed; rather, something in him had returned during the time he'd spent in the bathroom, retching until there was nothing left except the acrid taste of bile and grief.

So instead, he took her chin in his hand, as she had done to him, but more gently, and said, "Well, I don't believe it. I will never believe what you said."

The rain was still falling steadily when he stepped outside. He didn't bother to button his coat; at that point it didn't matter to him if he got wet. He walked in the rain to the stoop adjacent to her place. He sat on the top step and raised his face to the sky. He wished the rain could wash away everything he'd done wrong. It didn't take long for the cold water streaming down his cheeks and neck to soak under the collar of his coat and through to his clothes. He looked down at his feet. The rain had drenched his shoes and socks, too, and the exposed bottoms of his pant legs. Chilled, he began to shiver. He gazed out into the street and watched the morning's increasing traffic. He thought about his next step. Not his next step with Jenny, or his next step with Claire, or even how to get to Jefferson City in dry clothes so that he wouldn't arrive late for the seminar. He thought only about how he would get from the stoop to his car in the garage downtown. Whatever happened after that struck him as beyond his ability to comprehend. He tried not to, but he couldn't help but think of her again, of both of them, as they struggled on her bed, desperately trying to satiate the hunger that all their willpower over the past years couldn't make go away.

As if she knew what he'd been thinking, and she'd been assigned the task of reminding him of what she'd done to him, how she'd broken him, she appeared at her front door. She didn't see him at first. She opened her umbrella as she stepped out. She had on a raincoat, but he could tell from her pumps and her styled hair that she was heading to Newman. She had a small overnight bag slung over her shoulder. He realized that he'd been sitting there in the rain for quite some time, long enough, at least, for her to have showered and dressed for work.

She spotted him when she turned around to lock the deadbolt on her door. She stood motionless, her right hand still holding the key in the lock. He could tell from the startled expression on her face that she hadn't prepared herself for the possibility of seeing him again just then. They stared at each other silently.

A loud clap of thunder interrupted their standoff and she jumped. She looked down at her hand holding the key as if she didn't understand that it belonged to her. She slipped the key from the door and dropped her key chain into her purse. Without looking at him again, she walked down the steps and crossed the street to her car, taking care to avoid puddles. He waited for her to look at him one last time, to offer him a ride downtown, even though he knew he would refuse. But she didn't do either.

After she had driven off, he began the long walk in the rain to his car. Calling a cab just wasn't an option.

The clock on the dash read 11:52 A.M. when he exited the interstate onto Route 54. He'd reach Jeff City in a half hour, but he worried that he wouldn't be able to concentrate on what anyone was saying or, worse, that he'd get sick again. Before he'd left St. Louis, he'd called from his car and left a message that he'd be later than he thought, using the rain as an excuse. He knew it really didn't matter if he made it on time, but he was afraid that if he didn't call ahead, they'd notice his absence and call his office looking for him. On his way out of the city, after he'd made certain Claire was gone, he'd stopped by the house to change clothes. He knew it was foolish because there was a good chance a neighbor might see him, and it would most certainly get back to Claire. But he wasn't thinking clearly enough to cover his tracks adequately.

When he arrived at the seminar, he sat in the comfort of the small, dry space of his car and tried to compose himself. He thought that maybe he should wait until they took their lunch break before joining them; maybe then his entrance wouldn't be so noticeable. Even better, maybe he should just turn around and go home. The thought of sleep seduced him, and he wanted nothing more than to be in his own bed, alone in the quiet house, where he could slip into a dream, where everything made sense.

He leaned back against the headrest and waited until the windows had completely fogged up. And then, when he could no longer see out and he knew no one could see in, he started to cry, releasing the surging grief that had built up on the long drive. When he closed his eyes, he kept seeing Claire, the first time they'd ever made love, on a blanket under the stars in the middle of a high school football field near the university. He thought of her fair skin, damp from their mingled sweat, how it glistened in the blue light of the moon.

He had an overwhelming desire to tell her what he'd done, just skip all the pain they'd both have to go through and get immediately to the forgiveness. He longed so badly just to have that forgiveness, to tell her it had nothing to do with her, and have her know that, believe that. But he knew he couldn't skip the pain, and he knew she'd never grant him the forgiveness he so desperately needed. He was certain that if she ever found out, their marriage would be over.

"It's the ultimate intimate act, to let a man actually enter your body, become one with you, and to let him watch you, with all your inhibitions down," she had explained years ago, when she'd been questioning the casual sex lives of her friends. "How could you even want to do that with someone you didn't love deeply?"

"I guess you just get horny sometimes," Jack had answered then. Now the words seemed so flippant; she'd been trying to tell him something important to her. She hadn't been offended, but she had remained serious. She told Jack at that point that adultery was the one thing she could never forgive, even if she wanted to.

"I couldn't bear the thought of you experiencing that connection with another woman."

CHAPTER FIFTEEN

There were no messages from Jenny when he returned to his empty office at eight that evening, as there had been that Friday morning in the spring. There were no attempts to reach him, no entreaties to pretend that nothing had happened. He'd probably never hear from Jenny Dodson again, despite her pleas for him not to treat her differently. She wouldn't even give him the chance.

The call came at ten on Sunday night. He'd been struck low with a fever most of the weekend. When the phone rang, he knew it was her. Maybe she'd gone away for the weekend. Maybe she'd finally come to her senses. He didn't even stop to consider that his house was the last place she'd try to reach him, if she tried to reach him at all.

"I'll get it," he said a little too eagerly, rising from his chair in front of the television.

Claire narrowed her eyes at him and motioned for him to sit back down. "I think I can get it from here." She answered the phone on the table next to her without taking her eyes off him. He took his seat and listened carefully to her side of the conversation.

"Hi, Maria." *Maria?* Maria had been assigned to on-call duty that weekend. She was responsible for filing the charges against anyone picked up between Friday night and Monday morning. "Yeah, he's here. No, no, it's okay."

Why was Maria calling him? What couldn't wait until tomorrow? He tried to read Claire's face for clues when he took the phone.

"Yeah, Maria?"

"Jack, I'm really sorry to call you." Whatever she had to tell him, he sensed that she didn't want to be the one to do it.

"It's okay. What is it?"

"I'm at the police station, and they're saying I need to call another county because we can't handle this, and I don't know what to do." The words tumbled from her mouth.

"Slow down. Back up. Can't handle what?" He shrugged at Claire.

"I'm sorry, Jack. I'm sorry." She began to choke up. "They've brought Jenny in and . . ."

Her trembling voice reached through the phone and gripped his chest like a vise. "What?"

"They're saying I can't prepare the charges, that no one in our office should be involved with preparing the charges—"

"Stop! What are you talking about? Brought Jenny in for what?" He stared past Claire as she sat down on the footstool in front of him.

Maria hesitated. She lowered her voice. "For murder."

"*What?*"

"A lady named Maxine Shepard was shot on Thursday night."

Jack looked directly at Claire. What he'd thought couldn't get any worse just had.

"Supposedly she was a client at Newman," Maria added. Her voice seemed to come from far away. When he didn't respond—he was too busy panicking—she said, "Jack?"

"This is ridiculous! Let me talk to them," he demanded.

"Jack—"

"Let me talk to them, dammit!"

Claire set her hand on his knee.

"Mr. Hilliard?"

He didn't recognize the voice. "Who is this?"

"Officer Ryan, from the—"

"What do you think you're doing? You can't possibly have any evidence to warrant this."

"Well, sir, we think we do, but we're aware that Ms. Dodson helped you in your election, and Ms. Catalona here indicated she's also your close friend, so you know I can't discuss this with you or with her. I need someone to call another county so we can get the arrest warrant issued."

Jack stood. "Jesus, Ryan. She didn't commit a murder! What are you doing?"

Claire gasped and covered her mouth with her hand.

"I'm doing my job, Mr. Hilliard. With all due respect, can you please just do yours and inform Ms. Catalona how she can reach a prosecutor in Franklin County or somewhere?"

"Don't move. I'm coming down there."

"There's no need, I just—"

Jack hung up the phone before Ryan could finish his sentence. "I've gotta get down there." He headed for the kitchen and Claire followed him.

"What's going on? They think Jenny had something to do with a murder?"

He ignored her as he searched through the mess on the counter in a desperate attempt to find his car keys. "What is all this crap, anyway?" He shoved a pile of papers to the edge, causing one of Michael's books to fall on the floor. "Where the hell are my keys?"

"Jack." She placed her hand on his shoulder. "Calm down. You shouldn't drive when you're this upset. Why don't I call Marcia and she can stay here while I drive you?"

"No!" The last thing he needed was to have Claire with him as he tried to straighten this out. He took a deep breath. "I'm fine. Can you just find my keys for me?"

She opened the cabinet above the counter. The keys were on the bottom shelf, in the same spot as always.

"Sorry." Taking the keys, he turned and started for the door to the garage, but she grabbed his hand.

"Jack?"

"Claire, I'm in a hurry."

She leaned closer, kissed his cheek near his ear. "Just try to drive carefully, will you? You can't help her if you don't get there alive."

He nodded, stopping long enough to return her kiss.

When he burst through the door to the police station, the man he took to be Officer Ryan was in the middle of explaining to Maria that they had only twenty hours to file the charges, and then they'd have to let Jenny go. Maria, of course, already knew this. She had her arms and legs crossed, and she rolled her eyes at Jack when he entered.

"Where is she?" Jack asked.

"Mr. Hilliard?" Ryan offered his hand. "I'm Officer Ryan, Craig Ryan."

"Yeah." Jack gave him the obligatory shake. "Where is she?"

"She's in a holding cell." He smirked at Jack. "Same place they all go."

"What? Are you crazy? You don't have an empty room where you could've let her wait?"

Ryan stared at him, his face deadpan. "She's being held for murder, sir."

"She's a respected attorney in this town, in case you weren't aware of that."

Ryan shrugged.

"Take me to her."

"I'm not at liberty to do that. You're not her lawyer."

"No, goddammit! I'm the DA for this city. Which, if I understand correctly, means I'm also the chief law-enforcement officer. So let's just say I want to interrogate her."

Ryan exaggerated his sigh on purpose. "Mr. Hilliard, even—"

"Can you please call me Jack?"

"Jack, even if you were a complete stranger to her, you know I couldn't let you do that. Anyway, she's already said she's not talking to anyone except her lawyer."

Good for her. Right call. He'd known of enough lawyers who thought they were smarter than the cop interrogating them and ended up waiving their rights.

"How is she?"

Ryan brushed off the question. "She's fine. You should ask how the guards are. She's a tough cookie. Has quite a mouth on her."

Jack glanced at Maria, who wore a hint of a smile.

"Well, just let me in as a visitor, then. As a friend. Just to see she's okay."

Ryan shook his head. "Sorry, not till she's been booked."

Jack started to get angry again. There had to be some benefits to this job. "Get your boss on the phone. I'm sure he'll have no issue with me seeing her."

"I already called him, while you were on your way here. I'm following his orders."

Shit. Trumped again. "Can you at least tell me what you have, to haul her in like this?"

"Listen, Mr. Hil—Jack, I tried to tell you on the phone. I can't talk to you about this case. Given your relationship with the defendant—"

"And what relationship is that?" As soon as the question spilled from his mouth, he thought it sounded too defensive.

Ryan looked at Maria. "As I said, in addition to the fact that she worked on your campaign, I'm talking about the relationship as described by Ms. Catalona. She said you two are good friends, that you used to work together at the same law firm."

"Jenny didn't tell you that?"

"Ms. Dodson didn't even mention you, sir." Jack looked away, tried to hide a growing blush; when he didn't respond, Ryan continued. "Given that relationship, you know that your entire office will be required to disqualify itself from handling this case. Now, I'm asking you to please do the right thing and get a prosecutor from another county on the phone for me."

Do the right thing. Ryan had no idea he'd chosen the exact four words that would get the reaction he wanted. It had been a long time since Jack felt like he'd done the right thing.

"Okay. But I need to get over to my office to get the numbers. Can you at least get a message to her for me while I'm gone?" Ryan nodded. Jack liked him; he wasn't cocky, and Jack knew he really was just doing as he'd been instructed. "Can you tell her I'm trying to get in to see her, that I'm working on it?"

Ryan agreed, and back at his office Jack did as he'd promised. He reached an assistant DA for Franklin County; she lived just outside Pacific and promised to be there within the hour. He returned to the police station within twenty minutes, eager to hear if Ryan had kept his end of the bargain.

"I gave her your message, but she had one for you, and I don't think you're going to like it."

Jack felt Maria watching them as one watched a tennis match—back and forth, back and forth. He wasn't sure she should be in the room when Ryan relayed the message, but he didn't know how to get her out tactfully, without raising suspicions. Jenny wouldn't give anything away, though. If what she had to say was sensitive, he felt confident she'd code the message somehow.

"Well?"

"She said she's not expecting you, and she doesn't want you involved." He paused, and Jack waited, anticipating, praying there was more. "That was the 'edited for vulgarity' version, by the way."

On Monday morning the DA from Franklin County, Alan Sterling, arrived to take over where his assistant had left off on Sunday night, and it quickly became apparent to Jack that this DA had political aspirations which would affect how he handled the case. He, too, refused to allow Jack to see Jenny; he claimed to be fearful of tainting the case and wanted to research the issue first. Jack knew it had nothing to do with a fear of tainting the case and everything to do with asserting his newfound power over the new, young, big-city DA, who wasn't even able to handle the first high-profile case to land on his desk.

He spent the morning stewing over his impotence. His mind kept returning to Thursday night. He thought, too, of Jenny sitting in jail and of the story she'd told him about her family. The memory finally moved him to action.

The main file room buzzed with activity, as it did every Monday. The musty smell of old paper permeated the cavernous room. He'd always liked the smell; it usually reminded him that the thousands of brown files that lined the drawers and walls of the room had historical significance beyond the role he or any other lawyer had played in creating them. But today the smell assaulted him, made him think of something rotten and insidious.

Lawyers from all over the city stood at the long counter, jockeying for the attention of the clerks in charge of retrieving the requested files. Jack approached tentatively, mindful that most of them standing there had seen the morning's headlines with their first cup of coffee. As he waited for Rose, the file room's head clerk, he drummed his fingers nervously on the worn wooden counter and stared mindlessly at the doodles carved over the years by the pen points of impatient lawyers. The other clerks benevolently ignored him and helped others as they scribbled case names or file numbers on the little pieces of scrap paper lying around. They'd learned that Jack liked Rose best and would wait for her if she was busy helping another attorney.

Today she bestowed a sympathetic look on him as she leaned on the counter to greet him.

"Jack, rough weekend, I hear," she said, her voice raspy but low, as if they already shared a secret. "That lawyer gal they picked up is your friend, huh?"

"Yeah." He felt far too close to this one to talk casually about it with her, the way they did about everything else. "Look, Rose, I need some help locating an old file. I think it's probably from 1974 or '75. I only know the victims' names; I don't know the defendant's name."

"Anything for you, Jack." She picked up a pen, her hand poised to write.

"It's Dodson. A triple murder."

She wrote the name and then slowly looked up at him. "That's the lady's name, ain't it?" He nodded. She regarded him quietly and winked. "Give me a sec, okay?"

Despite her request, he knew a search by the victim's name alone could take a while, and he didn't wish to pass the time fidgeting where he felt all eyes were on him. He slipped into one of the phone rooms at the end of the counter and sat down to wait. He stared at the old tan phone on the table, its boxy shape a sharp contrast to the new, streamlined black phones recently installed in the DA's office. The simplicity of it comforted him. He shut the door for privacy, picked up the receiver, and called Claire at work.

"Hi" was all he said when she answered.

"Hi" She paused, and when he didn't say anything, she asked, "Where are you?"

"In one of those little phone rooms in the file room. I'm waiting for them to look up a file," he explained. "I miss you."

"I miss you, too."

He played with the buckle on his belt. He didn't know what else to say, but he didn't want to hang up. He thought of the past two days, how in bed he'd pulled her tightly to him, trying to imprint on his brain how her body felt against his so he could retrieve it later, again and again. "It's as if you're holding on for dear life," she'd teased. All he could think to himself at the time was, *I am, I am.*

The little room seemed to be shrinking around him. If he could just find a way to tell her before she found out from someone else, maybe then the outcome could be different.

"They'll straighten out this mess," Claire said, breaking the silence. Her voice was soft and comforting. "I'm sure of it, Jack."

"You believe she didn't do it?"

"Of course I believe she didn't do it."

"How do you know? How are you so certain?"

"It's Jenny, Jack. I know Jenny."

He closed his eyes. What was he going to say? *No, you don't, Claire. And you don't know me, either.*

"Jack? Do you have reason to believe she did it?"

"No, I have reason to believe she didn't." He'd just tested the water, and he waited to see if she'd understood.

"What do you mean?"

But he should tell Jenny first, shouldn't he? She should know that he intended to admit everything. It was only fair. "I mean what you mean. I know Jenny. I know she'd never do anything like that."

Claire fell silent at the other end, probably not quite comprehending what was going on but knowing there was more than what he'd just said. Finally, she said, "Did you see her yet?"

"No. The Franklin County DA is giving me the runaround."

"That's absurd. Why wouldn't you be able to visit?"

"Yeah, that's my question. I don't want to piss him off, though."

Claire huffed. "Piss him off! Do whatever you have to. She must be scared to death." He hunched his body over the table, propping his head on his one hand. "Did you hear me?" she persisted.

"Yeah." The phone rang in the adjoining room, and hearty laughs came from just outside the door. Suddenly he blurted, "She told me her parents and sister were murdered when she was a child. She witnessed it all."

Claire let out a gasp. "Oh my God. When? When did she tell you this?"

He hesitated. "Just after the election. We had lunch."

"God, that's awful. She's never talked about anything like that."

He rubbed his temples. Why had he told her? The energy he'd felt on his way down to the file room had dissipated, and exhaustion from the long night before was setting in. He'd told her because he didn't want to argue with her about his problems with the Franklin County DA. He'd told her because he wanted her to understand. What he wanted her to understand, he wasn't sure anymore.

"Claire?" He wanted to say, *I need you* and *Don't give up on me,* but he didn't. "I should go. If they found the file, they're probably wondering what happened to me."

"Okay. Hang in there. We'll talk more tonight, all right?

"Yeah, okay."

"If you get in to see her, tell her I'm thinking of her."

"I will." But he couldn't think of a single scenario in which he'd be able to say those words to Jenny on behalf of Claire.

Rose stood at the end of the counter, waiting for him, when he emerged from the phone room. She was engrossed in filing her nails with a long emery board. She spoke without looking up.

"I've got good news and bad news," she said. "The good news is that I found the file. The bad news is that it's off-site, in storage. It could take some time to have it sent over here, but I'll do my best to get it as soon as possible."

"Great. Thanks, Rose. You'll call me when you get it?"

She patted the top of his hand. "I'll call you. Hang in there."

Hang in there. The same thing Claire had said. As if everyone knew that he was barely holding on.

CHAPTER SIXTEEN

Jack's patience with Alan Sterling reached its limit on Tuesday morning, when the Franklin County DA began to build his case against Jenny on the front page of the newspaper. From a news article Jack learned that a scarf belonging to Jenny had been found at Maxine Shepard's house. He also learned that a neighbor claimed to have seen, on the day of the murder, Jenny and Maxine engaged in what the neighbor called a "heated discussion" on Maxine's doorstep. The worst and most shocking claim was that Newman had been investigating Jenny for embezzlement in connection with Maxine's investments.

When he arrived at the courthouse, reporters were waiting for him on the front steps. For the first time in the many years he'd been a prosecutor, he didn't stop. He pushed through the throng, stating only that he'd talk to them later. Once inside, he immediately called Sterling's office in Union, Missouri, and told the receptionist why he was calling.

"Sir, I'm sorry, but Mr. Sterling isn't here right now, so I can't really say—"

"Excuse me, ma'am. I really don't care if Sterling *is* there. Union's not that big. Find him if you have to. I'm merely calling as a courtesy to let him know that I'll take his nonresponse to my request to be a positive response, and if he has an opinion to the contrary, he'd better contact me within the hour with an explanation that has some basis in law."

She stuttered an unintelligible protest but he hung up on her.

"I'll be at the jail," he told Beverly after an hour had passed and no call had come. On his way out, he passed a few attorneys in the reception area. All eyes were on him and he had the urge to turn around and ask them what they were staring at.

He made it to the jail in less than seven minutes. They let him in without protest this time; he wondered if Sterling had called and given the go-ahead. He knew the guard who accompanied him from the many visits he'd made to the building over the years. They greeted each other courteously, but then Jack realized he was being led not to the interview rooms but to the row of phone carrels where he'd have to talk to Jenny through a Plexiglas window.

"No," he said, stopping abruptly. "I want to see her in a private room."

The guard winced; he'd anticipated this issue. "Mr. Hilliard, you know I can't—"

"Don't tell me 'can't.' I know Sterling's talked to you guys, and frankly, I don't care what he said. I'm seeing her in a private room or I'm going to start raising some major hell around here. I'm already a little pissed that it's Tuesday and I'm only now getting in, even though she's been here since Sunday." He paused and they regarded each other. "I'm supposed to be on your side, remember? You want to piss me off some more?"

"No."

"All right, then."

The guard's nostrils flared. Jack had never spoken to anyone like that before; he'd never had to. Finally, without another word, the guard led him in the opposite direction to a different corridor lined with doors, each with its own small window at eye level. He reached into his pocket for a set of keys and, after struggling with the lock, motioned Jack in.

"She'll be in shortly." All pretense of amicability was gone. He left Jack alone in the large gray room, empty except for a table and two chairs.

Jack sat on one of the hard chairs and fumed. He stared at the walls, their surfaces thick and chipped with old coats of paint. He wondered how this DA from Franklin County had managed to turn everyone against him. He suspected that he was now being handled the way they handled defense attorneys.

He stood when the door swung open. He glimpsed her first through the window in the door, and then she appeared fully, only several feet in front of him on the other side of the table. She wore the bright orange jumpsuit he was so used to seeing on other defendants. It was not orange like a pumpkin or even orange like the fruit. It was Day-Glo orange; it forced you to look away.

Her hair hung limply on either side of her face. It was clean, but un-kempt. She didn't seem as tall as he remembered. For a brief instant he saw her again, standing naked in front of the stove. He blinked to erase the image from his mind. When he finally looked into her chestnut eyes, she was already waiting for him to meet her stare. Her eyes were glassy, the skin around them swollen from crying or lack of sleep.

When the guards left, she sat down and immediately started talking. "I know exactly what you want to do, but I'm telling you now, don't do it."

He reached across the cold metal table for her hands, but she jerked them in fast, as if a spring had been released. Jack was stunned; touching had never been forbidden for Jenny.

"Why not?" he asked, his voice hoarse.

"I'll get out of here regardless," she said. "There's no use in you fuck-ing up your family because of it."

"As usual, your confidence scares me."

"How'd you get in here?" She leaned back in the chair and crossed her arms.

"What do you mean?"

"How'd you get in here?" she repeated. "In this room. Except for a defendant's lawyer, all other visitors are supposed to see the accused out-side, at the carrels, aren't they?"

He wanted to ask her how many visitors she'd had so far. "Yeah, well, they know me." Jack scanned the room for cameras or microphones. He knew some of the rooms were rigged for when the confessions came.

"My point exactly. They let you in, even though you're not my lawyer."

"So what is your point?" This wasn't how the meeting was supposed to go.

"My point is, I'm one of the privileged, just like you." Jenny's voice was sarcastic, bitter. He wanted to laugh; his difficulty getting in had taught him that he wasn't nearly as privileged as he believed himself to be a few days earlier. "I'm an almost-white, Yale-educated, female lawyer who works for one of the biggest firms in the city. I get special favors. They're not going to hang me."

"Or they might use you as an example—did you ever think of that? To show all those bleeding hearts like me that the law won't be unjustly weighted against poor black guys."

Jenny's cheeks blanched. Jack regretted his words; he knew she'd probably already thought of it and was trying to convince herself otherwise.

"Do you know something I don't?" Jenny asked. She'd dropped the sarcasm. "Around your office, have you heard talk about my case?"

"Are you kidding?" Now he was the one to scoff. "I'm a pariah. I come around a corner and I can tell they've been talking about it, but they clam up."

Jenny shook her head in disgust, and Jack began to worry that he had just given her another reason to insist he keep his mouth shut.

"Look, I'm just going to tell them I was with you that night," he said.

"No, you can't," she said. "You think you're a pariah now, just wait until they find *that* out. It'll be on the front page of the papers in seconds."

"Ha! Obviously you haven't seen a paper in a few days. Just the fact that we're friends has thrown them all into a tizzy. It won't be long before they create an X-rated relationship all on their own."

She looked down, and he suspected that he wasn't the only one thinking about the two of them a few nights before, tangled together in the darkness of her room. And then he couldn't help but think of how he had left that morning, and how she had left him, sitting there in the rain.

"Look, you'd be out of here by morning, Jenny. An alibi is much stronger if you tell them about it right off the bat. They'll give us both lie-detector tests and then drop the charges."

"No."

"You're being ridiculous."

"No, *you're* being ridiculous!" She leaned forward, her eyes narrowed. "I'm innocent, remember? They have to have some evidence to convict me."

He thought of the news article. "Evidence can be twisted or, worse, manufactured."

She glanced sideways. "Yeah, you ought to know."

Despite his efforts to remain calm, he started to get angry. He watched her right hand as it tucked her lifeless hair behind one ear; it trembled the whole way. When she looked at him again, he said, "Jenny, you know I've never tried a case in my life where I didn't believe completely in the defendant's guilt."

She rolled her eyes. "What a saint you are. Let me shake your hand."

"Fuck you." He hated her just then. He stood to leave, but her next words made him stop.

"You already did that, remember?"

He stared down at her; she glared at him. She didn't really believe that, did she? Is that why she'd turned on him that morning? He wanted to tell her, *No, you fucked me, but I made love to you.* But maybe she was right. Maybe it had been nothing more than that. Two people fucking. So instead, he said, "You can rot in here. You can rot in hell, for all I care."

He waited for her to say something, to say she was sorry or to ask him not to go. But she just sat there, staring at the wall on the other side of the small room as if transfixed on a tiny spot that only she could see. Finally she bent her head and rubbed her face. "I'm so tired. I need some sleep, but I can't sleep in here. It's so noisy at night." Her voice trembled with desperation.

Jack squatted in front of her. He took her hands and this time she let him. She rocked, just a bit, in her chair. Several moments passed before she spoke again.

"She'll leave you. She'll leave you and take the kids."

"No, she won't. We'll be okay." Jack knew his words weren't true. "It was just one night, one time. Other guys have done worse and their marriages survived. She'll forgive me."

Jenny shook her head. She finally began to cry. "You two are different, Jack. Other guys are jerks and their wives expect less from them. It's different with you and Claire." She started to wipe her nose with the back of her hand. Jack pulled out a handkerchief and handed it to her.

"See!" she said. "How many men still carry a handkerchief? You're just different."

He knew that Jenny was only partly right. It was Claire who was different.

Now here he stood, faced with the decision of whether to break the heart of a woman who had done nothing to deserve it—to tell her that he had, indeed, experienced that connection with someone else—or to let that someone else spend the rest of her life in jail—or, worse, to protect his butt.

"Jack, listen, just hold off for now, okay?" Jenny's pleading voice interrupted his thoughts. She had almost stopped crying. "Let's see what they come up with. Don't do anything you don't have to do, okay?" She paused, and when he didn't respond, she added, "Please?"

She was throwing him a lifeline. How could he not take it? He swallowed and nodded his acquiescence. He felt guilty for the ease with which he'd let her convince him. "I'm so sorry, Jenny."

"Don't be sorry. If it weren't for you, I wouldn't even have an alibi."

He thought of Alex. Maybe she would have had dinner with him, after all, if Jack hadn't been there. "If it weren't for me, maybe you'd have an alibi you felt comfortable using."

She squeezed his hands. Despite the solidity of the room, he couldn't tune out the sounds from the other side of the door: doors slamming, voices shouting, phones ringing, all magnified as a result of the barren surroundings. No carpet on the floors, no pictures on the walls, no wood furniture—everything was metal; there was nothing to absorb the noise. He'd never really noticed the noise before.

He moved his chair around from the other side of the table and sat next to her.

"When's your arraignment?"

"I'm not sure, next week sometime."

"What? That's crazy! You need to get your bail set and get out of here. You can't wait until next week." He remembered what he wanted to know. "Who's representing you?"

She looked scared, as if she was beginning to realize that perhaps everything that could be happening for her defense, wasn't. "I called Rob when they brought me in. He said they'd handle it through the arraignment, and in the meantime they'd find a criminal lawyer for me." Jack knew she meant Rob Kollman at Newman, and he now also knew she hadn't seen any papers. He held back telling her what he'd read.

"No. You need a criminal lawyer right now. You needed a criminal lawyer two days ago. It shouldn't take so long to get an arraignment scheduled." He stood and roamed the room. "The first few weeks are crucial." As his mind churned, he began to talk more to himself than to Jenny. "I'm going to call Earl. God, why didn't I think of that before? Yeah, I'll call Earl. He's perfect. You need someone who will think of you as more than just a client."

"Jack? Uh, in terms of experience, I mean . . . well, he hasn't been doing defense too long."

"No, you don't understand." He sat down again, facing her, and grasped her hands between his. "You couldn't ask for anyone more suited to this. The best criminal defense lawyer is a former prosecutor. He'll know exactly what they're thinking."

"Okay."

"You have to trust me on this one, Jen."

"I trust you."

"He'll have you arraigned and out of here on bail tomorrow."

"Okay," she repeated.

They both looked down at their hands. Neither made an effort to pull away.

"Listen to me. Did they give you any indication of what type of evidence they have against you?" He didn't mention what had been reported in the paper.

She shook her head without raising it to look at him.

"Is there anything, anything at all, that you can think of that they might be able to use to tie you to this? Is there someone who might want to set you up?" She continued to shake her head, but he sensed she wanted to tell him something. "What is it, Jen?"

She started to cry again. "It's crazy."

"Tell me. You have to tell me, even if it's crazy."

"I can't. I can't. You won't understand. You'll think I'm crazy. You'll hate me."

"I won't hate you. I could never hate you. You could tell me right now that you murdered Maxine Shepard and I still couldn't hate you."

She looked at him then, and it was the look he'd wanted so badly from her when he told her he loved her, but didn't get. A look that acknowledged how desperately she needed to hear what he'd said. And now it was too late, and they both knew it.

She lowered her head again and began to whisper; her voice was barely audible and he had to ask her to speak up. "I was at her house that day."

"Maxine's house?"

She nodded.

"What day? Thursday?"

He wanted her to hurry, just spill everything she had to tell him, but at the same time he wanted to run and pretend he'd never known her, because he feared what she was about to say. He tried to remember exactly what the articles had said. He was certain, yes, absolutely certain they all had said the murder occurred Thursday night or very early Friday morning.

"Before I met you in the garage that night?"

Another nod.

"Why, Jenny? Why were you at her house?"

She began to sob uncontrollably. He leaned closer and smoothed her hair to comfort her. His touch seemed to upset her more, but he couldn't stop. When he'd left on Friday morning, he'd thought he'd never touch her again.

"It's okay," he whispered. "Tell me anything. Whatever you tell me, it will be okay."

"I went because of Mendelsohn."

"Why?"

She began to shake her head, resisting. He grabbed her shoulders and shook her. "Why?" he repeated, more loudly this time.

"To tell Maxine what he'd done."

"What are you talking about?" He wanted to pry it out of her. Her fragmented answers were making him wild. "Did you find out more about Mendelsohn's involvement in the litigation you were handling for her?"

She tried to take a deep breath; her body shuddered when she exhaled. She nodded. "When I went back to my office—"

"When? After going to Maxine's?"

"No, after lunch that day. He was waiting for me. He was in my office." She blew her nose. "He was sitting in my chair, all smug-looking, and he says"—she imitated his voice—"'So, Ms. Dodson, have you heard the good news yet?' He was referring to the partnership decision. Stan had told me that morning that I'd made partner."

"You didn't tell me, Jen."

"Yeah, well . . ." She paused, as if reconsidering whether to say what was on her mind. "We were a little occupied with other things, wouldn't you say?"

Jack didn't respond, but he remembered her words: *You're very selfish*.

"Anyway, Mendelsohn told me I'd been voted in, but reminded me nothing was official until I signed all the papers and paid my equity. And then he says he got a phone call from Maxine that morning that could affect my partnership.

"He said that she had been reviewing her invoices from the firm and felt that I had billed way too much time on her cases. She wanted to know how I'd ever been allowed to rack up such exorbitant fees."

"What'd you say?"

"I defended the invoices." She laughed bitterly. "I told him, in so many words, to shove it up his ass. I hadn't done anything wrong and I knew it. And that's when I made my mistake."

"In what way?"

"I suggested that maybe it was he who had done something wrong."

The pieces of the puzzle were starting to fall into place, and what he'd seen so far scared him.

"The reason I'd billed so much to the files was because I was digging. I discovered that there was a reason Mendelsohn didn't try harder to dissuade Maxine from making those bad deals."

Jack waited, silent.

"It seems Maxine was investing in Mendelsohn, only she didn't know it."

"Whoa. You told him you knew?" he asked.

"Not really. I mean, I didn't come right out and tell him. But like I said, I did suggest that maybe he was the one doing something wrong." She started to cry again. "It was so stupid of me. I knew better, but he made me so mad. I let him get to me."

"What'd he say?"

She wiped her eyes with the damp handkerchief, trying to stop her tears. "Oh, you know, just what you'd expect from him. He lashed out at me. Threatened me. I think his exact words were something like 'You'd better be careful before making unfounded allegations against people, Ms. Dodson, or you might find it hard to get work in this city.' "

"Tell me how you ended up at Maxine's house," Jack said gently.

"I went to tell her what I'd discovered. I was afraid that because I'd hinted to him that I knew he'd done something wrong, he'd try to get to her first, and then she wouldn't believe me."

"Do you think he found out that you went there?"

"I don't know. Why?"

He looked at her. He didn't want to tell her. "Jenny, Mendelsohn's telling the papers that Newman has been investigating you."

"What do you mean? Investigating me for what?"

He hesitated. "For embezzlement. I think he's trying to make it look like you were the one bilking Maxine, not him."

Fear began to cloud her eyes as she began to understand. If Mendelsohn believed his scheme was crumbling, and if he knew that Jenny had already gotten to Maxine, he might have tried to use Jenny's visit to kill two birds with one stone. He could get rid of Maxine and at the same time make it look like Jenny had done it.

"Oh God." She began to wail again. "I was so stupid! How was I supposed to know? I would never have dreamed he was capable of something like that."

"Jenny, listen to me," he demanded. "Just because you were there . . . that's not enough. You know that."

She nodded but didn't look convinced. He reached up and touched her hair again.

"Tell me something. Why didn't you just go to Stan after this conversation with Mendelsohn?"

"I planned to, eventually. But I wanted to talk to Maxine first. I didn't want to go to Stan until I had all my ducks in a row, you know?"

"You went straight to her house after your meeting with Mendelsohn?"

Jenny nodded.

"Did you call her? Was she expecting you?"

"No. I was afraid if I called her ahead of time, she wouldn't see me."

"What happened when you saw her?"

"She was very rude to me when I first arrived. She wouldn't even let me in." She smiled sadly. "You would have been very proud of me, Jack. I kept my cool the whole time, and that's why she finally agreed to listen to me. I'd brought my files with me so I could explain to her what I'd discovered, and I asked her if we could go over them together."

Jack tried to process all the information she had given him. "Jenny, how much are we talking about? How much did he take her for?"

"It's easily in the hundreds of thousands."

"Jesus." He shook his head in disbelief. "Why would he do that? Why would he risk everything like that?"

Her head had been hanging low; she'd kept her eyes down through most of her explanation. But then she looked up at him, her sad eyes cutting into him laser-sharp. He looked away, and all she said was "I don't know; that's the part I haven't figured out."

There was a knock at the door and the guard shouted, "Two minutes, Mr. Hilliard."

"Jenny, tell me quickly. Did Maxine understand?"

"Yes, yes," she said, nodding vehemently. "She planned to come to the firm the next day, and we were going to meet with Stan to tell him what I'd discovered." She began to cry again, though she tried to contain it. "It's my word against Mendelsohn now."

"No, there are the documents."

"I don't know, Jack. He's not stupid. He's probably already gathered the files and destroyed them. I locked them in my office when I left on Friday. But if he'd commit murder, I'm sure he'd have no qualms about breaking into my office to find those files. I'm sure they're history now."

"There's gotta be a paper trail, Jen, or something. What about the other attorneys, the ones who were fired? They'll back you up."

"I don't know. We don't know how much they know."

He paused, thinking. "What happened Friday, when Maxine didn't show up for your meeting with Stan?"

"I tried to call her house, but of course she never answered. I left several messages."

"That can only help your defense."

"I didn't even see Mendelsohn. His secretary told me he was out all day speaking at some seminar. So I relaxed a bit. I felt maybe I'd been a bit paranoid and that he had no intentions of going to Maxine. I decided that he must have believed I'd back off after he threatened me. I left work that day around five and spent the weekend in Chicago. I didn't even know she'd been murdered until"—she paused to take a deep breath—"until they picked me up getting off the plane on Sunday."

"Jesus." He could just imagine the scene at the airport. He wondered what had gone through Jenny's head when she learned that Maxine had been murdered the same night she'd been with him. "Listen, the guard will be back any second. I'll call Earl as soon as I leave. I'll tell him all this, but you need to tell him, too, okay? Everything. Everything you can think of."

She nodded.

"You haven't told this to Rob or anyone else from Newman, have you?"

"No, no one's been over to see me yet. I keep calling them, and they say they're coming, but no one's showed up yet."

He looked at her in disbelief.

"I was afraid to call you."

"I'm sorry. I was trying to get in. I can't believe I didn't think to call Earl as soon as I'd heard. I was just so . . . after everything . . . I couldn't think straight. He'll get you out today. I promise, okay?"

"Yes," she whispered. "Can I ask a favor?"

"Anything."

"Will you feed my cats? They're probably getting a little hungry by now."

He smiled. "Yeah, Jen, I'll feed your cats." He reached to smooth a stray hair, but she leaned away.

"It's going to work out; don't worry. I'm sure of it." She stood. "You should go now."

The door opened without warning and the guard stepped in. "Sorry, Mr. Hilliard, the boss is going to be on my case if I let you stay any longer. I've already stretched it."

Jack nodded and turned back to Jenny. "I'll be at the arraignment," he whispered.

"Jack." She grabbed his arm as he started to leave. "Not even Earl."

He hesitated, unsure of her meaning. And then it dawned on him. "But—"

"Not even Earl, Jack. Promise."

"Okay." *I promise,* he mouthed.

When he left the building, he saw a late-model Chrysler parked at the bottom of the steps against the curb in the no-parking zone. He recognized the man in the passenger seat—Jim Wolfe, the legal reporter who had questioned him at the lake last summer. He must have staked out the court building and followed him to the jail. Jack turned quickly, hoping that Wolfe hadn't seen him, but when he reached the corner he heard the car door slam.

"Mr. Hilliard," Wolfe called to him.

Jack waved without turning around, to signify, *Not now.*

"Mr. Hilliard," Wolfe called again, closer this time. "Just a moment of your time, please."

In an instant he was next to Jack, walking with him.

"Mr. Hilliard, did you see Ms. Dodson? Can you tell me what was said?"

Jack stopped abruptly. "Mister, uh, what's your name again?" he said, though he knew.

"Jim Wolfe."

"Mr. Wolfe. You're aware that I'm a lawyer."

"Yes, sir, of course, but you're not Ms. Dodson's lawyer. There's no privilege attached to your communication."

"Thank you for that little legal lesson. I'm well aware there's no privilege in a court of law, but in the court of media, it's the privilege between friends not to have their discussions plastered on the front page of tomorrow's paper." He turned and started walking again.

"Was Ms. Dodson aware that authorities searched her home late last night?"

He kept walking, trying not to let Wolfe see his surprise. The cats. The gun. *There's no law against having a gun, Jack.* He wondered if she had it properly registered. Strike number two. One more, would she be out?

"Has anyone informed her that the authorities think they found the murder weapon?"

The murder weapon? Her gun? He struggled to maintain his composure.

"Sir?" Wolfe persisted.

"Mr. Wolfe, as I'm sure you're aware, my office has disqualified itself from this case. I don't think it would be proper to comment on it." He had to get away from the guy and call Earl.

"Do you know whether they're going to seek the death penalty? After all, it was you who said it would be enforced in appropriate cases."

Jesus, she hadn't even been arraigned, and they were already out for blood. He suppressed the urge to turn and slug the guy. "Yes, but I'm not handling this case, am I? So I'm not making the decision. Now, as I said, I won't be commenting. You'll need to speak to Mr. Sterling."

He climbed the steps of the courthouse, Wolfe still shadowing him. Just inside, he nodded to the guard as he bypassed the metal detector. "I think Mr. Wolfe has something on him that might set it off," he said to the guard.

Then, with one last look at the reporter, he added, "It's probably the belt."

CHAPTER SEVENTEEN

Jack had been in Clark & Cavanaugh's offices before, but not since Earl had joined the firm. He'd assumed his first visit would be of a more celebratory nature.

Earl's office was on the twenty-eighth floor of a twenty-eight-story building. As Jack rode the elevator, he considered whether to tell him the whole truth, despite his promise to Jenny. But he recognized that part of his desire to confess had more to do with unburdening himself than with advancing Jenny's defense.

His old boss greeted him when he stepped off the elevator. "Do you feel like the top banana yet?" Earl asked as they shook hands. They hadn't seen each other since just after the election.

"Not since this case broke." He followed Earl past the receptionist's desk and down a long hall of partitioned secretarial cubicles. He lowered his voice to avoid being heard. "They picked her up on Sunday night, and I just got in to see her today."

"What was the problem?" Earl stopped at the end of the hall and waved Jack on into the corner office without waiting for an answer to the question. Jack heard him request coffee as he wandered into the large room. His eyes were immediately drawn to the walls of glass and the pink reflection of the late-afternoon sun on the towering legs of the Arch. He edged closer to the windows and looked down at the river.

"They even gave you a corner office, huh?" he commented when Earl joined him.

"I don't have many clients yet, but I've got a name. That's worth just as much if not more."

Jack felt himself blush, but if Earl noticed, he ignored it. "So why'd you have trouble getting in to see her?" he asked. He sat on a leather couch in front of the south-facing window and motioned for Jack to take a seat.

"I'm not sure, exactly. That asshole from Franklin County kept jerking me around. Claimed he wasn't sure if I could see her, even though the whole office has disqualified itself."

"That's bullshit." Earl loosened his tie and undid his top button. "Can I give you some advice?"

"Don't you always? Why should it be any different now that you're here?"

"I'm serious, Jack."

"So am I."

"If you don't act like the boss, they're not going to treat you like the boss. I don't care if you're new to the job. No more Mr. Nice Guy. You need to assert yourself. Raise your voice if you have to. It's a different game now."

Indignation crept through Jack's body. It was as if Earl was accusing him of acting. "I am who I am, Earl."

"That's true. And I respect that, obviously. Just don't worry too much about making friends."

Jack nodded.

"So what's going on?"

"I don't know. I just know she didn't do it."

Earl cleared his throat. He leaned back into the couch with his hands behind his head and frowned. "Well, despite your friendship with her, I beg to differ about what you 'know.' As a prosecutor, you're well aware that stranger things have happened."

Jack tensed. "I said, I know she didn't do it. I don't want you representing her unless you believe that."

Silence filled the room. Jack's insistence that Earl accept Jenny's innocence without question was unwarranted, and they both knew it. It wasn't what he was paid to do. The challenge remained unanswered when a knock at the door announced the arrival of their coffee.

"Okay," Earl said when the secretary had left. "We'll just skip the topic of guilt or innocence for now. You're too close. Why don't you tell me about your visit to the jail?"

Jack considered repeating his demand but thought better of it. He *was* too close, but not in the way Earl thought. He feared that if he pushed the issue, he'd be tempted to reveal his involvement just to convince him.

"She told me some stuff that leads me to believe she's been set up."

"Go on. I can tell you already have a suspect."

"I know you'll think this sounds crazy, but I've got a feeling that Newman's involved."

"Well, there's obviously some connection. They claim they've been investigating her."

Earl's lack of shock at Jack's suggestion reassured him. "Right, right. *Mendelsohn* claims so. I'll get to that in a sec." Jack was eager to tell Earl everything at once; he tried to slow down.

"Listen, she was brought in Sunday night, right? She told me she called Rob Kollman, but no one's been over to talk to her yet. And get this: she told me she thought her arraignment was scheduled for sometime next week."

"What's that prove, except they're inept." He rolled his eyes. "I'll have her out by tomorrow."

Jack knew Earl never really respected the big firms that practiced only civil law. To Earl, if it wasn't criminal law, it wasn't real law. Everything else represented nothing more than a means of transferring wealth.

"No. Today. I promised her you'd get her out *today*."

"Christ, Jack! I'm not a miracle worker."

"She's scared. I have to get her out of there. You must have some favors you can call in."

"What else?"

"I find out from a reporter who snagged me leaving the jail that they've already searched her house. Jenny didn't mention it, so I don't think she even knows."

"Merely more ineptitude." Earl was unimpressed. "Let's hope they didn't find anything incriminating."

"She's got a gun," Jack blurted.

Earl shrugged. "And I'm sure it's being tested right now. Unless it's the same gun used to kill Maxine Shepard, it doesn't matter. You know that."

"The reporter said they think they found the murder weapon."

"Bullshit. He's just trying to get a rise out of you. Until they've tested it, he has no basis for saying anything like that." He got up and repositioned himself on the arm of the couch so that he could look outside. "Come on, Jack, nothing you've told me points to Newman. I'm right. You are too close to this, in more ways than one."

"I'm not done. I've saved the best for last."

"I'm waiting."

"Look, I'm not alleging a conspiracy. But there are those at the firm who I believe would do anything to protect their butts."

Earl's lips tightened. He was obviously waiting for the evidence to back up Jack's claims.

"You know, Earl, you never asked why they fired me."

"It didn't matter. I'd heard enough good things about you, and I never give much credence to the reasons a big firm gives for letting someone go. It happens too often, for political reasons."

"What'd they tell you?"

"I never called them."

"What?" Jack was incredulous.

"I told you. It wouldn't have mattered to me." He tilted his head and searched Jack's face. "Okay, so why'd they fire you?"

Jack thought back to the night Mendelsohn called him into his office, one just as big as Earl's but much more opulent. Jack had known, even before he reached the door, that when he left that night he wouldn't be coming back. He knew that after talking to Mendelsohn he'd return to his office to find a guard and a few empty boxes for his personal things. He'd be watched as he packed, and then they'd escort him from the building.

He remembered sitting on the other side of Mendelsohn's large glass-top desk, listening to him claim that Jack really didn't fit the firm's culture, that he really wasn't a team player, that he didn't share the same goals and probably would never be happy there, and that they were doing him a favor by letting him go. And all the while they both knew that it was doublespeak for, *You disobeyed me, you crossed me, and you must pay*. And they both knew, without it being said, that if Jack protested, tried to go public with what had really happened, Mendelsohn would deny it. As the older, more well known and respected attorney, he would be the one whom everyone believed. Back then, he had the power to ruin Jack's career.

"I'd worked on a product liability case with Mendelsohn. It was pretty obvious our client was going to lose, that they were negligent, but of course Mendelsohn insisted on fighting, on papering the plaintiff to death so they'd settle more quickly and, hopefully, for less money. But the plaintiff's attorney was smart and tough, and knew they had a strong case, so he papered us right back. I ended up doing massive amounts of document review at the client's manufacturing plant to respond to the endless document requests. I came across a very damaging intercompany memo. The minute I read it, I knew the case was no longer about negligence, but intentional tort. It wasn't what our client 'should have known,' but what they did know and didn't do anything about."

Earl was riveted. "The client showed you this memo?"

Jack shook his head. "No. You have to understand, I reviewed a lot of documents. A lot. This was a copy. I don't think they realized it existed. We never found the original. They had probably destroyed it, without telling us."

"What'd you do?"

"I went to Mendelsohn, of course, thinking we could brainstorm, figure out some privilege to hold it back or somehow justify to ourselves why it wasn't within the scope of the requests."

Jack stopped and thought of his statement to Jenny: *Evidence can be twisted*. At the time, he thought he'd done the right thing. That's what lawyers did, wasn't it? That's what they were paid for, to use the rules and bend them in their clients' favor. Now, for the first time, he wondered if he was only slightly above Mendelsohn on the low end of the ethics scale.

"Jack?"

"He told me to destroy it. Pretend like it never existed, that I'd never seen it."

Earl immediately understood the implications of Jack's accusation. "And?"

"And I didn't, of course. I spent a lot of unbillable time in the library researching how I might be able to legitimately withhold it, but, not surprisingly, I couldn't come up with anything. I agonized over what to do." He laughed bitterly. "You know me, Earl. Mr. Nice Guy."

"You produced it."

"Yes. Although I did bury it in the middle of a bunch of irrelevant junk. I figured I'd at least buy some time. I hoped the case might settle before they found it. I felt guilty just for doing that."

"Mendelsohn found out and fired you over it?"

Jack nodded. "But not right away. It took a while. Mendelsohn was furious. He assumed that I'd done what he instructed, so he never even discussed the memo with the client, or what could happen to the case if the plaintiff knew about it. Had he done so, he could have encouraged them to settle for what the plaintiff was demanding at the time. Which, needless to say, was a lot less than what the case eventually settled for."

"Or *you* could have."

"What?"

"You could have discussed it with the client."

Jack shook his head vehemently. "It wasn't like that. I wasn't at that level. The most I ever interacted with the client was at the plant, talking to the secretaries." He knew the point Earl was trying to make: Jack wasn't completely blameless. "But, yeah, you're right. After I was no longer in the middle of it, I realized I could have done things differently. Had I been thinking straight, I would have told Mendelsohn right away that I produced it, so that he could counsel the client. I still would have endured his wrath, but at least the client would have had the chance to settle before they came across it. If it had settled early, no one would ever have bothered to look in that pile of documents we produced.

"He waited a few months before getting rid of me, so it would look unrelated. But he made it clear to me, in his own cryptic way, what my firing was about."

"But he still contributed to your campaign." Earl spoke matter-of-factly, not as if he doubted Jack.

Jack smiled, again feeling the small sense of satisfaction he'd felt when Mendelsohn's check arrived. "Oh yeah. Given the recent stuff that's been going on with him, he probably thought he'd buy himself some extra insurance to maintain my silence. He doesn't need any more problems."

Earl sat straighter. He seemed more receptive now to Jack's suggestion that Mendelsohn could be involved in Jenny's case. "What recent stuff?"

Jack explained first what Jenny had told him last spring about Maxine and her bad investment deals, and then he relayed everything she'd told him in the jail. Earl rose and paced the room as Jack talked. At times he almost wondered if Earl was even listening to him. At one point Earl hovered behind his desk; it looked to Jack as if he was reviewing his calendar.

"If we start pointing the finger at Newman," he muttered, "it's not going to be pretty."

It's not pretty now, Jack wanted to say.

Earl moved over to the window and gazed down at the river. He frowned in thought and then walked back to his desk and pulled a cigar out of the middle drawer. Jack watched him. He'd never known Earl to smoke.

"Little housewarming gift from my new partners," Earl said in response to Jack's gaze. He struck a match and took his time lighting the cigar. "You're not going to like this question, but don't you think it's a little odd that she went over there?"

"Not really."

"Not really?"

"No."

The room fell silent, and Jack heard an attorney in the hall hollering for his secretary to find a file.

"What's Claire think about all this?" Earl asked.

The question caught him by surprise. He still held his coffee cup and he noticed his hand begin to shake. He set down the cup. "What do you mean?"

"Just what I said. What's she think about all this?"

"I haven't talked to her since seeing Jenny. She doesn't know any of this stuff I've just told you."

"I'm not talking about Newman. I'm talking about the murder charge."

"I don't know. She was shocked, upset. She knows Jenny didn't do it."

"Because you told her that?"

"No." Jack scooted up a bit in his chair, as if to get closer to the table in front of him. But he knew he was just fidgeting. "Claire's a good judge of character."

Earl crossed the room and opened the door to his office. He asked his secretary to get one of the judges on the phone.

When he returned, Jack braced for the inevitable, reminding himself of his promise to Jenny. The sweet smell of the cigar began to fill the room. Earl leaned up closer. "Look, Jack, I just need you to be straight with me."

"I am being straight with you." But he heard a falsetto note creeping into his voice.

"Why are you so certain she didn't do it?" Earl narrowed his eyes.

"I told you. I just know." He had to give him more. "Look, I've known her for over nine years. When she finds a bug in her house, she doesn't kill it, she puts it outside, you know? She adopts every stray she finds. And I'm not just talking animals. She practically sponsors this homeless guy who she runs into on her way to work. She talks tough, but she's not. She's a pussycat. I know she doesn't have it in her to kill anyone."

But it was as if Earl hadn't heard a word he'd said. "Listen to me. Are you involved in this case at all, in any way? I need to know everything if you want me to defend her."

"Yeah, I'm involved in this case." He felt his anger rising, although he knew he had no right. Earl was doing his job—the job Jack was asking him to do. "I happen to be a close friend of the defendant. And the media doesn't seem to want to let me forget it."

"From an evidentiary standpoint? I need to know."

"No."

"You're not trying to protect her in any way?"

Quite the contrary, Earl. She's protecting me. "Why don't you just come out and ask me whatever it is you want to ask?" But even as he spoke, he prayed that Earl wouldn't press it.

"I'm not going to suggest anything. Just don't keep me in the dark if there's something I need to know. Okay?"

Earl's secretary knocked and peeked in. "Judge Baxter is on line one, Earl."

Jack tried to relax as he listened to Earl's banter with the judge. He closed his eyes. *Get to the point,* he thought as Earl asked about the judge's wife and then talked about the last poker game they'd attended together. He finally stood and tried to calm himself by looking out the window again.

"Listen, Judge, I need a favor." Earl's tone was still chatty. He laughed heartily, and Jack wondered how the judge had responded. "The Dodson girl, brought in for her client's murder? It looks like I'm going to be representing her. She's been in since Sunday night, and I've been told that her arraignment isn't scheduled until next week. Do you have any time this afternoon so we can appear? I'd like to get her bail set and get her out of there."

Jack spotted a plane in the distance flying away from the city. He wondered where it was headed. He remembered his comment to Jenny about scheduling a trip to India. Get her out of there. And then what?

A change in Earl's tone brought him back to the phone conversation.

"No, Judge, I didn't know," Earl said, all hint of levity gone. "I haven't been in contact with Sterling yet." When he hung up, he said to Jack, "Two o'clock, as long as I can get Sterling to agree. Another inmate is coming over for a hearing, so the judge agreed to let her appear at the same time."

"Thank you," Jack said.

"There's something you need to know."

At Earl's ominous tone, Jack turned back him.

"The judge said . . . well, he said he's been advised that this could be a capital case."

"What?" Jack shook his head. "What are you talking about?"

"Just what I said. Sterling thinks he's going to ask for the death penalty."

Jack slowly moved away from the window and fell into the closest chair.

"The judge told you that?"

"Sterling was courteous enough to advise him of his decision before going to the press."

Courteous enough? This man from Franklin County, who knew nothing about Jenny, about her life, was somehow entitled to be the sole arbiter of whether a jury could be given the choice to take that life away, to put her to death for a crime she didn't commit? He hadn't even allowed the ink on the arrest warrant to dry, and here he was already talking about the punishment.

"Jack?"

He lifted his head slowly to meet Earl's eyes.

"Now would you like to tell me about your involvement in this case?"

When he just shook his head again, Earl said, "You need to tell me. I suspect she'll be a better liar than you."

Yes, she was a good liar, wasn't she? The way she'd turned on him that morning, so believable that he'd had trouble remembering the events of the night before. So convincing in her coldness that he had forgotten how just hours before she'd warmed and let him in. And even at the jail she had lied to him, persuading him that everything would be okay, that they could never come up with anything to convict her, that the two of them would be able to keep their secret. All to protect him. She was willing to sacrifice herself to protect him.

"I'm her alibi," he whispered.

Earl stood and went to Jack's chair. He sat on the arm and leaned in. "*What* did you just say?"

"I'm her alibi." Jack stared at the edge of the desk in front of him. If he blinked, he was unaware of it. "I spent that night with her, at her place. That's why I'm so sure of her innocence."

"Oh, Jesus." Earl dropped his head into the palm of his hand and rubbed the leathery skin of his face. "Does Claire know?"

Jack laughed bitterly. "Oh yeah. Sure. You know, the minister forgot to include the part about forsaking all others, so it's no problem."

Earl was silent. The silence didn't seem calculated; it lacked the manipulative tension that usually accompanied Earl's failure to speak. He walked to the credenza behind his desk and carefully lifted a picture. Jack hadn't noticed it before, but now, as he watched Earl, he knew that it was a framed snapshot Claire had given to Earl and Helen. Jack knew the picture without looking at it. It was of the four of them, from a Bench & Bar conference years before—before Jamie was born. Jack had stared into the camera lens while Claire was looking at him. Claire had always laughed about it and said they'd snapped the picture just as she was reminding him to smile.

Earl turned to Jack and a slight, nostalgic smile lit his face. "I don't think I've ever met a woman who revered her husband quite like Claire reveres you."

At that moment, Jack knew that Earl wasn't talking just about Claire. Like the instant when a foggy dream from the night before becomes crystal clear, he suddenly realized that Earl thought of him as the son he'd never had. What Jack had done dishonored not only Claire, but Earl, too.

He was about to attempt an apology, however feeble and useless it would be, but Earl's voice came to life first.

"I don't get it. She's willing to go to jail to prevent you from being exposed?"

Jack shrank with shame at Earl's question. How had he ever agreed to Jenny's crazy gag order? She'd made it sound so reasonable.

"Well, sort of. But not really." The words came out hoarsely. "Since she didn't do it, she thinks it's a given that she can beat it without my alibi."

"Unbelievable. And the two of you agreed that I didn't need to know this, even though you asked me to represent her? She's a naïve bankruptcy attorney, but you know better, Jack."

"Yeah, well, I've learned that I don't think straight in her presence." He looked down at the floor, embarrassed that he'd finally admitted what Earl had been accusing him of all along. Earl had seen it coming and tried to head it off at the pass, but Jack had just plowed on by.

"Do you love her?" Earl's voice was barely audible. He seemed afraid both to ask the question and to hear the answer.

How to respond? He'd told her that he loved her, hadn't he? Was it possible to love two women at the same time? Despite his confusion about Jenny, he was certain that he loved Claire, had always loved Claire. It was Claire, not Jenny, whom he couldn't bear to lose. He thought of Jenny's statement, *I'm not interested in being someone's mistress*, and knew that she'd understood this all along.

"Jack?" Earl's voice was gentler than Jack had ever heard it. "I need to get over to the jail and see her. We can talk about this later."

Jack nodded his acquiescence. Earl grabbed his coat from the back of the door and motioned for Jack to follow him. He put his arm around Jack's shoulders as they stepped into the elevator. The unexpected physical contact was almost more than he could bear.

"I'll take care of her," Earl said. "We'll figure this thing out. You just do your job; don't get sidetracked. I'll take care of her for you."

Jack knew then that if he went down and brought the Office of the District Attorney with him, Earl—like Claire—would never forgive him.

CHAPTER EIGHTEEN

After feeding Jenny's cats and trying to straighten the mess made by the cops in their search, Jack arrived at the courthouse with only twenty minutes to spare. He was so focused on getting to Judge Baxter's courtroom on time that he didn't even see Claire sitting on the granite wall that lined the steps to the entrance.

"Jack!" she called to him.

He stopped.

"Jack," she repeated when she reached him.

"What are you doing here?"

"Where have you been? Are you okay? Everyone's worried about you."

"What?" Everyone was worried about him? What was she talking about? She touched his arm and began to lead him the rest of the way up the stairs.

"I called to see if you ever got in to see Jenny, and Beverly said you had, but she hadn't heard from you since. So I asked her to call the jail, and they told her you'd come and gone already, but Earl was there. We found out about the arraignment from Earl. We'd both tried to call you on your cell phone, but it was shut off."

She paused in front of the metal detector, waiting for a response, but he merely pulled out his phone and looked to see if he'd turned it off. He had, though he didn't remember doing it.

"Jack?"

"Yeah?"

"Where have you been?"

He dropped his keys and phone in a small plastic basket and walked through the detector with Claire following him. He wondered if the cops had already come through the rear door with Jenny. Once they reached the elevators, he finally looked at Claire again.

"I went over to her house. She asked me to feed her cats."

Claire's face went blank. Jack knew what she was thinking: How long does it take to feed cats?

"They'd searched her place," he said. And then, in an effort to explain the time gap, he added, "I tried to put it back together a little for her."

They stood on opposite sides of the elevator. When the doors closed, he asked, "Why are you here?"

"I came here to support her. Why do you think?"

He nodded, bit his bottom lip. Of course.

They stepped off the elevator to a small crowd trying to work its way into the courtroom. He saw Jim Wolfe and knew there had to be more reporters. He wondered how they'd gotten wind of the arraignment so quickly and if Earl and Jenny were already inside.

"Hang back a bit," he instructed Claire. He didn't want any reporters to see him until the last possible minute, when it would be too late to question him.

When the hallway was all but empty, Jack grabbed her hand and led her in. Everyone was standing, milling about in the narrow aisles between the benches, but Jack could see well enough past the crowd to know that Jenny had not been brought in yet. He pushed past spectators to get to the front, keenly aware of the fact that, after Jenny, he was the next most-gossiped-about person in the room. He was suddenly grateful for Claire's presence; he gripped her hand more tightly and pulled her through.

He saw Rob Kollman sitting at the defense table and began to get nervous. Where was Earl? Rob saw Jack and nodded in greeting; Jack returned the gesture. He managed, with a smile and few handshakes, to secure seats for himself and Claire just behind the bar.

"This is a zoo," she whispered as they sat down on the hard bench.

Minutes later, the door to the back halls opened and Jack saw Earl standing in the entryway. When they emerged from the hall, Earl was talking to Jenny as if there wasn't another soul in the room. Despite the rising clamor, Jenny's expression was impenetrable, and she kept her eyes on Earl's face, nodding to acknowledge whatever he was telling her. Jack knew that Earl was talking nonstop to distract her and help her ignore the circus. Earl had obviously seen right through Jenny's tough act and knew how fragile she would be in this setting. He was taking care of her, just as he'd promised Jack.

The bailiff slammed the gavel and shouted for everyone to take their seats. Rob stood and pulled out the middle chair for Jenny, and Earl took the chair on her other side. It was then, just as she was about to turn and take her seat, that she allowed herself to look at Jack.

Less than five feet separated them. It lasted only a second, if that. He stared at the back of her head and tried by sheer mental force to know what she wanted him to do, all the while feeling ashamed because it really didn't matter. He knew what he should do. He just didn't have the strength to do it.

"Please be seated," the judge said loudly. He directed his attention to Earl. "Mr. Scanlon, it's going to take some getting used to, seeing you on that side of the courtroom." Nervous laughter hummed through the room. The judge saw Jack then, and for a moment Jack feared he was going to comment on him, too, but instead he just nodded and turned his attention to Sterling.

"Mr. Sterling, sir," he said, nodding politely to him, too. "Thank you for being available to handle this matter on such short notice. Is there anything either party needs to bring before the Court before we read the charges?"

Jack fidgeted, his foot tapping softly on the floor, while Earl explained that although Newman had initially acted as Jenny's attorney, he had subsequently filed his entry of appearance and his firm would be handling the case in its entirety. Rob confirmed Newman's withdrawal from the case.

The judge bent down and whispered to his clerk and then they both looked at Jenny.

"Ms. Dodson? Please rise for the reading of the information."

Earl leaned over and said something into her ear—words of encour-
agement, Jack knew. She stood up and teetered slightly. Did he imagine
it? The clerk stood, too, and in a slow monotone read the charges against
her for the first-degree murder of Maxine Carson Shepard.

When she finished, the judge spoke. "Ms. Dodson, how do you plead
to the charges?"

"Not guilty, Your Honor." She spoke the only four words she would
speak in court that day loudly and clearly. Somehow, Earl had instilled the
fight back in her.

Earl stood. "Your Honor, we ask that the Court dismiss the charges
for lack of evidence—"

"Denied," the judge interrupted, doing what both Jack and Earl had
known he would. Earl's request had been nothing more than a formality.

"We'd further ask the Court to set bond at this time."

The judge nodded and turned to Sterling. "Mr. Sterling?"

"Your Honor, since filing these charges, we have collected additional
evidence that links Ms. Dodson to this crime. In light of this, we would
ask the Court to hold Ms. Dodson until trial."

"To what additional evidence are you referring?" Judge Baxter asked.

"Police officers searched her home late last night, and at that time they
found a Walther PPK pistol, .380 caliber, which they suspected might be
the murder weapon. Test results received this morning confirmed their
suspicions."

Jack felt as if someone had just punched him in the gut. *That's impossible,* he thought. Earl whirled around and narrowed his eyes at him, but it
wasn't until Claire chastised him—"Jack, shh"—that he realized he'd
spoken aloud and that everyone else in the front of the courtroom was
looking at him, too. But he didn't care. More of a blow to him than Sterling's statement was Jenny's reaction to it—or really, her lack thereof. She
sat immobile, her back erect against the hard wooden chair, her hands still
crossed ladylike in her lap. She hadn't even twitched, for crying out loud.
As if she'd expected this bit of information all along. *As if she'd known her
gun had been used to kill Maxine Shepard.*

When he thought it couldn't get any worse, he heard Earl say, "Your Honor, Ms. Dodson has an airtight alibi"—the courtroom emitted a collective gasp—"which we will reveal at the appropriate time. When we do, it will become readily apparent to everyone that she had nothing whatsoever to do with this crime."

As Jack tried to process that Earl had used the word *alibi* in open court, the other lawyers moved on to arguing over the amount of the bond.

"Jesus," he muttered. Suddenly Claire was feeling his cheek and forehead with the back of her hand.

"Are you okay?" she whispered, her voice shaky. "You're as white as a ghost."

Was he okay? He looked at Claire as if she was a stranger. And really, at that moment, she was. He wanted to grab Jenny by the shoulders and demand, *Why aren't you surprised that your gun was the murder weapon?* He wanted to shout at Earl, *Why did you mention an alibi?* But most of all, he wanted to drag Claire into the hall and confess right there and beg her forgiveness. More than anything, he wanted Claire's forgiveness.

As it became clear the hearing was drawing to a close, he whispered to Claire to stay put, he'd be back to get her. He quietly left his seat and tried to slip down the outer aisle near the windows as unobtrusively as possible. He waited in the back corridor behind the courtroom; his plan was to intercept Jenny and her entourage as they came out.

But this was a part of the process he'd never seen as an attorney for the state. He'd always remained at his table after a hearing, until the guards escorted the defendants out of the courtroom, sometimes with their attorneys, sometimes without. He'd never seen or really thought about what happened once they disappeared through the door through which they'd come in.

He knew, of course, that she wouldn't be released immediately; she'd be taken back to the jail until arrangements were made to have the bond posted. And he knew that for a bond so large—the judge had set it at one million, though she'd have to come up with only 10 percent of that—it could take a while. What he didn't know was that they would handcuff her again as soon as they stepped into the hall, and even Earl would have only a brief moment to speak to her. For Jack to have a moment with her would be out of the question.

Their eyes met briefly as she walked through the door. But she ignored him otherwise and focused on Earl just as she had when she'd entered the courtroom. She pretended not to notice as one of the guards, a large, balding man with a red, shiny face and stubby fingers, cuffed her. In one smooth, practiced motion the guard slipped one cuff around her wrist and clamped it shut, and then he pulled her arms together and effortlessly did the same with the other. Jenny left her arms limp throughout the short maneuver, but Jack, believing the guard to be unnecessarily rough, felt his own arms tense, his fists clench. At least the jackass had left her arms in front.

"She's okay, she'll be fine," Earl said as the guard led her away. With a touch on Jack's sleeve, he tried to lead him in the opposite direction, back toward the large foyer outside the main entrance to the courtroom.

"What were you doing in there?" Jack said under his breath. "Are you crazy? Why didn't you tell me you were going to—"

"Calm down," Earl ordered.

"I can't calm down. In case you forgot, *I'm* the fucking alibi! Don't you think you should have told me? Why'd you bring up the alibi?"

"I'm trying to save that girl's life. I know what I'm doing." Earl was mad now. "I shouldn't have to tell you that."

"No, but you should have to tell me what—"

"Listen to me. I didn't use names, did I? Now relax." Though no one was around, he grabbed Jack's arm and pulled him closer to the wall for privacy. "I want to see how Mendelsohn reacts to the news, all right? If he thinks she has an alibi, he might start to crumble more easily."

It made sense but it scared him like hell. "What did she say about the gun?" he asked. "Did you have a chance to talk to her about the gun?"

"Yes, I—"

"Why the hell was she so calm in there when they trotted out that stuff about the gun?"

"She already—"

"She didn't even flinch!"

Earl crossed his arms, leaned back against the wall, and let out a large sigh. "Why don't you tell me? Why was she so calm? Why didn't she flinch?"

"I don't know!"

"So you expected her to be surprised?"

"Yes, of course I did."

"Why?'

Jack felt Earl backing him into a corner, but he wasn't sure how it was happening or why. "Because she's innocent," he said.

"And you know that with one-hundred-percent certainty?"

Jack swallowed. "Yes."

"And an innocent person would be surprised to learn that her gun was used to commit the crime, wouldn't she?"

A staring contest ensued. Was Earl insinuating that Jenny was guilty?

"She didn't do it," he insisted.

Earl studied him for a moment longer, and then, as if in the middle of his line of questioning he decided to take a different tack. He said, "For your information, she *was* surprised when I told her about the gun. In fact, it was the only time during my visit with her that she seemed visibly upset."

"What do you mean, 'when you told her'?"

"At the jail, before I went in to see her, I called Sterling about having the bail hearing today, and he told me they'd just received the results on the gun. I told Jenny about it, of course, when I saw her."

He must have seen the relief on Jack's face.

"Were you doubting her in there?" His tone was unfriendly, accusatory.

"No, of course not." Jack lowered his eyes. *Was he?*

Except for the muffled sounds of footsteps and conversations and elevators on the other side of the door, the hallway was quiet. He remembered that Claire was still waiting for him, and he wanted to escape Earl's penetrating gaze.

"I need to get back out there. Claire's waiting. Can you get a message to Jenny for me?"

"Certainly."

"Ask her to call me as soon as possible?"

"I'll tell her, but I wouldn't hold my breath if I were you. She's pissed at you for telling me your little secret. I had to persuade her to let me do what I did today in court. She wants me to tell you that she thinks it best if you keep your distance from her during all this."

"Really? She really said that?"

"Yeah." Earl stared hard at Jack. "She really said that."

CHAPTER NINETEEN

Jack followed Jenny's instructions, for the most part. It had been almost two weeks since the arraignment and he'd spoken to her only once. Their phone conversation had been short and polite; neither brought up how—or why—he'd confessed to Earl, despite his promise not to do so. She explained that Newman had given her a leave of absence and she was passing the time reading, taking walks, organizing her house, and screening calls. She asked about Claire. It was almost as if his visit to the jail had never happened, not to mention everything that had gone before. An eavesdropper would never have suspected what had transpired between them. He told her he wanted to see her, but she didn't think it was a good idea. She didn't allow him to argue. He wanted to plead, *I'm trying not to treat you differently, I'm trying to do what you asked,* but instead he said, "Yeah, you're probably right." The conversation had ended without plans to talk again.

His resolve weakened, though, as alibi rumors grew rampant. No one had thrown his name into the mix yet—despite his treasurer's woes, Jack still enjoyed the popularity left over from the election—but reporters eager to break the story cast the net wider each day. Jack knew it was only a matter of time before one discovered his late arrival at the Jefferson City seminar.

Sterling, in the meantime, used Earl's failure to name the alibi to his advantage. He portrayed Jenny to the press as the ambitious orphan girl who had made work her life and who, when faced with the loss of everything, including her newly earned partnership position, would do anything, even commit murder, to save it.

But what finally compelled Jack to ignore Jenny's directive was a call he received from Rose, the clerk in the file room. She informed him that the Dodson file hadn't arrived from storage yet, but the docket room had received another request for it and she wanted to make sure Jack had first dibs.

"Who wanted it?" Jack asked, presuming that it was Sterling.

He heard her fingering through some papers. "The request slip says 'J. Dodson.'"

Jack grabbed his coat and left the courthouse immediately. He didn't bother to call ahead. He remembered Jenny's comment about how she thought Maxine would refuse to see her if she told her she was coming.

At the steps to her front door, he bent and gathered the newspapers collecting on the walkway. It was at least a week's worth. If she was passing the time reading, it definitely wasn't the papers.

He rang the bell and waited. The biting wind numbed his cheeks.

"Jack." Her face betrayed no indication of her feelings about finding him on her doorstep. "What are you doing here?"

"I needed to return your key, from when I fed the cats."

"Oh." She didn't move except to cross her arms as a barrier against the cold, and he wondered if she was waiting for him to hand it to her and then leave.

"Can I come in?"

She lowered her eyes and he panicked. She was going to say no. He knew it.

"Jenny, please. Don't do this. Can't I just come in for a minute?"

She nodded and backed up. He stepped into a wall of warmth. A fire blazed in the fireplace. Her two cats were curled up together on the end of the couch closer to the fire; the blue-and-gray throw he'd covered her with that night lay haphazardly at the far end. A half-empty cup of coffee and a book, *The Sound and the Fury,* lay on the coffee table. The only electric light in the room came from the reading lamp at the far end of the couch.

"Where would you like these?" he asked, referring to the papers.

"On the hearth, I guess, so they'll dry out."

He pulled the plastic wrap from the papers before putting them down. He glimpsed her last name on one of the headlines and turned it over so she wouldn't see it. And then it dawned on him: that's why she'd stopped bringing them inside. He turned to her before finishing the task. "You'll never read all these. Would you rather I just put them out back in the trash for you?"

"No, that's okay, Jack. Thanks."

"Just keep the doors closed on the fireplace until you move them out of the way." God, this had to be the stupidest conversation they'd ever had.

She picked up her coffee cup. "I'm refueling. You want some?"

He didn't, but he figured he'd be able to stay longer if he had a drink. He followed her into the kitchen because he didn't know what else to do with himself. He leaned back against the counter, his fingers drumming under the ledge. After she'd poured the coffee, she set his cup in front of him and pushed the small carton of cream in his direction.

"Do you want sugar?"

"No, that's okay." He wondered, as they engaged in this meaningless banter, if she was thinking about everything that had happened between them in this kitchen, as he was.

"Shouldn't you be prosecuting some criminal, or something?" she asked.

He looked up from stirring his coffee. Her face remained emotionless. He ignored her question. "Did it take you long to get your place back in shape?"

She shrugged. "Not too bad." She laughed a little, and he was grateful for at least that. "I noticed you had trouble finding the cats' bowls."

"Yeah, I did."

"I should have told you. I keep them on the landing in the cellar. They use a cat door."

"I managed."

She nodded. "Yeah, thanks." She picked up her coffee cup and started toward the exit of the narrow galley. "Should we sit down?" she suggested politely.

He'd had enough. He stuck out his arm to block her passage, and with his other hand he took her cup and set it on the counter. He wrapped his arm around her waist and pulled her to him. The sensation of his palm on her back still felt new, thrilling. "Jenny, it's me."

Her bottom lip quivered. "I know it's you." She kept her head down.

"Then stop this nonsense. Talk to me."

She shook her head.

"Talk to me," he repeated.

"I can't. I can't. Don't you get it? I'm doing all I can just to keep it together, okay? You've gotta leave me alone. You can't keep doing this."

"What? Doing what?"

"This! *This!*" She waved her arms wildly, motioning at his grip, then at nothing. "It's not right. It's wrong. You've got to stop it."

"Jen—"

"No, stop it. Listen to me. If Claire were standing here with us, would you be holding me like this?" He opened his mouth, but no words came. "It's not fair to her," she continued. "It's not fair to me. You've got to stop it." She wiped her eyes with the heel of her hand. "It's not who you are, Jack. You're a better person than this."

Stung by her words, he let her go. "Than what?"

"Than this, than the way you're behaving."

"The way I'm behaving." He made it a statement, not a question. He couldn't look at her. He stared at the black grout lines on her kitchen floor.

She softened her voice. "What I'm trying to say is that how you might feel, how I might feel, is irrelevant."

It was the first verbal acknowledgment of her emotions.

"And how do you feel?" But his tone was too sharp.

"It doesn't matter."

"I deserve to know."

"You don't deserve anything. We made a mistake, and now look at what we're facing. Nothing good can come from what happened."

He knew she was right, but when he looked into her eyes, they were dark, and shadowed by mock sympathy, he imagined. He had the urge to hurt her as she'd hurt him.

"Why are you digging up old murder files?" he asked.

"What?"

"Your family's murder. You recently asked to see the case file."

Suddenly her empathy disappeared. "Who the hell do you think you are?" She shoved him. "Damn you, Jack! Get out of my life. Are you following me or something? You don't trust me?" Suddenly a look of recognition crossed her face. "Is *that* why you told Earl about us? You were starting to doubt me and you wanted him to reassure you? You needed to tell someone to believe it?" She started crying and hit his chest. "You promised me, dammit!"

"What can I say?" he said sarcastically. "I was trying to be a better person."

She burst past him and out of the kitchen. He tried to grab her, but she jerked her arm until he released her. She started yelling from the living room.

"It was *my* evidence to divulge, Jack, not yours! It's up to *me* to decide what to tell him." It sounded as if she'd thrown a pillow. "He's *my* attorney, remember? Not yours. You had no right!"

"I had an ethical duty to make sure the state doesn't prosecute the wrong person for murder." He knew he was making matters worse, but he couldn't stop himself.

She marched back into the kitchen. "You're a fuckin' asshole!" He tried to grab her again, but she pushed him away. "You and your fuckin' ethical duties. Bullshit! Why didn't you go straight to Sterling, then? Huh, Jack? You probably just couldn't stand to live with your guilt anymore and figured it'd be easier to tell Earl than your own wife!"

He'd hurt her, all right, and now he regretted it. His regrets were piling up, one by one. He reached for her and this time forcibly held her so that she couldn't get away.

"You're absolutely right. That was part of it. It helped to tell him. I hadn't planned to, though. But when he told me about Sterling's intentions, what was I supposed to do? Sit on the sidelines while he tries to have you fried?"

"He's just bluffing. You should know that. Anyway, once he learns about Mendelsohn, he'll drop the charges."

"Jenny."

She looked up at him, her eyes hot with distrust.

"He's not bluffing. A DA doesn't ask for death unless he thinks he can get it."

"No, he can't get it. There's no way he can get it. I *didn't* do it!" She began to sob, and her entire body shook. She finally relented and collapsed against him.

"You can't ask me not to help you," he whispered into her ear. "I can't stand by and watch this happen to you."

"I don't want to be the one responsible for splitting up your family."

"You're not. I am. I'll take full responsibility." Then he added, "It'll be okay. We'll work it out." He'd never sounded so unconvincing.

"I don't know what I was thinking, letting you come here that night." She was talking to herself now. "I thought I could talk you out of it, but you were so persistent. I knew it was wrong. I knew it was wrong from the start, last April. I knew we were playing with fire. And I feel like everything is my fault. I should have been able to tell you no. And I tried to, in my own way, but you were so persistent. God, Jack, you're always so persistent! And I know there were times when I egged you on. I think I finally told myself that if we just gave in, then maybe we'd lose interest in each other.

"But that's not what happened. Instead I found myself drawn to you even more, and then when you started telling me you loved me, I realized that all my evil wishes had actually come true and that I could have you, if I wanted. It hit me the next morning that if I didn't do something to push you away, you'd just keep pursuing me and I would be the reason Claire would lose a husband and your kids would lose a father. I couldn't take that. I can't stand to even think that I could be the cause of that." She looked straight at him. "I won't be the cause of that, Jack. Don't force me to be the cause of that. I'd rather they send me to the chair."

He wiped her wet cheeks with his thumb. She turned her face away.

"You've got to stop. I know you mean well. I know you're trying to make me feel better, but your touch just makes it harder for me. You've got to leave me alone." She paused. "She loves you, and you might be going through a rough time, but you love her, too. I could see it the first day I saw you two together, and I can still see it."

"Isn't it possible to love two people at the same time?"

She shrugged. "I don't know. Does that matter?"

He loosened his arms around her and she moved away slightly. He tried to take in everything she'd said to him. *You're a better person than this.*

"Jenny . . ." He started to reach for her but stopped. He wouldn't touch her anymore. "I can't let Claire find out from someone else. I have to tell her. And once I do, I'll have to tell Sterling. So if you don't tell him, I will. I don't have a choice."

She stared at her cat as it rubbed against her ankle.

"Are you listening to me? I *will* tell him if you don't."

"I'll deny it. I'll say you're just trying to cover for me. You'll look even more foolish."

He couldn't understand why she was being so stubborn. He was willing to admit to everything to ensure her freedom, but she didn't seem to want that.

And then it hit him. She didn't believe her own words—*I could have you, if I wanted*—so she wanted him to make the choice. And she needed him to do it now, on his own, before circumstances forced a choice on him, before Claire decided for him. She didn't want him if he merely came to her after losing Claire.

He took a deep breath. It was time to be that better person. What he was about to say was brutally honest and, ironically, would mean that he would lose both of them. But it would also ensure that she didn't get convicted of a crime she hadn't committed.

"You know, you're right about something. Claire does love me and I love her, too, more than anything." *More than you, Jenny.* But he couldn't say that part; he swallowed and tried but he couldn't be that cruel. "That's why I have to come forward." They held each other's gaze as he spoke. "If I want any chance of salvaging my marriage, I have to do the right thing, even if it causes pain to my family. She would expect me to do the right thing."

He waited for her to nod or indicate her acquiescence in some other way. When she finally spoke, the words weren't what he'd expected. But they told him, nevertheless, that he'd succeeded.

"Get out." Her trembling hand tucked her hair behind one ear. "Just get out, will you?"

He dug into his pants pocket and fumbled wordlessly to extricate her key from his key chain. He placed it on the counter. When she reached for it, he tried to touch her hand in a final attempt to convey his sorrow, but she pulled away. He merely looked her in the eyes and then let himself out the front door.

By the time he returned to the courthouse, his mind was so preoccupied with his world imploding around him—slowly but steadily, he could feel it beginning to suffocate him—that he didn't even notice Jim Wolfe waiting for him on the top step leading to the entrance. The reporter had to step in front of Jack and block his entry to get his attention.

"Mr. Hilliard, did you hear the news?"

Jack stared blankly at the small man. "Maybe you should tell me which news you're referring to, Mr. Wolfe," he asked, putting emphasis on the reporter's name.

"Well, of course, that the DA in Ms. Dodson's case has announced he will seek the death penalty." A look of understanding crossed Wolfe's face. He opened his eyes wide. "Is there other news, Mr. Hilliard?"

There's going to be, Jack thought, *when I haul off and land you on your ass*. That would certainly make the front page. He tried to maintain his composure. "Is there a question on the table?" The voice reaching his ears didn't sound like his own.

"Do you have any comment about Mr. Sterling's intent to seek the death penalty?"

"Yes; I think it's not very well thought out." He shouldn't have said it; he should've just kept his mouth shut. After all, he was still the DA, even if he wasn't the prosecutor on this particular case.

"Can you elaborate?" Wolfe had the look of someone who believed he'd just stepped into something good and unexpected, and Jack had a sudden, inexplicable desire to make the guy's day.

"Yeah, I'll elaborate. You might want to turn on your tape for this one, Jim." Was this what it felt like to have a nervous breakdown? Complete awareness, yet no control?

The reporter fumbled in his coat pocket and pulled out his Dicta-phone. Jack grabbed it out of his hand and turned it on. "She didn't do it," he said into the speaker, but with his eyes on Wolfe. And then more slowly, more loudly: "She . . . didn't . . . do . . . it." He turned off the machine and smiled. "How's that?"

"Mr. Hilliard . . ." The reporter's mouth hung open.

"Not enough?" He handed the recorder back. "Here, ask me anything. Anything." A part of him realized that what he was doing would end up in tomorrow's paper, but he couldn't stop himself. He already envisioned the headline: HILLIARD LOSES MARBLES OVER DODSON MURDER CASE.

"Well, okay," he stammered. "Do you know who her alibi is?"

Jack looked at the recorder to see if Wolfe had turned it back on. He had, of course; the tiny red light blazed out at him. *You're a better person than this.* He wondered what Claire was doing just then. He wanted to go over to the university now, sit in the privacy of her office and talk to her. Tell her everything. Slowly let the air out of the balloon of lies he'd created, instead of waiting for someone else to pop it. "No, I don't," he managed to say. "I just know she didn't do it."

Wolfe seemed more intent on processing the look on Jack's face than on the content of his response. "What if she confesses?"

"What if she confesses?" He repeated the question as if he hadn't heard it or didn't understand it. But he did. What he didn't understand was how he'd managed not to think of it himself. Because it suddenly occurred to him that if Jenny also thought of the idea, and if she felt desperate enough to protect him, she just might be crazy enough to do it.

Wolfe pressed him. "Yes, if she confesses, admits she murdered Maxine Shepard. Then would you concur in Mr. Sterling's opinion that her crime warrants the death penalty?"

"No, absolutely not."

"Because she's your friend?"

"No." He glared at Wolfe. He could see where the conversation was heading, but he was too distracted by the countless thoughts playing pinball in his head to collect himself and give the media-savvy answer. "No."

"Mr. Hilliard, I don't have to remind you of your campaign promises."

The mob was getting closer. He just wanted to take those few steps through the courthouse doors and leave Wolfe standing there, but his legs wouldn't move.

"I believe my campaign promises were to represent the city to the best of my abilities."

"And I believe that included asking for the death penalty in an appropriate case."

Shut up now, Jack. Just shut up. "This isn't an appropriate case, Mr. Wolfe. I think we're finished." He willed himself to reach for the tarnished handle in front of him. His arm felt heavy, slow. He could see his hand trembling and he hoped that Wolfe didn't notice.

"One more question, Mr. Hilliard."

Jack raised his eyes.

"Is there *any* set of facts that would, to your mind, warrant the death penalty?"

He asked it as if he already knew the answer, as if he knew that Jack had lied all along but now had an overwhelming need to come clean. Jack looked beyond the reporter's head, to the cars driving by on Walnut Street; they drove slowly, but to him they were a blur. The wind picked up and blew through the back vent of his coat. He thought of Claire again and wondered if she thought of him during the day when they were apart. Maybe it would all be okay. Maybe she wasn't even aware of her capacity to forgive. They had so much invested, so much history. Something special, something indescribable between them. Even Jenny saw it. He couldn't believe that Claire would just turn her back on that. *Will it get better?* He had to believe that she'd give him the chance. But it had to be all or nothing. *You're a better person than this.* It had to be all or nothing.

When Jack refocused, Wolfe was fumbling with his briefcase and had started down the steps. He mumbled something about catching up with him later, but Jack called his name to get his attention. Wolfe turned.

"Your question?" Jack said.

Wolfe nodded, almost undetectably.

"To my mind?" Jack slowly shook his head. He almost imagined he could hear the slow creak as his world began to collapse. "No, there's not."

CHAPTER TWENTY

The story made the next morning's paper—the bottom half, but the front page nevertheless. Unable to concentrate on his work, Jack spent most of the morning staring at the newsprint in front of him, even though he'd finished reading it long ago. HILLIARD CHANGES STANCE ON DEATH PENALTY, the headline read. The accompanying story reported his death penalty flip-flop and recounted his unsupported defense of Jenny.

But he'd done it, hadn't he, and survived? Somehow he'd found the strength to admit that he'd lied about his position on the death penalty. Now he just had to find the strength to admit to everything else. Now all he had to do was tell Claire.

A knock on his door startled him. It opened and Beverly leaned her head in.

"Can I come in?" She spoke gently. "I know you don't want to take calls, but Earl's on the line. He says it's urgent." She waited. "Jack? You okay?"

He looked at her without really seeing her. "I'm okay. I'll be okay. You can send it in."

He picked up the receiver in the middle of the first ring.

"Listen to me and listen carefully," Earl's veteran voice barked at him. "You've got to get hold of Claire immediately. You need to tell her not to take any calls unless you want them to get to her before you do."

"What are you talking about?" But he knew. He didn't know the specifics, but he knew. He began to tremble. The ice on that big frozen lake he'd been trying to cross—all the while thinking he could see the other side—was beginning to thin, and he felt the cracks forming beneath him.

"I just got a call from a reporter. He wanted to know if it was true that you were Dodson's alibi. He might call you next, but if he's like most reporters, he'll call Claire first."

"Oh God." Jack bolted from his chair. "What happened? How'd he know?"

"I'm still trying to find that out. Right now, you need to hang up and find her. Hear me?"

"I can't," he said, looking at his watch. "I can't. I can't even think straight."

"Jack, you can't talk to her if you don't calm down." Perhaps realizing that Jack wasn't in any condition to speak to Claire, he tried to keep him talking. "Listen, try to think. Who else knows?"

"No one." His jaw tensed; he'd told Earl that repeatedly.

"How about Jenny?" Earl asked, his voice lower now, aware of the heresy of his suggestion. "Would she have leaked it?"

"No. No way. She wouldn't do that to me." Sensing this wasn't enough for Earl, he added, "She's the one who practically made me take a blood oath not to tell, remember?"

"That would be consistent with someone who didn't want you to think she was the leak."

"No," he said more forcefully, "she wouldn't do that." *Would she?*

"Listen, we'll worry about 'who' later. Just hang up and call Claire. Do you think you can?"

"Yeah, okay, I'll try," he said, talking himself through it. "I think she's teaching a class now."

"That won't stop someone who really wants to talk to her." And he knew that Earl meant the reporter, not Jack. "They have their ways."

He dialed Claire's number and waited impatiently through each ring. Everything seemed to be in slow motion, yet he still didn't have the time he needed to think.

"Hold on, Jack, she's in her office now," said the receptionist. He looked at his watch again, certain that she was supposed to be in class.

"Hello?" Her voice was hesitant, cautious.

"Claire, it's me."

"Jack." She seemed relieved to hear from him, and he thought this was a good sign.

"Listen, don't take any more phone calls and don't talk to any reporters if they show up at the school. They might be trying to reach you about Jenny's case."

She was quiet, and he thought this was a bad sign. "They already called," she said finally. "He pretended to be someone with a message from you, so they pulled me out of class."

"Oh God, the asshole." The line fell silent, and he heard her take a deep breath.

"Is it true?"

Giving him a chance. Willing to trust him still, willing to believe whatever he said. If he'd had two options before, if he was going to lie to her, he lost the opportunity in the instant he hesitated. The ice broke and he fell in.

His hands gripped the steering wheel; he tried to stay focused on the highway. Ten minutes to the university if there was no traffic, another five from his car to her office. How do you contain a bomb that has already exploded? His car was not capable of going as fast as he wanted it to go. It was December, and he was sweating profusely. *I can't talk to you right now* was all she'd said before she hung up. *I can't talk to you right now.*

He burst into the lobby of the Dean's office, then stopped abruptly when the receptionist and the secretary looked up at him in unison from the eerie quiet of their desks.

"She left right after you called," the receptionist told him. She leaned back a bit, alarmed by his flushed face. "Is everything okay?"

"Yeah, great," he said and ran out.

Back in his car, back on the highway. It was at least twenty-five minutes to their house. And how did he even know she would be there? That might be the last place she'd want to be. But he couldn't think of where else she might have gone. He thought of Jamie. Maybe she'd gone to pick him up from school. No; being with the kids didn't have a calming effect on her, as it did for him. Something about them, Jamie especially—his curly towhead, his new skin, his dewy smell, his laugh—they always had a way of making everything else fall away. But he knew it was different for her; she spent so much more time with them. She'd want to be alone.

By the time he turned onto their street he had no memory of driving there. He realized he was driving ridiculously fast when he passed a woman pushing a stroller and she hollered at him. He didn't actually slow down, though, until he reached the crest of the hill near their house and saw a car parallel parked on the street out front. He recognized it immediately as the same car that had waited for him outside the jail the first day he'd visited Jenny. He couldn't believe it.

He sagged against the headrest. He had the distinct sense of time passing at an uncontrollable rate and a feeling that the longer he sat there, the more irretrievable she became. He reached for his phone on the seat next to him. Even as he punched in the numbers, he knew it wasn't wise, that there was a good chance the reporter had a police scanner in his car and might pick up the conversation. But he couldn't think clearly enough to see any other options.

The answering machine came on and he heard Michael's voice telling him to leave a message. He choked up upon hearing it. The long beep sounded.

"Claire, babe, pick up. Please, pick up." Silence. He knew he had to keep talking or it would switch off. "Claire, please. Please." Maybe she wasn't even in there. But where else could she be? "There's a reporter outside the house." Silence, still. "I want to come in and talk to you, but I need to know you're there. Okay?" Silence, again. "Okay? Claire, please pick up. You can hang up on me, but just pick up first." He thought about calling Marcia, across the street. Maybe she'd seen Claire come home. "Babe, please. *Please*. We need to talk." Inhale. "I love you."

He heard a crashing sound in his ear when she picked up; she must've dropped it.

"If you ever say those three words to me again, I swear I'll cut your tongue out." The venom in her voice wormed its way into his head. He was stunned. "Don't even try to come into this house. I've disconnected the garage opener and locked the garage. I know you have a key for the front, but I'm sure your reporter friend would love the opportunity to talk to you as you struggle to get in."

He stared at the steering wheel. Her voice had been calm when she'd hung up on him at the university, but he'd known it would be bad when he found her. He'd expected her to yell and scream and call him names and tell him what a fuck-up he was. He'd expected to have to explain what he'd done, to come up with some half-brained explanation for it, even though he had none. He'd thought she might even try to take her anger out on him physically. He would almost have preferred that; physical pain might blunt the emotional pain. He knew that she would probably tell him to pack his bags and find somewhere else to sleep—that's what women did, wasn't it, when their husbands cheated on them? Yes, he had expected it to be bad, but not like this. Not so fast. He didn't think for a moment that in her cold calm she would lock him out of the house first thing.

"Don't hang up," he managed to croak.

"I'll give you one sentence. Don't waste it."

He resisted the urge to just start talking. He recognized immediately that if he didn't say the right thing, he'd never get in. Ever. He knew this wasn't the time to try to justify or make excuses for what he'd done. He glanced at the reporter's car.

"There's a reporter sitting outside the house and we'd be much better equipped to deal with him if we act as a team and it's very important that we do this before Michael gets off the bus and he accosts him and I promise you he will because they have no scruples." Then he let out a deep breath; for fear that she would cut him off, he'd said it all in one long desperate go.

"Yeah, and you're swimming in them, aren't you?"

He waited. He didn't say anything because he knew it was just an editorial and not her real response. He had appealed to her mother-bear instincts, putting his money on his belief that her desire to protect the kids would prevail over her anger at him, and he was praying that he'd bet right.

"Fine. If you can get around to the deck without him seeing you, I'll let you in. But I don't want him to know you're here."

"Okay, I'll—" She hung up without letting him finish.

Trembling with relief, he drove out of the circle and onto a street that came within several hundred feet of the side of their house. From there, it was merely a matter of cutting through a few yards and some woods to approach the house from the back. He killed the engine, stepped out of the car, and quietly closed the door. The cold air hit his sweat-drenched body; he shivered and pulled his coat tighter.

He saw her as soon as he reached the deck. She stood inside the house, just on the other side of the sliding door, and stared at him. Faint red blotches marked her face, and the swollen rims of her bloodshot eyes were angry with tears. Strands of hair on each side of her face stuck to her wet cheeks. Her ethereal innocence, her invisible light that had served as both his beacon and his compass, had vanished. She was not the same woman he'd kissed that morning before he'd left for work. She was the most beautiful and tainted thing he'd ever seen.

He tried to pull the door open but found it locked. His eyes began to well up, and when she saw this, she banged repeatedly on the glass with her fists.

"Don't you dare! Don't you dare cry. You have no right to cry!" Her screams seeped through the glass, slightly muffled but clearly audible.

He pulled on the door with one hand and struggled to wipe his eyes with the other.

"Let me in, Claire. You can hit me, but just let me in." He feared that she would break the glass, and then they'd have an emergency-room visit on top of everything else.

She unlocked the door and pulled it open. He started to approach her but she was on him in an instant, hitting his chest and pushing him backward, farther out into the middle of the deck. Not one long push but a series of pushes that were really open-palmed strikes.

"I hate you! I hate you!" she said with each contact. Tears flooded her cheeks. "I hate you!" she repeated over and over, and he began to wonder if she really was speaking or if it was merely the echo of her voice playing in his head. "Don't you cry! You have no right to cry!" He tried to hold back his tears because he wanted to do whatever she wanted him to do.

He grasped her wrists and held her arms in midair. "Stop it."

She twisted to free her arms but succeeded only with the right one. She promptly began hitting him again with it. "Let me go! Don't touch me!" Her voice and her energy began to wane. He now had a firm grip on her left arm. "You . . . have . . . no . . . right . . . to . . . touch . . . me!" She said it slowly, methodically, and with each word she punched him, but the punches were less forceful, as if she was finally surrendering to the reality of his treason.

"What have you done?" she sobbed, and he guided her unaware back into the house. She jerked her left arm and he let it go. She backed herself to the kitchen table and collapsed on a chair.

"I've done something terrible, but it's not what you're thinking," he said. He stayed by the door. "It wasn't an ongoing thing."

She covered her ears. "No, no, I don't want to hear this. Don't you dare try to minimize what you did, what you've done to us." She inhaled, the short, quick breaths of one who's been crying hard. "You've destroyed us."

The last words hit him hard. "I'm not trying to minimize it. I just thought you should know. It was just one time."

She must have refueled because she went at him again. In one quick motion she was on her feet in front of him, pushing, striking at him with her open hands. She pressed him against the slider and he had nowhere to go.

"Tell me, Jack! Why should I know that? Huh? Tell me why! What's the difference?" She tried to catch her breath. "You're a fucking cliché, you know that? What are you going to say next? It didn't mean anything? Well, fuck you! It meant everything." He tried to block the punches— she'd progressed once more to fists—but his heart wasn't in it because he knew that she was entitled to every one of them and more. "One time, huh? Too bad for you, Jack. You should've fucked her brains out a million times to make it really worth it. Because you've destroyed us. I hope your one time was worth that."

He closed his eyes and just let her do it—let her hit and punch and flail at him until she'd drained her reserves again. When she finished, he listened to her cross the room and climb the stairs, and then he slid his back down the glass and sat with his head between his knees for a long time. He'd never known such pain.

Later, he heard her footsteps and looked up to see her coming down the stairs with a small satchel in her hand. He panicked. Somehow, the thought that she might be the one to leave hadn't occurred to him.

"I've packed a change of clothes for the kids." Her voice was flat. "I want you to meet Michael at the bus stop; don't let him come to the house. Then pick up Jamie at Christopher's; he's supposed to play there after school. The directions are in the side pocket of the bag. Where you go with them after that is up to you. Just don't come back here tonight. You can drop them off tomorrow." She set the bag on the table and turned to go back up the stairs.

"Claire, you can't barricade yourself in here."

"Once the story breaks, he'll leave." She spoke with her back to him. "Anyway, they already got my 'no comment' at the university. It's you he's waiting for." Her voice, though steeped in sarcasm, wavered, and he thought she was about to cry again.

"What do you want me to tell them?"

She turned. Her usually bright eyes were darker than he'd ever seen them. They both knew he was talking about the kids, not the reporters.

"I think I'll leave that up to you. How 'bout that, Jack?"

When he finally went upstairs to rinse his face and pack a change of clothes for himself, he found her sprawled facedown across the bed. He stood in the doorway of the bathroom, trying to send her a telepathic message to turn her head, to look at him just once. Except for the sporadic rise of her back when she sniffled, she lay motionless. He knew she was awake.

He went into the bathroom to compose himself. After splashing his face and drying it, he looked in the mirror and was frightened by what he saw. His eyes were bloodshot, and his fair skin lacked even a hint of color. But it was more than physical. He'd lost something inside.

With his toothbrush in hand, he crossed the room to his closet and grabbed a pair of jeans, a shirt, socks, and underwear. He shoved it all into a small overnight bag that he found on the floor behind yesterday's dirty laundry. He looked at her again. He had to say something.

"Claire?"

She didn't respond, didn't even flinch at the sound of his voice.

"Claire? Can we talk?"

Her silence scared him more than her outbursts downstairs. He sat down on an old wicker chair. The room was quiet enough for him to hear the ticking of the grandfather clock in the front hall downstairs.

When she finally spoke, her voice dripped sarcasm and was raspy from prolonged crying. "Yeah, sure, what do you want to talk about? How was the weather when you drove home?"

"Claire—"

"I have just one question for you." She sat up and faced him. Seeing the hollowness in her eyes again filled him with an insatiable longing for her, a longing to hold her until she had no choice but to forgive him. "I want to know how it happened. I mean, did you plan it? Or, you know, did circumstances throw you together, and then you just couldn't resist? How did it happen?"

It was as if she asked so that she could weigh the evidence to determine whether he should be charged with manslaughter or murder. Were his actions heat-of-the-moment or premeditated? Jack understood that her ability to forgive him was perhaps dependent on the answer.

"I didn't plan it, not like you're thinking, but . . . it wasn't an accident, either."

She turned to the window with a grunt. "What's that supposed to mean?"

What *did* it mean? He hadn't planned it, at least he didn't believe he had. He thought back to what Jenny had said about everything being so calculated. He'd never felt that way and still didn't. He'd thought about it a lot, that was true, but until that moment in the garage, when words he hadn't planned to speak fell from his mouth, it had never been anything but fantasy. It was as if he'd snapped, as if he'd temporarily lost the use of his brain and his common sense had taken a leave of absence. In Jenny's presence he'd lost all ability to appreciate the wrongfulness of his behavior.

That was it. It was like temporary insanity. That wonderful defense he'd always scoffed at.

"I don't know," he said finally. There was no way now to explain his thoughts.

After another two chimes on the clock, she said, "I want you to leave."

His heart beat furiously. He'd expected more questions, a real discussion of what he'd done, but now he realized that he'd messed up again by not giving her a satisfactory answer to what she claimed was her only question. "Don't you want to—"

"I mean leave. Not just leave right now. But leave. I can't share the same space with you." The sharpness in her voice had dulled. Now she just sounded weary.

"Claire, come on, don't do that. We need to talk." She'd never even asked him why. He wanted the chance to try to explain himself.

"I can't have you here. It hurts too much."

"But the kids will—"

"You can come over when you want to see the kids. I won't keep you from them."

She pushed herself off the bed and trudged to the bathroom. Her face revealed no emotion; he preferred the anger. At least then he knew he still provoked feeling in her. His greatest fear was that she would stop feeling anything for him.

"I don't want to just 'see' my kids. I want to live with them."

She grabbed the molding on the doorway, and for a moment he thought she was going to faint right there. "I guess you should have thought about that before you decided to screw her, huh, Jack?" She spoke with her back to him. "See, I've always believed building a life with your wife and kids to be mutually exclusive from screwing another woman. The two just don't mix. I always thought you believed that, too. Silly me."

She closed the bathroom door. Within a few minutes he heard the shower running. He walked to the door and let his weight fall against it. It was as close as he could get to her. He listened as she slid the shower door open and then closed. He tried the doorknob, but she had locked it. He took a few steps to her side of the bed and picked up her pillow. He buried his face in it. The scents were subtle, mixed, but there. The clean smell of her skin after bathing, the faintly citrus fragrance of her cologne, the balmy scent of her sweat after they made love.

He heard her crying. Her sobs were contained at first, but he could detect them nevertheless over the pattering of the shower. He lowered the pillow as the muscles in his chest tightened and he imagined that having a heart attack must feel like this. When her cries metamorphosed from uncontrollable sobs into intentional wails, as if she was trying by sheer will to force the pain from her body, he went back to the door and placed his palm on it. He tried to absorb it all—all the hurt that poured from her body. He could never tell her so, but he felt it, too: the grip on the lungs that made it hard to breathe, the excruciating hole in the heart where the blood and emotion tried to escape. Except he knew that her pain seared from anger, while his burned from shame. And that made all the difference in the world.

CHAPTER TWENTY-ONE

He did exactly as she had instructed. He parked his car near the bus stop, but out of sight of the reporter, and waited for Michael to get off the bus. He told him only that a reporter had staked out their house because of developments in Jenny's case and that he'd explain more later, but he already felt an unspoken accusation in Michael's stare. Michael was old enough to perceive when Jack and Claire were fighting, and Jack knew that his son was also old enough to figure out, by the looks on their faces alone, who was probably to blame. Right now, Michael blamed Jack.

He left Michael in the car when he picked up Jamie. He held on to him tightly while the mother of his playmate made small talk in her foyer. He kept trying, unsuccessfully, to read her face for clues of having heard the latest news.

Back on the road, he racked his brain, trying to figure out where to take the kids for the night. The thought of a hotel room was just too depressing. He drove in no particular direction, with no particular destination.

"What are you doing, Dad?" Michael asked. The disgust in his voice was palpable.

"I'm trying to decide where we're going for the night." Jack kept his eyes on the road.

"Where's Mom? Why isn't she coming, too?"

"She wanted to stay home. The reporter wants to talk to me. I'll explain later, Michael."

"I want to go to Uncle Mark's."

Jack finally looked over at Michael, who was sulking against the passenger door. Strands of his sandy-colored hair fell across his forehead—he was in desperate need of a haircut—but Jack could see the resentment in his eyes. He knew from hours spent on the job with therapists that Michael was at a very impressionable age. The odds were now greatly increased that he would follow in Jack's footsteps as an adult. He would hate what his father had done, but, ironically, he'd be doomed to repeat it.

Go to Mark's. It was a pretty good idea. Why hadn't he thought of it? Mark was going to find out everything anyway, and Jack doubted that reporters would come looking for him there.

"Okay, we'll go to Mark's."

Michael didn't even acknowledge him.

Jack drove to his brother's house without bothering to call first. Mark worked from home, so he decided to take his chances. If he wasn't there, well, he'd worry about it then.

When Mark opened the door, he looked from Jack down to the kids and then back. Jack suspected, from the look on Mark's face and the fact that he didn't automatically step back to let them in, that he had a visitor.

"Can we come in?" Jack asked, walking in without waiting for an answer.

Mark eyed the bag slung over Jack's right shoulder. "Yeah, what's going on? Where's Claire?" He nodded to Michael and picked up Jamie and cuddled him.

Jack shook his head to indicate that it could wait. "You've got someone here, don't you?"

"Yeah. It's okay. She's in the kitchen."

"Why don't you two go downstairs and see what's new?" Jack suggested to the kids. He would never have allowed such a thing in the past.

The endlessly growing and changing stash of toy samples in Mark's basement office was usually off-limits to the kids until they'd spent some time with Mark himself. But today was different.

"What's going on?" Mark repeated as he set Jamie on the ground to follow Michael.

"You're gonna have some houseguests tonight, if you don't mind."

Mark cocked his head. Jack could see that he was already making guesses in his head. He motioned in the direction of the kitchen. "Can you get rid of her first?"

"I intend to. But give me a clue, will ya?"

Jack dropped his bag onto the floor. "There's been a major leak to the press in Jenny's case, and I'm trying to avoid the reporters."

"Why are *you* trying to avoid the reporters if the leak is about Jenny's case?"

Mark had more than an inkling. Jack waved again toward the kitchen. "Mark, please."

Mark's eyes drilled into him for a few moments more before he turned and walked to the back of the house.

The woman, dressed in a pumpkin turtleneck and black slacks, her wheat-and-honey-colored hair pulled back loosely at the nape of her neck, smiled warmly at Jack from under the glow of a halogen lamp. She seemed out of place in Mark's cold, stainless kitchen.

"Of course I recognize him, Mark," she said, laughing, when they were introduced. "I voted for him." Her smile faded when they shook hands and she felt Jack's nervous trembling. Evidently sensing that he wasn't there for a simple social visit with his brother, she gathered the papers scattered on the table and shoved them quickly into a black briefcase.

Jack remained in the kitchen while Mark walked her to the front door. He sat in her vacated chair and listened to their murmurs from the front hall. He couldn't hear their words but he knew the tone: intimate and easy.

All at once he became overwhelmed with the enormity of the mess he'd created. He rested his elbows on the table and let his head fall into the palms of his hands. What had he done?

"So you've moved on from accused murderers, huh?" Jack said when Mark returned to the kitchen and sat in the chair across from him.

Mark balanced the chair on its rear legs, rocking it back and forth gently. "For your information, she dumped me." He folded his arms across his chest. "So? You gonna let me in on why you're here?"

Jack picked up a crumb from the table and played with it between his thumb and forefinger. "I think you probably already know."

"Tell me."

"I was with her, the night of the murder."

Mark leaned back and looked at the ceiling. He shook his head in disbelief.

"I'm her alibi."

"Aw, shit! What the fuck were you thinking?"

He flicked the crumb onto the floor and stared at the table in front of him.

"Jack!"

"I don't know!"

Mark glared at him and then abruptly stood up and went around to Jack's side of the table. He slapped the back of Jack's head hard and hollered, "You don't know? What do you mean, you don't know?" He yanked the refrigerator open violently, grabbed two bottles of beer in one hand, and slammed it shut. On his way back to his chair, he hit Jack's head again with the base of his palm. Jack winced—it was even harder this time—but he was grateful that Mark hadn't used one of the bottles. "You don't mess around with someone who's not your wife and then say you don't know, goddammit!" Mark spoke low this time, hissing, Jack guessed, so the kids wouldn't hear.

Jack twisted the top off the beer Mark set in front of him. "It's not like you're thinking. I—"

"Oh my God, listen to yourself, will you? Isn't that what they all say?"

Jack felt himself getting defensive. "Who's 'they,' Mark?"

" 'They'? 'They' are all the assholes like you who get married too soon and then discover they're not done wanting to screw other women."

"You don't know what you're talking about. I've been married over thirteen years and I've never wanted to 'screw other women,' as you say. Just because you want to do every female that passes you on the street doesn't mean I do."

"No, Jack, you just had one particular one in mind, didn't you? And then you try and tell yourself that somehow that should make it different. Did you try that excuse on Claire? No wonder she threw you out of the house. You're pathetic!"

"She threw me out of the house because there was a reporter waiting for me out front, just as Michael was coming home from school. We're trying to protect the kids."

"Oh, yes, and I'm sure that once the story breaks, she'll welcome you home with open arms."

Jack sighed.

Mark took a swig of his beer and regarded his brother coolly. The kids' shrieks rose from the stairwell. Jack thought of Michael again, and wondered what he was going to tell him.

"How long has it been going on?"

Jack walked to the window above the sink and looked out onto the barren patio. The wrought-iron table and chairs were still there, but the cushions and the umbrella that shaded the table in the summer were gone. Two large planters sat in each far corner, the remains of last season's annuals lying brown and frozen in the hard potting soil.

"You've probably ruined those planters. They'll crack when it thaws."

He turned and leaned against the sink. He looked into the neck of his beer bottle and took a long drink. Maybe if he got drunk, he could get through the rest of the day more easily. Maybe Mark had some bourbon in the house. He liked it better, and it would do the job more quickly.

"Jack."

He looked up at the sound of Mark's voice.

"What happened?"

Staring at the refrigerator on the other side of the kitchen, Jack suddenly realized why Mark's kitchen, and his entire house, for that matter, always seemed so cold. It was the lack of kid things. Despite Mark's business and the number of toys in the basement, the upstairs had no evidence of children. No pictures or poems graced the front of the refrigerator. No backpacks, sneakers, or stuffed animals cluttered the floors.

"I was trying to tell you. It was just once. I realized it was wrong . . .

and that would have been the end of it if Maxine Shepard hadn't been murdered."

Mark shook his head, not believing what Jack had said. "Something was going on last spring, Jack," he insisted, "at your house."

"No. Not like that."

Mark tilted his head, still skeptical.

"Look," Jack continued, "a few weeks before Claire invited you over to meet Jenny, we had been at an awards dinner—it was the night my boss said he was leaving. We all got a little drunk. Well, actually, Jenny got a lot drunk, and I ended up walking her to her car and eventually taking her home."

"Oh man, Jack, not drunk."

"No, no. That's not what happened." He stopped, wondering how much to tell Mark. "She'd wanted me to dance at the bar, and I wouldn't. So when we got to her car, she asked me again, and I just felt bad saying no again. So we danced, and, well, you know how it is when you're buzzed. We ended up kissing. But that was it. That was it, Mark. We stopped and I drove her home. That was it. I swear."

"You told Claire?"

"No."

"She knew something."

"Yeah, I guess. Maybe she just sensed we were getting too close."

"Hell, you'd have to be blind not to sense something was up between you two."

Jack shook his head. "It wasn't like that. We've always been friends. And we both agreed it'd been a mistake and we'd never mention it again. Nothing was 'up' between us."

"You're in denial, bro. Maybe nothing happened between that night last spring and the night of that lady's murder, but somehow you still ended up in bed with her."

Jack took another drink of his beer. Yeah, somehow he had, hadn't he?

"How'd Claire find out?" Mark asked.

This was the part he couldn't talk about. He could still see Claire's face through the glass door, her eyes hollow, drained of love.

"Did Jenny tell her?" Mark suggested.

"No!" Why did everyone think that? Jack could understand Earl's suspicions; Earl knew Jenny only as a woman who could get Jack in trouble. But Mark knew better. He knew her.

"Did *you* tell her?" Mark asked then, his voice incredulous.

Jack raised his hand to stop Mark's inquiries. He just didn't want to talk about it now.

"The leak?" Mark persisted, finally understanding the connection to what Jack had told him when he'd first arrived. Jack nodded.

"God, you really fucked up this time." He stood, and Jack thought Mark was going to hit him again.

"Dad?" They both turned to see Michael standing in the wide doorway of the kitchen. His voice sounded younger than usual. Jack wondered how much of their discussion he'd heard. "There's nothing for me to do. It's all kid stuff downstairs."

Mark put his arm around Michael's shoulders. "Why don't we go outside and play some hoops?"

"No." He wriggled away. "I wanna go home, Dad. I don't want to stay here tonight."

If it had been Jamie, he could have gone over and hugged him, lifted him into his arms. But he couldn't do that with Michael. Michael was too old, too big. There was a distance between them now which Jack hadn't figured out how to bridge.

"Mark, I want to talk to Michael, okay?"

"Yeah, yeah." Mark's movements as he rinsed his bottle in the sink exuded forced cheer. "We have to eat, right? And I know I have nothing here to feed you guys. Why don't I take Jamie and go pick up some pizza for dinner?"

They both knew that pizza could be delivered. "That'd be great. Thanks." He tossed Mark his keys. "Take my car. You won't have to move the car seat, then."

Michael had come into the kitchen during their brief conversation. He sat on a bar stool beneath the phone on the wall. They remained silent as Mark gathered up Jamie. They remained silent even after the front door slammed shut and a lonely quietness settled on the house. Jack took nervous swigs of beer and then realized that Michael was probably thirsty, too.

"Do you want something to drink? We can see if he has some soda or something."

"Why can't we go home?"

Jack had the feeling that somehow Michael already knew everything and was just waiting to see if Jack would be honest. "The short answer is that—"

"I don't want the short answer. I want the real answer."

"Let me finish." Michael nodded. "The short answer is that a reporter was parked outside our house just before the bus came. He wanted to talk to me about Jenny's case, and we were afraid he'd try to talk to you." Michael shrugged his shoulders; he didn't care about this part of the explanation. "The long answer is that Mom is a little mad at me right now, and she wanted to be alone. I'm involved in the case in a way I shouldn't be, a way that upsets her. Okay? So we're here tonight. We'll go home tomorrow, and I'll talk to her. We'll work it out."

"What does that mean?"

"What does what mean?"

"That you're involved in the case in a way you shouldn't be?"

"I'm probably going to be a witness."

"What do you mean, Dad?" His voice was shrill, desperate. It suddenly occurred to Jack that Michael might think his father had something to do with the murder. He clarified his explanation.

"A witness for Jenny. A witness who can explain to the judge that she didn't kill that lady."

"Why would that make Mom mad?" Had he told Michael that Claire was mad—or just upset? His ability to think straight weakened as Michael kept pressuring him for more explanation.

"Michael"—Jack sighed—"I know that Jenny didn't kill that lady, couldn't have killed that lady, because I was with Jenny at her house at the same time the lady was killed. But Mom thought I was somewhere else. I was supposed to be somewhere else." Michael was staring hard at Jack, the way one stares at someone he thinks he knows, but isn't sure. "You know"—Jack thought of a comparison—"like when you tell Mom you're gonna be at Danny's house but instead you go to Kevin's." He waited, but when Michael didn't say anything, just looked at the floor, he added, "She gets upset, right?"

Michael mumbled something without looking up.

"What?" Jack asked.

"I said"—his head jerked up at Jack quickly—"yeah, but she still lets me come home!"

"Michael—"

"Stop talking to me like I'm five years old, like I'm stupid!" He began to cry.

Before Jack could respond, Michael stood and leaned against the center island. "You think I'm so stupid! She's your girlfriend. I know she's like your girlfriend."

"No, that's—"

"You're a liar!" He wiped his tears with the back of his hand; it reminded Jack of when he was a little boy. "Why can't you just tell the truth? Why do you talk to me like I'm a little kid?"

"I have told you the truth," Jack said. He started around the island, unsure of what he'd do once he got to him.

"Get away from me!" Michael yelled when Jack approached. "You're a liar. I know you like her instead of Mom now."

"Michael!" Jack shouted at him as he moved away; when he turned, Jack stretched and grabbed him by the arm, pulling him back. "That's wrong. I love Mom. I've always loved Mom and I always will." Michael wouldn't look at him, so Jack shook his arm. "Are you listening to me?" Michael kept crying, but Jack shook his arm again. "Answer me. Are you listening to me? Jenny's not my girlfriend. I love Mom." Michael tried to twist his arm away, but Jack grasped harder and shook it one more time. "Do you hear me? I love Mom."

"You're a jerk," Michael said, his eyes narrowed. "And I hate you."

Jack's hand went limp on Michael's arm and he let it fall from his grip. Michael ran out of the kitchen and left Jack standing there, stunned. At one time or another Jack had been told by his older son that he hated him. This was the first time he'd ever felt that Michael really meant it.

Jack woke to a dense fog blanketing the ground outside the guest-bedroom window. So much for his fantasies of catching a plane to some faraway place today; he doubted that any plane would take off in such a mess. He gazed trancelike at Michael sleeping, mouth wide open, on the opposite edge of the bed, and Jamie flung out sideways across the middle, his feet resting peacefully in the space where Jack's waist had been.

He found Mark in the kitchen, making coffee.

"I'll probably be back tonight, without the kids, if that's okay."

Mark poured the coffee with his back to Jack. "You can stay as long as you want. But I would think it'd be a lot easier to patch things up if you're in your own house."

"I don't think there's a patch big enough." He reached out for the cup Mark handed him and watched him pour another for himself. Mark sipped his coffee standing in front of the window above the sink, his eyes searching the yard as if he was looking for something. After a moment, he retrieved a small bag of cat food from the pantry and went out the back door.

"You have a cat?" Jack asked when he came back in, bringing the cold air with him.

"A cat has me. I don't know where he came from, but he hangs out here so I feed him."

It occurred to Jack that maybe Claire understood Mark better than he did. Maybe Jenny and Mark *would* have hit it off had Jack not been in the picture.

"Do you remember when I used to be home from school, and we used to have coffee like this together in the morning, before Mom and Dad got up?"

"You mean before Mom and Dad got up and began to harass me about why I couldn't be more like you." Mark stared at him over the rim of his cup. His bluntness irked Jack.

"It wasn't quite—"

"Okay," Mark interrupted. "I'm exaggerating. Their tactics were much more subtle."

"Yeah," Jack said quietly. "And I encouraged it, didn't I?"

Mark shrugged. "Sometimes. Not always." He laughed then and added, "They'd be singing a different tune if they could hear about what you've done now, wouldn't they?"

"It's not funny."

"Relax, I didn't mean anything by it."

He started past Jack toward the sink. Jack took a step forward to block his passage. "Yes, you did. You think it's funny." Even as his body moved, even as he spoke the words, he knew that he was issuing a challenge and he knew what might happen, but he ignored the warnings in his head.

"Get outta my face, Jack, or else."

"Or else what?"

Mark stared at him as if deciding whether to take it further. Finally, he said, "You need to chill out." He turned his back and set his cup in the sink. "You're a little too sensitive right now." He pushed by, grabbed the cat food from the counter, and headed to the pantry.

"I have a right to be sensitive."

Mark stopped. He walked right up to him, close enough to force Jack to tilt his head back, and stuck his finger against his chest.

"No, you don't. You don't have any rights anymore. You gave them all up the minute you fucked Jenny Dodson." He jabbed him a few times. "The only right you have is to go home and get down on your knees and beg your wife to forgive you. In fact, you don't even have a right to do that. If she lets you, if she even listens to the miserable-ass excuses you come up with, it'll be a privilege. You understand that, Jack? If she even lets you look at her, that's a privilege."

"Get your fucking hands off me." He knocked Mark's finger away, but Mark grabbed his wrist.

"I'll put my fucking hands on you if I want to, got it? You're in my fucking house, sleeping in my fucking bed, drinking my fucking coffee. I'll do whatever the hell I please."

Jack tried to pull his wrist from Mark's grip, but Mark only held on tighter and with his other hand knocked the side of Jack's head gently. It was meant to taunt, not hurt. He laughed in Jack's face. "You need to be knocked around a bit, and I think you know it."

"Yeah, and you also think you're the one to do it, don't you?"

"It would be my pleasure."

"Let me go," Jack stated in the calmest voice he could, faking resignation.

Mark released him, and as soon as he did, Jack was on him. In one flowing movement he slammed his coffee cup on the island as his right fist headed for Mark's jaw. But Mark was fast. He grabbed Jack's arm and stopped it. With his other hand he tried to push Jack back. They moved as one in a mass of flying arms and grunts first toward the sink, then back toward the island, where one of their arms knocked the cup and sent it tumbling off the edge.

"You're cleaning that up, you know," Mark said, laughing between grunts as he grabbed hold of Jack's right arm and twisted it behind his back.

"What are you two doing?" Michael's voice came from the archway into the kitchen.

Jack made the mistake of turning his head, and Mark took advantage of it by forcing him to the floor. He placed his knee at Jack's crotch, ready to exert pressure.

"I've been working out, bro," Mark said, and he winked as he gave one last little jerk. He left Jack lying on the cold tiles, staring at the ceiling and wondering how he could possibly muster the drive required to stand up and begin piecing together the remnants of his life.

Jack eyed the morning paper on a neighbor's driveway as he and the kids went out to the car. He restrained himself from crossing the lawn to take a peek. He considered buying one at the 7-Eleven on his way to drop the kids at school—if only to know beforehand what schoolyard gossip Michael would have to contend with—but decided against it. The last place he wanted to endure scrutiny was at the convenience store buying a paper that might have his picture on the front page.

The fog remained thick on the drive out to the far suburbs, and Jack grew impatient with having to go slowly. He dropped Michael off at his school first, getting the cold shoulder. That morning, when he'd composed himself enough to get up off Mark's floor, he'd tried to tell Michael that they'd only been goofing off, but he had merely regarded Jack with disgust and left the room. He hadn't spoken to his father since.

Jamie's good-bye was entirely different, but not any easier. After Jack pulled up in front of his preschool and released him from his car seat, Jamie gave him a long hug.

"That's for tonight, too, since I might not see you," he said, smiling sweetly at him, only inches away from his face. Jack smelled his toothpaste.

The words took Jack by surprise, although they shouldn't have. "What do you mean?"

"Mommy said you might not be home tonight, you might have to work late."

He'd had the kids call Claire the night before to say good night, and now he wondered what else they'd talked about. He hadn't told Jamie very much. Despite her instructions, he wanted to let her decide what to tell them. He knew she'd do it tactfully and wouldn't be one of those women who encourage her children, directly or indirectly, to despise their father as much as she did.

When he returned to his brother's house, the newspaper was still lying on the neighbor's lawn, and the car that had been parked in the driveway was gone. He crossed the yard and picked it up. He waited until he was inside the house before pulling it from its plastic wrapper. The paper trembled in his hand and he began to have difficulty breathing. HILLIARD POSSIBLE LOVER & ALIBI FOR ALLEGED MURDERER. Under the headline, above the story, were three headshots in a row: him, Jenny, and Maxine Shepard. He closed his eyes and tried to breathe slowly. It wasn't working and he started to get dizzy. He made his way to the kitchen table and sat down, letting his head hang between his knees. He dropped the paper to the floor and began to read the article from there.

Recently elected St. Louis District Attorney Jack Hilliard spent the night at the home of his campaign treasurer, Jennifer Dodson, on November 16, the same night Dodson is alleged to have committed the violent murder of Maxine Shepard, says an unidentified source. Mr. Hilliard, whose office has disqualified itself from handling the murder case because of his previously reported friendship with the defendant, was unavailable for comment. Defendant Dodson, when reached last night at her home in Lafayette Square, vehemently denied the claim.

Ms. Shepard was a client of the prominent law firm Newman, Norton & Levine, where Dodson practices law and was up for partnership. Sources have indicated that the firm is investigating her for possible embezzlement. Other attorneys at the firm, who asked to remain anonymous, have stated that Dodson represented Ms. Shepard in several matters, but the two did not get along well.

When questioned about how this development might affect his prosecution of the defendant, Alan Sterling, the out-of-town district attorney brought in to handle the case, stated that unless Dodson indicates she will claim Mr. Hilliard as her alibi, nothing will change.

"We believe we have sufficient evidence to prove that Ms. Dodson committed the murder. Whether Mr. Hilliard and the defendant have an improper relationship is not my concern."

Kevin Tyler, a former District Attorney and an expert in criminal law, told the *Post-Dispatch* that in many cases, when the defendant claims an alibi that appears plausible, officials will administer polygraph tests and, depending upon the results, often dismiss the charges. He further stated that he was puzzled by Mr. Sterling's response to this development, because the defendant's denial of the alibi is understandable if she is trying to protect Mr. Hilliard, who is married with two children.

"As the District Attorney, I would think he would want to investigate the claim independently, even if the defendant denies it," he said.

The next couple of days were a lesson to Jack in understanding the phrase *a living hell*. He spent each day in Mark's guest room, trying desperately to think clearly but unable to do so. Even though his alibi had been Jenny's best chance to avoid a trial, to avoid what was looking more and more like a sure conviction, she'd outright denied it.

He turned off his cell phone, and though he heard the house phone ring over and over again—and knew that the calls were probably for him because Mark had a separate business line in his basement office—he just ignored it. He considered driving into the city, just walking into his office as though nothing had happened and trying to go on with his life, but he abandoned the idea as quickly as he'd thought of it.

It wasn't until near the end of the second day that he summoned the courage to listen to his voice-mail messages, and that's when he realized that he'd been avoiding more than just reporters. There were messages from assistant district attorneys and from defense attorneys complaining about those assistant district attorneys. An angry judge had left several messages wanting to set up a teleconference about a plea bargain; Jack was supposed to have called him the day before. Dunne had called twice and Earl had called several times, sounding more aggravated with him in each message. There were numerous frantic messages from Beverly, begging him at least to call her. And there was a single message from Jenny, calmly asking him to return her call. "I need to talk to you" was all she'd said. Her voice, low and smooth, reminded him that although he felt his life had ended, she was still fighting for hers. And he was the only ammunition she had.

But he didn't call her and he didn't go into the office. Then, early on the third day, Earl called to inform him of the lie-detector tests scheduled for later that day.

"She won't do it," Jack mumbled into the phone after Earl explained why he'd called.

"I'll worry about her. You just drag your ass over to the police station by quarter to one. They want to question you first."

"She won't do it. She told me she won't do it, and if you try to force her, she plans on lying. She's gonna say I'm just covering for her."

Earl grunted. "She thinks she can beat the machine now, does she?"

"I guess." Jack raised the shade as he talked, but when he saw how sunny it was in Mark's backyard, he pulled it back down with an agitated yank.

"Do you ever plan on facing the music?" Earl asked. "The rumblings are that the Republicans are going to call for your resignation." Jack pretended not to have heard him. "Jack?"

"I'd better take a shower now if you want me there on time. I've got some calls to make."

Earl's sigh on the other end was loud, exaggerated. "I can imagine."

Afterward, Jack finally tried to call Jenny back, but he hung up when her answering machine picked up.

Despite his certainty that she would skip the test, even under order of court, she was sitting in the lobby waiting for her turn when he emerged from the testing room. He sat next to her but received only a brief glare. When he began to speak, the proctor who'd followed him out of the testing room scolded him. Jack cut him off.

"You can listen to every word we say," he assured the man. Then he turned to Jenny. "Earl talked you into coming, huh?" he asked.

She ignored him.

"Jenny, if you tell the truth, they'll dismiss the charges by the end of the day. I can almost guarantee that."

Jenny directed her stare to the proctor, who sat across from her. "I intend to tell the truth."

Muzak played from the speaker just above Jack's head and he couldn't think of anything that could have been more aggravating just then. He glanced at the proctor. He wanted to reach Jenny but wasn't sure how personal he wanted to get with this guy sitting there.

"I'm staying at Mark's now."

He knew that would get her. Her eyes landed on him like a magnet.

"By choice?" Her voice was barely above a whisper.

He shook his head.

The door to the testing room opened and the examiner poked his head out.

"Ms. Dodson, I'm ready for you."

The proctor stood to accompany her but she hesitated, holding Jack's gaze with her own. "Why didn't you ever call me back?" Her eyes welled up.

"I did, but . . ." There was no satisfactory answer. He could have left a message; he could have called again. So he said simply, "The damage has been done, Jenny. You can't protect me anymore. Just worry about protecting yourself."

She lowered her eyes as she followed the proctor into the testing room. Jack didn't know whether it was enough. He didn't know whether he'd persuaded her to come away from the front or whether he'd merely pushed her farther into the line of fire.

He learned later from Earl that Jenny had told the partial truth. She'd maintained her innocence, repeated that she had nothing to do with Maxine Shepard's murder, and, to Jack's relief, the test results bore that out. But when it came to Jack's alibi, she'd continued to insist that he was lying. Just as she'd told Jack she would, she claimed that he was covering for her; that as a staunch death penalty opponent, he'd do anything to make sure she wasn't convicted of a crime she hadn't commited. She'd explained the wineglasses by admitting he'd been at her place early in the evening, when they'd shared a bottle of wine to celebrate the partnership decision, but then he'd left for Jefferson City. She had tried to explain the presence of the glasses in the bedroom by claiming they'd gone upstairs so she could show him the house, and that he had left abruptly once he re-alized he was behind schedule.

In the end, her lies—detected easily by the machine—helped in Earl's bid to have the charges dismissed. When Earl relayed the good news, Jack almost wondered if she'd known all along that they would.

PART 4

WINTER

CHAPTER TWENTY-TWO

The first thing Jack noticed as he approached the house was the Christmas lights. He knew they'd be up. She wouldn't have disappointed the kids. They lined the windows on the first floor and draped the bushes in front. She'd even wrapped a strand of lights intertwined with garland around the light pole near the front walk. But it still seemed bare to him, though, because no lights were strung along the roofline, none hung from the gutters or were wrapped in a spiral fashion around the towering pines at the edge of the woods to the west of the house. There were no lights whatsoever in the spots for which he'd always been responsible.

He parked in the driveway because she'd taken his garage opener when she took his keys. At the front door, he debated what to do. She was expecting him, but he still felt he would be invading her privacy somehow if he just strolled in as though he were coming home from work.

He pulled on the screen door. Just as his knuckles were about to make contact with the wood, the door opened. Claire stood right in front of him, with Jamie on her hip. He was too big for that now, but Jack wasn't surprised to see him there. What surprised him instead was Claire's hair—or rather, her lack of it. She'd had it all cut off. In the thirteen years they'd been married, in the fourteen years they'd known each other, he'd never known her to have anything but long hair. Now it was short, and curlier, too, without the weight of length. It reminded Jack of Jamie's hair when he was a toddler, before he'd had his first haircut.

"You cut your hair" was all he said, still on the porch, waiting for the invitation to come in.

Jamie released Claire's neck and dived for Jack.

"Come in so I can close the door," she said, her voice betraying nothing.

He moved farther into the front hall, away from the path of the door as she swung it shut.

"You cut your hair," he repeated, thinking that maybe she hadn't heard him the first time.

She reached up with both hands self-consciously. "Yes, I know."

"Daddy, come see my new LEGOs. Grandma let me open them early."

Jack nuzzled his nose in Jamie's neck; he smelled of soap, as if he'd just had a bath. "Go get it set up for me, okay? I'll be right there. Let me talk to Mommy first."

"No. Now, Daddy." His voice was whiny, but it didn't bother Jack as it sometimes did.

"Hey, two minutes. I promise." Jamie acquiesced and wriggled free. Jack stood there, not sure what to do with his hands.

"Why'd you cut it?"

She crossed her arms and leaned against the front door. "I needed a change."

He finally shoved his hands into the pockets of his jeans. "It's easy for women, isn't it?"

"What?" Her voice was venomous, daring him to say the wrong thing.

"To make a change. You just need a new hairstyle."

She laughed sarcastically. "Yeah, it's that easy. Chop, chop, chop and it's gone. So easy."

He kept trying to see her as before, to remember what she looked like with it long, but he couldn't see her clearly. It was just some imagined Claire in his mind.

"You're an idiot, coming in here and saying that to me." Her eyes narrowed. "I think your two minutes are up, and I'm sure Jamie knows it. I'll find Michael to tell him you're here."

Jack heard footsteps in the hallway and he turned, expecting to see Michael. Instead, Claire's parents rounded the corner, then halted when they saw him. She hadn't told Jack they'd be there, and from the surprised looks on their faces, she must not have told them that he'd be stopping by, either. Jack hadn't seen them since the day of the election.

"Why, Jack," her mother said. "Hello."

She didn't look particularly angry with him, just uncomfortable, and he momentarily considered whether to go to her, to give her the customary hug and kiss on the cheek. But the stern look on Harley's face made him think better of it.

"Hi." He could think of nothing more to say. "Merry Christmas" or even "How are you?" just didn't seem appropriate.

"What is he doing here?" Harley asked, speaking to Claire as if Jack weren't standing there.

"I'm here to see Claire and my children," he answered before Claire had the chance. Harley had every right to be angry at him—he knew he'd feel the same if it had been his daughter—but this was still his home, his family, his problem, and he couldn't help but be defensive. "And I'd like some privacy."

Harley ignored him, looked to Claire for guidance. She nodded her acquiescence.

"We'll be in the family room, then," Harley said, as if his daughter might need rescuing.

When they left the foyer, Jack stood silent, watching Claire and waiting for her to look at him. When she finally did, he said, "What I said about your hair . . . I didn't mean it like that." He took a step toward her. She put her hand out.

"Don't touch me, Jack. I cringe at the thought of you touching me."

"Claire . . . I just meant it's easy to change how you look. That's all." She crossed her arms again and looked away. "Can we talk before I leave?"

"No."

"Claire . . ."

"What, Jack? What do you want from me?" Tears began to form in her eyes.

That was the question, wasn't it? There were a lot of things he wanted, but he knew she couldn't give them to him. He wanted to go back to the night in the garage, back to April, and tell Jenny no when she asked him to dance. No, he wanted to go back even further than that. He wanted to go back to the banquet, to go home right when he'd first planned. Or maybe just a bit more, to before Earl said he was resigning. That's what he really wanted. He simply wanted his old life back.

But he knew this wasn't the answer she was looking for. He thought that maybe she was giving him an opening, cracking the door just a bit to let him back in. It was a test, only he hadn't studied for it. All he could do now was wing it. All he could do now was pick one little thing, one small desire that might enable him just a glimpse inside. And it had to be honest. It had to be true.

"I just want to hold you again."

She pulled a tissue from the pocket of her cardigan and dabbed her eyes. "Well, I've got a news flash for you. Jack Hilliard doesn't get everything he wants." She crossed in front of him to the stairs. "I'm going up to the bathroom so the kids don't have to see me cry again. You can let Michael know you're here yourself."

"What's wrong with them seeing that their mom's sad?" he asked.

She stopped abruptly in the middle of the steps. The house had seemed cold before, but now it was as if every window had been left open. Her jaw tensed; her hand gripped the railing as if she were trying to draw strength from it. He knew something bad was about to happen. It was like those minutes in the courtroom before the jury announces the verdict, but not one juror has looked at him, not one has smiled. The only difference was that now, he was the one on trial.

She screamed. It was not a loud, high-pitched scream, but a low, rumbling growl of frustration from deep in her chest.

"God! How can you be so smart but so dense?" she yelled. And then, as if struck by inspiration, she wheeled around and grabbed a ceramic vase resting on the shelf of a small, rectangular alcove. She hurled it over the railing. He ducked, and it shattered on the wooden floor behind him. "There! Does that look like sadness to you?" She ran the rest of the way up the stairs, but before turning the corner into their bedroom, she added, "And I wasn't aiming for you this time. If I was, I wouldn't have missed."

He retreated to Mark's "country" house, about five hours southwest of the city in the middle of the Missouri Ozarks. It was a few miles outside a little spit of a town known as Cape Fair, which Jack had always called Cape Fear to irk his brother. It hovered at the top of a large hill overlooking one of the skinny fingers of Table Rock Lake. It was a large barnlike structure built into the slope of the hill, and the only livable space was the small, dank apartment in the bottom part, which was cut into the ground.

Mark had bought the place for a few thousand dollars with dreams of someday renovating it and turning the barn into the main living area. But Jack didn't see much to renovate; Mark would probably have to tear it down and start over. Pieces of the barn were missing, exposing the interior to the elements, and what remained was rotted and hanging precariously from rusting nails.

In the meantime, Mark used the place for parties—big, wild, drunken beer bashes he staged for his friends and clients. He'd invite them all down for the weekend, hire a local bluegrass band, and make sure the food and alcohol flowed into the wee hours of the night.

But those parties had been in the summer, when the grass was green and the trees exploded with leaves. It was now January; winter had settled on the house and the surrounding hillside, and, at Mark's suggestion, Jack had gone there to seek refuge—to "get his shit together," as Mark was so fond of saying. But it hadn't turned out the way Mark had expected, or the way Jack had hoped. He'd originally planned to stay for a long weekend, maybe a week at the most. But the place began to grow on him. He began to enjoy his desolate isolation, the way the wind howled up from the valley and over the hill, rattling the weak slats of the barn as he tried to sleep at night. He'd lost track of how long he'd been there, but he suspected it was approaching a couple of weeks. Long enough, at least, to stretch the limits of his leave.

Within fifteen minutes of his arrival on New Year's Day, he'd moved a plastic Adirondack chair to a spot at the edge of a yard, just in front of a short, crumbling stone wall that blocked the steep embankment on the other side. Each morning he made instant coffee and went to the chair, where he remained for the length of the day with his feet propped on the wall, looking out over the dead valley. Sometimes he closed his eyes, but more often he stared straight ahead, for he found it was easier not to think that way, at least not to think about things he didn't want to think about. With his eyes open he could think instead about the landscape in front of him, the brown gnarly trunks and branches of the trees that he couldn't identify without their leaves. He could wonder why his brother had bought this place and then let it go to ruin.

Most days were gray, and he had trouble getting his bearings, knowing which way was north, which way was south, east, or west. It was on one of those gray days that Jack noticed the sound of a slowly approaching car on the long gravel drive leading to the house. He'd spent the morning shooting at empty beer cans with a shotgun he'd discovered in a closet.

There were a lot of people he could imagine coming down there, if he bothered to think about it. His brother, or Claire, maybe, if only to serve him with divorce papers. He could believe she'd want to accompany the process server herself, for the satisfaction of it. Even Jenny, possibly, if he stayed there long enough, to chew him out for something or other. But when Earl stepped out of the car and slammed the door behind him, Jack was surprised. It wasn't that Earl seemed out of place. To the contrary, he fit right in; he had always been more Fort Leonard Wood sergeant than St. Louis District Attorney. But Jack had long ago decided that Earl had given up on him. The surprise was the first emotion Jack remembered feeling for a while.

As Earl's stocky figure closed in on him, Jack turned back to the valley. He wondered what they could possibly have to say to each other.

"Christ, you look like you're about to waste away," Earl said when he reached him. When Jack didn't acknowledge him, he added, "Have you eaten anything since you've been here?"

"Enough."

Earl picked up the cup from the armrest of the chair and tossed what little bit of coffee was left into the grass.

"What are you doing here?" Jack asked.

"Claire told me where I could find you."

"I've got a phone, you know."

"She says you never answer it."

Well, that was true. But he'd never thought it might be her. Had she tried to call?

"Is this how you spend your time down here? Sitting in this chair? What about your children, Jack? Your responsibilities?"

Jack didn't answer. He watched a blue jay alight on a tree in the distance. He sneezed.

"You're going to catch pneumonia." Earl noticed the shotgun and picked it up. "What's this for?" He held it high and aimed.

"Earl, what are you doing here? Making sure I pay my child support? Or did you come to offer me a job?" Jack was surprised by the bitterness in his own voice. "You're about a year too late."

"No, I think you're a long way from being ready for that offer."

Jack closed his eyes. He wasn't up to the verbal sparring, but out it tumbled. "Yeah, well, it seems I wasn't ready for the other one you made me either, was I?"

Earl picked up the cup again, walked over and set it near the end of the wall, and then came back near Jack. He lifted the gun again, aimed, and this time pulled the trigger. The cup burst, shattering into pieces on the wall and in the grass below it.

"Hey!" Jack said.

Earl sat down on the wall just in front of him. "You been down here feeling sorry for yourself, Jack?" he asked quietly.

Jack stared at Earl. He seemed older, but he couldn't figure out what was different. Maybe the sadness permeating his pale eyes was more than a mere reflection of Jack's own. Looking at him, Jack realized that they'd both aged in the last few months.

"No; I know I have only myself to blame. I'm just trying to figure out what to do next."

Earl nodded. "Mind if I look around?"

Jack waved—an "it's all yours" gesture. Earl's footsteps crunched through the dry grass as he neared the house. Jack heard the door to the little underground apartment open, and then heard it slam shut.

"Your brother owns this shack, huh?" Earl was right behind him; Jack hadn't heard him come back out. He'd dragged over the matching chair and now he sat.

"What's up, Earl? I really don't believe you drove five hours to talk about my brother's real-estate holdings." God, he was doing it again. Why couldn't he just ask a simple question?

"Listen, you have to remember that you're still a father, even if you don't feel like a husband anymore. When's the last time you saw your kids?"

Jack narrowed his eyes. "Claire send you here?"

"Would you have liked that?"

Jack looked at the hard ground between his legs. "Of course," he said quietly.

"Look, no matter what happens with you and Claire—"

"You talk like there's still more to come. What happens with me and Claire has already happened."

"Well, I didn't get that feeling when I talked to her."

Jack felt something flip in his stomach. "Why's that?"

Earl looked out into the valley, focusing as if he saw something in particular. "Nothing I can put my finger on. Just a feeling I got from her. She obviously misses you."

"No, she misses who she thought I was. She hates who I am."

"She knows neither of you can go back. I think you should give her more credit."

Jack sighed. The longing he felt for her overwhelmed him.

Earl turned to him. "You said you were trying to figure out what to do next. What do you want? Do you want her back?"

"Of course." He nodded his head fervently. "That's all I want. That's all I care about." He looked right at Earl as if his old boss had the power to grant his wish. "Did she ask you to come here, to ask me that?"

"No, Jack, she didn't ask me to come here. She doesn't have any idea why I'm here. I made up a work-related excuse. I just asked the question because your answer is important, something you need to figure out before you can decide what to do next." He paused. "A marriage can survive infidelity; it just has to be for the right reasons." His eyes drilled into Jack's. "What about Jenny?"

"How do you know?" Jack asked, ignoring his mention of Jenny.

"How do I know what?"

He knew that Earl understood what he was talking about. "That a marriage can survive infidelity." Earl stood up, took a step to the wall, and put one foot up on it. He leaned down and retied the lace on his shoe. Jack had never seen him so fidgety. "Earl?"

"Because mine did." He turned around and sat again on the wall, facing Jack. "You didn't answer me." He ignored the look of shock on Jack's face. "What about Jenny?"

"I don't know." He couldn't think past what Earl had just revealed to him.

"Dammit, you'd better know! It's important that you know."

"I know, I know, I mean I do know." Jack dropped his head again. "I do." The weight of his despair crushed him. He'd kept it at bay until now, but Earl's appearance had caused him to surrender to it, to allow it to break through his resistance. "Something Claire said to me, that I've thought about a lot while I've been here. She said, 'Jack Hilliard doesn't get everything he wants.' And now I understand, I know she's right."

An urgent need to make Earl understand gripped him. He lifted his head.

"Listen to me," he implored. "You know that old question? You know, the one where you're asked, 'If your wife and your mother were both drowning and you could only save one, who would you save?' Or some variation of that. You know what I'm talking about?"

Earl nodded sadly, and Jack scooted to the edge of his chair, closer to him.

"I've been here a long time, and I've been thinking a lot about that question. If it were Claire and Jenny who were drowning, who would I save? What would I do?"

Two months ago he would have felt like a fool, spilling his emotions like this to his old boss. Now he just didn't give a shit. "It took me so long. I tried to exclude certain factors in Claire's favor, you know, like her being the mother of our kids. I tried to isolate it, just the two of them. But I couldn't choose. I couldn't do that to either of them. But I kept telling myself, you *have* to choose. That's what Claire was saying. I can't have everything. I have to choose. I'm forced to choose or they both drown, you know? We all drown.

"Well, I chose. I finally chose. I don't want everything anymore. I just want Claire." He closed his eyes tightly. "I'd let her drown, Earl. If I had to, I'd let Jenny drown."

The next day, Jack resumed his vigil in the chair out by the stone wall. The air was cold but damp with the scent of snow. Gray, thick clouds hung heavily in the sky, and he wanted to be outside when the tiny flakes began to fall. Earl sat with him, bringing him hot coffee and soup from a can that he heated on the stove. Sometimes Jack drank the coffee, but the soup got cold and Earl ended up returning to the house with it. After a morning of silence, Earl finally spoke.

"Jack, you're needed back in St. Louis," he said bluntly, without preface.

Jack looked at him and shook his head. He assumed Earl referred to his job, and he hadn't thought about whether he'd fight for it.

"Jeff and Frank are trying Alex Turner for Maxine Shepard's murder. The trial starts in a few weeks."

Jack stared at him in surprise. "Alex?" *What happened to Mendelsohn?*

"Yes, Alex." Earl smiled slightly, pleased that he'd managed to pique Jack's interest. "They ruled Mendelsohn out pretty quickly. He's being charged with fraud and embezzlement, but he's not a murderer. They ran all the prints found on the gun against the prints on file for anyone who knew Jenny. As you know, because Alex is an attorney, his fingerprints are on file. They matched."

"Why would Alex murder Maxine Shepard?" Jack asked calmly, not wanting Earl to see the fear growing inside him.

"Seems Mr. Turner has a few screws loose. Once they tied his prints to the prints on the gun, they searched his house. They found a journal that revealed—well, let's just say he was a little obsessed with Jenny. He thought that if he could get rid of Maxine, he could win her back."

Jack's head swirled with emotions: disbelief, anger, and, even though he didn't want to admit it, a sort of understanding. He knew well Jenny's power to inspire obsessions.

Earl continued. "I guess she shared her Maxine troubles with Alex one too many times. He thought he'd be saving the day—you know, knocking off her nemesis, I guess."

"What about Jenny?" Jack asked.

"There's nothing in the journal to suggest she knew anything about Alex's strange scheme. In fact, there's not even anything that would constitute an outright admission by Alex, and therein lies the problem. He's denying it and pointing the finger at Jenny. And since she's gone—"

"What do you mean, she's gone?"

"She skipped town," he added before Jack misunderstood.

"She ran?" Jack couldn't believe it. It was impossible.

"She ran, not long after the charges were dropped. And that doesn't look good for her."

"But what about the lie detect—"

"Alex's attorney knows it's inadmissible, Jack. And he knows he doesn't have to prove she *did* do it. He just has to put the reasonable doubt in the jurors' heads that perhaps Alex *didn't*."

Jack suddenly knew why *he* was needed in St. Louis. Earl must have seen the realization on his face. "He's counting on you not to show up," he said.

"I can't do it," he said. "I can't get on the stand and testify about it. I can barely think about it."

"It wouldn't be any different from what you told the examiner at the lie-detector test. Jeff just needs to establish that you were with her."

"It would. It would be very different. It'd be in front of a courtroom full of people, and I'd be subject to cross-examination. A defense attorney would have a field day with my testimony."

"True, but Alex would have a field day without it," Earl replied.

Jack shook his head. "I'm already the laughingstock of the city. And Claire—"

"You'd be surprised how much public support you still command. They've taken the story and managed to romanticize the whole thing, to the dismay of Steve Schafer and his camp."

"Oh, great. I'm sure Claire appreciates *that*."

Earl stared hard at him. "Claire's instinct is a bit stronger than yours in terms of separating out what's really important, what matters."

Jack sighed. On that point he needed no persuading.

He looked out over the valley. The sky was darker in the southwest, and he guessed the snow was already falling there. It wouldn't be long now. It was moving in their direction.

"When Jenny was a child she saw her parents and little sister murdered," he said. He wanted Earl to know that about her. "We'd known each other for nine years and she didn't tell me until the night of Maxine Shepard's murder. I pressured her to tell me." He could see her sitting on the bed, her back to him, every ridge on her spine visible as she hunched over, trying to keep him out. "She didn't want to tell me, but I wouldn't let up." He laughed sarcastically. "Good 'ol Jack. 'Tell me, Jenny, so I can be there for you.' Except she knew all along I wouldn't be there for her. She resisted, but I pushed and pushed until she gave in." He paused, remembering. "Everything happened that night because I pressured her."

"Jack, she's an adult. You can't—"

"No, it's true. She told me I was selfish, and I didn't even understand what she meant. I practically begged her to let me stay the night." He saw them together in the garage, her cold hands in his. *Jenny, please*. And later her look of resignation, when she asked, *Do you want to go upstairs now?* "It's like she already knew the road we were on, but she didn't have the strength to tell me no."

"She's a strong woman. She made her own choices."

I'm a big girl. "You're wrong. I always thought so, too. But she only pretended to be strong." He looked straight at him. "She *didn't* do it, Earl."

Both of them knew that it really didn't matter what Jack wanted or was willing to do. Both of them knew that as long as he stayed in Missouri, he could be subpoenaed to appear at the trial, and that Earl was asking him to come back voluntarily merely as a courtesy. But Alex had to know that, too, didn't he? Perhaps he thought Jack, like Jenny, would run before he'd subject himself to that ordeal.

Jack felt wetness on his hand and looked down to see a snowflake melt against his red, chapped skin. The snow started to fall slowly, the feathery crystals settling intermittently on their coats and legs, but within minutes they were surrounded by white rain. It didn't float but rather appeared to be pushed down from the sky.

Jack finally nodded. Of course, he would go back. He had to. He had no choice. He would tell no lies. He would give them what they wanted, and he would finally hammer in the last nail of the coffin he'd started building for himself nearly a year before.

CHAPTER TWENTY-THREE

Judge Lehman's courtroom seemed larger than Jack remembered. He hadn't set foot in any courtroom since Jenny's arraignment. That had been mere weeks ago, really, but he felt so out of place, it could have been years. This particular courtroom boasted floor-to-ceiling windows with a southern exposure. In the summer, the room's sweltering heat forced the bailiff to lower the large, ancient blinds to block the sun; they were yellowed with age and dust flew whenever he fiddled with them. But it was March now; the blinds were pulled tight against the top of the window frame, their frayed cords hanging loose. Beams of dusty light penetrated the room.

When he passed through the heavy double doors in back, he focused on the judge's bench and on the empty seat in the witness box waiting for him. In his peripheral vision he saw the faces of the crowd, small, round blurs watching his entrance. He saw shoulders leaning against one another and heard hushed mumbling. He knew that if he looked, he would recognize many of the faces. But he didn't look. The only person he wanted to see was Claire, and he felt certain that she would stay away.

The only time he allowed his eyes to leave the front of the courtroom was when he passed the defendant's table. He deliberately turned to Alex. If there was one person he blamed more than himself for what had happened to Jenny, it was Alex. Jack had fantasized a lot about physically harming him in some way, and now it was possible. He could do it, if he wanted to. He knew he could manage to inflict a lot of pain on Alex before they pulled him away.

But Jack had let his emotions control his actions one time too many, so he took the one step up into the witness box and stood waiting for the judge's clerk to administer the oath. As he listened to her recite the familiar words, he maintained his vigilant refusal to look into the audience. He trained his eyes instead on the jurors.

He answered the oath and sat down. Judge Lehman nodded toward the prosecution table. Jack took a deep breath as Jeff McCarthy stood up and began to approach the witness box. Jeff moved hesitantly, apologetically, as if he'd been given the job of executing an old friend, but Jack thought he'd probably insisted on being the one to question him, rather than allow Frank Mann, who sat at the table with him, the opportunity.

"Hey, Jack," Jeff said under his breath so that only Jack could hear. And then loudly, for everyone: "Could you state your full name for the record, please?"

"John William Hilliard."

"But you go by Jack, is that correct?"

"Yes."

"For the record, can you tell us what you do for a living?"

"I'm"—he paused because he wasn't sure whether to use the past or present tense—"I'm the District Attorney for the City of St. Louis." Technically correct, for now.

"Are you familiar with the defendant in this case, Alex Turner?"

"Yes."

"How do you know him?"

"I first met him because he works at the university with my wife." *My estranged wife.*

"Are you familiar with him in any other capacity?"

"He once dated and lived with a friend of mine, Jenny Dodson." He heard his voice waver when he spoke her name. Had the microphone amplified it to everyone in the audience? In the silence between questions and answers he heard something drop, the creak of the old benches as people shifted positions. He stayed focused on Jeff.

"So how long would you say you've known Mr. Turner?" Jack knew it really didn't matter. But Jeff wanted to go slowly and get him into a conversational tone so that maybe some of the old charm would shine through. Jack just wanted to answer the relevant questions and leave.

"I knew *of* him probably within the first year that my wife started working at the university, about nine years ago."

"Did you ever have occasion to socialize with him?"

"He came to a party at our house. My wife invited him with the intention of setting him up with Jenny. After that, the only time I saw him was at a university or law function."

"You and your wife didn't socialize with Ms. Dodson and Mr. Turner?"

"As couples? No." Jack knew the next question on everyone's mind would be *Why not*? But he also knew Jeff wouldn't ask it; the defense attorney would.

"Jack, I'd like you to think back to the day leading up to Ms. Shepard's murder. November sixteenth of last year. Do you remember that day?"

"Yes." Did he remember it? It played over and over in his head like a broken record. He'd memorized every moment, had tried to determine at what point he might have reined himself in. There had been so many opportunities and he'd missed them—no, ignored them—all.

"Did you see Ms. Dodson that day?"

"Yes." His throat began to tighten and he had trouble swallowing. This was the easy part; how was he going to survive the cross? He glanced at the small thermos and empty Styrofoam cup in front of him. He wondered if he could still his hands enough to pour some water.

"When did you first see her?"

"That night."

"How did you happen to see her that night?"

"I met her at her car, in Stadium East garage."

"What time was it when you met her?"

"About eight thirty."

"What was Ms. Dodson's mood when you met up with her?"

Jack hesitated. *What happened? Is something wrong? You're scaring me.* He knew Jeff was trying to dilute the cross-examination by bringing up

Jenny's nervousness now. But Jack was afraid Alex's attorney would use his testimony later to argue that perhaps Jenny was nervous because of what she'd done or was planning to do: murder Maxine Shepard. All Sanders needed was that reasonable doubt. He didn't have to prove Jenny did do it, to suggest that Alex didn't.

"She was a little nervous. When she first stepped off the elevator, it was dark—"

"He's giving a narrative, Your Honor," Les Sanders, Alex's attorney, interrupted. Jack stared at Jeff. Though technically the objection was valid, they both knew Sanders was merely objecting because he didn't want the jury to hear a different explanation for Jenny's nervousness.

"Overruled." Judge Lehman knew it, too. "Go on, Mr. Hilliard."

"When she got off the elevator, it was dark and she couldn't see me well. She seemed scared to approach her car, but once she realized it was me, she was okay." *Sort of.* He hadn't lied, really.

"What did you do after you met her?"

"We talked for a few minutes and then we left."

"Where did you go?"

"To her house in Lafayette Square."

"How did you get there?"

"In her car." He'd hoped the straight questions and answers would help make everything seem matter-of-fact, just a normal, average day after work, but he felt the jurors staring at him, thinking he was slime. They must have been asking themselves, *Didn't this guy just mention a wife?* He also knew that with the next question, he would forever become to them and every other breathing body in the courtroom just another lawyer on the make.

"How long did you stay at her house?"

"Until morning. I'm not sure what time it was, but it was light when I left."

Murmurs rose like a mushroom cloud from the audience. Jack closed his eyes, tried to block out the static, but in the self-imposed darkness the voices only seemed louder. He wanted to object to their comments. Speculation! Hearsay! And then there was Jenny, on top of him, whispering in his ear, frightening him with her demands.

"You were both there, the entire time?"

"Yes."

Jeff nodded, his way of letting Jack know he was almost finished. "So you were with Ms. Dodson from eight thirty on Thursday night, November sixteenth, until the morning of November seventeenth, Friday morning? Is that correct?"

"Yes." *Yes, yes, yes, yes. I was there. I admit it. I was there.*

"One more question." Jeff paused as if he were thinking, though they both knew what it would be. "The entire time you were with Ms. Dodson, did she ever mention Maxine Shepard?"

"No." At least not to Jack. "Not to me." He glanced at Alex.

"Thank you." Jeff looked at the judge. "That's all, Your Honor." He turned and winked at Jack, and that would have been nice, except Jack knew the worst hadn't even begun.

M r. Hilliard." Sanders enunciated Jack's name slowly as he rose behind the defense table and strode nonchalantly to the witness box, waiting until he was right in front of it to ask his first question. "You said it was eight thirty when you met Ms. Dodson at her car in the garage?"

"Yes. Around that."

"How do you know?"

"I know how to tell the time." Little chuckles from the jurors and audience. But Jack hadn't meant to be funny. He just wasn't going to make it easy for the guy.

"That's cute. I'm sure you do. But really, Mr. Hilliard, I'm curious how you know exactly when you met her."

"I had a watch on." He pointed to his wrist. *Not a Rolex, but pretty accurate nonetheless.*

"Did you actually look at your watch that night, to know exactly what time you met her?"

"Yes."

"Really? Tell us about that."

"What do you want to know?" *Fuck you, Les. I'm not going to do your job for you.*

"What time did you first arrive at the garage? Did you notice that?"

"Yes, it was between seven and seven fifteen."

Sanders furrowed his brow. "But you didn't meet her until eight thirty?"

"Right."

"What were you doing between seven fifteen and eight thirty?"

Jack didn't want to admit that he'd gone to end a friendship but instead had started an affair.

"Mr. Hilliard?" Sanders repeated the question: "What were you doing between seven fifteen and eight thirty?"

"Waiting."

"For Ms. Dodson?"

"Yes."

"Was she late?"

It suddenly occurred to Jack that they all thought he and Jenny had *planned* to meet in the garage—a rendezvous. Why hadn't he realized that before now? He knew Sanders pursued this line of questioning under the guise of pinpointing the time, and thus Jenny's opportunity to commit murder. But Jack now understood that his other goal was to make Jenny look just as sleazy as Jack and then be lucky enough to get him also to testify that she was late for their little liaison. Then even Jack couldn't testify to where she'd been. "I don't know what you mean by late."

Sanders sighed heavily, partly to express his frustration but more for theatrics. "Late, Mr. Hilliard. Did she arrive in the garage later than you thought she would?"

"I was not expecting her at any particular time."

Sanders threw a thin manila folder onto the table behind him. He waved one hand helplessly toward Judge Lehman. "Your Honor."

The judge shrugged. "So phrase your questions better, Mr. Sanders."

For the first time in many months, Jack felt a slight smile cross his lips. Sanders grunted.

"Let's back up, why don't we. Had you and Ms. Dodson agreed to meet in the garage?"

"No." The hum began anew.

"So why did you go to the garage to meet her?"

"To see her." Only Jack saw him roll his eyes at the useless answer. "Why?"

Jack looked at Jeff for an objection. But Jeff just stared back, as if he, too, wanted to know what could have compelled Jack to do such a stupid thing. "I . . . I needed to talk to her. To tell her I couldn't be around her anymore."

Sanders laughed. "You mean to tell me, you went to the garage to tell her *you couldn't see her anymore*, and yet you just testified to Mr. McCarthy that you spent the night at her house?"

God, it did sound ridiculous. Jack determined that he would get Jeff's attention, regardless of how he did it. He turned to the judge. "Judge, I don't see how—"

The judge raised his hand to cut him off. "Could counsel approach the bench, please?"

Jeff scrambled out of his chair; Sanders sauntered over. The judge leaned over the bench and whispered, "Mr. Sanders, how is this relevant?"

"I'm trying to establish the time they met in the garage," Sanders hissed. "And he's just giving me the runaround."

"So establish it. But how's that relate to *why* he was meeting her, unless you're trying to insinuate he had something to do with the murder, too? I assume that's not what you're doing."

"No, Your Honor."

"Then get on with it. Why he met her isn't relevant. Trying to titillate the jury doesn't qualify."

Sanders looked down, only slightly embarrassed at having his intentions exposed so blatantly. He moved closer to Jack to continue his questioning. "When you first arrived at the garage, how long did you think you'd have to wait for Ms. Dodson?"

"I didn't have an opinion about that."

"But you looked at your watch while waiting for her?"

"Yes."

"How many times?"

"Several. I don't recall the exact number."

"Did you look at your watch because it was taking her longer than you thought it would?"

"I didn't think about how long it would take her."

"Then why did you look at your watch?"

Jack shrugged. "I don't know. I had been there awhile. I was wondering how late it was."

"So it was eight thirty when she finally arrived?"

"Yes."

"Did she say she'd just come from her office?"

"No. But I assumed that."

"Your assumption could have been wrong, couldn't it?"

"Sure, I suppose."

"Was she surprised to see you?"

"At first, maybe."

"Why?"

Jack narrowed his eyes. "I think that would be speculation, wouldn't it, Mr. Sanders?"

"Well, then, sir, let me rephrase it. Why do you *believe* she was surprised to see you?"

"I guess you could say we had a nine-to-five friendship. It was unusual for us to get together in the evening unless we were both at some law-related event."

"A nine-to-five friendship?"

Jack shrugged.

"Sir, the court reporter can't transcribe a shrug."

"Well, I think the question was already asked and answered."

"How did she look when you first saw her?"

He saw her in his mind then. The black from head to toe, the hesitation in her step when she saw him on her car. Good. He'd never known her not to look good. "Can you be more specific?"

"Her hair, her clothes. Were they in place, or did she appear to be disheveled?"

"Everything seemed in place to me."

Sanders walked away from Jack. He crossed slowly in front of the bench to the defense table, where Alex sat. For a moment Jack wondered if some miracle had occurred—that Sanders was finished and he would be spared the agony of testifying about the night at her place.

But it became apparent rather quickly that Sanders wasn't finished. He opened the manila folder he'd thrown down earlier and pulled out a piece of paper. Jack looked at Jeff, who began to fidget in his chair. Neither had expected Jack to be questioned about any documents.

Sanders approached the witness box. "Mr. Hilliard, how long have you known Ms. Dodson?"

"About nine years."

"How would you describe your relationship?"

"We were friends."

"Good friends?"

"Yes."

"Did you confide in each other about things?"

"Certain things. Mainly job-related things."

"In all that time you knew her, nine years, did she ever talk to you about Maxine Shepard?"

Jack wanted to know what the document in Sanders's hand said. He tried to think back. Had she e-mailed him some rude comments about Maxine, saying that she wished she were dead, or that she wanted to kill her? He couldn't remember anything like that. In fact, he and Jenny hardly ever e-mailed each other. He now realized that they'd always wanted to hear each other's voice.

"Yes."

"What did she say about her?"

"I don't know. A lot, I'm sure. I can't remember everything."

"Was it your impression that she liked Ms. Shepard?"

"She wasn't Jenny's favorite client, if that's what you mean."

"How do you know that?"

"They just didn't click. Some people click, some don't."

"Like you and Ms. Dodson, you clicked?"

"Objection!" Jeff sprang up from his chair. *Finally*, Jack thought. The crowd began talking again; the hum of the circling bees grew louder.

"I withdraw the question, Your Honor." Smirking, he turned back to Jack. "Mr. Hilliard, let me ask you something. I'll get to the point. You cared for Ms. Dodson very much, didn't you?"

"Yes." His body told him to shut down or run away.

"You would do anything to protect her, wouldn't you?"

"No, I wouldn't do 'anything.'"

Sanders pretended to have received a positive answer. "Indeed, you've always been jealous of Mr. Turner and his relationship with Ms. Dodson, haven't you?"

"No."

"You don't like Mr. Turner, do you?"

"As we speak, no, I don't."

"You never liked him, did you, when he and Ms. Dodson dated and were living together?"

"I didn't have an opinion about him."

"She was your friend for nine years, and you had no opinion about the man she lived with?"

"I didn't think about him much."

"But you said yourself that you and your wife . . ." Sanders paused. "What's your wife's name, Mr. Hilliard?"

Jack thought his head was going to blow from the pressure building up inside it. Of course Sanders knew Claire's name. "Claire."

"You said yourself that you and your wife, Claire, never socialized with Ms. Dodson and Mr. Turner as couples, isn't that so?"

"That's correct."

"Why not?"

What was he going to say? *I only wanted to spend time with her alone. I didn't want to share the time with some other guy.* He suddenly remembered one of Jenny's complaints about Alex. "They never socialized with anyone as a couple, that I know of."

"Let me go back to Maxine Shepard again. Were you aware that Ms. Shepard tried to have Ms. Dodson fired?"

Jack debated how to answer. Jenny had told him that Maxine complained about her, but never that she'd tried to have her fired. Only Mendelsohn had done that. "No."

"Ms. Dodson never mentioned that to you?"

"No."

"So she didn't confide everything to you, did she?"

"I didn't say she did."

"There were a lot of things you didn't know about Ms. Dodson, weren't there?"

You have no idea.

Jeff was on it. "Objection. I think we've gone a little bit beyond the scope of my direct."

"I disagree, Your Honor. It was Mr. McCarthy who first asked Mr. Hilliard if Ms. Dodson ever mentioned Maxine Shepard. He opened up the issue of what Ms. Dodson might have said."

"But it's all hearsay, Judge," said Jeff.

"I'm not trying to prove the truth of what she might have told him, just the fact of whether or not she confided her feelings about Ms. Shepard—what he knew."

"How is that relevant? Except to use the testimony as a way to suggest she didn't like her, and then it's hearsay, as I said." The muscles in Jeff's jaw tightened.

"I'll tie up the relevancy shortly, Judge," Sanders said, a little too confidently.

The judge raised his hand to halt their banter. "I'll allow it, but get to the point."

But Sanders seemed already to have made his point, and Jeff's objection had only helped drive it home. Sanders walked over to Jack and handed the paper to him.

"Objection!" Jeff slammed his palms on the table. "Excuse me, have I seen that?"

While they argued in front of the bench, Jack quickly read the document: a letter from Maxine Shepard to Stan Goldberg, and copied to Newman's managing partner and to Rob Kollman and Steve Mendelsohn. In it, she rambled on about Jenny, how she was mishandling her cases and billing too much time, her bad attitude, her failure to return her phone calls, even an accusation that Jenny had tried to sabotage Maxine's attempts to reconcile with her stepchildren. There was so much negative information that it was readily apparent that the writer of the letter was, at the very least, exaggerating, and at the most, paranoid and delusional.

Jack was struck by the thought that Maxine must not have been too smart; her first mistake, if she wanted to get rid of Jenny, was sending the letter to Stan. Stan was a well-respected attorney, but he was not well liked by those who didn't really know him. He came across as gruff, barking orders at new associates he passed in the halls, more out of a desire to scare them than because he needed some work done. He'd made many a new female associate cry. It took years for them to understand that in order to gain his respect, they had to stand up to him; some never learned.

But Jenny had known right off the bat; she'd been at Newman only a few months when she told him to go fuck himself after he'd ordered her to get him a cup of coffee in the middle of their meeting with a client. Jack remembered her telling him the story. She'd said it only because the client was on the phone in the corner of the conference room, not paying attention, and she'd blurted it under her breath, only partially intending Stan to hear. Her first thought was that she would be fired on the spot, but then she detected the start of a smile on Stan's face. Her boldness earned his immediate and lasting loyalty. He'd never give her up, despite the demands of some rich client.

Jack looked up just as Judge Lehman was saying he would allow Sanders to use the letter.

"You can question him about his knowledge of the letter, or to refresh his recollection, and that's it," the judge said to Sanders. "Otherwise, the document is hearsay."

Jeff returned to his seat, his body radiating his frustration. Sanders approached Jack.

"Mr. Hilliard, have you had a chance to look at this document?"

"Yes."

"Can you tell us what it is?"

"It appears to be a letter, written about one year ago, from Maxine Shepard to Stan Goldberg, with copies to some other attorneys at Newman."

"Who is Stan Goldberg?"

"He's the head of the bankruptcy department at Newman. To my knowledge, he was Jenny's direct boss."

"Can you summarize the letter for us?"

"Summarize it? It sounds like Maxine Shepard was trying to make a case for getting Jenny fired. Indeed, she suggests her dismissal at the end."

"Have you ever seen this letter before?"

Jack shook his head, suppressing the urge to mouth off. He wanted to point out that the letter wasn't addressed to him. He was also beginning to wonder if Maxine Shepard was even the true author of the letter. "No," he said.

"Ms. Dodson never showed it to you?"

"No." It wasn't addressed to her, either. He wondered if Jenny even knew about it.

"Did she ever mention its existence to you?"

"No."

"Isn't it possible, Mr. Hilliard, that what you took to be a simple dislike of a client was actually much more?"

"No, it's not possible, not for Jenny Dodson."

Sanders walked around, trying to look like he was thinking deeply about that answer. Jack knew he was just dramatizing. "Let's go back to the garage," Sanders said then.

Jack's stomach churned.

"You testified that you went with Ms. Dodson in her car to her house, is that correct?"

"That's correct."

"Did you stop anywhere on the way?"

"No."

"What time did you arrive there?"

"Around eight forty-five, I think. It only takes about ten minutes to get from downtown to her place, and we were only in the garage a few minutes before leaving."

"What did you do when you arrived at her house?"

Jack, Jeff, and Frank had discussed how they would deal with this line of questioning. They knew Sanders had a right to ask Jack about his time spent there, to try to find any cracks in Jack's story. But they had agreed to ask the judge to limit it as much as possible.

"We talked a bit and then ordered dinner."

"Ordered?"

"To be delivered."

"How long did it take the food to be delivered?"

"I don't know."

"Do you know what time it arrived?"

He thought of what Jenny had said to Alex: *It's nine thirty. I'm not usually at work this late.*

"I think it was a little after nine thirty."

"Would the delivery person be able to testify that you were there?"

"No."

"Why not?"

"I didn't go to the door; Jenny did." Jack had a hunch that Alex hadn't told Sanders about his visit to Jenny's that night; indeed, Jack hadn't even told Jeff or Frank. Although it was risky, he wanted to control the timing of the information coming to light. He considered bringing up Alex now but thought better of it. Not yet. He lay in wait, ready to pounce.

Sanders was quiet for a minute, letting the jury absorb Jack's inability to produce a corroborating witness. "And then what did you do?"

His answer was a harmless lie: "We ate the food."

"And then what?"

"We talked some more." Simultaneously spoken with Jeff's "Objection."

Everyone turned in Jeff's direction. "May I approach, Your Honor?" he asked calmly. When Sanders and Jeff reached the bench, Jeff said, "Your Honor, I understand where he's heading. He wants to see if there's any point at which Ms. Dodson might not have been with Mr. Hilliard. But can't he just ask the questions directly? After all, it is cross-examination. He's allowed to lead." He paused, glancing at Jack. "I don't think it's necessary to make him testify about every little interaction between the two of them."

The judge looked at Sanders, raised his eyebrows, and waited for a response.

Sanders cocked his head and shrugged. "I think what he did that night goes to his character." He glanced at Jack with a smirk.

Jack looked down at his lap, fidgeted in his chair. He finally poured some water to prevent himself from butting in, but he couldn't get much down when he tried to swallow.

"I don't think his character is at issue, Your Honor," Jeff said. "I sure didn't make it an issue on my direct."

The judge looked at Jack now, who looked back at him. "I tend to agree with Mr. McCarthy, Mr. Sanders," he said, turning back to the bat-tling attorneys. "It leans to the inflammatory side, and I'm not sure it serves much of a purpose, from an evidentiary standpoint." He was quiet for a moment and then added, "Why don't you just ask him specifically what you need to know? We'll see how that goes."

Sanders nodded in resignation, but he didn't look too upset. He prob-ably thought he'd still find a way to have some fun with Jack. "Mr. Hilliard, were you awake the entire night?"

"No."

Sanders smiled. "You fell asleep?"

"Yes."

"Then how are you sure she was there with you the entire time?"

How *was* he sure? He wasn't really, was he? He struggled to reconcile what he thought he knew with what could have happened. No, he was sure. He knew she'd been with him the whole time. He hadn't slept much that night, but when he had, it was with her in his arms. But then he also remembered waking up surprised to find her on top of him. He remem-bered her scent, how she'd smelled of the cold, November night. How could he be sure?

"I didn't sleep much—only in very short intervals. And she was with me. She was asleep, too."

"How do you know that?"

"She fell asleep first." He needed to be clearer so that the jurors knew she was there, even when both of them were asleep. "I held her," he whis-pered.

"Could you speak up, please? I couldn't hear you."

Jack turned and looked directly at the jury. "I held her," he said, louder this time.

Sanders didn't like that; he rushed past it. "What time was it, the first time you fell asleep?"

Jack looked away from the jury, back to Sanders, but his mind was in Jenny's bedroom, on her bed, staring at the sheers while he waited for her to fall asleep. *These voices must be my soul.* He'd forgotten the music playing in the background, but now it came back to him clearly. He had trouble concentrating on Sanders's question. "I don't know for sure. Around eleven."

Sanders frowned. "The food arrived a little after nine thirty, you ate it and were asleep by eleven?" His voice conveyed his disbelief. It sounded crazy even to Jack.

"Yes," he answered emphatically.

"Do you make it a habit to rendezvous at the homes of women friends and then just go to sleep when you get there?"

Jeff jumped to his feet, but before the word even had time to leave his lips, Judge Lehman's voice bellowed from above them all: "You're out of line, Mr. Sanders! Get up here!"

"I withdraw the question," Sanders said on his way to the bench, but his face made it clear that to he just hadn't been able to resist.

The judge pointed his finger over the bench at Sanders; he lowered his voice but his anger was palpable. "Mr. Sanders, I'm only going to say this one time. You've just crossed that thin line you've been straddling. Don't do it again or I'll hold you in contempt."

"Yes, Your Honor."

"The jury will disregard defense counsel's last question," the judge called out. Jeff took his seat and Sanders, looking appropriately admonished, returned to his position in front of Jack. "Okay, you said you slept in very short intervals. What time was it when you woke up after the first interval?"

Jack closed his eyes for a split second, saw the clock on her nightstand, the big red digital numbers. "One fifty," he said without hesitation, without thinking about it. He didn't need to; his thoughts had completely left the courtroom. The clock acted as a Play button on an imaginary tape machine, and the night played again. His mind fast-forwarded the tape, and there was his head between her legs, his tongue inside her, his eyes open and watching her from below. She let out a cry—a howl, really, like an animal in pain—and it scared him, so he backed out, but she grabbed his head and pressed him back down to her. The stereo played the music, and he had trouble distinguishing her cries from the sounds of a saxophone.

A shiver traveled the length of his body. It reminded him of how cold he'd been afterward.

He imagined sleeping in his own bed then, but someone kept trying to wake him up, repeating his name the way Claire used to sometimes, except they were saying "Mr. Hilliard" instead of "Jack." Finally, one voice alone, softer now: "Jack?"

He opened his eyes. Judge Lehman leaned over his bench in Jack's direction. "Jack, are you okay? Do you need a break?"

But the words wouldn't form; his mouth wouldn't open. He shook his head, no.

"Do you want Mr. Sanders to repeat the question?"

He nodded and gazed at Sanders vacantly.

"How did you know it was exactly one fifty?"

The question wouldn't register. He wanted to say, *What?* but he still couldn't speak. The muscles in his throat just wouldn't push the word up and out. He reached for the water.

"Mr. Hilliard," Sanders said insistently, "you said it was one fifty the first time you woke up. How did you know the exact time?"

"I looked at the clock when I woke up." The words croaked out.

Sanders turned around slightly so that the judge couldn't see and made a face for the audience. "You take note of the time quite often, don't you?"

Jack didn't respond, thinking the judge would hammer Sanders. But Judge Lehman's head was leaning over to the other side as he whispered something to his clerk. He hadn't heard the question.

"I suppose."

"So you were asleep almost three hours. Did you fall asleep again that night?"

"Yes."

"Did you happen to notice the time you fell asleep the second time?" His voice oozed sarcasm.

"That was one time I didn't notice the clock."

Sanders laughed. Jack knew that he should have just simply answered no. He was letting Sanders get to him. But reliving the night exhausted him. And he was beginning not to care.

"Can you make an estimate?"

Jack thought about it. Their first round on the bed had been urgent, and fast, but then how long had they been in the kitchen? And then up-stairs again, before they dozed off? They'd spent more time in explo-ration the second time, once she'd unburdened herself to him and they'd worked through their little spat. He struggled to calculate the hours, but his mind kept trying to play the tape again; computing time seemed out of the question. "Probably close to four, but I'm not certain."

"And what time did you wake up?"

"I don't know, but it was light out."

Sanders walked back to the defense table and picked up another docu-ment, but this time he approached Jeff first. Jeff nodded his assent after glancing at it. When Sanders handed the paper to Jack, it fluttered in his grasp. He quickly read it and set it on the wall of the witness box. "Mr. Hilliard, do you know what this document is?"

"It's a report from the National Oceanic and Atmospheric Adminis-tration."

"Did you see the portion of the document I have highlighted?"

"Yes."

"Can you tell us what it indicates?"

"It indicates that on November seventeenth last year, the sun rose at six fifty-four a.m."

Sanders grabbed the document from the wall. "Your Honor, I'll get this into evidence later, during our case." Judge Lehman nodded. Sanders turned back to Jack. "So do you think it was six fifty-four or after when you woke up the second time?"

"It appears that way."

"So you were asleep for almost three hours the second time, too, cor-rect?"

"Approximately."

"So, for a total of almost six hours, you really can't say where Ms. Dodson was, can you?"

"I told you, she slept at the same time I did."

"Both times?"

"Yes."

"That's just an assumption, isn't it, Mr. Hilliard?"

"No."

"You can't really testify honestly, can you, that she was there next to you every minute of the time you were asleep?"

"I think I can."

"You think?"

"I would have noticed if she got up; she would have stirred me."

"How are you so sure?"

"I'm a light sleeper." Not that night. He'd slept like a baby.

"Mr. Hilliard, tell me something." Sanders held one hand to his chin and rubbed it. "In the morning, did Ms. Dodson look any different to you? You know, did she exhibit any signs of having struggled with someone during the night?"

Jack stared hard at Sanders and remained silent.

"You're under oath," Sanders reminded him.

He remembered her coldness, her muscles tensing when he brushed the hair from her back and saw the marks he'd made. He continued to stare at Sanders. He couldn't look at the jury; he couldn't even make himself look at Jeff to plead for help. A simple *yes* implicated Jenny. A *yes* with explanation implicated Jack. A *no* constituted perjury. But only if it could be proved. Did Sanders somehow already know the answer to the question? Had they examined Jenny for telltale marks when she was first arrested?

"Mr. Hilliard?"

"Yes, but it was—"

"Thank you, Mr. Hilliard. You've answered my question."

"It was my fault." Was it, though? "The struggle was with me."

Sanders smirked, but didn't ask for further clarification. Jack had just tainted himself and they both knew it.

"Mr. Hilliard," Sanders continued, before Jack could try to rehabilitate himself, "was that the only time you ever spent the night at Ms. Dodson's home?"

"Yes."

"Really?" Sanders raised his eyebrows; apparently he had expected a negative response.

"Yes," Jack insisted.

"Had you ever spent the night with her anywhere else?"

"No."

"Had you ever had any type of intimate relations with her before, at all?"

Jeff stood, accidentally knocking a file to the floor. It hit the floor with a thud. "Your Honor, I object. First of all, I don't believe Mr. Hilliard ever testified that he was intimate with Ms. Dodson—in fact, this is the same type of testimony Mr. Sanders was trying to get earlier, and you disallowed it. Second of all, what's the relevance of this question?"

Judge Lehman sighed and waved them up. "Sanders?" He'd dispensed with the "Mister."

"Judge, I should be able to show the extent of their relationship, to show motivation for being her alibi, and—"

Jeff interrupted. "She's not on trial, remember? We dropped those charges."

Sanders threw him a mean glance. "No, but my client is, and she was never acquitted. I'm not convinced she didn't do it. Mr. Turner should be entitled to use all available evidence that supports his innocence. And if Jack's relationship with Ms. Dodson might affect his testimony, I should be able to point that out."

"Judge, you disallowed this earlier as too inflammatory," Jeff said, his voice rising.

"Well, Mr. McCarthy, I'm entitled to change my mind," the judge said. "I think I now agree with Mr. Sanders." His tight-lipped grimace suggested that he didn't want to, though. Jeff rolled his eyes at Jack and shook his head in apology. Jack shrugged. He had nothing left to lose.

The judge continued, this time directing his comments to Sanders. "But Mr. McCarthy is right about your question, in terms of putting words in the witness's mouth. I think you first need to establish intimate relations, if there were any, which you haven't done." He paused. "Just keep it limited, Sanders. Don't try to get this courtroom all worked up, or I'll cut you off."

Sanders nodded and looked almost gleeful. "I'll withdraw the previous question, for the time being," he said when he returned to his spot near Jack. "Were you intimate with Ms. Dodson on the night you described, the night you spent at her home?"

"Yes."

"Were you ever intimate with her before that night?"

Jack stared at Sanders; he refused to look away, to betray his thoughts. It seemed almost worse to have to testify about the first time in the garage, in April. It was bad enough to admit to Claire what had happened in November, but he'd told her it'd only been one night, and it had been, really. But he knew the knowledge that something had happened more than seven months earlier, even if it had been only a kiss, would add insult to injury. "You'll have to define intimate."

"You didn't need a definition for my previous question."

"I was certain that whatever the definition, what happened on that particular night would qualify."

Sanders smirked. "Well, I'll ask *you* the question. How did you define it, in order to answer the previous question?"

"I assumed you meant sexual intercourse."

"Are you testifying that you and Ms. Dodson engaged in sexual intercourse on the night you described at her home?"

"Yes."

"Had you ever had sexual intercourse with her at any other time?"

"No."

"But you were intimate with her on other occasions?"

"As I said, you'll have to define intimate."

Sanders walked over to the defense table, turned around, and leaned against it nonchalantly with his arms crossed.

"Well, I suppose the best way to ask it is this: Did you ever, before that night, engage in any activity with Ms. Dodson that you didn't want your wife—Claire, was it?—to know about?"

Jack's heart pounded, pumping the blood hard through his veins and causing him to grow warm. He knew the color in his face betrayed his anger. How low could this asshole go?

"Mr. Hilliard?" Sanders persisted.

"Yes. Once only; we exchanged a kiss."

"And when was that?"

"Last spring, April."

"Was that the only other time you had any kind of intimate relations with Ms. Dodson?"

"Yes."

"A kiss in April, and then nothing until sexual intercourse in November, seven months later?"

"That's right."

Sanders smirked again, and Jack braced himself for another rude comment, but Sanders must have thought better of it. "Mr. Hilliard, let me ask you this. Don't you think it's a little odd that Maxine Shepard would be murdered on the same night you claim to have spent the entire evening engaging in sexual intercourse with Ms. Dodson? Especially given that you testified you'd never done that before?" He paused. "Isn't that just a little too convenient?"

A spark ran up Jack's spine; he sat up straighter. This was it; this was his chance. He hoped his instinct was right, that Alex hadn't told Sanders about stopping by Jenny's that night.

"Well, Mr. Sanders, you're right. At first I thought it was really odd. And, in fact, after Jenny was first charged with the crime, I couldn't believe it." Maybe he should just own up, too, while he was at it. "But my disbelief at that time stemmed more from my fear of being found out, since I knew I was her ticket to freedom, than from the coincidental nature of the two events." He paused, finally, to add his own effect. He spoke more slowly. "But then later, when the other evidence pointing to Alex was presented to me, I thought about how he'd stopped by that night"—Jack watched as Sanders turned to Alex in surprise—"how he sneaked into her bedroom, where she kept her gun, like some cat burglar." He couldn't believe that Sanders hadn't objected yet. He was probably still processing the fact that Alex had been at Jenny's. "And how he spoke to her that night, asking her if Maxine Shepard was still bothering her, and accusing her of having someone at her house. She told me afterward that he was 'insanely' jealous of me. She used that word, *insanely*. And then it all started to make sense."

Jack vaguely heard Judge Lehman say something like, "That's enough, Mr. Hilliard," but it sounded far off and he ignored it. He noticed Sanders approaching the judge and then Jeff jumping up to join him. Out of habit, Jack glanced at the jury to gauge whether they understood the relevancy of what he'd said. And that's when she smiled at him. The woman in the rear, far left seat, a middle-aged redhead with freckles on every inch of the exposed part of her skin. It was a warm smile, a sympathetic smile, the kind he remembered getting whenever he was the interrogator, so long ago, it seemed. It came more from her eyes than her mouth. It enveloped him, gently washed over him like a cleansing bath. He found himself smiling back.

Jack turned back to Sanders and realized that Sanders, even as he listened to Judge Lehman's whispers, had seen the contact Jack and the red-haired woman had made. The wild look in his eyes told Jack that Sanders knew he was losing control over his examination, that Jack was on the offensive. The realization spurred Jack on.

"So to answer your question, no, it's not odd. I know you want the jury to think I'm here testifying because of some vendetta I have against your client but—"

"I said enough, Mr. Hilliard," Judge Lehman ordered.

"I'm testifying against Mr. Turner to make sure a murderer goes to jail. You really think I'd get up here and put myself through this for any other reason?"

"Mr. Hilliard!" The judge was yelling now. But Jack didn't care. He wasn't going to shut up, now that he'd finally let loose.

"Do you really think I'd get up here and testify in front of the world that I betrayed my wife's trust, that I would actually make that up to somehow get back at your client for the simple reason you think I don't like him? My *wife*, Sanders!" Sanders backed away from the bench. "You know, the one whose name you have trouble remembering. You think I'd intentionally destroy her, the woman who matters the most to me, merely because I don't like your client?" Out of the corner of his eye he saw the guard approaching the witness box. Sanders turned his back to Jack and waved one hand in the air to indicate his belief that Jack spewed gibberish. "Or even to somehow protect the reputation of a woman who's already been to hell and back? When she was a child she watched her family be executed. Has anyone told the jury that yet?"

Jack's voice broke with the last sentence and he collapsed back against his chair. Judge Lehman had given up on him and was now telling the bailiff to remove the jury from the courtroom. He called a recess and ordered everyone out into the hall. Jack knew he'd caused a quiet chaos to erupt, but it was all outside the little boxing ring he'd created in his head for himself and Sanders. The guard came around to the witness box and grabbed Jack's arm just above his elbow.

"I'm done." Jack jerked his arm away.

"Let it go, they're almost gone," he heard the judge say, and the guard stepped back.

The jury had been taken out quickly. For the first time, Jack let his eyes fall on the audience as they made their stunned way into the halls. They departed in relative silence, their voices low and respectful. Only a few were brave enough to turn around and steal a glance at him, to consider one last time if what they'd just witnessed was real.

And then he saw her. Standing in the corner next to the last window in the row, bringing up the rear of the spectators filing out from that side of the room. Her body was turned to the side, facing the crowd, but her head was turned to the front and she'd been watching him. Mark was next to her, his arm around her, trying to lead her out. She'd dressed for work; she'd probably been at the university earlier, he guessed. She wore straight black trousers and a brown turtleneck. She'd obviously taken care not to stand out, so unusual for her.

In the instant they made eye contact, he lost his breath. He hadn't expected her to be there; indeed, he'd been certain she would stay away, wouldn't subject herself to listening to him rehash a night spent with another woman.

But there she was. Her hair had grown slightly since he'd last seen her; it was now just below chin length, one side tucked behind her ear, and her big, sad eyes pierced him, but the anger they'd radiated since she'd learned of his betrayal was gone. He searched to see if the anger had been replaced by forgiveness, but couldn't tell. He saw something new and struggled to identify it.

"Ma'am, you'll have to leave the courtroom during the recess." She started at the voice of the bailiff next to her, shooing them along. The shuffling crowd in front of her just moments before was now fifteen feet ahead, passing through the doorway. Neither she nor Jack had noticed. She nodded politely to the bailiff and made her way to the door with one last look in his direction.

Then, in an instant, he realized. He slumped into his chair.

It was pity. That's what he'd seen in her eyes. Pity.

CHAPTER TWENTY-FOUR

Claire and Mark were the last ones out of the courtroom. As soon as the bailiff closed the doors behind them, Sanders began screaming.

"I demand a mistrial, Your Honor!" he yelled as he paced in front of the judge's bench. "What the hell just happened in here?"

Judge Lehman had had it with outbursts; he seemed to have even less patience with this one, since he probably suspected it was all for show. "Why don't you relax and go back to your seat, Mr. Sanders, and we'll see if we can figure it out."

Jeff headed back to the prosecution table before being told to, but Sanders kept on.

"First he starts spewing information that we haven't been told about, and then he has the audacity to make eyes at one of the jurors before he goes into a little monologue about his love for his wife! Not to mention this comes after his testimony about his tryst with the other one. This is simply unbelievable! It's like he's some fucking Lothario!"

"Mr. Sanders! You watch your language in my courtroom. We might be at recess, but I can still hold you in contempt. Sit down!"

"Me? What about him?" Sanders pointed at Jack. "He's the one who needs to be held in contempt."

"For the last time—sit down."

He finally did, leaning over to Alex and quietly discussing his outrage with him.

The judge pushed his chair away from the bench and wheeled around to face Jack.

"Would you like to explain to us what that was all about?"

"He asked me a question. I answered it." Jack looked out into the empty gallery.

"I'll give you another chance, since I like you. Would you like to explain what that was about?"

Jack wondered if Claire was still in the courthouse.

"Jack?"

"I'm sorry, Your Honor," he said, looking up at the judge. "I don't have an explanation. I'm not trying to be smart, but I guess I think it was pretty self-explanatory."

"It might have been self-explanatory," the judge said, "but it was wholly improper, and you of all people know that. I expect better from you."

"I apologize, Your Honor."

He wondered if she would return when they let everyone back in. Maybe she'd seen enough.

"Did you have an improper communication with a juror?"

"No."

"What is Mr. Sanders referring to, then?"

"I looked at the jurors and one of them smiled at me. That's all."

The judge turned to Sanders. "Mr. Sanders, is that accurate?"

"He smiled back at her."

The judge grunted in exasperation and shook his head. "Is that it?"

Sanders stared at Jack; Jack sensed his frustration. "Yes, that's it."

"Well, here's what I'm going to do. Mr. Sanders, if you think you have cause for a mistrial because of whatever he said or because he smiled at a juror"—the judge rolled his eyes—"then you can submit any motions you'd like after the trial is over, if it's necessary. But frankly, I don't think anything he said tainted the jury beyond repair, so I'm not going to stop the trial at this point and make the State start all over with a new jury. I—"

"He called my client a murderer, Your Honor," Sanders interrupted.

"Well, that's what the case is about, so I don't think the word is too shocking for them."

"Judge," Sanders's voice rose, "what about all that stuff about Mr. Turner stopping by Ms. Dodson's house on the night of the murder?"

"What about it? He's *your* client. You had full access to that information." The judge paused for a moment. "You'll have the opportunity to question him about it." He turned to Jack. "Jack, would you like to take a few minutes before we get started again?"

"Yes. Thank you."

Judge Lehman nodded his permission. Jack stepped down from the witness box and strode to the rear doors. He avoided looking at Alex; he'd already exerted the little bit of power he'd had left.

"Mr. Hilliard," the judge called to him from the bench, just as Jack was about to leave the courtroom, "you're still under oath."

"Yes, Judge," he acknowledged, and braced himself for the crowd outside as he pushed through the doors.

The noise of gossip dimmed as Jack stepped into the wide, open hall. Bodies stepped aside and eyes fell to the floor when he cut a path toward the bathrooms, as if everyone thought he carried some highly contagious disease. He scanned the small groups of people milling about to see if Claire was among them. He saw Mark and Earl standing together at the end of the hall; she wasn't there. They began to approach, but he shook his head to send them away. When he didn't see Claire anywhere, he walked down the hall near the elevators, face forward and pretending not to hear the murmurs. He passed through a door into the long corridor he knew led to the judges' chambers and to bathrooms more private than the ones in the front hall.

And that's where he saw the redheaded juror, the one who had smiled at him and caused Sanders to lose it. Her face lit up when he approached and she opened her mouth to speak. He raised his hand to stop her.

"I can't talk to you, ma'am. It could be cause for mistrial." He surprised himself by laughing a bit, thinking of Sanders's ridiculous outburst. Even as he attempted protest, he knew he was taking it too lightly. Very unchar-acteristic of him. "On top of all the other sins I've testified to in there, I don't need to add jury tampering."

She laughed, too. He reached down to open the door to the men's room, but it was locked.

"My fellow jurors," she said, nodding at the door to the ladies' room. "I'm waiting, too."

He looked down at his feet. He knew he should retreat to the bath-room out in the main hall and deal with the stares. If the bailiff caught him standing with her, there'd be hell to pay. He turned to leave.

"Your remorse is evident, even if you don't realize it, and she saw it, too. If you meant what you said in there, give her the time she needs to forgive you."

She spoke softly, almost in a whisper, but he heard it as clearly as if her lips had been an inch from his ear. He stopped, but kept his back to her. He wanted to pull her into an empty room and interrogate her. Who was she? What did she know? Why did she say these things? What did she see in Claire that he couldn't? He heard a toilet flush and knew he had to get out of there.

When he reached the turn in the hallway, he looked back at her one last time. She waved slightly, and he finally felt that if she was right, this impropriety, this blatant flouting of the rules of ethics, was perhaps one of the times when the ends could justify the means. If she was right. He mouthed *Thank you* and left to endure the crowd as they regathered by the courtroom doors, waiting for the rest of the show.

When he approached the witness box the second time, he was still thinking of the juror's words outside the bathroom. At first he tried not to look at her, partly for fear of upsetting Judge Lehman but more for fear of losing it all over again. He finally gave in, though. When he was certain that Sanders wasn't looking, and suspected that Judge Lehman wasn't either, he glanced at her and was surprised to find that their brief eye contact comforted him. He began to search the back of the courtroom for Claire but didn't see her. When Sanders resumed his questioning,

Jack responded quickly. He'd accomplished what he'd set out to do and now he just wanted to get out of there.

When he'd finished answering Sanders's questions—which, to Sanders's dismay, included testimony about Alex touching the wineglasses and most likely being seen by the guy who delivered the Thai food—and the judge had finally excused him, he didn't wait around to hear more. He'd returned to the city only to play his small role in the trial. He hadn't really cared what ultimately happened—it had all seemed so irrelevant. Jenny was gone, Maxine Shepard was gone, and he'd believed his marriage to be irretrievably broken. He had testified merely because they had asked him to.

But the exchange with the redheaded juror changed things. It instilled hope somewhere deep inside him.

His impatience compelled him to hurry down the stairs instead of waiting for the elevator. He jogged through the downstairs lobby and past security. The guard called to him, a cordial good-bye—some people stuck by you no matter what—but he merely waved as he pushed open the heavy door and stepped into the sunlight.

It was March and the bulbs were in bloom; the yellow daffodils refused to be quieted by the persistent chill in the air. The tulips, though not yet gracing the streets with their brilliant colors, were pushing their green stalks through winter's protective mulch.

He scanned the area in front of the courthouse. He didn't see her, but he knew she was near, that she was waiting for him somewhere. He felt her pull like a magnet, and he was certain now that she felt his, too. It had compelled her to come to the courthouse, to sit through his testimony and find out just how bad it was. Why would she have bothered, if what the redheaded juror had told him wasn't right?

He'd parked in an open lot several blocks from the courthouse. He was still on the sidewalk when he saw her, six rows deep in the middle of the lot, leaning against his car. A fence surrounded the lot and he quickened his pace, all the while keeping his eyes trained on her.

She watched him approach with the same expression she'd worn in the courtroom. He almost expected her to open her arms to him, but when he finally stopped a foot in front of her, she looked down and then to the side to avoid his eyes. He felt an inkling of doubt creeping in, but the pull was still there, leaving him no choice but to rely on its force.

"Claire." He said it not to get her attention or as a prerequisite to any other statement, but simply as an expression of relief that she was finally so close to him again, after so much time.

She looked up at him, and her eyes looked like an ice sculpture that had stood too long in the afternoon sun. So many times over the past year he'd stared into those eyes without really looking.

He shifted awkwardly from foot to foot, pushing his hands into his trouser pockets and pulling them out again. In his haste to leave the courthouse, he'd left his coat in the DA's office. He crossed his arms to ward off the creeping chill, but he knew, and she knew, that he had nothing else to do with his hands anyway. Perhaps winter was not over yet.

He was afraid to ask the one question he needed to ask. Maybe the kind juror had been wrong. Maybe Claire had already discarded what might have been salvageable, tossing it into a heap of what was but is no more.

But if he didn't ask, what then? He'd never know where he stood.

"Why did you come?" His voice was barely more than a whisper.

She didn't say anything, but he thought he heard her swallow. She unzipped her purse and pulled out a manila envelope. The lawyer in him told him exactly what it had to be, and his stomach began to turn, his heart began to claw against the walls of his chest. Tricked. He took a step backward.

"I found these." She held the envelope out to him, but he merely stared at it and then glanced at her. She nodded for him to go ahead and take it, so he did, letting his fingers brush against hers when he reached for it. "Please, open it."

But he didn't want to. He thought that not knowing whether he'd ever be with her again was better than knowing for sure that he wouldn't. He sensed that certainty lay somewhere in the envelope.

"Please, Jack, just open it."

A reluctant gentleness seeped from her voice; she wanted to be angry still but had either grown too weary to maintain it or, he hoped, had exhausted it all in the past months. He fumbled with the clasp and slowly opened the envelope. His fingers were cold and he had trouble sliding the contents out, but as soon as he saw them he knew what they were.

"Where did you get these?" he asked. He didn't look up from the top photo—a picture of the ice-encased rose bushes, the ones she'd planted the spring before. He hadn't thought of those bushes or of the photos he'd taken since the day of the ice storm. He realized now that he'd forgotten to have them developed for her birthday. The bushes, he remembered, had survived.

"The film was still in your camera when I dug it out for Christmas." She shrugged. "So I developed it." As if it was something she'd always done: develop photographs that he'd taken.

He tried to imagine the scene as he wished it might have occurred. Claire alone in the house one day near Christmas, missing him but not wanting to. Coming across his camera while looking for her digital one. Holding it, feeling the weight of it in her hands, the silence of the large house surrounding her and making his absence more palpable. Deciding to develop the film on the off chance there might be pictures of him— pictures she'd never seen before that might provide some clues to what had happened to him, to them.

He wanted to set the photos on the car and step closer to her. He needed to know if she'd even let him do that. Instead, he continued to stare at the tiny, tender buds that had somehow managed to bloom vibrant pink by August.

"There's more," she said, motioning tentatively with her hand for him to look at the others. He shuffled through the photos of the bushes, of the trees, of fallen debris on the ground, and, of course, the ones of Jamie. When he came to the first picture of Jamie he closed his eyes. It was too hard. It reminded him too much of his shame, of his ache to see his kids, and of his fear that he'd allowed himself to become a stranger to them.

But he forced himself to look at the rest because he sensed that she wanted him to. He knew he'd come to the photo she wanted him to see when she looked away.

It was a picture of himself. The picture Jamie had taken, so close and so vivid. It had a grainy texture, though it was hard to tell if this was a result of the mist or of the lack of distance between photographer and subject. He had a wide, easy smile on his face. He remembered that he'd been laughing at Jamie when the picture was taken. His eyes had been laughing, too, he noticed now. They were clear and bright and betrayed no evidence of the emotional seesaw he'd been riding in the weeks leading up to that day, and for many months thereafter. His happiness during the hour spent in the yard with Jamie had been fragile but pure.

"I'm so confused," Claire said suddenly, a gush of silent tears following her words. Her pain ripped through him and he finally did by instinct what he'd been yearning to do since first approaching her. He reached for her and slowly pulled her close. She didn't resist.

"Why did you come?" he repeated.

She backed away as if she'd just heard the question for the first time. She began to speak in one uninhibited rush.

"All this time, I've wanted to ask you why. I wanted to scream it at you. I wanted answers from you. I wanted to force you to give me answers, even though I knew there were none. But I told myself that it was the one question I'd never let myself ask, because I knew—no matter what you said—it would never satisfy me, never justify what you'd done."

"Claire, I—"

"Be quiet." It was an order. "You asked me a question. Let me answer it." She retrieved a tissue from her purse before continuing.

"I knew I could never understand, so why bother asking? Plus, I knew you'd lie. I knew you'd try to sugarcoat it for me. But then . . . Mark told me you'd finally come back to town to testify.

"I realized your testimony would be the only opportunity I would have to hear the truth, because I knew you, of all people, wouldn't be able to lie on *that stand*." She waved one hand in the direction of the courthouse, as if the witness stand was another object worthy of her contempt. She did not at that moment admire his loyalty to the law; perhaps she never had.

She paused, but his shame only intensified in the silence because he knew that she was right. He had been more truthful on the stand than he would have been with her, and he was beginning to understand how she could hate him for that.

"That picture of you? It haunts me. I look at it, and as much as I don't want to, I still have feelings for the man in the picture. And I don't know what to do about those feelings. I don't even know what the feelings are. Are they love? Or just love's remnants? And what am I supposed to do with them?"

He knew these questions were rhetorical. Besides, anything he might say, no matter how he tried to say it, would be exposed for what it really was—the attempt of a desperate man willing to say anything to get his wife back.

"You know, certain things used to be so black and white for me. There were good guys, and there were bad guys. Men who cheated on their wives were bad guys. Pigs. No questions asked, no excuses. A woman who stayed with a pig deserved whatever shit he kicked in her face. But now, I don't know." She carefully wiped her eyes with the tissue. "I don't know what to think, what to do. Everything I knew to be true, well, it isn't. I feel like someone's played a cruel joke on me.

"And the worst part of all is that I wonder whether the man in the picture is the same man standing in front of me right now. And do I even want him to be?"

"He's not," Jack whispered. "He's not the same."

The next thing she did was so unexpected that he thought he would lose any composure he'd been able to maintain up to that point. She placed her palm on his cheek. "I think I just might believe you."

He grasped her wrist so that she wouldn't take her hand away.

"Tell me what you want, Claire. Tell me what to do."

"I don't know. I don't know what either of us should do." She looked him in the eyes. "I just don't know if I can handle the constant reminders that would be inevitable. I don't know if I'm a big enough person to get past it. Even now, I know you're mourning her, as if she died. Maybe for you she did. But how am I supposed to deal with that? I guess I can't deny you your feelings for her, but I can't bear watching, either."

She pulled her hand away and stood up straighter. "Here they come."

"Who?" He turned around. Streams of men and women were heading to the parking lot. The trial must have recessed for the day. Jack saw Jim Wolfe in the middle of the bunch and it was clear that he'd seen them, too.

He grabbed Claire's hand and pulled her to the other side of his car. "Get in," he said, opening the passenger door for her. But as soon as he'd spoken the words, they brought it back. Just like that, it was April and he was back in the parking garage, trying to coax a drunken Jenny to get into her car.

Claire noticed. "What is it?"

"Nothing," he said, shaking his head, shaking off the memory.

He glanced at Wolfe, who was approaching quickly, and then at Claire, sitting in the front seat. He realized that she'd gotten into the car willingly. Wolfe was breathing down their necks, but Jack knew she was strong enough to stay and handle the reporter if she really didn't want to go with him. Despite her pain and confusion, despite everything she'd said, she'd gotten into the car. And that one action told Jack everything he needed to know.

EPILOGUE

LATE SPRING

Jack sat sideways on the top step of the deck, his back against a post-rail, and gazed into the backyard where Jamie played in the water. The community pool wouldn't open for another week, but the heat of summer had arrived early, so Jack had bought a wading pool to tide him over to Memorial Day.

The file lay next to him on the deck. He fiddled with the elastic string but didn't open it. He'd had the file in his possession for several weeks now. He'd forgotten that he'd asked for it, until Rose had called him one afternoon and apologized profusely for its taking so long to arrive from storage. She didn't know if he still wanted to see it, she'd said, but she promised to hold it until he let her know. It took him about a week to decide to pick it up from the file room; two weeks later and he still hadn't opened it. Until the day before it had sat on the corner of his desk, blending in with the other files, but always within his line of sight.

He wanted to read it at home, away from the office, but he also wanted to read it when he was alone, or rather, when Claire wasn't home. He knew he'd have the opportunity soon enough. Since moving back, the routines he'd been used to had changed. Claire spent more time away from the house now, sometimes leaving Jack to take care of the kids and sometimes taking them with her. If she took the kids, it was usually to spend an afternoon or evening at her parents' house. When she went out

alone, he didn't always know where she went. Sometimes she would mention that she was going out with one of her girlfriends, but at other times
she didn't say, and he didn't ask.

He knew eventually they would reach a point when they could talk
about everything again, when they could do so matter-of-factly, without
reopening their wounds. But for now the topic was untouchable, though
ever-present. It was the elephant in the room. Sometimes at night, lying
in the same bed but miles apart, he'd wake to hear her crying softly. He
wondered if maybe he'd been talking in his sleep, saying things he shouldn't
say. He'd reach for her, and sometimes she'd let him and sometimes she
wouldn't, and he had no choice but to accept her decision.

He still thought of Jenny daily, wondered where she was, and he knew
that Claire must know this. For a time he resisted the thoughts, but once
he learned to accept the intrusions they became easier to bear. What surprised him most was the sheer number of reminders that popped up
when he least expected them. Accidentally hitting her office number on
his speed dial at work; the sight of her homeless friend camped out under
the walkway to the stadium; even the brochure for that summer's Bench &
Bar conference, with a full-color picture of the lake on the cover. The
obvious reminders he could prepare himself for; it was the ones that
sneaked up on him that threatened his ability to cope.

Jamie's giggles and shrieks coming from the yard reassured him that
life was as close to normal as it could be. In moments of tenderness with
Claire, which, as time passed, became less bitter and more sweet, she told
him that although Michael still held a grudge, the kids were behaving
better since he'd returned. He worried that this was the only reason she'd
allowed him back, but, as with his recurring thoughts of Jenny, he accepted those doubts as something he'd have to deal with until they went
away. He stared at the file and debated whether to risk the possibility of
stalling their fragile progress.

Most of the time he believed that he knew everything there was to
know. The jury had convicted Alex of Maxine Shepard's murder and sen-
tenced him to death. Based on reports both from Jeff and from the newspapers, Jack knew that the verdict had been decided, in part, on the
strength of his testimony. And though Alex's appeals could take years,

that knowledge didn't even begin to alleviate Jack's guilt over the sentence.

He'd even learned that the alibi "leak" hadn't been a leak after all. It had merely been a hunch by Jim Wolfe, who'd tested his theory by suggesting it to the interested parties and then watching to see how they reacted.

But then there were the times when he'd sit up in bed in the middle of the night, seeing again the fingerprints on Jenny's back, trying to remember if he'd gripped her hard enough to cause them. He'd think about the story she told of her family's murder, and it bothered him that she'd left out more details than she'd put in. He'd tell himself it didn't matter; the rest of the details were irrelevant. Whatever had happened over a quarter of a century ago was just history.

But then Rose had called, telling him she had the file.

He glanced at Jamie, who had left the pool and was chasing a butterfly near the edge of the woods. It was Saturday, and Claire wouldn't be home for a while; she'd taken Michael shopping for the supplies he needed for camp that summer. Jack picked up the file and held it in his lap for a long time before finally slipping the string off.

His hands trembled as he opened it. He started to leaf through some of the pleadings, but a few yellowed newspaper articles fell out and he grabbed them before they blew away.

The first story, published the day after the murders, confirmed what Jenny had told him. With a reporter's distance, it told the facts of the crime more clinically than she'd been able to, even given her attempts at detachment. He read the article with the same emotion with which he read a police report or a witness-impact statement, the sadness of one who can sympathize but cannot understand. Until, that is, he came to the first reference to Jenny and her brother.

Two other children, nine and eleven years old, survived the massacre by hiding in a closet.

She'd told him how she and Brian had managed to be spared, and how they'd watched from their hiding spot. She'd told him how it felt, both at the time and afterward, when the inescapable guilt set in. She'd told him how the only good thing to come from it was the bond forever formed between her and her brother, a bond she thought must be similar to that shared by twins. But despite everything she'd told him, he hadn't been prepared for the impact of this one simple sentence. He stared at the word on the brittle paper: *massacre*.

He closed his eyes but he still saw her, crouched in a dark closet with her brother's hand clamped over her mouth. Unable to help, unable to scream, unable to join her mother and father and sister, wherever they were going.

Massacre. She'd told him they had watched, but now he realized that she hadn't told him what, exactly, she'd seen. She'd shown him the pictures of her parents and her sister, and he'd been so thrilled that she was finally letting him in that he hadn't stopped to consider how painful looking at the photo album must have been for her. He hadn't considered that she might have seen in her mind's eye much more than was on the page. He tried, but even now he couldn't imagine what the scene would have revealed to the eyes of a nine-year-old.

Looking up, he quickly scanned the yard; Jamie was oblivious to his presence. Jack hastily fumbled with the other few stories, squinting to find the one with the most recent date as he simultaneously skimmed the headlines. He was trying to find a story about the trial or maybe the sentencing. He held his breath. He felt certain that the words *death penalty* or *capital punishment* or some other euphemism for the ultimate revenge would jump out at him from the headline. He realized, with shame, that he wanted—he was hoping—to see it.

> Just four days before trial, prosecutors in the Dodson triple murder case that shocked the city last spring announced a plea bargain with attorneys for defendant Anthony Vaughn. Although the exact terms of the agreement were not disclosed, prosecutors have indicated that in exchange for Vaughn's testimony against reputed mob boss Salvatore Ronzini on other charges, the multiple first-degree murder charges against him will be reduced to second-degree murder and they will recommend the minimum sentence of 10 years.

Nothing, however—not the despair of revisiting the facts of her family's murder, not even the shock of learning how the murderer had managed to escape a meaningful sentence—could have prepared him for what he read next. Even with the details laid out in front of him in black and white, he had to reread the paragraph to be sure he hadn't misunderstood.

> Although Ronzini's connection to the murders has been merely speculative, Vaughn's attorneys have suggested that their client was acting for the reputed mobster when he broke into the victims' home last summer and murdered the three family members while two other children looked on. Some sources have claimed that Harold Dodson was heavily in debt to the mob for money borrowed to maintain a secret mistress, identified as Maxine Carson, and that the crime was orchestrated in retaliation for his failure to pay. Prosecutors have repeatedly denied this, even though the particular nature of the murders was consistent with Ronzini's modus operandi, in which victims are usually killed execution-style. Miss Carson, reached at her apartment in the city, refused to comment.

Except for the increasing rise and fall of his breath, Jack sat perfectly still and gazed, unseeing, at Jamie at the edge of the yard. He thought back to Jenny's arraignment, to when the clerk had read the charges. They hadn't referred to the victim as Maxine Shepard. They'd referred to her as Maxine *Carson* Shepard. He remembered it as clearly as if he still sat in the courtroom.

Beads of perspiration formed near his temples and he was acutely aware of the sweat dripping down the side of his face. *I'm not interested in being someone's mistress. Especially not yours.* He stood only after he was certain that his legs would bear his weight. *He was a full-fledged American. As Waspy as they come. Like you, Jack.* He mumbled something to Jamie about staying out of the pool and then walked numbly into the house with the file under his arm.

They said he had a mistress. Standing in front of the kitchen table, he put the papers back together and tucked the file into his briefcase. *I'm not just saying that because we're friends, although that would be an added benefit, wouldn't it?* It was unthinkable. *If I ever got in trouble . . .* He went out to the garage and put the briefcase on the passenger seat of his car. *If I ever got in trouble.* He returned to the house, picked up the receiver from the phone in the kitchen, and called Jeff at home. An answering machine picked up.

"Jeff, it's Jack." The sound of his voice was foreign. He swallowed, but it was difficult. "Give me a call, will you?"

It was simply unthinkable.